DARK VISION

Gift's heart was pounding against his chest. He had never gone into the palace before, not in his own body. He had only walked—Linked—with Sebastian, inside the golem's body, the case of stone.

Gift didn't know what would happen if they caught him.

But he had to try. He had to get Sebastian out of here, at least until he knew who the strange Fey in his Vision was. The Vision had happened in the near future. And the only thing Gift could do to prevent his death and Sebastian's was to keep them away from Islander buildings, away from the palace, away from the cities.

He had to get Sebastian to Shadowlands.

And he knew Sebastian couldn't get there on his own. . . .

Also by Kristine Kathryn Rusch

The Fey: The Sacrifice
The Fey: The Changeling

STAR WARS: The New Rebellion

THE
RIVAL

THE THIRD BOOK OF
THE FEY

Kristine Kathryn Rusch

BANTAM BOOKS
NEW YORK   TORONTO   LONDON
SYDNEY   AUCKLAND

THE FEY: THE RIVAL

A Bantam Spectra Book / April 1997

SPECTRA and the portrayal of a boxed "s" are trademarks of Bantam
Books, a division of Bantam Doubleday Dell Publishing Group, Inc.

ISBN 0-553-56896-5

Published simultaneously in the United States and Canada

Bantam Books are published by Bantam Books, a division of Bantam
Doubleday Dell Publishing Group, Inc. Its trademark, consisting of the words
"Bantam Books" and the portrayal of a rooster, is Registered in U.S. Patent
and Trademark Office and in other countries. Marca Registrada. Bantam
Books, 1540 Broadway, New York, New York 10036.

PRINTED IN THE UNITED STATES OF AMERICA

RAD   0   9   8   7   6   5   4   3   2   1

For Jerry and Kathy Oltion, whose enthusiasm for this project has been invaluable.

ACKNOWLEDGMENTS

Thanks on this one go to Chris York for waiting all these months; to Tom Dupree and Carolyn Oakley for their insights; to Nina Kiriki Hoffman for her honesty and her trusty red pen; to Dean Wesley Smith for letting me steal from a lifetime of mountain experience; and to all the readers who let me know how much they liked *The Sacrifice*.

THE ARRIVAL

ONE

THE mountains rose before him, an impenetrable stone wall.

Rugad clung to the fine strings holding the front part of his harness. Above him, the strings' ends were looped around the talons of twenty-five Hawk Riders. The swoop of their magnificent wings sounded like cloaks snapping in the wind. They bore him hundreds of feet above the raging ocean toward the mountains that lined the southern end of Blue Isle.

He angled toward the sun, but it brought him no warmth. Instead, its harsh light covered everything with a clarity that was almost eerie. The mountains themselves seemed to be carved out of the blueness of the sky.

Nothing had prepared him for those mountains. Not his Visions, not all the talk of the Nyeians, not even a visit to the Eccrasian Mountains, the Fey's ancestral homeland. These mountains were sheer gray stone, rubbed smooth on the ocean side by centuries of storms, waves, and severe weather. The ocean slammed into their base as if the water wanted to pound a hole through the rock, and the surf sent white foam cascading into the air. Even at the birds' height, angling upward to reach the top of those peaks, Rugad could feel the spray pricking his exposed skin like tiny needles.

The higher they climbed, the colder he got.

That was one contingency he hadn't prepared for. He had ordered the harness chair from the Domestics back on Nye. They had spelled a dozen different models. Some of the rope was too thick for the Hawk Riders to hold. Some had been so thin that it cut into the Riders' talons. This material supported his weight and didn't put too much of a burden on the Riders above him.

The Riders had two forms. In their Fey form, they looked nearly human, except for their feathered hair and beaked noses. In their bird form, they were all bird except for the small human riding on the bird's back. They looked like tiny Fey riding on a bird, but they were, in truth, part of the bird, their legs and lower torso subsumed into the bird's form. The only danger they posed in bird form was that they had two brains—and sometimes the bird's instinctual one took over.

Rugad hoped that wouldn't happen here. He had wanted the Domestics to create a rope that the human part of the bird could hold in its hands. But the hands were too little. They couldn't carry anything of substance.

They needed a strong, magicked fiber to lift him from the ship to the top of those peaks. Rugad swallowed, glad he swung from the harness alone. He wasn't certain he could mask his nervousness. His feet dangled over the ocean. He was flying higher than he had ever been in his life, and he would have to go higher still.

He had sent a scouting party to the top of those mountains. They had reported a small level landing area, but he couldn't see it from here. From here, the mountains looked as if they rose to jagged points, sharp as the teeth of a young lion.

The birds changed their angle of flight, and his harness swung backward, making his breath catch in his throat. He gripped tighter, remembering the Domestics' admonition not to pull on the ropes. An exhilaration rose in his stomach, a lightness that he almost didn't recognize.

He was frightened.

He hadn't been frightened in over seventy years, not

since his first battle as a teenage boy before he came into his Visions, when his youth and lack of magick forced him into the Infantry.

Frightened.

He grinned. Somehow the feeling relieved him. He had thought that part of him was dead. So many other parts were.

Logic conquered fear, he remembered that much. They had tested the harness, put in a strong wood base and an even stronger back, making it like a sedan chair carried by Hawk Riders. Above him the ropes looped over a small ring and then attached to the talons of an inner circle of birds. Another group of ropes ran higher, to a larger ring, and then to a larger circle of birds. Right now, they were angling upward in perfect formation, as if they shared a brain, the tiny Fey riders on their backs laughing and shouting across the air currents.

In all of his campaigns, Rugad had relied on Beast Riders more than any other form of Fey. He had brought most of his Bird Riders along on this trip, knowing that he would need them to traverse the distance between ship and shore.

The Hawk Riders had a majesty the other bird riders did not. From this angle he could only see one of his own men on the hawk's back, his lower body vanishing into the hawk's form. Only the man's torso and head were visible, looking as if he were actually astride the hawk. The hawk's own head bent forward slightly to accommodate the unusual configuration, but that was the only concession to the difference. The Rider and the Hawk had been one being since the Rider was a child.

These Hawk Riders had flown him dozens of times before, testing the final harnesses, but never this high, never at such risk.

Landre, head of the Spell Warders, had tried to talk him out of this course. He had suggested that Rugad listen to the Bird Riders, and send a few Scouts, then trust their opinions. Rugad had discarded that idea before the fleet left Nye. Then Landre had suggested that Boteen do some sort of Enchanter spell that would enable Rugad to share the Bird Rider's sight. But he had rejected that as well.

He had to see Blue Isle for himself.

Blue Isle. It had a reputation as being impenetrable. The

river that ran through the center of the Isle was navigable, if
the ships had a current map of the harbor. The first Fey
invasion force, sent almost twenty years ago, had had such a
map, but still the Isle had defeated them.

Just as Rugad had known it would.

The Isle would not defeat him.

The Hawk Riders' angle grew steeper. The harness swung
back, making him giddy. The mountains were close now.
Their sides no longer appeared smooth. They were made of
volcanic rock, polished by the elements, with cracks and
crevices, and broken edges all along the face. Nothing grew
on the ocean side, no scraggly trees, no windswept bushes
struggling to survive. There was no soil here, and probably
hadn't been since the mountains rose out of the sea, thousands of years before.

His grin grew. The sheer cliff faces of legend were not
smooth as tempered glass. They had flaws. Imperfections.

Handholds.

Then the Riders pulled him over the top of the mountain, and his breath caught in his throat. The mountains still
rose beside him, but beneath him was a plateau, and
through it, a long narrow crevice. If he squinted, he could
see blue sky through that crevice.

The Gull Riders and Scouts had been right. A concealed
landing place that gave the Fey access to the entire valley.

Gently, the Hawk Riders lowered him onto the plateau
until his feet brushed the rocky surface. He pressed a lever
as he landed, and the boards of his sedan chair flattened.
The ropes collapsed around him, and he staggered forward
before he caught his balance. The Hawk Riders landed
around him, the narrow circle first. Rugad was surrounded
by ten hawks, tiny Fey riders on their backs. Hawks were not
designed to land on flat surfaces, so they had to time their
change to the moment their talons touched the stone.

In unison, the tiny Riders straightened their arms and
loosened the rope loops around their talons. The ropes slid
open as the Riders grew to Fey size. As they stretched to
their full height, the bird bodies slipped inside their own.

Then they stood around him, in fully human form, taller
than he was. They had a not-Fey quality to them. Their hair
was feathered as it flowed down their backs. Their finger-

nails were long, like claws, and their noses were long and narrow, hooking over their mouths like beaks.

They watched as the remaining Hawk Riders landed and went through the same transformation.

Within the space of three heartbeats, Rugad went from being surrounded by hawks to being surrounded by Fey. They were a small fighting force, standing on the plateau.

The wind blew through the crevice, ice-cold despite the fact that it was summer on Blue Isle. The Hawk Riders were naked, but they didn't seem to feel the chill. Rugad did. He shuddered, and wished that he had brought gloves.

The other peaks towered around him like tall buildings, blocking the sun. It was as dark as dusk on the plateau.

The leader of the Hawk Riders, Talon, clicked his fingernails together. The Riders grabbed their lines to prevent the ropes from tangling. Rugad kept his harness on—it was too difficult to reassemble—and stepped forward until he could see through the crevice.

A valley spread before him, as green and lush as anything he had seen on the Galinas continent. The air, even at this elevation, had a fertile, marshy smell. Several villages dotted the valley, looking like insect colonies from this height.

"The mountains are sheer on the valley side," Talon said. His voice was piercing, and his sibilants whistled through his small mouth. "But they are only half the height. Going down will be easier than coming up."

Coming up was the problem. Thirty thousand troops, most with little or no flying ability, scaling the rock face, the frothing ocean below.

"Are there other plateaus like this?" he asked.

"No," Talon said. "Not within a reasonable distance."

Rugad nodded. Only a hundred men could fit here at any given time. That would slow the progress into the valley tremendously.

"And what is directly below?" he asked.

"A town of perhaps four hundred people. I have one of my men watching the site. These people do not seem to venture toward the mountains."

Rugad cautiously stepped over lines. The wind was strong here, so strong that he could lose his balance if he weren't careful. He peered down the side of the plateau, into the crevice, and felt that jolt of fear again. Nature would be his most formidable opponent here. He had never, in all his ninety-two years, seen terrain as mighty as this.

He would beat it, as he had beaten all the other challenges that had arisen in his life. A tiny island in the Infrin Sea would not stop him. If he lived a normal Fey span, he still had fifty years of life ahead of him. He planned to live out his old age on the Leut continent, across the sea from Blue Isle. He would conquer Blue Isle, and half the countries on Leut, and then he would retire, the greatest Fey leader of all time, the only one to circle nearly half the globe.

And when he retired, his great-grandson, Jewel's boy, would become Black King. Rugad had Seen it.

"So," Talon asked, "Do you think we can invade this place?"

Rugad raised his chin, and gazed down the valley. Near the horizon, the green disappeared into a white mist, suggesting further riches beyond.

"We will invade," he said. "And we will conquer."

He knew that much to be true. He had Seen the invasion and the victory. Standing here, on this mountain plateau with the valley that had haunted his Visions for fifty years spreading below him, he knew that the plans he had made on Nye were perfect.

The Black King had arrived.

And nothing would stand in his way.

THE INVASION
[TWO WEEKS LATER]

TWO

ARIANNA peered into the wavy silvered glass and jutted out her chin. The birthmark was the size of her thumbprint, darker than the rest of her already dark skin, and as obvious as the pimples the new hearth boy had.

She pulled her dressing gown tighter, then glanced behind her. Still no maid. Good. Her bedroom was empty. Sunlight poured in the open window, and the birds in the garden chirruped. The bed was made, and she had thrown her new gown on the coverlet. The dress had a low-cut bodice, which her father wouldn't approve of, and a cinched waist that tapered into a flared skirt. The dressmaker had begged her not to use that pattern, but Arianna had stared the woman down.

The last I knew, Arianna had said in her best haughty voice, *I was the Princess. Has someone given my title to you?*

The dressmaker had had the grace to blush. She had done what Arianna wanted, knowing that if she didn't the palace wouldn't hire her again.

The palace might not hire her again anyway. Arianna had heard the woman curse when she thought Arianna wasn't in the room.

Demon spawn.

Even after fifteen years, the Islanders didn't know what to make of Arianna. She was the second child of Nicholas, the Islander King, and Jewel, the granddaughter of the Fey's Black King. Arianna had never known her mother. Jewel had been murdered the day Arianna was born.

Arianna wished her mother had lived. If her mother had lived, no one would call Arianna demon spawn. No one would look at her sideways as she went down a hall. No one would say that she wasn't really Islander, that she was pure Fey.

But it was easy to see how they thought that. Arianna didn't look like her father. She had dark skin like the Fey. She had pointed ears and upswept eyebrows like the Fey.

And, most importantly, she had magick.

Like the Fey.

Her birthmark was the sign of that. It identified her, according to her Fey guardian, Solanda. Only Shape-Shifters had such a mark. It was the sign, Solanda said, of the most perfect Fey. Yet no matter what shape Arianna Shifted into, the mark remained on her chin. Sometimes it was a faint outline, a suggestion of a mark, and sometimes it was a stamp, as vivid as a charcoal slash against the skin.

And it was ugly, ugly, ugly.

She was the Islander Princess, the most perfect of the Fey, and she couldn't get rid of the mark on her face. Solanda said she should look on it with pride. But Solanda wasn't fifteen. Solanda didn't understand how the boys stared at the mark, and how the girls giggled at it. Solanda didn't know that Arianna had overheard all the conversations about the King's strange daughter with the witch's wart on her face.

Maybe if the witch's wart went away, people would see Arianna for who she was, instead of who they thought she was.

Demon spawn.

She glanced around the room a final time. No cats, no maids, no hearth boys. She was still alone. She leaned over and pulled open a drawer in the bottom of the vanity.

The pot was still there, untouched.

She smiled, wrapped her hand around the ceramic, and

pulled the pot out. She set it on her dresser, pulled off the lid and winced at the sharp tang of aliota leaves.

The cream inside was a muddy brown. An awful color for skin. Skin should be a pale golden white, like her father's. Then her blue eyes wouldn't seem so startling, so out of place.

She dipped her fingers in the cream, and rubbed some on the back of her left hand, as the dressmaker had instructed her to. The cream blended in, hiding the tiny cut she had gotten the day before. She held her hand in front of her, tilting it at different angles, trying to see the blemish. So far it seemed natural. If it looked good in the light, she would slather some on her chin before she put on the dress. She would go to her brother's Coming-of-Age ceremony looking as regal as she could.

No witch's wart to remind them she was different.

She would be beautiful for the first time in her life.

She stood and, holding her hand out in front of her, crossed to the window. The stone floor was cool beneath her bare feet. She glanced once at the slippers resting beside the bed. Shoes were the most uncomfortable contraptions ever invented. Her feet weren't meant to be bound. But they would have to be soon. A Coming-of-Age ceremony, as her father kept reminding her, was an Important Event. She would have to wear the shoes he had ordered to go with her dress.

The window was large. It ended near the ceiling and stopped about waist-high. Solanda had had it built specially, with long hinged glass panes that opened over the garden. She believed that air was important to well-being—a Fey thing that Arianna's father reluctantly agreed with. A tapestry depicting the coronation of Constantine the First was tied back. Arianna hadn't looked at it in weeks, disliking the square poorly stitched faces and the symbols of Rocaanism that dotted the tapestry.

Rocaanism, the state religion, was tied to her father's family. Her father was a direct descendant of the Roca, God's first representative on the Isle. Rocaanism was also deadly to her mother's people, the Fey. Some believed that the union of the Fey and the Roca's descendent polluted the blood, and resulted in Arianna's brother, Sebastian. Many believed that Sebastian was stupid. He wasn't stupid, but he was slow. Rapid movement—and rapid thought—seemed impossible for him.

She sat on the piled cushions of the window seat and tilted her hand toward the sun. Then she frowned. A stain discolored the skin over the cut. It looked as if she had spilled Solanda's root tea on her hand. Everyone would know that Arianna was covering up the blemish instead of having found some way to spell it away.

She clenched her fist and felt the skin pull. The cream dried hard. Her skin would have felt like caked mud by the end of the evening. She would have to go to the ceremony, witch's wart and all.

Then the hair rose on the back of her neck. Someone was watching her. She didn't move, but pretended to study her hand. The birds had stopped singing. The scent of roses was overpowering, like it was when the gardener was working with the flowers.

Someone was in the garden.

Slowly she tilted her head and looked down.

Sunlight dappled across the flowers. The roses spotted the green with color—red, pink, white, and yellow. Pansies littered the ground with purple. The oaks, maples, and pines were still; there was no wind. The garden, her father's pride and joy, the place she had spent most of her childhood, appeared empty.

Then she caught a flash of movement near the birdbath. She squinted. The bath was clear, the water smooth. The shade of the nearby oak trees covered the marble inlay, making it look gray. No birds were in the trees, none were overhead, and clearly none had been in the water moments before.

She leaned back and scrubbed her hand with the sleeve of her dressing gown, keeping her gaze on the garden below. Then a tree branch rustled, but she forced herself not to turn her head. Instead she watched, as seemingly preoccupied with cleaning as she could be when she was in her cat form. After a moment, her patience was rewarded.

A man stepped out of the small copse of trees near the birdbath. Not a man, exactly, more a boy.

A teenage boy.

Her brother, Sebastian.

This time, she did turn her head. Sebastian was supposed to be in his rooms, dressing for his Coming-of-Age ceremony. It took him longer to dress than it took anyone else because he insisted on doing it himself.

She placed her palms on the window seat cushions and leaned out. "Sebastian!" she yelled. "You're supposed to be inside!"

He looked up, and her breath caught in her throat. For the first time in his life, Sebastian's eyes were filled with a quick intelligence. They were blue pools of flashing light. That was odd. Sebastian's eyes had never looked blue before. They were a stone gray.

His dark hair was mussed, as it always was, hiding his faintly pointed ears. The exotic features of his face—his dark skin, his swooping eyebrows, his small nose—blended perfectly with the slight roundness their father had given to his bone structure. For the first time in his life, Sebastian looked integrated, whole, not like something slapped together from mismatched pieces of clay.

He made a small panicked noise in the back of his throat, a noise that echoed in the silence of the garden, and disappeared into the trees.

"Sebastian!" she called again, but he didn't come to her like he usually did. Something was wrong. And her internal sense warned her that if she ran down the steps, through the halls, and into the garden, he would be gone.

So she slipped out of her gown and Shifted. Her bones compacted and lightened. Her arms stretched out, the fingers melded into tips, and feathers sprouted all over her body. Her mouth stretched into a beak, and her vision changed as her eyes moved to the side of her head.

This was her robin form, one of two dozen shapes she had never told Solanda about. Shape-Shifters were supposed to have only one alternate form—Solanda could only turn into a small tabby cat—but so far Arianna had experienced no limitations. She could Shift into anything she chose, as long as she practiced the form in advance. She had been playing at her robin form since she was six years old.

The change happened within a heartbeat. She hopped to the edge of the window and flew. The air currents ruffled her feathers and she felt the warm kiss of freedom. She longed to rise with the wind and explore the city of Jahn, looking for food, looking for other birds, but she quelled the instinct, landing instead on the edge of the birdbath.

She cocked her head and looked into the trees. The long, cool shadows hid nothing. She could see the smooth tree trunks, the sloping branches, the carefully tended grass.

Sebastian wasn't quick enough to hide from her.

Was he?

"Sebastian!" she called again. "If you're not dressed when Dad comes for you, he'll really be mad."

No answer. The strangeness made her stretch her wings, then tuck them back against her side. Sebastian always answered her, and he hated displeasing their father. Normally just the sound of her voice would have made him appear.

"Sebastian!"

She took one small, mad hop, then nearly lost her balance. She put spindly leg out to steady herself and tottered over the water for a moment before she remembered her wings. She opened them and flew into the trees, landing on a maple branch. A jay landed above her and cawed at her; he thought she was too close to the bath and he wanted to use it.

Another robin landed on a nearby oak tree. That was confirmation enough. She would circle the garden and the courtyard to make certain, but she already knew what she would find.

Sebastian was gone.

He had disappeared in less time than it normally took him to move his arm.

Maybe he had finally come into his powers.

Maybe all the abilities he was supposed to have as a mixed Fey had been dormant all these years.

Or maybe something had gone wrong.

No matter what, he would be terrified. Change always frightened Sebastian. He would need her.

She wouldn't rest until she found him.

THREE

GIFT huddled in the hole near the stone fence. He was breathing through his mouth, as quietly as he could. Sweat ran off his nose and dripped on the ground, making dark spots in the dirt. She would fly above him. He knew she would. One thing he had learned about Arianna over the years was that she was brilliant.

And she had seen him.

She thought he was Sebastian, and he supposed in a way he was. Gift was the baby born to Jewel and Nicholas, Arianna's older brother, but he had been stolen by his grandfather Rugar when he was only days old. Sebastian was the Changeling who had been left in Gift's place.

Birds returned to the garden. Their shadows passed along the ground, their cries echoing overhead. They couldn't see him. Maybe Arianna wouldn't either. He could only hope. He didn't know what she would do when she saw him. He was wearing Fey clothes, and he wouldn't be able to explain that. And the clothes were only the beginning. Even though he and Sebastian looked alike, they were not identical. In fact, the only things they had in common were their strange beginning, Gift's birth family, and the mental Link between them.

And maybe their future.

He shuddered despite the afternoon's heat. The Vision still weighed heavily on him. He had been a Visionary since he was a little boy—unheard of in the history of the Fey—and none of his Visions had scared him like this one.

Except the one in which he saw his mother die.

He swallowed. A robin circled overhead, coming lower and lower, its head cocking from side to side as it descended. Despite being raised by the Fey, he had never gotten used to animals and birds speaking with human voices. When that robin had called out Sebastian's name, Gift had jumped in alarm. He had nearly tripped in his mad dash to his hiding place.

He couldn't let her find him. She would want explanations, and then she would drag him to their father to show the poor man that the boy he thought was his son was really a stone.

Or maybe she wouldn't. She loved Sebastian despite his faults. She was his best friend and his protector.

She might see Gift as a threat. She had never been to Shadowlands, the artificial home of the Fey. She had never been around Fey, except for Solanda and a few others. She thought like an Islander, not like a warrior, and that, he suspected, would hurt her when the time came.

Although she had not been in his Vision.

Which led him to believe that the Vision might be about him.

The robin circled lower and finally landed on top of the stone fence. If he tilted his head slightly, he could see the tips of her claws, her feathered breast, and the underside of her beak. The beak had a strange white mark at the base, like a birthmark.

The bird was Arianna, then, and she was directly above him. If he so much as moved, she would see him. His throat tickled with a sudden urge to cough. His body wanted to give him away. He wanted to talk to his sister for once, as half-breed to half-breed. But now was not the time.

He had to find Sebastian, and then he had to think of a way to protect them both.

The Vision had been a simple one, and unusually clear. Visions were usually impressions, fleeting images, puzzles to be put together. This one was an entire event, and he saw it two ways, which terrified him more.

In the first, he was standing in front of a Fey he had never seen before. They appeared to be in the Islander palace, in a large room. The room had a lot of Fey guards. Behind them, the walls were covered with spears. A throne rested on a dais, but no one sat on the throne. On the wall behind it was a crest: two swords crossed over a heart.

He had never been there before, but he recognized the crest. It belonged to his father's family.

The Fey was a man with the leathered skin of a fighter. His eyes were dark and empty, his hands gnarled with age. He had the look of Gift's long-dead grandfather. He was staring at Gift, hands out, eyes bright, as if Gift were an oddity, almost a religious curiosity.

Then Gift felt a sharp, shattering pain in his back. The Fey man yelled—his words blurring as his face blurred, as the room blurred, and then the Vision disappeared into darkness.

The second Vision was somehow more disturbing, even though it felt impersonal. He wasn't in his body. He floated above it, as if he were looking through a spy hole, or were a spider on the ceiling. His body stood below, taller than the strange Fey man. His body was exactly the same age it was now; it belonged to a teenager, not a fullgrown Fey. The man and Gift's body stood close together. Fey guards circled the room. Two were at the door. The Fey carried no weapons, but some of them looked like Foot Soldiers, with slender, deadly, knife-sharp fingers.

No one seemed to see him.

The older Fey wasn't speaking. He was examining Gift's body as if it were a precious and rare commodity. The body—and Gift—were studying the man in return.

Then someone in a hooded cloak slipped through the door. The Fey guards stepped aside, and the old man didn't see the intruder. A gloved hand holding a long knife appeared from inside the cloak, with two quick steps, the intruder had crossed the room and shoved the knife into the body's back.

Gift was screaming, but he couldn't get inside the body. The old man was yelling, the door was open, and the intruder was gone.

The body lay on the floor, eyes wide, blood trailing from the corner of the mouth. It coughed once, then its breath wheezed through its throat. The wheeze ended in a sigh, and all the life disappeared from the face.

Gift's face.

And then the Vision ended.

Two versions of his own death. One from inside his body—where he felt the final deathblow—and one from out. The Visions had started almost a month before. Finally—yesterday—he went to the Shaman as she had taught him to do with difficult Visions long ago. She had looked at him with compassion.

Did you know that each Visionary sees his own death? she had asked.

He nodded. He also knew that the death Vision could be changed. He had seen his own death as a boy—when his real mother died, he should have died with her—but his friend Coulter had changed the path of that vision.

So this is mine? he asked.

She shook her head. *Two Visions, two paths. In the second, you do not die. Someone else does.*

Sebastian did. Sebastian—good, innocent, and childlike. Sebastian, the golem who should not live and did. Sebastian, whom Gift loved like a brother. Sebastian, who had so much of Gift inside of him that Gift wasn't certain if one could survive without the other.

How do I stop it? Gift asked.

You must change the path.

But how?

The Shaman shrugged. *I have not seen this path. We cannot compare. The future is too murky. Everything is changing now. By next week, our lives will have a different meaning.*

Try as he might, he could not get her to explain that last. The job of a Shaman was to safeguard her people. And sometimes, safeguarding her people meant keeping their leaders in darkness.

Overhead, the robin sighed. Gift resisted the urge to look up. His arms were cramping, and his neck ached. She had to leave sometime soon. She had some sort of ceremony to go to, something Sebastian had tried to explain during the last Link. But Gift's understanding of Islander rituals was poor at best, and he hadn't understood this one at all.

"By the Powers, Sebastian," Arianna said. "You'll get us both in trouble."

And then she shook off, stubby wings outstretched. She had a grace, even in flight, that marked her as Fey. Fey were so different from other races. The Islanders, Gift knew, regarded the half-breeds as something less, as not quite worthy. But the Fey, the Fey knew that half-breeds were stronger, that the magick flowed pure in mixed blood. The Shaman had once told him she thought it a cultural imperative for the Fey to continue conquering. They had to move on, to find the purity that gave their power its ferocious strength.

But she spoke as if she disliked the Fey desire to conquer. She spoke as if she had used the idea as a way to understand the warrior culture.

Gift was a half-breed. He had had Visions younger than any Fey, and he had built a Shadowlands without practice, by simply holding his grandfather's creation together. His Links were fine and strong, and he could travel along them with no effort at all.

Arianna Shifted into more than one form, unheard of among the Fey. He didn't know what her other talents were. He wasn't sure he wanted to find out.

But they were the only two half-breeds on the Island. The Fey still hadn't comingled with the Islanders. Most of the Fey still lived in Shadowlands, hiding in their protective Fey-made fort for nearly two decades now, sorry in defeat.

The Shaman said the Fey had never been like that before.

She warned that when the Black King came, he would slaughter them all for behavior unworthy of warriors.

All except Gift, whom he could not slaughter, because Gift was of his own blood. If the Black King's family turned on itself, all of the Fey would dissolve into chaos and insanity. Gift and Arianna. They were safe. None of the other Fey were.

He couldn't see her anymore. The birds were again

chirruping in the garden. He stretched slowly, then eased out of the hole. He glanced up for good measure, and saw nothing but blue sky. Perhaps the garden wasn't the best way to go. It was the only way he knew for certain. But if he played this right, the guards would think he was Sebastian.

Gift's heart was pounding against his chest. He had never gone into this palace before, not in his own body. He had only walked—Linked—with Sebastian, inside the golem's body, the case of stone.

Gift didn't know what would happen if they caught him.

But he had to try. He had to get Sebastian out of here, at least until he knew who the strange Fey was. The Vision had happened in the near future. And the only thing Gift could do to prevent his death and Sebastian's was to keep them away from Islander buildings, away from the palace, away from the cities.

He had to get Sebastian to Shadowlands.

And he knew Sebastian couldn't get there on his own.

FOUR

NICHOLAS adjusted the cuffs of his sleeves. Lace fell over his wrists and onto the backs of his hands. He tugged the sleeve of his waistcoat to his wristbones, and made certain that nothing touched the lace. The ring Jewel had given him after the birth of Sebastian glinted on his left hand.

He tucked the shirt into his pants, then pulled his boots out of the wardrobe. His dressing room was large, almost a room in itself. This suite had been filled with laughter once, when Jewel was alive. Hard to believe fifteen years had gone by. He still saw her in his dreams.

And he still missed her, with a visceral ache. He had the children, of course. Sebastian, even though he was slow, was a model son, and Arianna looked like Jewel. The girl acted more like Solanda, though, imperious, proud, and too confident. Sometimes he wondered if he had done the right thing, letting Solanda act as a foster mother. But he didn't know how he could have done otherwise. Arianna was a special child, even for the Fey. She had Shape-Shifted as she came out of the womb, and continued to do so at random during her first few years of life.

He leaned against the dressing room door. He had asked

to be alone this afternoon because he had known he would need it. Sebastian turned eighteen this week. Eighteen years since his birth, since he and Jewel realized that a single child wouldn't unite the two nations. Eighteen years since they learned, bitterly, and finally irrevocably, that uniting the Fey and the Islanders would take a lot of work—work that Nicholas hadn't been able to do alone.

The Fey and Islanders had reached a silent truce since Jewel died, since her father Rugar died. Many of the Fey stayed in Shadowlands, which was a magickal construct, an artificial and invisible place to hide. A few Fey lived on the Isle. Those who did though, were treated like pariahs much of the time, and often threatened with holy water. Holy water killed the Fey with a single touch—and the death was devastatingly horrible.

The Fey melted.

The Fey were so frightened of it that the mention of holy water deterred them. The Islanders made certain that the Fey kept their distance.

He grabbed his boots, sat down on the upholstered chair, and pulled them on. They were calf leather, new and tight. His feet would ache by the end of the day. He hoped it would be worth it.

He had designed the ceremony himself, something the Rocaanists were already protesting.

The religion and the kingdom were tied. For centuries, holy water had been part of every ceremony held in Blue Isle. But it hadn't been used in Nicholas's marriage to Jewel, and he had thought it wasn't going to be used in his coronation either. But Matthias, the Fifty-First Rocaan, had had other ideas.

Jewel had died that day, hideously. If the Fey Shaman hadn't arrived, Arianna would have died too. After that, Nicholas forbade the use of holy water anywhere near the palace.

And that still caused problems. He sighed and ran his hands through his curls. The Fifty-Second Rocaan, Titus, had already sent a letter of protest because the Prince wasn't going to be anointed as per ancient custom. Nicholas had been anointed on his eighteenth birthday, confirmed as the heir to the throne by custom and tradition. But holy water had never touched Sebastian, and Nicholas wouldn't trust his son's life to some theory that a half-Fey child could survive the touch of holy water.

Hence the Coming-of-Age ceremony. It was essentially the same thing as the Anointing, only it was done without Elders, Auds, or, most importantly, the Rocaan.

A handful of the lesser lords had already refused his invitation to attend. He would deal with them later, after the ceremony, when he had a chance to think. Lord Egan had advised him, ages ago, to strip these upstart lords of their lands. Nicholas had refused, thinking that it would make tensions worse. But tensions had grown worse anyway—the lords still slurred him for his "unclean" marriage to a Fey, for his "illegitimate, half-breed" children, and for his non-traditional ways. They were, in Egan's words fomenting dissent, and as lords, they had a platform. And maybe quite a bit of support. Nicholas wasn't certain how much support they had, and he wasn't sure he wanted to find out. He knew he would find out, though, the moment he took away their titular holdings and their titles.

A sharp knock made him start. He frowned at the door.

"I told you not to disturb me, Sanders," he said. His chamberlain sometimes had a mind of his own. Nicholas hated to be nagged, and Sanders was a master at it.

"Forgive me, Sire." Sanders' voice, through the door, had a supercilious tone. "But Lord Stowe has information that cannot wait."

"I'll see him at the ceremony."

"He claims it is important, Sire. He is in your outer chamber."

Nicholas sighed. Stowe was one of the older lords. He had been Nicholas's father's trusted colleague, and was now one of Nicholas's. But Stowe had the unlucky fortune to always bring Nicholas the worst news.

"Tell him I'll be right out," Nicholas said.

It probably had something to do with the ceremony. So many people opposed Sebastian's position as heir. But Nicholas had no choice. The kingship always went to the oldest son, the direct male heir to the Roca. Sebastian was slow, but he was thorough. Arianna had already agreed to be his right hand, and Sebastian trusted her. She was brilliant and unbeatable at anything she tried.

She would protect her brother, and the country, and keep them both safe.

Although Nicholas hoped that wouldn't happen for a long time. Unlike his own father, Nicholas planned to live to a ripe old age. Maybe by then the succession could skip over Sebastian and fall onto one of his children.

He braced himself a final time, then stepped into the sitting room just off the bedroom. The room was cooler than the dressing room. Sanders had opened the window, and beams of sunlight filtered in like halos. There was enough of a breeze to make the entire suite smell like the garden below.

Lord Stowe stood and bowed. He too was wearing his finery, a long black coat with matching pants and narrow shoes based on the Fey model. Nicholas thought it odd that they could steal the Fey's clothing ideas but not accept any other part of their culture.

"Stowe," Nicholas said, not caring for protocol. "We have a ceremony in two hours, and I have to prepare my son."

Most of the lords did not know the extent of Sebastian's mental disabilities, but Stowe did, just as he knew how very powerful Arianna was. Stowe had been near both children since the beginnings of their lives, and had advised Nicholas about them more than once.

"I know, Sire, but you need to hear this now." He waved a hand at Sanders, who hovered near the door. Sanders bowed and backed out, pulling the door closed behind him.

Stowe waited until he was gone, then said, "Is this room safe?"

Nicholas glanced at the door. Sanders could be—and probably was—listening in. Nicholas crooked a finger at Stowe and led him through the dressing room into the royal bedchamber. The room was neat, even though Nicholas had not left it that way in the morning. The windows were closed. The room was dark and stuffy. It had an unused feel, which, Nicholas supposed, was appropriate.

He hadn't brought any one into his bedchamber since Jewel died.

"All right," he said to cover his own discomfort. "What's so hush-hush? Has Titus done something to disrupt the ceremony?"

Stowe pulled the dressing room door closed. "Not that I know of, Sire, but I could check for you."

Nicholas shook his head. He already had twelve people keeping an eye on the Rocaan, and another group watching all the Elders. He wouldn't let the Tabernacle get close to his son.

"There's no need," Nicholas said. "Just get on with this."

Despite his fine clothes, Stowe looked a bit haggard. In the last few years he had lost most of his hair, and his scalp shone in the dim light. He also hunched. Long lines were carved into the skin by his mouth, frown lines, showing his difficult and serious life.

"A man's come up from the Kenniland Marshes. He says the Fey have invaded down there."

"The Fey?" Whatever Nicholas had expected, it wasn't this. The Kenniland Marshes were on the far southern end of the Isle. The Fey armies had never gone that far, not even in their first assault on the Isle. "How did they get there? We would have had reports of an army moving south."

"I don't know, Sire," Stowe said, "but the man said they came over the mountains."

"Over the mountains?" The sea was on the other side of those mountains. They were impossible to scale from the valley side. And the only reports of their far side had come from ships that had circled the Isle trying to get in.

Large mountains with sheer cliff faces, disappearing into a treacherous sea.

A chill ran down Nicholas's back despite the heat in the room. He had seen the impossible ever since the Fey arrived on Blue Isle. Before they arrived, he thought that holy water was benign, that the body was a stable mass of tissue, and that Blue Isle was impenetrable.

Stowe was watching him. The lines on Stowe's face seemed deeper than they had even moments before.

"This is not an internal attack, then," Nicholas said.

Stowe shook his head. "Our people watching the Shadowlands have seen no real changes there. An occasional Fey leaves, but always returns."

"And what about the enclave south of Jahn?"

"The Outdoor Fey?" Stowe said, using the nickname those Fey got from their own people. These Fey weren't able to suffer through life in the Shadowlands any longer. They had to live outside of it. "The enclave split up nearly five years ago. They've spread out all over the Killeny's Bridge area."

"And they haven't gone south separately, then attacked?"

"Sire," Stowe said, his voice lowering. "The man says every village in the Kenniland Marshes is overrun. He says he's seen hundreds of Fey on the mountains."

Nicholas clenched his fists. His children's people. His wife's people. Invading. "How do we know he's sane, Stowe? Is there any proof that he's telling the truth? We've heard these tales before only to discover they were warped visions from a fevered mind."

"I know, Sire," Stowe said. "I believe him."

"Based on what?"

"The logic of his tale," Stowe said. "He says that the Fey started pouring out of the mountains two weeks ago. He went into hiding in the Marshes. I've been there. I've seen that area. The natives could hide there for weeks."

Nicholas didn't need to know how well people could hide in the marshes. His father had died there, murdered by a hidden assassin. Stowe had been beside his father at the time. "The insane can be logical," Nicholas said.

"Sire—"

"If the Fey were invading again, why didn't they come down the river, like they did the first time? It's impossible to scale those mountains, Stowe. And even if the Fey found a way to scale them, it's impossible to bring a ship close to them."

"Some Fey fly," Stowe said.

"Yes, but not all of them. Some have no magick at all. You know that. And your man says they've been coming down the mountains for two weeks. Do you know how big a force that would be? Do you have any idea?"

"Thousands," Stowe said, softly.

"Tens of thousands," Nicholas corrected. "The first invading force didn't have that many people in it. Why would a second? And why would a second come so many years after the first?"

But he already knew the answer to that. He had known it for nearly two decades. Jewel had warned him that the Black King would come. But she hadn't known who the Black King would be, or when he would arrive.

Nicholas had asked her during the marriage negotiations when the Black King would arrive.

Three years, five, ten, she had said. *I don't know. If my grandfather has died, it will take a bit longer because my brother has to get used to the reins of power. Once he is used to being Black King, he will come here.*

But it was the memory of what Rugar had said next that chilled Nicholas.

Eventually, Jewel's father had said, *the Fey will come to Blue Isle in such numbers that we will rule this place.*

Tens of thousands. More than enough to rule this place. More than enough.

"Jewel always said they would come," Stowe said. "She said your children would protect us."

Nicholas shook his head. "Only if she were alive to designate the Isle as part of the Fey. As already conquered. But she's dead, and so's her father."

Stowe looked at his hands. "But your children, they're part of the Black King's family. He can't touch them, right?"

The True Black King—or Black Queen—has to be ruthless, Jewel had said just before she died. *It is the only way to survive. No one wants to kill a Black King more than his closest siblings or his child. But the Black King's family cannot kill within its ranks. That causes untold turmoil. So we have to do it subtly, by hiring assassins and not giving direct orders, or by finding other methods.*

Like invading.

Death by ignorance.

It might work.

"Can he touch them?" Stowe asked again.

"I don't know," Nicholas said. He swallowed. His children were younger than he had been when the Fey first came to Blue Isle. His son didn't have the capability to fight the most ruthless of all Fey. His son would never be much more than a baby himself.

The Black Throne is held together by Blood Magick, the Fey's Shaman had told him after Arianna was born. *That Blood flowed through Jewel. It flows through your children now. If the Blood turns on itself, insanity reigns. And when insanity reigns, whole cultures die. If you cause the Blood to turn on itself, you will unleash a fury.*

Nicholas shook himself. There had been other false alarms in the last twenty years. One actually had them sending an army to the mouth of the Cardidas River to find only mist and the figment of an elderly man's overactive imagination. This might be another.

Nicholas couldn't panic.

Not now.

Not ever.

"Get someone to corroborate this story. Find out who has been to the Marshes lately. See if you can find the Auds who travel through there or a bartering merchant who buys from the south. A force of thousands can't stay hidden forever."

"Unless it's in Shadowlands," Stowe said.

Nicholas shook his head. "The Shadowlands are a bivouac for a regular army, not a hiding place like it's been used here. If the Fey came over the mountains and conquered villages, they're still in those villages. If this has been going on for two weeks, we should have heard before now."

"Unless no one could get out."

"You said the Marshlanders were good at hiding. If they saw a force of ten thousand coming, they would have taken to the marshes and escaped. We would have heard within days."

"The Fey are cunning," Stowe said, sounding skeptical.

Nicholas nodded, remembering all the twists and turns of Jewel's planning. The last thing he had asked her before she died had been if she would someday betray him.

She had promised she wouldn't.

But he had wondered for fifteen years if she had been telling the truth.

"We defeated them once," Nicholas said. "We can do so again."

"Do you think that was a true defeat?" Lord Stowe asked.

"They negotiated out of weakness, Stowe," Nicholas said. "Jewel would never have sacrificed herself and her unborn children to life in Jahn if she had thought there was another way. The Fey are warriors, remember?"

"I'm having trouble forgetting," Stowe said.

"Find me proof," Nicholas said, "and set up a meeting of the lords after the Coming-of-Age ceremony. We'll settle this thing as soon as we can."

At least, he hoped they would. This invasion from the south sounded implausible.

Which made it all that more likely that the Black King had arrived. The Fey never did things the expected way, and they had more abilities than Nicholas knew of.

I know the Black King lives and I know he has not abandoned Blue Isle, the Shaman had said.

He will come, Jewel had said.

In such numbers that we will rule this place, her father had said.

Nicholas had been dreading this for a generation. And if it were true, if the Black King had arrived with an army of thousands, Nicholas didn't know what to do.

The Fey are sworn to protect anyone in the Black King's family, the Shaman had said.

Anyone.

Sebastian.

Arianna.

And the Black King himself.

Instead of solving the war between Blue Isle and the Fey, Jewel and Nicholas had made it worse.

Their marriage, and their children, and turned an invasion into a civil war.

A fury, the Shaman had called it.

Insanity.

Nicholas closed his eyes.

This was only the beginning.

FIVE

TITUS, the Fifty-Second Rocaan, sat on his balcony in the heat of midday. His chair was a specially designed lounge, made for relaxation and afternoon naps. A red berry punch sat on the table beside him, untouched, even though he usually drank two glasses as part of his afternoon ritual. He was staring across the courtyard, over the Cardidas River, and into the main section of the city of Jahn.

He was staring at the palace.

This afternoon the half-Fey would be celebrated as the next head of state. The creature with the little brain, who carried the Roca's blood mixed with the blood of murderers, the creature who could not touch holy water for fear of death, would be designated the Prince.

Someday he would rule Blue Isle.

Titus was not certain that day should come.

Although he didn't know how to prevent it. His predecessor, Matthias, would have gone to the ceremony and somehow—presumably accidentally—touched the heir with holy water. Matthias had done that once before, to the King's consort, Jewel, and her death had been hideous.

But not as hideous as the slaughter of the Fey in Daisy

Stream. That had been the worst Titus had ever seen. The bodies melting around them, the stench of decaying flesh, and the cries of pain. That had been the only time he had touched one of them.

He had couched over a dying Fey. Its body had twitched as it had gone through its throes. Like a sand sculpture after someone had poured water on it, the Fey had lost definition, until it was unrecognizable as a living being. It was only flesh and bone, lumps of skin-colored debris, littering a wet floor.

He had thought to Bless it, but instead he had found himself cursing it with the Words Written and Unwritten: *When you touch water,* he had told it, *you touch the Essence of God.*

And he believed that. He believed that God's essence filled the holy water, and it let God's people live, while slaughtering others.

In fifteen years of study, however, he had been unable to determine how—or why—God's people could mate with God's enemies and produce issue. The only answer he had come up with was that God had cursed the firstborn by removing his brain, and had abandoned the secondborn, allowing evil to flourish within her monstrous person. The fact that King Nicholas had mated with a Fey in the first place, and allowed her children to live, only showed that he was as godless as Matthias had once claimed.

Only now the King was condemning the entire country to live under tainted rule.

Titus did not know what to do about that. He had prayed for weeks, hoping to hear the still small voice telling him how to resolve this problem. He could not kill—he believed that death was God's provenance—and he could not blaspheme the direct heir to Roca's throne on this earth. All he could do was withhold his approval, and hope that would be enough.

So far, it had not been.

So far, all the palace had done was ignore the Tabernacle as if the Tabernacle had no place in this society.

Nicholas forgot what gave his Kingship power.

Titus picked up his juice and took a sip, wincing at the bitter taste. The afternoon's heat was fierce—he was sweating under his robes—and the shade didn't provide much cover. It was hotter in the Tabernacle itself. At least on the balcony, he could feel the breeze off the Cardidas, with its faintly marshy scent. If he were still an Aud, he would go to the riverbank, and wade into the water, allowing the water to cool his hot, tired feet.

But he was not an Aud. He hadn't been one since he was a teenager. He had become Rocaan because of a fluke, because the Fifty-First Rocaan had run away from his duties, leaving only Titus in control of the Secrets. Titus could have taught the Secrets to his superiors, the Elders, but he felt that none of them had the spiritual grace to follow God's commands.

God had appointed him, in the most difficult circumstances, and Titus could not turn away from divine order.

Just as he could not turn away now.

If only Nicholas really understood. It seemed so simple to Titus. The Roca, before he was Absorbed, appointed his eldest son as the heir to the throne. He had made his second son the head of the newly formed religion. The first Rocaan, the Roca's second son, did not have children, and so appointed a worthy second son as his replacement. The Rocaans traditionally did not marry, nor did they have children. The line of Rocaans was handed to second sons for generations, true believers who had joined the Tabernacle, who had only the interests of the religion, the Tabernacle, and Blue Isle at heart.

But Nicholas could trace his heritage, in an unbroken line, to the Roca himself. The Roca, beloved of God, who had allowed himself to be killed by the Soldiers of the Enemy so that he could be Absorbed into the Hand of God. The Roca, who lived still, and now had God's Ear, and spoke for all his people. Nicholas should have been proud of that lineage.

Instead, he had polluted it. The Fiftieth Rocaan had believed that the Fey were, metaphorically, the Soldiers of the Enemy. Instead of defeating them with the Hand of God, as the Roca had done, King Nicholas had married them.

In a ceremony only partially sanctioned by the Tabernacle.

The children had never been Blessed, never been Converted, never been Touched by the Hand of God. How could they rule, then? How could they lead the Roca's people if they were not in touch with the Holy One? Titus had tried to discuss this with Nicholas once, and Nicholas had dismissed him as lacking in understanding.

Titus understood. Nicholas feared for his children's lives, believing them to be Fey. But they carried the blood of the Roca within them. His holy water might not kill them, but strengthen them.

If, of course, they were truly God's Anointed, and not demons as some believed.

But Nicholas had refused the holy water. He had refused the test. And he was flying in the face of tradition, celebrating his son's heritage with a fake ceremony.

Titus would do nothing yet. Nicholas was a still a young man, only a few years older than Titus himself, and would probably live a long life. Titus would begin his campaign now, and finalize it before the girl came of age. She was truly the dangerous one. The boy couldn't rule without her help—or the help of a powerful wife.

He stood slowly, decision made. His robes felt heavy across his shoulders and somehow the heat of the day seemed fiercer. He took one final sip of the bitter juice, determined to take it inside, when he heard cries below.

He leaned over his balcony. An Aud, his robe filthy with mud and grime, staggered across the courtyard. Other Auds hurried out, talking rapidly. The dirty Aud cried out, his voice rising, screaming of danger. Titus scanned the road. Except for a handful of people going about their daily business, it was empty.

The other Auds ushered him inside, his cries fading as the doors closed behind him. Titus put his juice glass down, adjusted his robes and hurried through his rooms. He pulled open his door, startling the Aud guards, and hurried through the corridor and down the stairs.

The Aud's cries continued. He kept repeating something about danger and Fey and death. The hair rose on the back of Titus's neck. Something had changed. An Aud shouldn't have anything to worry about the Fey. The Fey were frightened of any representative of Rocaanism, but they were particularly frightened of the Auds, who often went from kirk to kirk carrying holy water, and bringing the message of Roca to the believers.

Titus found them in the servant's chapel. The filthy Aud was on his knees before the altar, weeping. The Roca's sword, hanging from the wall behind the altar, shone cleanly in the candlelight. There were no windows in the servant's chapel. They hadn't even had services here for the first ten years after the slaughter of the Fey that had taken place in this room.

It had been here that Matthias had discovered the properties of holy water. He had had no weapon, and the symbolic sword had already been stolen by someone else for use against the Fey. So he had grabbed vials of holy water and had thrown them like rocks, hoping to knock out the approaching group.

Instead, he had melted them.

Titus had been an Aud then, and after the battle, he had had to clean up this room. The memory still turned his stomach.

But he had been the one to reinstate services here, to hide the memory of all those deaths.

The others hovered around the sobbing Aud. His bare feet, a sign of his position, were black with grime and dried blood. His robes were torn, and his sash was missing.

He couldn't have been more than fifteen.

Rusel, an Officiate, came in through the worship room door, a Danite at his side. Officiates were in charge of running the Tabernacle. They were two steps above Auds (the lowest of the low), a step above Danites, but below the Elders. A good Officiate could expect to fill a vacancy in the Council of Elders, just as a good Elder could hope, one day, to become Rocaan.

Rusel was portly and balding. His robe fit snugly over his round frame. He stopped when he saw Titus. "I did not realize anyone had sent for you, Holy Sir."

"I saw the commotion, and decided to see what caused it," Titus said. He walked down the aisle and sat on the steps beside the sobbing Aud.

"Son," he said softly, "you're safe here."

The boy shook his shaved head. He gulped and wiped his face with a filthy arm, smearing the dirt. The rug below him was already stained with mud. "It was awful," he said.

"What was awful?" Titus kept his voice low, soft. He

remembered feeling this kind of terror when he was about the Aud's age, when the Fiftieth Rocaan had sent him with a message to the Fey.

The boy looked up. His eyes, wide and blue, grew wider when he saw who he was talking to. "Holy Sir," he breathed. "Forgive me. I had no idea—"

"You're upset," Titus said. "Tell us what happened."

The boy nodded, then wiped at his face again. Some of what Titus had thought of as dirt was more blood.

"Get him a cloth and some water," Titus said.

"I have holy water," Rusel said, his tone vaguely disapproving. Titus should have touched the boy with holy water before sitting beside him. It was an old precaution, one that dated from the Fey invasion, and it kept Fey interlopers out of the palace. Any Fey touched with holy water would, of course, melt.

The boy held out his hand. It was shaking. "It doesn't matter any more," he said as the Danite crouched beside him, and poured a bit of holy water from Rusel's vial onto the boy's skin.

"It matters," Titus said. "I'm sorry we have to do this."

The boy shook his head. "You don't understand."

"Holy Sir," Rusel said pointedly. "His title is Holy Sir."

"Titles don't matter right now," Titus said. "This boy has been through something terrible. What's your name, son?"

"Dimitri," the boy said.

"A name of kings," Titus said.

The boy smiled, just a little. "My people were never kings."

"We all are," Titus said, "in God's eyes."

The boy did not melt or even flinch as the holy water touched him. An Aud came into the room with a basin filled with normal water and several large cloths. He handed one to the boy. The boy looked at Titus, as if asking for approval.

"Wash your face, Dimitri, then tell us what happened."

The boy dipped a cloth into the water, then scrubbed the dirt off his face. It came away red.

Not dirt.

Blood.

Titus frowned. He touched the boy's ruined robe, and scraped off some of the dried flakes. Mud.

"Are you injured, Dimitri?" he asked, nodding at the water.

The boy shook his head. "It's not mine, Holy Sir," he said softly. "Would God that it were."

"Whose is it?" Rusel asked.

"I don't know," the boy said, his voice quavering. He sounded as if he were going to burst into tears again.

Titus glared at Rusel, making the Officiate step back. Titus wanted to be the only one questioning the boy. "Where were you stationed, son?" Titus asked.

"The Kenniland Marshes."

"With Gregor?"

The boy nodded. He dipped the cloth in the water again. The splashes were the only sound in the room.

"Where is Gregor?" Titus asked, hoping the boy wouldn't make him work for every answer.

"Dead. They're all dead." The boy's voice was flat. He took the cloth out of the water and scrubbed his hands. Drops fell on the carpet. Rusel moved toward them, as if he were dismayed by them, but Titus impaled him with a look. Again.

"Who killed them, Dimitri?"

"The Fey." The boy whispered the word, as if he were afraid of being overheard.

"What Fey?" Titus asked. That prickly feeling at the back of his neck had grown.

"You don't know, Holy Sir?"

Titus glanced at the others. They looked as confused as he did. "We've heard nothing different about the Fey," Titus said.

The boy dropped his cloth in the bucket. He closed his eyes and winced as if he were trying to hold back tears. Then he took a deep breath.

"The Fey came out of the mountains," he said. "Hundreds of them, maybe more. They were waiting for us in the kirk at the south end of the marsh."

"They went into a kirk?" Titus asked. He remembered their reluctance to do so years before.

"They'd been there a few days. They were waiting for us. They already had the village."

"I'm confused," Rusel said. "Who were these Fey? Did they come from Shadowlands?"

"Rusel," Titus cautioned.

"They came from the mountains," the boy said in that flat voice.

"The Snow Mountains?" Titus asked.

The boy nodded. He opened his eyes. Tears lined them.

"They came from the sea?" Titus couldn't believe it.

"Hundreds of them," the boy said. "And they were waiting for us. In the kirk."

Rusel leaned against the altar. His face was ashen, as if he knew what was coming.

"And then?" Titus asked.

"They attacked," the boy said. "With their fingers. Did you know they can rip skin off a living person with the edges of their fingers?"

No, Titus hadn't known that. And he wasn't certain he wanted to know.

"We got out the holy water and threw it on them, but it didn't do anything. They kept coming. I grabbed the Roca's Sword, God forgive me, and hit one of them. Then I ran. They followed me to the edge of the marsh. I ran in, then dove under the reeds. My grandfather taught me how to grab a reed and breathe through it like a straw. I did. When I didn't come up, they must have thought I was dead. By nightfall, they were gone. I went back to the kirk. Everyone was dead."

He shuddered as if the memory were too much.

"Most of them had empty holy water vials in their hands."

"The Fey didn't come after you, even then?" Rusel asked, as if he found this story incredible.

"They wanted him to get away," Titus said. "They wanted someone to inform us." He leaned toward the boy, not entirely sure he believed either. "Are you certain the holy water was made properly?"

The boy shrugged. "We got it from the Tabernacle as we always do. I picked it up before we left for the marshes."

"Send for Elder Reece," Titus said. "I want his help testing the holy water. Let's make certain no one substituted their water for ours."

It had happened once before, years ago. A Fey had sneaked into the Tabernacle and replaced holy water vials with river water. Reece had discovered the problem then. He would be able to discover if there was one now, too.

One of the Auds left in search of Reece. Rusel's face had grown even paler. "We need to inform the palace."

"Of what?" Titus asked.

"Hundreds of Fey have invade the Isle. Surely they need to know."

"We don't know if Nicholas sent for them, now do we?" Titus asked.

"He's our King," Rusel said.

"And the father of Fey children. He has been close to the Fey too long. We don't know what he's planning."

"Are you saying we should keep this invasion secret, Holy Sir?"

"I'm not certain this is an invasion," Titus said. "We don't know how many Fey are in Shadowlands. It might be easy for them to seem to appear out of the mountains. The Kenniland Marshes have little experience with the Fey. We'll find out what's going on, and then we'll contact the palace."

Rusel bit his lower lip. He frowned. Titus stared at him. Rusel nodded once. "As you wish, Holy Sir."

"No one will discuss this matter," Titus said. "Reece and I will see what's happening with the holy water. Call the Elders together, Rusel. After Dimitri is fed and suitably clothed, I want him to tell the Elders everything he remembers. That's every detail, son. Can you do that?"

The boy nodded. He was courageous, Titus had to give him that. And young.

So very young.

"That's all," Titus said. "Please take Dimitri to the kitchens. He needs to eat. Then make certain he is not injured before you bring him to the Elders."

Everyone looked at him.

"Please leave me," Titus said. The boy stood, along with the Auds. Titus put his hand on the boy's arm. "You did well, son," he said. "I'm pleased you came to us first."

A tear slid down the boy's newly scrubbed cheek. "Where else would I go, Holy Sir? I belong here."

"That you do," Titus said. "I will see you shortly." He nodded at the Auds, and they led the boy out of the room. "Stay for a moment, Rusel."

Rusel glanced at his Danite, who bowed and left. The two of them were alone in the room. It seemed larger now that it was empty. The stain Dimitri left on the rug gave off a muddy, iron smell.

"What do you think of his story?" Titus asked.

Rusel shook his head. "It's too incredible to be true."

"I think he's telling the truth. A young boy cannot fake that kind of deep fear."

"If he is, indeed, a young boy."

Titus smiled. "We tested him with holy water."

"The water might be tainted."

"But the boy was the one who told us that."

Rusel's hands were gripping the side of the altar so tightly that his knuckles had turned white. "The Fey are cunning, Holy Sir. They might tell us the truth while concealing a greater lie."

"You think he's a Doppelgänger?" Doppelgängers were Fey who picked a host, murdered it, and then duplicated its features exactly. Titus had seen a Doppelgänger attack a host only once. The Doppelgänger wrapped itself around the host's body, and sucked the very life out of it. The host's bones had fallen to the floor, and the Doppelgänger had landed, naked, looking exactly like the host.

It had been terrifying.

"Perhaps," Rusel said. "It would explain many things."

"But why make up an attack that never happened? It would be too easy to check."

"Still, Holy Sir, once Elder Reece has checked the holy water, I would like your permission to test the boy again."

"Granted," Titus said. He leaned back, resting his elbows against the top step. "What if the boy's story is true? What if the Fey have taken over the Marshes?"

"I would wonder how they got to the Marshes. The Mountains are impassable."

"The Fey are cunning," Titus said. "You said so yourself."

"That does not convince me that they can achieve miracles," Rusel said.

"What if they left their Shadowlands months before,

switched the holy water, and staged this attack to look as if
they were coming from the mountains?"

"To what end, Holy Sir?"

"To send us in panic to the Kenniland Marshes. The boy
did not go to the palace. He came here."

"And he said they were waiting in the kirk."

Titus nodded. He no longer looked at Rusel. He was
staring at a pew. It still bore faint scars from the attack so
many years ago. "They let him get away."

"You think the palace is behind this, Holy Sir?"

Titus shrugged. "The Tabernacle has become quite a nui-
sance to them, has it not?"

"The King would never dare dispute the authority of the
Rocaan."

"The King has done so many times. Once he even toyed
with declaring himself head of the Tabernacle."

"But that was under the Fifty-First Rocaan. The Fifty-
First Rocaan was crazed."

"Was he, Rusel? He had never seemed crazed to me.
Merely tortured in body and spirit. And he hated Fey, even
more than the rest of us did."

"I cannot believe you're suggesting this, Holy Sir."

Titus turned, leaned on one elbow and looked up at
Rusel. The Officiate's face had gone from a stark white to a
brilliant red. His hands still gripped the side of the altar.
"Would you prefer the alternative?"

"That the boy is lying? Yes, Holy Sir."

"And if he's not? Would you still prefer the alternative?"

Rusel's Adam's apple bobbed once as he swallowed nervously. "That the Fey are doing this on their own?"

Titus nodded.

"They can't be, Holy Sir. The holy water would have
killed them."

"And what if they've found a way to survive it. What if it
no longer has any effect on them?"

"That's not possible," Rusel said.

"It's always been a fear, that they would learn a way
around holy water," Titus said.

"If they have . . ." Rusel said, his voice trailing off.

"We'll die," Titus finished for him. "We'll all die."

SIX

GIFT slipped behind a column on the fourth floor. Finally he was on familiar ground. Sebastian's suite was nearby. Sebastian rarely went anywhere other than his suite, his sister's rooms, and the garden. Sometimes, Gift knew, Sebastian ate in the royal dining chamber or used the audience room, but Gift was never with him at those times. Gift had only been to the suites and the garden. The rest of the palace was a mystery to him.

Getting inside had been amazingly easy. He had imitated Sebastian's halting gait and kept his eyes averted. His body, even though it looked like Sebastian's, wanted to move quickly, and he knew he had the gait wrong. But no one noticed. In fact, the few servants who saw him had bowed or curtsied. Gift ignored them, as he knew Sebastian would have.

To do something out of the ordinary took additional energy for Sebastian.

But now Gift was at the tricky part. He had to be careful to avoid the servants, and even more careful to avoid seeing Sebastian in the hallway. No one outside of Shadowlands (except Solanda) knew that Gift was really the child of

Nicholas and Jewel. They all thought Sebastian was a living being instead of a golem. He was a special golem, but a golem all the same.

The corridor was empty. It smelled stuffy, as if it wasn't used much. The columns were placed in the center of the corridor, one past each major doorway. Eventually the corridor widened into a gallery. Portraits of the royal children hung along the wall. Dozens of the portraits were artificially posed scenes: two or three children cuddling a dog, or holding extremely large flowers. None of the children looked happy.

Gift and Sebastian had studied all of these portraits. The later ones had more life to them as the part of portraiture improved. Gift's father, an only child, had the best portrait. He sat at the edge of a brook, knees drawn to his chest, staring pensively into the water. Gift didn't know if the portrait caught the essence of his father—he had only seen the man a few times—but it did make him look the most relaxed, the most real, of all of them.

The portrait of Arianna and Sebastian hung at the top of a flight of stairs. Sebastian sat on a stone stairway, so motionless he looked like stone himself. Arianna stood above him, her hair flying behind her as if she were caught, alone, in a breeze. The artist had captured the essence of both of them: Sebastian's innocence and uncanny ability to be still; Arianna's brilliance and constant motion. Gift loved the portrait as it was. Sebastian had told him, in his slow, stilted manner, that he wished Gift could be in the portrait as well.

The gallery was empty. The windows at the far end stood open, letting sunlight fill the hall. Sebastian's door was also open, and Gift heard nothing from inside. Sebastian had to be dressed and ready, then. Otherwise Gift would have heard a gaggle of servant voices, and the nurse who seemed to grow more commanding each year that her "precious boy" did not make significant improvements.

Gift sprinted across the hall, past the railings over the stairwell, and slipped inside Sebastian's door.

The suite felt as familiar as home. This was the only place Gift had ever been that was filled with light and color. It had prevented him from suffering the Overs as Coulter did when he left Shadowlands, a strange paralyzing fear that came from living his entire life without stimulation.

The Fey weren't meant to live in Shadowlands. Visionaries created Shadowlands as places to sleep during battles, as places to store weapons or to protect leaders. Shadowlands was a box built with the mind of the Visionary, and linked to that Visionary like a body was linked to a mind. Gift's grandfather had built the Shadowlands Gift had grown up in, and when his grandfather died, Gift had held the Shadowlands together. If Gift hadn't been there, Shadowlands would have been destroyed, killing all inside.

Because Shadowlands wasn't a natural place, nothing could grow inside. The walls, floor, and ceiling of the box felt solid, but were invisible. The lack of light made Shadowlands a place of gray, a colorless domain. Air could seep through the walls of Shadowlands, but nothing else. Gift grew up in an opaque mist that leached the color from even the most brilliant things. He wouldn't even have known what color was if it weren't for his Links with Sebastian.

Gift loved this suite. The sitting room had become the nursery when Arianna was old enough to walk. The distance between the nursery and the stairs was longer here than it had been in the official nursery, giving the nurse a chance to catch her, something that hadn't been possible before.

Gift slid inside the doorway and carefully, quietly pulled the door closed. He couldn't see Sebastian yet, but that didn't worry him. The servants had probably helped Sebastian dress and then had given him orders not to move until someone came to get him. That was the way these events worked in the past. No sense in believing they would change the pattern now.

Gift peered around the corner into the dressing room. No Sebastian. He hurried through the dressing room into the bedroom. This too felt familiar. The bed was a large, soft four-poster with several thick blankets. Sebastian was constantly cold, and piled the blankets on, even in the summer. When Gift was visiting along the Link, he often had to pull the covers off.

The room was built on a turret that extended over the garden. Two windows, one on either side, looked down on the blooms. Their tapestries were up, letting strong breeze flow through. Sebastian stood beside the window to Gift's left. He stared straight ahead at the blue sky and the circling birds as if he wanted to be part of them. His arms hung at his sides, looking useless even though they weren't.

Gift had never seen this Changeling, this golem, this creature he loved like a brother, in the flesh. The Link was like a string that attached them, a string Gift's consciousness could ride across, but Sebastian could not. They had learned, as children, that Sebastian owed his own consciousness to Gift. Every time Gift visited Sebastian's body, Gift left a tiny part of himself. Those parts gained a life of their own. Sebastian thought for himself, and saw himself as a separate being from the moment Gift's mother held him. He used to hide that conscious self from Gift, thinking Gift would take over his body permanently. When Gift discovered that, the boys were five, and Gift corrected that idea. From that moment on, they were fast friends, and close confidants.

Brothers.

Or perhaps more. Two parts of the same whole.

But they had never seen each other face to face.

Gift had warned Sebastian that he was coming, but that hadn't really impressed Sebastian. Sometimes actions were the only things that were clear to Sebastian.

Sebastian hadn't heard him come in. Gift took a moment to orient himself. Sebastian was as tall as he was, more solid than Gift was, and seemed steadier.

He was also wearing a long, embroidered white robe, which would make the afternoon very difficult.

"Sebastian?" Gift said.

Sebastian tottered, then turned awkwardly, moving his feet in tiny intervals. It was Sebastian's equivalent of a whirl, and it often made his more mobile sister laugh. Finally he faced Gift, and his eyes widened.

His mouth opened, and Gift knew what would come out.

A scream.

Gift was across the room in a heartbeat, and placed his hand over Sebastian's mouth. The scream started a second after, a raspy grinding sound that sent shivers through Gift. His hand muffled most of it.

"It's me," he said. "Gift."

Sebastian shook his head slowly, but with such strength it threatened to dislodge Gift's fingers.

"Gift," he said again. "I'm Gift."

Sebastian kept shaking his head, his eyes rolling with fear. Sebastian had never thought of Gift as anything but a second self, not as a separate being. Because Gift could travel along their Link, but Sebastian couldn't. Sebastian was rooted to his own body. Gift knew that, but he thought he had explained all of this to Sebastian.

Apparently he hadn't explained well enough.

Gift glanced at the open doors, hoped no one had heard the raspy muffled scream, and closed his eyes. He reached for the Link, a pattern that was as old as Gift himself. Then he slid along it, startled at the shortness of the trip. One moment he had been in his own body, the next he was in Sebastian's.

From the inside, Sebastian's body seemed huge. They always met behind the eyes. Sebastian's inner self was a partially formed child with a ghostly pale body and haunted eyes. Gift crouched beside him, this more familiar form of his friend and companion.

It's me, he said, gesturing at the view through Sebastian's eyes. *The man there. That's me.*

Sebastian shook his head—he could move rapidly outside of his stone body—and buried his eyes in his hands. Gift touched the ghostly, childlike chin and raised Sebastian's face to his own.

Remember what I told you, about the danger?

Yes. Sebastian's voice had grown deeper with the years. It sounded like a man's voice coming from a child.

I had to come to you in my body. I have to take you out of here. The city?

Gift could feel the childlike excitement rising around them. Sebastian had only made a few trips into the city, and he had loved all of them. His family hadn't loved it, though, and the taunts that Sebastian had received had broken Gift's heart.

My home. You want to come to my home? It's where you were born.

And you were born here.

Gift smiled. *That's right. Then they switched us.*

Sebastian smiled back. They were on familiar territory now. They had told this story to each other many times. *Can Arianna come?*

Not right now, Gift said. *Maybe later.*

And my father?

He has to stay here. He's in charge here.

He won't like it if I leave.

He won't like it if you die.

Sebastian's gaze flickered, and before them appeared the slender form of Gift's mother, supine, her head melting from the holy water. Sebastian had cried for her for months. Gift's father stood beside her, looking lost.

Then the image disappeared.

Will I die like that? Sebastian asked, a shiver running through his real body and shaking them like the wind would shake a leaf.

Gift shook his head and thought of the Vision. The image of Sebastian on the floor, a knife in his back, filled the space between them.

That's me? Sebastian asked, his voice small.

If you don't come with me.

Who are those people?

I don't know, Gift said. *They look like Fey, but they aren't any Fey I know.*

I don't know any Fey.

Except Solanda.

She calls me lump, Fey are mean people.

We're part Fey, Gift said. *Your mother was Fey.*

Gift's mother's face rose between them. She was peering at them, her narrow features beautiful in the half light. *He's smiling,* she said. *I love it when he smiles.*

You look funny, Sebastian said softly. *I didn't think you were real like everybody else, I thought you were like me.*

I am like you, Gift said. He was still staring at his mother's image, floating behind him. She looked young, but ferocious somehow. Her Fey features were pronounced. Her entire face was upswept—her eyes, her cheekbones, even the edges of her mouth. She had been a mother to Sebastian. She hadn't even known Gift was alive.

You have your own body, Sebastian said. He leaned against

his mother's image, as if needing her support. *If you have your own, how come you need mine?*

I don't need yours, Sebastian, Gift said, feeling desperate. He wanted to go to Sebastian's eyes and see the room. Any moment now someone would come looking for Sebastian. The ceremony had to start soon. *I visit yours because we're Linked.*

Then how come I can't visit yours? Sebastian had his tiny ghostly arms crossed. Gift had seen this stubbornness before. If he didn't answer it, they would never leave.

It's a Link, Gift said. *You should be able to visit my body. You just didn't know I had one until now.*

So why can't I stay here and Link to you? They'd hurt my body but not me.

Gift shook his head. *That might shatter the Link and kill both of us,* he said. *It's better that you come with me.*

Can I tell my dad? Sebastian asked.

After we leave, Gift said. *I'm afraid if we don't go soon, something will happen to both of us.*

I don't want to go, Sebastian said.

I know, Gift said, *but I think we have no choice. I love you, Sebastian. I don't want anything to happen to you.*

Sebastian got up and put his arms around Gift. The ghostly arms felt light and not quite solid. *I love you too, Gift.*

Then come with me.

Sebastian nodded against Gift's chest. *Bring me home quick, though.*

As quickly as I can, Gift said. He took Sebastian's tiny shoulders and moved away from him. *I'm going to break the Link now. Then I'll take your hand, and we'll leave together. We're going to go out the window. You have to climb like I taught you, all right?*

Sebastian nodded. He was biting his lower lip. Those climbs out the window had been precarious, and Sebastian had never done one on his own.

All right, Gift said. *The next time you see me, I'll be in my own body.*

Sebastian nodded again. Gift slid along the Link and arrived in his own body with a jolt. His hand was still over Sebastian's mouth, and his head was still turned toward the door. He brought his hand down. Sebastian closed his mouth.

"It's me," Gift said. "Just like I told you."

Sebastian's eyes were wide, but he brought his head up and down once. He looked terrified and lost.

"All right," Gift said. He took Sebastian's hand. "We'll go now."

"I . . . can't . . . get . . . the . . . robe . . . dir-ty." Sebastian spoke as fast as he could, which was still slow by most standards. His mouth didn't form the words well, and he had trouble creating sound in his throat. The problem had gotten worse as he had gotten older, not better. Gift suspected it had something to do with Sebastian's size, and the fact that a golem wasn't supposed to live this long or grow this big. The strain on the magick was simply too much.

"Tell them it's my fault," Gift said. He tugged on Sebastian's arm. Sebastian took one step toward Gift and then stopped.

Gift turned.

Arianna stood in the doorway, her dressing robe wrapped tightly around her, her hair messed and tangled.

"Who are you?" she asked, a small tremble in her voice revealing her surprise. "And what are you doing to my brother?"

SEVEN

MATTHIAS stood, shirtless, in the door of the smithy. The furnace roared behind him, making the open room unbearable in the afternoon heat. Sweat poured down his back. His breeches were damp, and his bare feet left prints on the straw-covered dirt.

The moment of truth had arrived: Yeon had finished forging the sword. Now he was about to plunge it into the cool water bath. The last five times he had done this, the sword had shattered.

Matthias stepped closer. Yeon's broad, muscular torso glinted with sweat, and was covered with black grime from the fire behind him. He used tongs to plunge the hot sword in water. Hissing started immediately, and steam rose, blinding both of them, and making the area even hotter.

Yeon glanced at him, eyes nearly hidden in his filthy face. Matthias said nothing, just watched the steaming trough. If Yeon could stand the increased heat, Matthias could too. Yeon was doing this at Matthias's suggestion. It was long, hard, hot work, but they had made some progress.

At first, Yeon had thought the strange metal from the Cliffs of Blood was unforgeable. It had taken them nearly a month to find the right combination of heat and tension to make the metal into a sword in the first place.

But they had done it. They simply hadn't been able to finish the process.

Matthias discovered the metal, called varin, during his long sojourn in the Cliffs of Blood. After he resigned from his position as the Fifty-First Rocaan, he ran home, to the Cliffs. He had no family left. He hadn't even been back in decades, but the villages looked the same, nestled near Blue Isle's northeasternmost mountains. The Cliffs of Blood were tall and imposing; the jagged, blood red stones lining the peaks gave the cliffs their name. They were actually part of the northern range, the Eyes of Roca, taller than the Snow Mountains to the south and much more deadly.

The people up there had a hard edge to them, a lack of belief in anything, including Rocaanism. It had been a perfect respite for him after a life in the Tabernacle.

But he had continued his scholarship. It had been more of a religion to him than the real religion anyway. And he had learned some things that would surprise the true believers. Things that had surprised him.

The steam kept rising from the bath. Matthias leaned closer. The stench of Yeon's body rivaled his own. They had been at this too long. Fortunately the smithy stood at the edge of a dead-end street in the farthest reaches of Jahn. Auds rarely came here, and lords never did. This was the poorest section, the kind of place forgotten now that the Fiftieth Rocaan—with his focus on the less fortunate—was long dead.

Matthias had been here for two months, unnoticed and unrecognized. Fifteen years had changed more about him than his appearance. Then he had been a high-ranking Elder, finally appointed (unwillingly) to Rocaan. His finery and the status of his office gave him his identity. Now he was like all the rest in the kingdom, with rough fingers from hard labor and a face lined from too much time in harsh weather. His clothes were still fine—the followers near the Cliffs had some excellent seamstresses—but grimy with use.

"Back!" Yeon shouted, and with a meaty arm shoved Matthias toward a pile of straw.

Matthias let himself tumble backward and covered his

head with his arms. Yeon landed with a grunt behind him, and then the sword exploded.

Boiling water fell on them like rain. Mixed with the droplets were hardened bits of varin. Matthias kept his face covered and protected the most vulnerable areas of his body. The varin pellets had hit him before and left welts the size of fists along his back. He would get welts again.

Yeon was cursing, his words muffled by his position under the straw. Matthias knew what the smithy was saying; he was casting aspersions on the Roca's parentage, on the Tabernacle's holiness, and on the King's love of the Fey. A hissing echoed behind them as the bulk of the water fell toward the furnace. It would take some cleaning before the smithy was ready for use again.

And then it was over. Matthias raised his head. He had small burns along his right arm, where the water hit, and a lump was already forming on the back of his left hand. Despite the pain from the welts, they pleased him. It meant that people had the same reaction to forged varin as some had to holy water.

The Fey's reaction might be even stronger.

He pushed the straw off Yeon.

"I don't know why I let you talk me into this," Yeon said. "It's a fool's project, and it will never ever work. No one can make varin into a sword. No one can make varin into anything."

"That's why Old Lady Fice had varin tools in her stable," Matthias said. He had shown Yeon the varin tools over a year ago, when they had first discussed this project.

"Find her smithy and have him make the sword for you."

"Her smithy is dead, and I have you."

"I'm a scholar just like you, holy man. My smithing days are long gone."

Matthias smiled. "They were long gone. But you've had six months of practice now."

"Six months of exploding metal." Yeon picked straw off his skin. He had welts too. He wiped an arm over his face, leaving a long black streak on his forehead. "Most metals don't explode."

"I suspect that's what makes this one so special." Matthias picked some straw off his stomach. He was in the middle of the straw pile on the outside of the smithy. The water had exploded backward, into the smithy, putting out the forge fire, but leaving the furnace running. Steam and smoke still poured out.

They would have quite a mess to clean up.

"I think you're chasing your tail," Yeon said, as he pushed himself to his feet. "I really do."

"Maybe," Matthias said, "But if I am, you're chasing with me."

Yeon grunted, put a hand over his mouth, and went inside.

Sometimes it did feel as if they were chasing a dream. But Matthias's scholarship had turned up interesting changes in Rocaanism over the centuries. The Fiftieth Rocaan had pointed the way by resurrecting the original recipe for holy water. Once he put in an ingredient missing from the common recipe, some people started to have skin reactions. Elder Reece had the worst one, and it was his lack of a reaction that led the Fiftieth Rocaan to know that a Fey had tampered with the holy water in the Tabernacle.

The reactions intrigued Matthias. What if the Islanders' reactions were merely a mild form of the melting the Fey suffered? If that were the case, then perhaps there were other ways of attacking the Fey, ways forgotten or not yet discovered.

He brushed the last of the straw off himself. He had started pursuing this theory when he couldn't get that Fey's voice out of his head. Burden, the Fey he'd murdered, had said Matthias had Feylike magick, and that he had used that magick to create the poisonous qualities of holy water.

You changed the water's properties, Burden had said. *Your magick is now part of the mix, and that is a sign of a very powerful magick maker.*

His voice mingled with the voices of so many others.

Demon spawn.

They had called Matthias that from childhood because of his unusual height. That had been one of the reasons he'd decided to join the Tabernacle.

You're tall, Burden had said. *Islanders usually aren't tall. Height seems to go with the magick for reasons we don't understand.*

Matthias had killed him for saying that. Or at least, the

Fey had tried to make Matthias believe he had killed
Burden. There had been another Fey in the room, a spark of
light known as a Wisp, and it had flown into Matthias's face
before Burden's death. Who knew what kind of magick the
Wisp had imparted? Who knew how they had tried to warp
his mind?

He had resigned as Rocaan. He hadn't been able to continue anyway, not after Jewel's death. But he hadn't lost his
interest in the history of the Tabernacle. And that interest
had gone from the history of the Tabernacle to the history of
the Secrets.

So many of the Secrets the Rocaan held were useless
pieces of information. The Tabernacle no longer held the
Feast of the Living nor did it celebrate the Lights of Midday.
Those sacraments had disappeared during the time of the
Twentieth Rocaan, although the Secrets to the ceremonies
were still passed from Rocaan to Rocaan. There were two
dozen such Secrets, of which the Rocaan still employed
about five.

The one that had intrigued Matthias most was the Secret
of the Sword. The Eighth Rocaan had discarded this one,
saying that Rocaanists no longer needed to carry weapons.
But the Sword-Making ritual was passed on from Rocaan to
Rocaan in an unbroken line from the time of the Roca's
death. Forty generations of unused knowledge.

Matthias was trying to resurrect it all. Five years of
research had finally revealed the material used in the Roca's
sword.

Varin.

Which made sense. The legends about the Roca—of
which there were many not recorded in the Words Written
and Unwritten—made his Cliffs of Blood origins extremely
clear. Seze, the missing ingredient in the holy water, was
native to the Kenniland Marshes now, but in the Roca's day,
it was grown in the Cliffs of Blood as well.

Detail upon detail. The Cliffs of Blood held the center
of the religion, only Rocaanism didn't acknowledge them
any more.

Matthias did.

He stood. He was a bit weak in the knees from the heat
and the steam and the bruises. He gulped hot air, felt it

singe his lungs. The smoke was clearing inside, and he could hear Yeon mumbling.

"We're doing something wrong," he said as he headed to the smithy.

"Using the varin."

"No, something in the process," Matthias said. "Maybe we should go over it again."

Yeon emerged from the smoke and steam, his body shining. His pants, once a fawn color, were black with ash. "I think we've done it your way long enough," he said. "I think we should go to the fallback plan."

"There's no need," Matthias said.

"There's plenty need." Yeon wiped his hands on his pants. "Every year we wait, the Fey get more cunning."

"They haven't tried anything in decades."

"For all we know, they're growing little Fey so that they can come after us with an army." Yeon crossed his thick arms. He looked solid, indomitable, like the leader he had been until Matthias stumbled on his little group. "I say it's time you mix us up gallons of holy water and we saturate their hiding place."

"It's been tried. It didn't work."

"Twenty years ago," Yeon said. "Maybe it'd work now."

"No," Matthias said. "I won't risk lives."

"You already are. We're lucky this stuff doesn't kill us."

Matthias sighed. "I don't want to fight old battles."

"We won't be," Yeon said. "What if I can get my people to kill the Fey one on one?"

"Then you'll alert the full body of the Fey and they'll come after us."

"Right," Yeon said. "They can't do anything to us if we've got holy water. Wipe them out. What'll it hurt?"

Nothing. It would hurt nothing if they did it right.

"We'd have to plan it down to the last campaign," Matthias said. "I don't want them coming out, slaughtering innocents."

"Leave that to me."

"No," Matthias said. "I've done that too much in the past. We do it my way."

"We stop playing with strange metals and get on with what we know."

This fight had been building for months now. Matthias might win it this time, but he wouldn't win forever. And he didn't know how long it would take to get the sword right. "All right," Matthias said. "You devise your plan, I'll make the holy water, and by the end of the summer, we'll go after the Fey. But I want a sword to take along."

"We can't have it done by the end of the summer. I don't think it can be done at all."

"Nonetheless," Matthias said. "I won't make holy water until you make me a sword."

"That's the same agreement we had."

"No," Matthias said. "Before we had no deadline on it. If at the end of the summer, you can't make me a sword, I won't make you holy water. If you can find someone else who'll make the sword by my deadline, I'll have more holy water than you could ever use."

"You don't even know the water will work without being Blessed," Yeon said. "You're not Rocaan any more."

"The Words say the Rocaan is Rocaan until he dies." Matthias had never quoted that passage aloud before. No one had resigned before him. Part of him feared, the superstitious part, feared that God was angry with him.

Most of him believed that there was no such thing as God.

"So the current Rocaan is a pretender?"

"He's just a placeholder, not the real thing at all," Matthias said.

"What's that mean to the religion?"

Matthias shook his head. "I haven't been able to figure that out. I just hope that his skills as Rocaan will never have to be tested."

"Well, I don't think it matters much to us in any case," Yeon said. "What matters is getting rid of those Fey once and for all."

"And you think your tactics will do it?"

Yeon nodded.

"You don't think they're prepared for an assault?"

"I think they've lost their preparedness. So many of them have gone Outside anyway. The rest seem to have forgotten why they came. I think we can get them, yes."

"And if your method fails, then what?"

Yeon narrowed his eyes. "I think you're too frightened, holy man."

"And I think you're too rash." Circles. They had been going in these circles forever. Matthias wiped his damp hands on his own filthy pants. "Get me my sword and I'll get your holy water. Let's do this before the winter rains begin."

"I won't work on the sword. I'll get someone else to." Yeon spoke as if that were a bad thing. Matthias merely nodded. He had wondered if part of the problem were Yeon, but hadn't quite known how to go around him.

"Do what you have to," Matthias said. "The quicker we get a sword, the quicker you get to attack the Fey."

"The less chance the King's men catch us, too."

Matthias laughed. "The King's men have no idea that we exist. You worry too much, Yeon."

"His children—"

"Aren't our targets. They'll have no kingdom if the Fey go."

Yeon nodded. He turned back toward the smoldering forge, then stopped. "Why'd you agree to this now?"

Matthias froze. Sometimes, Yeon was smarter than Matthias gave him credit for. "I'm sorry?"

"You've been fighting me for nearly six months on my plan. Why give in now?"

"Because," Matthias said, "something tells me we have to move quickly." That much was true. He hoped that Yeon would ask no more.

"I've had that feeling too," Yeon said. He walked across the wet straw. Strands stuck to his feet.

"Yeon, do me one more favor," Matthias said.

Yeon stopped. He kept his back to Matthias as if he were expecting this to be the real reason that Matthias gave in.

"Get me some strands of green ota leaves."

"I'd have to send someone to the Cliffs," Yeon said.

"Do that." Matthias smiled. "I want to hold a feast."

Yeon shrugged and went into the smithy.

Matthias watched him go. If they couldn't make a Sword that worked, they could try another Secret. The Feast of Living would do nicely. The followers wouldn't even know he was experimenting.

Therefore, only he would know if he succeeded.

EIGHT

MISERABLE, smelly villages. Rugad wore his fighting boots, the ones the Domestics had spelled to keep clean in all conditions—mud, blood, and piss. This village had more piss running down its middle than any he had seen on Galinas.

That wasn't entirely true, of course. Poverty in any country smelled the same.

He crossed the river of waste running down the middle of the street and headed toward Shadowlands. It was behind the tottering, and now empty, kirk. Appropriate, he thought, considering what he planned to do to this religion that had cost him so much grief.

And given him such an opportunity.

He waved a hand to open the Circle Door as he went. The door, a collection of blinking lights a moment before, widened into a full circle, surrounded by lights. It opened like a mouth behind the tottering kirk and he dove in, rolling on the opaque floor and coming up inside his tent. He still didn't trust these villagers enough to camp in their buildings.

Since he arrived, he had created eight Shadowlands, one for each village along the Snow Mountains. There were other assemblies of huts, places so small they didn't even have names, but those residents didn't seem to care who ruled them as long as those people provided food. The attitude and the poverty here shocked him. He had thought Blue Isle rich. That's what the Nyeians had told him. Somehow he hadn't thought poverty a part of life here.

But it clearly was. Malnourished children with distended stomachs, young mothers with rotted teeth and boils on their necks, and men with legs bowed with rickets. Poverty, starvation, and hopelessness, and all of it blamed on the government in Jahn. Until two weeks before, most of these Islanders had never seen Fey. They had thought the Fey a myth to justify the cutoff of trade to Galinas. They had thought their government had arbitrarily ended the villagers' livelihood to destroy life in the Snow Mountains.

They had starved for two decades, held on by sheer determination, and hadn't even known why.

By the time they saw the Fey invaders, they didn't care who ruled them. All they wanted was food and shelter and a promise that the days of prosperity would begin again.

He sat down on the cot inside his tent and pulled off his boots, massaging his feet. He had walked the length of this village and found it no different than all of the others. They had blurred so much that he couldn't even remember its name. He had spent part of the last five years learning Islander so that he could be a politician as well as a conqueror. But these apathetic creatures didn't care if he was either.

This lack of resistance took some of the joy out of his effort. He hoped, when he stopped at the garrisons his troops were establishing on the roads north, that he would be able to make use of his learning. Blue Isle couldn't be a simple, pathetic place. His estimate of Rugar's abilities was low, but not that low.

Rugad leaned back and stared at the tent's brown ceiling. He had learned long ago to make his quarters in Shadowlands as dull as possible, because the Shadowlands leached the color out of everything. He hated being inside, hated it almost as much as he hated dwelling in the same place too long. Shadowlands, particularly the way he constructed them, were tight, narrow, economical boxes. Some Fey couldn't even stand upright in them. From the outside, they were invisible to the naked eye. They were marked by a few blinking lights that looked, to the uninitiated, like fireflies winking off and on.

The only time he felt his age was at rest. He knew he still had years yet—he had at least fifty Visions unfulfilled, and in them all he looked older than he was now—but sometimes he felt as if he were on the cusp of old age. He was still vigorous, and could fight Fey one-quarter his age, but his bones ached when he stopped moving, and when he got up in the morning he was stiff, even if he hadn't fought in battle.

Old age was the curse of the warrior and the blessing of a cunning man.

He smiled. He was cunning. So far, things had gone almost as well as he could hope. His son, Rugar, was out of the way, and his granddaughter Jewel had lived long enough to mate with the wild magick in this place to produce a great-grandchild worthy of the Black Throne.

Rugad had waited nearly two decades to invade Blue Isle. He had several reasons. He wanted the Islanders to become complacent. He wanted them to forget how to fight. And he wanted his great-grandson to become an adult, to come into his power.

Now that his great-grandson was a man, it was time to bring him into the fold. Rugad didn't want to rule forever, nor did he want his other grandchildren to take over. Rugar's other children were as foolhardy, impulsive, and reckless as he was. None of them would take the Black Throne to Leut. Only his great-grandson would.

Rugad had Seen it.

The Circle door opened. It whistled faintly, a warning only Rugad could hear, a safety feature he added into all his Shadowlands. He sat up as Wisdom, one of his advisors, entered.

Wisdom was so named not because of any added intelligence but because, as an infant, he had the look of an elderly Shaman. He still did, even though he was Jewel's age, mid-thirties, still a child in Fey years. He was slender and strong, his magick the subtle power of Charm, a power that didn't work on other Leaders, but one Rugad found invaluable in his own advisors. It kept the troops happy, something Rugad always valued.

"This is not a victory," Wisdom said, "It's an acquiescence." He flipped his long, thin braids, done in Oudoun warrior style, off his face and down his back. Wisdom was an example of all that was good about the Fey's conquering. He was named in the L'Nacin tradition, wore his hair according to the Oudoun, and dressed (until recently) like the Nye. The Fey took what was best about a culture and used it.

So far, Rugad saw nothing here to use.

"It's just the beginning. The Isle is big."

"Not as big as Galinas."

"But as big as Nye."

"Bigger, if the old maps are to be believed." Wisdom leaned on the small chair beside Rugad's cot and crossed his arms. They were covered with scarification from his heroics in the Battle of Feire.

"We won't be staying here now. We have much to do before this Isle is completely ours."

"We shouldn't have stopped at all. We should have maintained the momentum."

Rugad shook his head. "We needed to take the time. The mission is a delicate one here. I have never completely Seen my great-grandson. The Visions are unclear, and I know him only in shadow. I do not want to risk a death in my family, even an accidental one."

Wisdom shuddered. "What of their King? Is he family?"

"He will determine that. He's not of the Blood."

"But his children are."

Rugad nodded. "A dozen Shamans have been unable to determine what his fate will be. The swirls are thick here. We have to tread carefully. Each action will send us in a different direction."

Wisdom scowled. His delicate, almost female features looked suddenly fierce. "Once you have found your great-grandson, put me in charge of the Failures." He touched his arms. "I know ways to make their deaths particularly unpleasant."

Rugad smiled but made no promises. The surviving Fey, if there were any, were another problem. If they believed that Jewel had made her bargain in good faith, they were not

Failures. But if they knew that the invasion had lost, they should have died long before. Failures had the duty to die when their mission failed. That way the enemy could not learn about the Fey.

What Rugad feared was that the Failures believed that he would never arrive, that they would be long dead before the Fey tried ever again to invade Blue Isle. That would be the worst crime, and punishable by severe torture and death.

They knew it too. Which made his invasion of Blue Isle doubly difficult. The Failures had lived here for a long time. The Black Throne was represented in the King's family as well as in the Fey. The Failures could, legitimately, fight for the Islanders.

The Failures could also start a second front.

Rugad had been careful not to bring family here. His army had no attachment to his son's. All they wanted to do was correct the Fey disgrace. He would have to use all his powers of persuasion to convince the most bloodthirsty to take prisoners first, kill later. That way he could make certain there were no Blood bastards among the Failures. All he needed to do was accidentally kill one of his own family.

The entire world would erupt into flames.

He hadn't Seen that, of course, but he was savvy enough to know there were many things a Visionary never saw. Visionaries were not all-knowing, despite their wish to be so. They were fallible like everyone else. The only difference was that they had more opportunities to make things right.

"We shall deal with the Failures after we locate my great-grandson."

"You think this pause will warn him, make him come to you?"

Rugad shook his head. "I suspect he knows nothing of me. His mother and grandfather died when he was still a child. No. I need to have him brought to me."

"Brought to you?" Wisdom asked. "Who would do that? A Failure? You would want one of those Fey in camp?"

"No," Rugad said. "We can't trust them. This is what I want to happen. I want you to send Flurry to their King and demand his surrender."

"Surrender," Wisdom repeated, as if the word were a curse.

"Surrender. We are not giving him a chance to build an army or even to get out of this. We are giving him the opportunity to show us my great-grandson. He will, of course, protest. Jewel told him that he would be family, and he will say that."

"A Wisp can't argue with their King. Flurry isn't the man. We should send a delegation."

"They'd never let a delegation in. A Wisp can get through any closed door. Flurry doesn't need strength. He needs courage. And he's a good observer. He will find my great-grandson for me."

Wisdom sighed, and shook his head. His scowl had grown deeper. "I don't know why you think their King will act this way. We've heard predictions about behavior before. You're the one who told me that we should never believe how someone is going to act until they do act that way."

"True enough," Rugad said. "But I saw Jewel make her bargain with him. I know what she told him. He will act according to that. There is also a Shaman here. I'm sure the Islander King has been warned about making war on the Blood."

"And if he hasn't?"

"He's not my concern," Rugad said. "He is not my Blood nor shall he ever be. In-laws can die. My son proved that in the Oudoun campaign. It must be the Blood, the true Blood, like my great-grandson. Once we find him, we're free to conquer these hopeless people."

"What if he doesn't want to conquer these people?"

"What choice does he have?" Rugad said. "He's a boy who has no warrior training. I have fought battles since I was twelve. He'll listen to me. He'll go to Leut, just as I told you, and he'll go as a conqueror."

Wisdom was quiet for a moment. Then he raised his head, his dark eyes bright. "The plan does have a symmetry."

"Of course it does," Rugad said. "And I've only told you a tiny portion of it. We've only just begun here, Wisdom. By the time we're through, the Fey defeat on this Isle will be more than a memory. It will be known as a lull in the battle."

"So you expect to win where Rugar did not."

Rugad smiled. His son had been a failure as a Visionary and as a commander long before he came to Blue Isle. The comparison was unfair. But Rugad didn't dare say so, or the Fey would start to question then why he had sent his son.

It certainly wasn't because he trusted him to succeed.

He had relied on him to fail.

And Rugar had failed.

Spectacularly.

"Of course I expect to win," Rugad said. He leaned back on the cot and closed his eyes. "Have you ever known me to lose?"

NINE

ARIANNA took a step deeper into the room. The air had a wild scent, the smell of loam and pine mixed with something she had never smelled before. The light shining through her brother's open windows cast halos around the two men. She felt an odd lightness, as if this were all a dream.

The Fey beside her brother was as tall as Sebastian, and his hair was as dark. They looked startlingly alike. Only the Fey's face was alive in ways that Sebastian's wasn't. And the Fey's eyes were blue. Sebastian's were a stone gray.

Solanda hadn't told Arianna about all the different kinds of magick. Was there a kind that stole the essence of a person? Was this a Doppelgänger?

"Get away from my brother," she said in Fey, hands clenched. "Get away from him now."

"Sebastian," the Fey said in Islander. His voice was deep, warm. Familiar in a way she couldn't place. "Come with me."

Sebastian turned his head slowly. The light caught the webbed lines on his features, faint cracklike marks he had had since their mother died.

Since Arianna was born.

"Ari . . . too?" Sebastian didn't seem worried. He accepted

the presence of this strange man when he never accepted the presence of someone he hadn't met.

The Fey seemed to take Sebastian's question seriously. "Arianna can come only if she asks no questions. We have to go."

"Of course I'm going to ask questions," she snapped, not liking their closeness, not liking the way they talked of her as if she weren't there. "I'm not running off with some strange Fey based on his word."

"Sebastian," the Fey said. He continued to ignore her. "Please?"

Sebastian's mouth worked. His eyes moved from the Fey to Arianna and back again. "Can't . . . choose."

"Well, I can," Arianna said. She walked up to the Fey. She was almost as tall as he was. He looked down at her, and she saw Sebastian in his face.

Sebastian and their father.

But she didn't have time to comprehend it. She shoved the Fey's chest, expecting it to be rock-solid like Sebastian's. It wasn't. She could feel the lines of his ribs, the softness of his skin. That familiarity washed over her again.

"Get out of here," she said to cover the strangeness.

"Don't send me away. You don't understand—"

"I understand enough," she said. "I understand that you're trying to kidnap my brother. I know what Fey can do, and you won't harm him, no matter what you want. Now get out."

She shoved again. This time he had to take a step backward to keep his balance.

Sebastian moaned, and reached a hand up in protest. Then the nurse's voice echoed from the hall. The Fey shot a panicked glance to Sebastian, then dove out of the window on his own, catching a tree branch and shimmying down it.

"Gift?" Sebastian said and started toward the window.

Arianna beat him there. The Fey was running through the garden. She wasn't going to let him get away this time. He would tell her what he was doing in the palace. If he didn't, she would assume he was trying to kidnap her brother.

And he would pay.

"Tell nurse that I went after him," she said to Sebastian. "Have her send guards."

Arianna's body compacted down into its robin shape. Her robe pooled around her, and she leapt out of its restraining folds. Then she took one step back and flew out the window.

Behind her, she thought she heard Sebastian wail, "Noooooo," but she didn't know why. She could either go back and protect him or find that Fey and see what he really wanted.

He had left a swath of destruction in the garden. Trampled flowers, shorn bushes, and broken tree limbs. Birds were circling above, cawing at her, complaining about his bad manners. When she finally saw him, he was running through the final copse of trees.

She had chased him this way before.

Somehow he had outwitted her and made his way back to the palace.

Her anger flared even more.

He knew the grounds. He had been here before. Who knew how long he'd been coming to see Sebastian? Did it take a long time for a Fey Doppelgänger to Shift into his prey? She had always understood that the process was quick, but she had never seen it happen.

She was flying as fast as she could, but her wings were growing tired. She had never been a robin for long, always preferring to circle the garden, stare out at the city, take in the river, and return home. For the first time, she was getting winded. What happened to birds when they couldn't breathe?

The Fey reached the fence and rolled into a hole beneath it. That's where he had hid. She had been right above him. She cursed, unable to form the words properly through her beak. A jay near her screeched and flew away, over the line of squat guard buildings on the other side of the fence.

Beyond the guard buildings were shops and one-bedroom homes. People were going about their business, oblivious to the Fey man in their midst. They probably couldn't even see him in his protected spot under the stone fence.

Then he crawled out on the other side, clawing his way

up the dirt embankment to the guard buildings, and she dove at him, heading for his face, his eyes. She would peck his eyes out for attacking her brother. He would—

Suddenly she couldn't move her wings. A fine gauze web was wrapped around her, stopping her momentum. It was attached to tiny sparks of light. She snapped at the web, her strong beak cutting through it. She shoved her feathered body through the hole, freeing a wing, as the lights encircled her again. Then she snapped at one of them, and with a puff of smoke, it turned into a tiny being, no bigger than her beak, naked, with blue wings rising off its back.

"Stop," the tiny woman said, "we're friends."

"Friends don't kidnap my brother," Arianna said.

"He is your brother. We've never kidnapped him."

Arianna couldn't make sense of the statement, so she didn't even try. She freed the other wing, then flew at the Fey man again. He raised his arms to his face.

Someone screamed above her. Someone else yelled her name and a phrase in Fey.

Beware the Chaos.

Arianna didn't know what it meant, so she ignored it. She gripped the Fey man's finger in her feet when a hand grabbed her. She pecked at the hand, and it released her. She flew above it, and saw a shadowy woman, tall and thin, her features indistinct.

The shadowy woman shouted in Fey, "Gift, run!" and the male Fey did, his feet churning the dirt beneath him.

Guards were running from the palace and the guard buildings. People were shouting from the side of the road. Arianna flew after the Fey man, determined to get him in a more private spot.

He had brought an entire Fey attack force with him to get her brother.

Or to turn into her brother.

If they got him before his Coming-of-Age ceremony, if they replaced him, then that Fey would lead the country. No slow half-breed, but a quick agile full-Fey.

She wouldn't allow it. Her father had sacrificed a lot for her, and even more for Sebastian. These Fey couldn't take it away. Solanda had always said the Fey were cunning, but Arianna had never realized how cunning.

Now she did.

She was part Fey. She could be cunning too.

She let herself rise on an air draft, to get out of sight of the ground, and then she followed the running Fey.

TEN

SOLANDA was sleeping in the garden, against the stone of the palace wall. The sun had warmed the stone, making it radiate heat. She had her paws outstretched, and one eye barely open, so that she could watch the bugs swirl around her. She was too tired to hunt—it was nap time—but she might bat at one or two if they came close.

She had been in the garden long enough to find a sunny patch and long enough to get drowsy. She knew she had to watch the position of the sun. Good King Nicholas would never forgive her if she failed to attend the lump's Coming-of-Age. Who'd have thought a golem would last that long? Who'd have thought it would develop such a personality of its own?

Solanda had monitored it ever since it saved Arianna's life. It had a core being of its own, too, and that hadn't come from Jewel's magick. It had come from somewhere else, somewhere she hadn't been able to pinpoint in fifteen years.

That bothered her.

Making the lump King bothered her too. Especially since the Islanders considered it part Fey. Solanda didn't know what it was, but she knew what it wasn't. It wasn't Fey.

Then she heard Arianna's voice, high and demanding. She raised her head. Arianna was, in all important ways, her baby. She had never intended it that way, but only a creature as charming, intelligent and challenging as Arianna could have held Solanda's interest for so long. And buried in Arianna's tone was an imperiousness she only used when she was frightened.

Solanda sat up, debating whether or not to get out of her cat shape.

The lump answered Arianna, only it spoke quickly.

The lump never spoke quickly.

The hair rose on her ruff. Solanda was full awake now. She backed up so that she could see the window above her. She was lying under the turret that was the lump's room. The light blinded her. She could see two shapes of the same height, but couldn't make out who they were.

Arianna spoke again, her voice growing closer.

The lump responded, quickly again, and Arianna snapped at him.

Then the lump spoke—slowly. The hairs on Solanda's ruff stood completely on end. The lump hadn't spoken the first time. It was—

Gift threw himself out of the window, grabbed a tree branch, and shimmied down it. Arianna yelled after him. Solanda backed out of the way. Gift had never been to the palace. Nicholas was too stupid to know that the lump wasn't his son. Solanda had tried to tell Nicholas, but he hadn't believed her.

She hadn't even bothered to tell Arianna.

Gift had the look of Jewel at that age, thin and beautiful, the way the lump would have been if he were real instead of a cracked piece of stone. Gift reached the bottom of the tree.

"Gift," Solanda hissed, but he didn't hear her. He took off at a full run. She was about to change to her Fey form when she glanced up. A robin was shaking itself out of Arianna's robe.

A robin.

The girl had said she only had two shapes: a cat and Fey, just like Solanda.

Arianna had lied.

The robin flew over the tree tops, hurrying after Gift. Gift was crashing through the garden growth, more speed than agility. If Arianna caught him, and she didn't know who he was . . .

"By all the lights in the Empire," Solanda snapped. She took off after Gift. It might be too late already. He didn't know who his sister was, his sister didn't know who he was, and they were both of the Black Throne.

Chaos would reign.

Solanda doubled her speed, using the crashing sounds of Gift's progress and the shadow of the bird as her guide. She was in good shape; she'd been hunting with Arianna, and they always made it a game to see who got the birds first. Solanda only hoped that the hunting would pay off.

The crashing stopped. She caught up to Gift as he rolled in the hole under the fence. The robin circled above, waiting to attack.

"No, Arianna!" Solanda yelled, but her voice was too small to carry to that height. Gift ignored her too. He shoved his way through the hole and disappeared under the fence.

"Damned half-breeds," Solanda said as she crawled on her belly through that hole. She would have to clean the dirt off her fur, and the Powers knew what else.

There was a slight embankment on the other side of the fence and a string of guard barracks that cast a shade on the road leading to the shops. She could see them all from her position in the hole, but she could no longer see Gift or Arianna.

Then Solanda heard cawing and screeching and crying. She pulled herself out of the hole to see Wisps attacking Arianna in the air. It wasn't a real attack—they knew who she was and were trying to prevent her assault on Gift. Gift's arm was over his face, and two Spies were beside him.

Other Fey had to be hidden in the area.

Something was happening. Something she didn't understand. Were they trying to substitute Gift for the lump before the ceremony? Had Arianna caught them?

Someone yelled at Gift to run, and he stumbled forward, down the Islander street, his eyes wild and his hair flying behind his back. Islanders appeared in their doorways, and more Fey Spies appeared around them, shoving them back. They were protecting Gift, making certain he was all right.

Her girl had broken free and was pursing him. Soon Gift would arrive on one of Jahn's main streets. Solanda didn't know how the Islanders would react to a young Fey running through the center of town. She wasn't sure she wanted to find out.

"Curse them all, and their ancestors too," she mumbled, not sure if she was swearing at Gift and his sister or the other Fey or the Islanders. She ran along the cobblestone, grimacing at the pain the sharper rocks caused in her pads. She hadn't run outside the garden in a long time. She was getting old.

And soft.

Maybe she should return to Fey form. Maybe she had a better chance of catching him then.

Arianna was screaming as she flew above them. She would catch him soon, and if his protectors weren't around, she might do actual damage.

Solanda didn't know what the damage would mean to the rest of the Fey. All she knew was what kind of problems Gift's death would cause.

Especially if Arianna killed him.

The Empire would erupt in chaos. Families would slaughter each other. Insanity would rule.

Solanda ran faster, nearly flying, her paws off the ground. Behind her, Islanders were screaming. Some Fey were flanking her—she suspected they recognized her—and others had moved ahead. They all knew how crucial this was. It was like a bad dream. There seemed no way out of it.

The road wound into the business district, and still Gift ran, knocking into Islanders carrying their wares. Baskets spilled, curses filled the air, and the bird dove, narrowly missing.

"No, Arianna!" Solanda yelled, but she was too far away. Islanders heard her, and a few Fey, but no one else seemed to. She was getting winded, and she couldn't afford to.

Everything rested on her.

She doubled her speed, ignoring her tired legs. Adrenaline was pumping through her. She wove beneath the feet of a dozen bystanders, keeping Gift in her sight.

He was staying close to buildings, to other people, so that he could duck if Arianna attacked him again. He glanced over his shoulder, features so like his mother's that Solanda was startled for a moment. Arianna was flying low, sometimes skimming the heads of Islanders as she passed. She had an agility she shouldn't have, not if this was a new form.

The girl had been holding out on her.

Solanda let the anger from that thought fuel her tiring limbs. She was having trouble seeing. The Fey flanking her were growing tired as well.

Gift had to be in fine shape.

Or he truly didn't want to get caught.

He leapt over a pile of broken cobblestones, but his foot hit an edge. He seemed to move in slow motion, tottering forward, arms pinwheeling as he tried to gain his balance.

Solanda cursed and used the last of her energy to speed to him. Arianna was smart. She would use this moment.

Solanda was almost to Gift's side when Arianna dove.

Solanda leapt, mouth open—

—and caught the robin in her powerful jaws.

ELEVEN

THE cat came out of nowhere. It leapt impossibly high. Before Arianna could get out of the way, the cat's mouth closed on her right wing, ruining her momentum and sending her sprawling. She would have Shifted in midair, but there were Islanders around. They didn't need to see their Princess, naked and vulnerable, kicking a cat in the middle of the street.

She landed on her left side with such an impact that the wind went out of her body. The cat hadn't hurt her yet, but it would. But she could outthink it.

If she could breathe.

No wonder a cat could so easily kill birds. It dazed them.

But the cat didn't go for her neck as she suspected. Instead it backed away and sat on its haunches on the cobblestone. "You all right?" it asked softly.

"Solanda!" Even though Arianna shouted the word, it came out as a whisper. She really didn't have much air in her body. And the cobblestone was hard. "What did you do?"

"I saved you, you stupid little fool." Solanda was whispering too. "Now shush. The Islanders are used to Fey, but not to Fey like us."

Arianna rolled her eyes, and raised her head slightly. The Fey man was gone. Long gone. "He got away," she said.

"And good thing, too."

"You know who he is?"

Solanda nodded. "I just don't know what he wanted."

The Islanders were picking up the spilled baskets and making a wide berth around the remaining Fey. Those Fey were trickling off in different directions, an obvious ploy to keep Arianna from knowing where the Fey man went.

One Fey, a shadowy woman with indistinct features, knelt beside Solanda. "Need help?" she asked. Even her voice had a shadowy quality. Arianna squinted, but the woman didn't come into any clearer focus.

She was female, and Fey, and that was all Arianna could tell about her.

"I don't need help," Solanda said softly, "but I think my friend does."

The woman nodded. She bent over Arianna. "I'm going to pick you up. Tell me if it hurts."

Up close, the woman's features looked as if they were made of sand that water had washed over. They were distinct enough to seem like features, and yet they were blurry around the edges. Arianna almost felt as if she were perceiving the woman through a thick fog.

The woman's hand closed around Arianna. The woman's skin was warm and soft. Arianna's wing ached where she had landed on it, but the wing that Solanda had touched didn't hurt at all.

The woman set her upright.

"Stretch your wings," Solanda said.

Arianna did, slowly. She could feel the tiny muscles straining.

"Can you fly?" Solanda asked.

Arianna nodded.

"Then meet me in your room, as soon as you can."

"But what about—"

"We'll deal with him." Solanda turned her small, triangular face toward the strange Fey woman. "Thanks for your help."

"Anything for the Black Throne," she said.

Solanda grunted. Arianna fluttered her wings, testing them. They felt fine. Tired, but then she was tired. She had never flown so far, so fast, in all her life.

Or had been that angry.

That Fey man had somehow threatened her brother's life. He would pay for it. She would make him, without Solanda's interference.

"You won't find him," Solanda said softly. "They've got him hidden now. Meet me at the palace."

Arianna frowned, unhappy that her thoughts were that obvious. She hopped, then fluttered her wings again and rose into the air. She circled over the city once, peering at roads, at dwellings, at the river. But Solanda was right. The Fey man was nowhere to be seen.

"I'll find you," Arianna murmured. And she would. Without Solanda's help. That comment about the Black Throne worried her. Solanda had helped the man get away. She had nearly hurt Arianna. And she had mentioned the Black Throne before, saying that all Fey loyalty had to go there first.

But Arianna was only part Fey. And the Black Throne wanted her brother.

She couldn't do this one alone. Her father knew more about the intricacies of the Fey than she did. As much as she loved Solanda, her own family came first. Her brother, her father, and herself.

Arianna would talk to her father and tell him what happened. He was King. He could decide what to do next.

TWELVE

HE moved faster in the heat of the day.

Flurry flew over the Island countryside, following the roads carved through the rolling land. He was the size of a small spark, invisible even to the most practiced eye, following the updrafts and air currents, using the power of the wind to propel himself forward.

The wind blew south to north today, and it was perfect for him. Rugad wanted him in the capital city by nightfall, a push even for the fastest Wisps. By horseback, the journey took three to four days. Getting there in one would rely on wing-speed, favorable winds, and luck.

He had the speed—he had been one of the fastest Wisps on Galinas—and he had the favorable winds.

Now he needed the luck.

The countryside was startlingly different the farther he flew. The marshes were green and brown, the water thick and murky from his height above the ground. Scraggly trees grew inside the marsh, and from the air he could see small roads, bridges, and solid areas that enabled knowledgeable Islanders to cross the marsh.

A wide, well-traveled north-south road spanned the

marsh, and he followed it. The Islanders had told him, and the Warders had confirmed it with the few recalcitrant prisoners, that the road went directly to the capital city.

If he stayed on the same path, he would get there.

Through the marshes, he saw very few Islanders. Those he did see were heading north, like he was, as if they were fleeing the Fey army.

They probably were. Rugad had said he wanted Islanders to escape. He had a plan for this Isle, a plan he hadn't shared with anyone outside of his advisors, and it differed from other campaigns Flurry had been on. In those, the Fey never asked for surrender.

Surrender was assumed.

Surrender was the end result of a Fey victory.

Surrender, sometimes, wasn't even necessary. There usually weren't any leaders left to capitulate.

But Rugad was exercising caution here. Some said it was because his son got trapped and died here. Others said it was because the Islanders had special powers.

A few years back, word had leaked through all the ranks that the reason the Fey never returned from Blue Isle was because the Islanders had their own magick. That magick came in a bottle, in the form of poison that killed Fey with a single touch. Flurry had thought the rumor untrue until he spoke to one of the Warders a year later.

It seemed that a handful of the Nye had practiced the Islanders' religion. The religion never really got off the ground in Nye, and the missionaries from Blue Isle returned to their home. But a few of the Nyeians still practiced, still believed, and still hoarded the magick poison, or holy water, as they called it. Only the Nye had never learned its Fey-killing properties.

They never learned those properties at all.

The Fey executed the religious Nye and confiscated the magick poison. And then experimented with it.

The Warder had told Flurry that Rugad's people had solved the riddle of the poison. They had a neutralizer, an antidote, and a warding spell. The Warder said that as soon as the neutralizer and the antidote could be produced in large enough quantity, Rugad would have his troops warded and invade Blue Isle. Flurry had scoffed. Everyone had heard how impossible Blue Isle was to invade. And, at that point, everyone had thought the first Fey force had died in the ocean crossing. It wasn't until later that the failure of the first force became clear.

And then Rugad had said he wanted to conquer Blue Isle.

Some Fey had been surprised by Rugad's decision to invade. But Flurry hadn't. Rugad was a warrior, and even though he felt the armies needed a rest after they conquered Nye, he also knew that the Fey would have to fight again. The Galinas continent belonged to the Fey. They had nowhere else to go.

Except to Blue Isle, and on to the Leut continent.

Rugad's grandsons weren't capable of taking the Fey onto the Isle. Rugad had to do it himself.

Flurry dipped and followed a twist in the road. The tall marsh grass was thinning, and the water had receded into small puddles. The ground was rising, and ahead he saw it level out in a sort of plain. The land was divided into different colors, like a quilt made by Domestics, and gradually the divisions resolved themselves into patches of land with a small clumps of buildings.

Farms.

Prosperous farms from the looks of them, with healthy midsummer crops. This was the Blue Isle that the Nye talked about, not the poverty-stricken hovels near the Snow Mountains. These farms obviously kept themselves fed and shipped crops all over the Isle. No wonder the Islanders hadn't starved without trade from Nye.

They hadn't needed it in the first place.

Trade had only made them richer. Now their prosperity had leveled off.

Flurry smiled to himself. The Fey could use this land. The Fey could use this place. His moods were rising. He had served with Rugad for four decades now, and he had never seen Rugad make a mistake. If the Islanders had to be approached differently from anyone on Galinas, so be it.

Rugad would help the Fey not only win, but thrive.

The wind dropped for a moment, putting a strain on his tiny wings. He flew low over one of the farms, seeing the large stone house and the large grain storage buildings beyond. Animals grazed on a small patch of ground behind the storage buildings. Wealth.

His wings ached. Without the wind, he couldn't maintain this pace. He would burn himself up.

He toyed with the idea of stopping, of resting, and he would have to soon if the wind didn't pick up. This was why winged Fey couldn't fly across oceans and other great distances. They tired. Their endurance lasted only so long. Rugad was asking Flurry to fly to the edge of his endurance and beyond.

Flurry would try.

But he might have to stop.

As he lowered himself toward the grain silos, the wind picked up again, and carried him forward. The great effort he had performed a few moments ago seemed less now. He wasn't as tired. And, by his calculations (and if the tortured Islanders were right) he was probably halfway. He just might make the capital city by nightfall.

Then his problems increased. He had to find the palace based on someone else's description, and he had to find the King. Somehow, a blue-eyed, round-faced, middle-aged, yellow-haired man, unusual by Fey standards, didn't seem so unusual here. He only hoped the Islanders acted differently toward their King, treated him as if he were a Shaman or something. He was related to their great religious leader. That might count for these people.

Even though Flurry had been forced to study the Islanders for the year before this journey, he still felt as if he didn't know enough. He was proficient in their language, he had been taught their odd religion, and he knew details about their culture.

Still things surprised him. Like Rugad, he hadn't expected poverty. And unlike Rugad, he hadn't expected this great wealth.

The farmlands seemed to extend forever. He would know he was getting closer to the city of Jahn when he came to a series of bridges. Then, the Islanders told him, he would be able to see the city in the distance. The Tabernacle was on this side of the great Cardidas River. He was to avoid that place, even though it looked like a palace. The palace was the other big building, on the far side of the river.

If his luck ran true, the day's heat would continue into the night. Then he would be able to fly through an open window and search the palace.

He would deliver his message and leave.

Rugad would take care of the rest.

THIRTEEN

GIFT stopped at the edge of the river, under the great bridge. He was panting hard. He doubled over, grabbed the backs of his legs, and stretched, feeling the blood rush to his face.

She had nearly pecked out his eyes. If Solanda hadn't stopped her, his own sister would have blinded him.

Such ferocity. Arianna loved Sebastian too. Maybe he could use that. Maybe he could tell Solanda what was happening and she would get Arianna to protect Sebastian.

Or maybe she wouldn't. Solanda considered him unnatural, and not real. She seemed to have a pure hatred for him, based on what he had been, not on who he was.

Gift leaned against the stone of the bridge. His heart was pounding hard. The river had a marshy stink here, hovering under the stone itself. There was a smell of decay, of urine, of old forgotten places. He had hidden here before, on his few trips to the city, because Islanders rarely came here, and those who did were the unfortunate, the unloved, and the homeless.

He had failed. He hadn't expected to. He had thought he might have difficulty convincing Sebastian, but he had thought they would get away.

Now he didn't know what to do. It felt as if every moment he waited doomed Sebastian.

Or himself.

If only he had found the room from his Vision. If only he could tell exactly when the Vision occurred. If only Arianna had left him alone.

If only.

Now he didn't know what to do. He could go to the Shaman, but he doubted she'd be much help.

She hadn't been any help before.

She knew that Visions could be changed, but she didn't know how this one could be. Or these two, since they represented a fork.

And he understood the fork.

Either he or Sebastian would be killed that day.

Unless they were both out of the palace, away from Jahn.

He took a deep breath. The humid air had a thickness here, along with the stench. It almost felt as if he were breathing the river.

Getting Sebastian out of the palace would be difficult. He hadn't realized Sebastian's resistance went so deep. He had seen Sebastian follow others' suggestions, but they had never been about abandoning his family or the only home he'd ever known.

Maybe Gift could convince Arianna.

He would have to explain who he was. That would be difficult. And he didn't know what her reaction would be.

His breath was beginning to return. His legs still felt wobbly, uncertain, weak. He hadn't run like that ever, at least that he could remember. And he had never been so terrified in all his life. If she had caught him, if she had harmed him, the magick would have stirred in the Black Blood.

If she had killed him, she would have destroyed the Fey.

Sweat trickled down his chin and dripped onto his shirt. He needed to rest before he went back to Shadowlands.

If he went to Shadowlands at all.

He still had one solution. He could get Coulter. They hadn't seen each other a lot since they were boys, but they were close, as close as Gift and Sebastian were. Maybe closer.

Coulter was an Islander whom Solanda had brought to Shadowlands when he was just a baby. She claimed he had magickal abilities. The Fey scoffed at her. No one had magick except Fey. Then the Domestics confirmed his magick and his age. He was too old to have been born to a mating between Islander and Fey.

Solanda abandoned him, and the Fey ignored him. He ran wild through Shadowlands, and an Islander prisoner, Adrian, took care of him. But on that day Gift's real mother was killed, Gift nearly died because his Link with his mother had not been properly severed. Coulter broke into Gift's house, severed Gift's Link with his mother, and forged a new Link, Binding Coulter and Gift together forever.

Only Enchanters could do such things. Gift's grandfather decided to test Coulter, to see if he was an Enchanter. But the tests amounted to torture, and the prisoner Adrian helped Coulter escape from Shadowlands. Since then, Coulter had lived at Adrian's farm, as Adrian's son, and was, for all Gift could see, extremely happy.

Gift had never been to the farm. But he had seen Coulter in Jahn a few times, when Coulter was bringing in the harvest for sale in the city. They usually talked across the Link, so it felt odd to talk face-to-face.

Just as it had been odd to talk to Sebastian face-to-face.

Two other Fey ducked under the bridge. They weren't panting as hard. The first was a Spy, Epla. He was as old as Gift's grandfather would have been. Young Spies had indistinct features that could be molded into other faces, not replicas of faces they saw, but something close. Older Spies like Epla had evolved a face of their own, one that took the best features of all the faces they had once worn. Epla could still change his face to look like someone else's, but in response, he was among the most handsome of the Fey.

Spies had their uses. They could watch and gather information. But they couldn't fight without damaging their delicate magick, and they couldn't kill without losing it.

Gift hadn't expected to need fighters on this trip. He had only wanted people who could blend in with the crowd. That was why he had brought so many Spies with him.

The other Fey was Prey, a Foot Soldier. Foot Soldiers killed with their fingers. They often tortured their victims to death. Gift had brought Prey as his only real protection, thinking she would be enough.

She had her hands clasped under her arms, the sign of a Foot Soldier in distress.

"You were supposed to guard me," Gift said.

"I can't guard you against the Black Throne," Prey said. "I will not kill your sister, even if she's trying to peck your eyes out."

"You should have warned us," Epla said.

"I did warn you. We were going to the palace." Gift took a shaky breath. He didn't mean to blame them. It wasn't their fault things had gone wrong. "Where're the others?"

"Coming," Prey said. "I wanted to get away from there."

"She was shaking with blood lust," Epla said. "You're lucky she has control."

"*I'm* lucky I have control," Prey said. "It wouldn't have mattered to him if I killed her. It would have been my choice. I'm the one who would have died for it."

"You were in her brother's service," Epla said. "We all might have died for it."

Prey sucked in her breath, as if that thought hadn't occurred to her. Then she wrinkled her nose. "Stinks down here."

"That's why Islanders rarely come here," Gift said.

"You could have picked a better spot for regrouping."

Epla shook his head. "Gift may be young, but he knows what he's doing. He's saved us countless times, Prey."

She shrugged. "Only in the Shadowlands. It's not like he's battle-tested."

Gift let that slide. He wasn't battle-tested, and he knew most of the Fey put stock in that. If he hadn't saved Shadowlands at such a young age, and if he hadn't had Visions from childhood on, none of the older Fey would take him seriously now. They knew he had enough of the Black King's blood to make him part of the line, and they attributed his lack of battle experience to the situation on Blue Isle, to the mess his grandfather had gotten them into, not to his own inabilities.

But many of the older Fey did consider him strange, and that they blamed on his parentage.

On his father.

On his Islander father.

"This is a safe place," he said. "No one will bother us here."

He wiped the sweat off his forehead and took a deep breath. His system was slowly returning to normal.

Two more Fey showed up, another Spy, Dolny, and an Infantry member, Leen. Dolny was younger, his features less distinct than Epla's. Leen had not come into her magick yet. She was five years younger than Gift, one of the few Fey born on Blue Isle. She hadn't reached her full height yet, either, but her body showed hints of it, with her long bones and narrow frame.

"We're missing Cover," Prey said.

"She stayed behind to make certain the girl was all right," Dolny said.

"What were they doing, letting Black Blood chase Black Blood?" Leen asked.

"It's my fault," Gift said. "She doesn't know who I am. And she probably doesn't know about the Blood."

"Well, she needs to learn," Prey said. "And quickly. What if she tries this again?"

"What if she succeeds?" Epla said softly.

"She won't." The new voice belonged to Cover. She came down the slope, using one hand to brace herself as she slid under the bridge. Her features were swirling. She had to have been wearing a different face before she got to the river. "I talked with Solanda. She'll explain everything."

"To whom?" Gift asked. "To Arianna? Or my father?"

"It doesn't matter if the Islander knows," Prey said. "Just the girl."

"That won't help Sebastian at all," Gift said.

"Clearly you can't go in there again," Epla said. "We can't afford to lose you."

"You won't lose me," Gift said.

"We might if the girl learns who you are," Prey said. "She might want to keep you."

"She wouldn't be able to do that," Gift said.

Prey shook her head. "Your sister has strength. She doesn't need battle testing. She came after you fiercely. Solanda has taught her how to hunt."

Gift glared at her. "Hunting isn't everything."

Prey spat on the ground. "Clearly untested, youngling."

"Leave him alone," Epla said. "The boy does the best he can."

"I think we should go back," Cover said. "Epla, Dolny, and I. No one will notice us. We'll get the golem out."

Gift shook his head. "He wouldn't come for me, and he knows me. He won't come for you."

"He's a golem," Prey said. "Golems have no choice."

"He does," Gift said. "He's no ordinary golem. He's lived long beyond his usefulness to his creator. He has a life of his own now. And with that life comes an ability to choose what he wants to do. He doesn't leave the palace. And he relies on Arianna."

"So we bring the girl," Dolny said.

Prey laughed. "Spies. You saw her. She'll fight you. And you can't fight back. She'll eat you alive. If any of us go to the palace, it would have to be me."

"And think of the carnage you'd leave," Epla said.

"No one goes back except me," Gift said.

"We can't risk you," Epla said.

Gift lifted his chin. He raised his head. He had heard that statement all his life, and it made no sense to him. So many of the Fey didn't trust him because of his parentage, because he had Islander blood. And yet they couldn't risk losing him. "Why not?" he asked.

"Because of who you are," Epla said.

"And just who is that?" Gift asked.

Prey glanced at Epla, her features set in a straight line. She obviously hadn't liked what he said. "You hold Shadowlands together," she said.

"And you hate living there."

She spat again. "I would hate living here more."

There was something they weren't saying. And he knew what it was. He just wished someone would admit to him that they were still afraid the Black King would come. They didn't want to be the ones who fought anyone with Black Blood. They didn't want to be the Black King's Blood enemy. It didn't matter what Gift did. From the moment he was born, he was protected within the Fey, so much so that they took him as their leader even as they argued with him.

"I'm going back in," Gift said. "But I'm not going alone. I'm taking Coulter with me."

"That Islander boy?" Epla asked. "He won't help you."

"Yes, he will," Gift said.

"He'll get you killed," Prey said.

"You don't know him," Gift said. "He saved my life before."

"When you were children," Prey said. "He won't do that now."

Gift clenched his fists. No one fought with other leaders. He knew for a fact that no one had fought with his grandfather. Half the Fey complained about that. They said they would never have come to Blue Isle if his grandfather had allowed the people around him to give advice. He also knew that no one argued with his real father either.

But they argued with him.

The Shaman said it was because he came to Leadership so young. They all saw him as a child instead of a Visionary. But she hadn't helped him find a way to change that perception. Even when he wanted to be strong, the arguments got out of hand. He always found himself defending his position instead of ordering it into being.

"I'm going to get Coulter, and that's all there is to it," he said.

"I don't think that's wise, Gift—" Epla started.

"I don't care what you think," Gift said. "It's what I'm going to do."

The older Fey glanced at each other as if he were a recalcitrant child. He hated that. But he couldn't argue with it. He would have to prove to them that he was right.

"You can't travel across the Isle without protection," Epla said. "Dolny and Cover and I will go with you."

"Spies are not protection," Prey said. "They are eyes and nothing more. Take me and Leen. That's all you'll need."

He glanced at them. "I'm going by myself," he said.

"You can't," Epla said. "If—"

"I'm going by myself," Gift repeated. "I don't want any of you with me. I don't want protection. I want to go alone. If I have any chance of saving Sebastian, I need to do it on my own."

"You've never faced Islanders and their poison. You'll need eyes," Epla said.

"And someone to fight."

Gift resisted the urge to smile. He finally had them where he wanted them. "All right. Cover, you come with me, and you too, Leen. There. Eyes and protection. The rest of you can go back to the Shadowlands."

Prey shook her head. Her hands were pressed tightly against her armpits, as if she were trying to control them. "You don't know—"

"Then I'll learn, won't I?" Gift snapped. "You never argued with my grandfather like this."

"And look where it got us," Epla said.

"Well, it's not helping me. Go away, all of you. Except Cover and Leen. You two stay. I don't want to see the rest of you until I get to Shadowlands."

They stared at him for a moment, as if he had sprouted horns.

"I mean it," he said.

They glanced at each other, then Epla shrugged.

"As you wish," he said, as if Gift were crazy. He started up the bank, Prey and Dolny beside him. When they reached the top, they did not look back. Gift felt an odd pull. He had expected more argument, more difficulty. Maybe he liked the tussles as much as they did.

He shook the thought from his head. "All right," he said. "First we need some food and something to drink. Then—"

The world shifted. One moment he was standing on the bank, the next he was on a barge in the river, Coulter beside him. Coulter was taller than Gift, and so blond it was blinding. The sun had darkened his skin from a translucent white to a soft brown.

"Over there," Coulter said. "I've heard that there's a group of assassins on the Tabernacle side."

They were floating near the bridge. Gift turned to look at the Tabernacle. Its white walls were streaked with soot. The upper towers had fallen in. It looked empty.

"I can't kill him," Gift said.

"No." Coulter smiled. "But I can."

Then the world shifted back, and Gift was leaning against the stone, his feet splayed in front of him. His hands were in wet ground. He didn't want to think about the filth he was picking up.

His mouth was open and dry, his chin wet with drool. He swallowed, licked his lips, then wiped off his chin.

Cover knelt beside him. Sympathy made her vague features almost clear. "They said you could do that, but I had no idea."

"That was a Vision?" Leen asked. Her voice held disgust. "It looked like a fit."

"It was a Vision," Cover said, "and a powerful one, I think."

Gift nodded. The heat and the dizziness had grown worse. "Do me a favor, Leen." His voice was raspy. The Vision felt as if it had only taken a moment, but he knew from experience that a moment in a Vision could be half a day in real time. "Look at the Tabernacle. Have the windows fallen in?"

Leen wandered along the edge of the bank, her hands clasped behind her back. When she was in sight of the tabernacle, she stopped, squinted, and shook her head. "Everything's fine," she said. "It's in good repair."

"That was a clue," he said, more to himself than to anyone else. "That was some sort of clue."

But to what he did not know.

Assassins, murder, the empty Tabernacle. And whom couldn't he kill? And why? And why would Coulter, that gentle soul, be willing to?

"Was it about our journey?" Cover asked.

Gift shook his head. "Visions happen out of order, Cover," he said. But he knew the Vision was tied to the journey. The moment he decided to take this trip with only Cover and Leen, the Vision had come. That decision led to this future.

The trouble was that he didn't know if it would be a good or bad future. Unlike the other Vision, the one he was trying to prevent, he didn't know if he should change this one, leave it alone, or use it as a guide.

He extended his hand, and let Cover pull him up. The

Spy's skin was cooler than his, a fact he had forgotten. "Do you still want to leave?' she asked softly.

The image of the ruined Tabernacle flashed through his head. That place had frightened him since he had first seen it, home of the holy poison and the death of the Fey.

"Yes," he said. "I want to go. I think it's more important than ever."

FOURTEEN

SOLANDA wore her cat form into the palace and slipped through the main doors unnoticed. Her tired paws left dusty prints on the newly cleaned marble floors. She padded across, ears flat, tail down. Her mouth still tasted of feathers, and she hoped she hadn't hurt Arianna too badly. Even though Solanda was as angry as she could be at that girl, she still didn't want to cause any physical harm.

A robin. Arianna had lied to her. She had said that she had settled on a cat form, just like Solanda, and Solanda had felt flattered.

By a three-year-old.

Arianna had maintained the lie for twelve years.

Solanda ran up the steps quickly. Twelve years, the most difficult years for a child to cover her Shifts. Arianna had hidden her abilities from Solanda that long.

What else had she hidden?

Solanda wasn't sure she wanted to find out. But she had to. And then she had to break the news to Arianna about her brother, a task she had hoped she would never have to face.

It would be ugly.

She might even be banished from the palace.

Although that wouldn't be as great a tragedy as she had originally thought. Apparently Arianna didn't need her as much as Solanda had once believed she did.

At the top of the stairs, Solanda ducked into her own suite. She had acquired it sometime after Arianna started walking on her own. At that point, Solanda realized she would be a part of this palace for a long time. She got the unused suite and made it hers by keeping the windows open constantly, using as much natural light as possible, and bringing back Domestic made sheets and blankets from Shadowlands. Now, after thirteen years, most everything in the suite was Fey-made, and it had the feeling of home.

Only Solanda didn't stop long enough to relax. She moved away from the window, closed her eyes, and Shifted. Her mass expanded. Her paws slid into hands, her limbs lengthened, and the fur absorbed into her body. The feelings were so familiar now that she barely noticed them.

When she was done, she was kneeling, naked, near the dressing room. She stretched, arching her back, and wished she had time for a bath. Then she stood, shook the day's dirt from her limbs, and grabbed fawn-colored pants and a cream top. Not what she had meant to wear to the Coming-of-Age ceremony, but if she didn't have time to change, it would have to do.

Then she hurried down the hall to Arianna's suite.

The door was open, and Arianna's gown was still on her bed, the hated shoes peeking out of the folds of the dress. Arianna hadn't been back.

Solanda knew where she was. She sighed. Arianna wouldn't take Gift's presence in their lives very well. She loved Sebastian too much.

Love, for the Fey, was always a problem.

Solanda went back to the stairs and took them two at a time. The hallway was empty, and Sebastian's door was closed. Solanda didn't knock. She turned the knob and entered.

The room always smelled like rock to her, dry, dusty, with a bit of history. It had a lovely setting, in one of the turrets over the garden. Both windows were open—Sebastian liked air as much as Solanda did—and the room was bright.

Arianna sat on the bed, a robe wrapped tightly around her. She was holding Sebastian's hand and murmuring softly to him.

The lump was shaking.

He looked as if he'd been crying. Solanda was glad she missed that. He had a raspy, grating cry. It sounded both anguish-filled and unnatural. He had cried like that the night Jewel died, and it had frightened Solanda then. Now, whenever Solanda heard that sound, she thought of that night, the night she got her Arianna, the night she watched a woman of Black Blood die in the most horrible agony imaginable.

"Isn't this cozy?" Solanda said, in part to announce her presence, and in part to banish the memory. She grabbed a wooden chair, turned it, and straddled it. "Sebastian, I need to talk with Arianna."

The lump's eyes were wide and liquid. Tears still stained his gray-brown face. "Did . . . I . . . do . . . some-thing . . . wrong?"

"No," Arianna said firmly.

"You tell me," Solanda said. "You're the one who let Gift in here."

"He . . . says . . . he . . . should . . . be . . . here."

"Does he want to be here?" Solanda asked, ignoring Arianna's perplexed expression.

"No!" The lump made it sound as if being in the palace was the most horrible thing that could ever happen. Maybe, for Fey, it was.

"You know what's going on," Arianna said. "You knew those Fey."

"Of course I did." Solanda rested her arms on the chair back. "I came here with them. I've known all of them longer than I've known you."

"What are you scheming?" Arianna asked. Her blue eyes were flashing.

"What am I scheming?" Solanda straightened her back and gripped the top of the chair. "I'm not scheming anything. I'm not the one who has hidden her abilities since she could talk."

"I haven't hidden anything," Arianna said.

The lump looked at her. He put his massive hand over her small one.

"A robin? What else can you turn into?" Solanda asked. "How many other shapes do you have?"

"I don't think that's any of your business." Arianna sounded haughty, but she looked scared.

"It is my business," Solanda stood, slowly, and pushed the chair down so that it was out of her way. It fell with a clatter. The lump watched her, fear all over his stone face. But he didn't move, and he gathered Arianna close to him, protectively.

Solanda approached Arianna and then stopped, hands on hips. "I gave up everything for you. I live in this horrible place with these ignorant people, for you."

"I didn't ask you to," Arianna said.

"You wouldn't have survived if I hadn't," Solanda said. "You were Shifting when you came out of the womb. The Shaman gave you to your father and told him to care for you. He didn't know what to do. He begged her to stay, and she said it was his destiny to care for you."

Solanda took a deep breath. "Without me, you would have died."

"I'm not a baby anymore," Arianna said. "I can Shift without you."

"Yes, you can, but there's a lot more to Shape-Shifting than settling in new forms."

"What do you know of it?" Arianna said. "You can only Shift to one form."

"And how many can you be?" Solanda asked.

The question hung between them, the moment of truth. Solanda was breathing hard, her anger a live thing. The lump was watching her, but leaning against Arianna. It was impossible to tell who was protecting whom.

Arianna stared at her, chin jutting out, the birthmark a livid red against the darkness of her skin. The mark had always changed color with Arianna's moods, but it was worse here, now.

"Ari?" the lump said.

"Shush," Arianna said. "This is between me and Solanda."

"But—"

"Shush."

"How many?" Solanda asked.

"What does it matter to you?" Arianna asked. "You didn't need to know before.'

"I didn't know you could Shift like that before."

"Yes, you did." Arianna spat the words out. Solanda hadn't seen the girl that angry since she was a child. "You always said it. When I was a baby, I Shifted all the time into all sorts of different forms. Remember? Did you think that changed?"

"You told me you had chosen one form. That's natural for a Shifter. You said you were a cat."

"Because you wanted me to be one. Like you."

The lump's lower lip was trembling. "Ari—" he said again.

"Wait, Sebastian. Let me finish."

The lump bowed his head. Solanda glanced at him. She hadn't seen him that animated in a long, long time.

"I wanted you to be safe. You didn't have to be a cat."

"What about the time I Shifted to look like nurse? You yelled at me."

Solanda smiled involuntarily at the memory. She had yelled, and then she had laughed. Arianna's playfulness got her into so much trouble. Solanda had simply wanted to head off more trouble. "Think about it," Solanda said softly. "If a child could look like her baby-sitter, then no one would ever punish her."

"I realized later that's why you yelled at me," Arianna said. "But what it did was made me think you wanted to control me."

"I did want to control you," Solanda said. "You were a child. Do you know how many times you nearly died from your Shifts?"

"More than you know."

Solanda gasped. She hadn't thought of it. Arianna had Shifted into other forms without Solanda's help for years. A child shouldn't have done that.

"It's natural," Solanda said, "for a Fey Shifter to try all sorts of forms before settling on one. Then that one becomes the only Shift after time. A Shifter can either do dozens imperfectly, or one perfectly."

"Was my robin imperfect?" Arianna asked.

Solanda looked away. Through the window, the sky was clear. The sun was setting, and clouds the color of amber were floating over the river.

"Was it?"

"No," Solanda said. "Except that you didn't anticipate an attack by a cat."

"By you," Arianna said. "I knew it wasn't any old cat."

"Are you hurt?" Solanda asked, remembering finally the reason she had come up.

Sebastian raised his head. His movements were glacial. By the time he had turned to look at Arianna directly, she had raised the sleeve of her robe.

Small chunks of skin were missing all along her right arm. The wounds were superficial—probably from the places she had lost feathers. One long gouge ran from her elbow to her shoulder. A toothmark that would have been small on the bird looked large on Arianna's skin.

Solanda bent over the wounds. "Does it hurt?"

"A little," Arianna said. "I've had worse." And then she let her sleeve fall back into place.

The lump took one of his hands off hers. "Ari . . . what . . . ?"

"I'm fine," Arianna said. "Just fine."

"You didn't know what you were doing," Solanda said.

"You didn't know it was me until too late," Arianna said. "You chased after a flying bird, and then when you discovered it was me, you stopped."

Solanda shook her head, wondering how she was suddenly on the defensive. "I knew it was you from the start. Do you think I'd run into the center of town for a bird when I can catch as many as I want in the garden?"

"So I was right. You knew that Fey boy. You stopped me on purpose."

"Yes, I did," Solanda said. "You didn't know what you were doing."

"I was saving my brother."

"Ari," the lump said.

"Sebastian, please," Arianna said.

Solanda looked at the lump. He knew. He knew who Gift was, and he was trying to tell Arianna.

"You don't own me," Arianna said. "You shouldn't even control me. You're not family. You just have this thing in common with me. And I hate it."

Solanda frowned. This was all going too quickly for her. "You hate it? Arianna, it's what makes you special."

"No, what makes me special is being the King's daughter. What makes me different is being so tall and so dark and so strange. Everyone looks at me funny, and no one would even talk to me if I weren't a princess. They all hate me because of what I am. And if they knew I could be anything I wanted, they'd hate me more."

"Can you be anything you want?" Solanda asked, almost afraid of the answer.

Arianna shrugged. She had lowered her eyes, as if she were ashamed of her outburst. Solanda wondered how long that had been building, and how come she hadn't seen it coming. Being a teenager on Blue Isle was different than being a Fey teenager. A Fey teenager had to cope with getting her magick and with finding her place in life. Her magick determined that. Solanda had skated over that part of growing up. A Shifter knew what she was from birth. So while the others were agonizing and learning, Solanda was moving forward, acting like an adult.

The Fey didn't care if they were liked. They grew up in communities where they were often hated. And they didn't have popularity contests with each other. Some personalities worked well together, and others didn't. Some magick types worked well together, and others didn't. Budding Charmers always offended Leaders and attracted followers. Always. But once a Leader knew that the Charmer had come into his magick, the antagonism went away.

"Arianna," Solanda said, "can you be anything you want?"

"Only if I practice," she said.

"Anything?" Solanda couldn't believe that. The magick didn't work that way.

Arianna was obviously uncomfortable with the questioning. Her head came up and her face was flushed with anger. "Now, obviously, I don't know that, do I? I haven't tried to be everything."

"But have you ever failed to become something?"

"Lots of times. But I keep practicing until I succeed at it."

She kept practicing until she succeeded. Solanda grabbed her chair, the fight gone out of her. She put the chair upright and sat on it properly. The lump watched her as if she were going to hit him.

"I'm asking you what the limitations are," Solanda said, in her best, most patient voice.

"I'm telling you I don't know," Arianna said. "I haven't found any. I've tried to be everything I could see. Except my father and you, of course."

Of course. Solanda didn't know why she and Nicholas were so obviously not a choice.

"Magick always has limitations. If you're not limited as to form, you're limited somewhere else." Solanda kept her hands open in her lap. She made certain her voice was calm. This both distressed her and pleased her. There were a lot of possibilities if what Arianna said was true. A lot of possibilities and a lot of dangers.

Arianna sighed and extracted her hand from the lump's grip. She leaned back on the bed as if she too were pretending to be calm. But her young body was filled with tension, and her bare foot tapped nervously against the side of the bed.

"If I'm not careful, I'll lose weight," she said. "And if I try too many forms too fast, I can't change at all for about a week."

"You could be stuck in your shape," Solanda said. She shuddered. Much as she loved her cat shape, she liked being able to change it whenever she wanted.

Arianna nodded. "It happened once. I was ten. Sebastian hid me until I could change back."

Solanda glanced at the lump. He was quite a little pocket of secrets. He was watching her, the cracks in his face showing more than usual. Strong emotion made him look like a shattered stone.

"You were ten?" Solanda said, sure she would have had memory of this.

Arianna nodded. "I talked to you, but I wouldn't show myself to you. You didn't get it, even then."

Solanda didn't even remember the incident. Arianna had been adept at fooling her from the beginning.

"Why didn't you tell me?" Solanda asked.

Arianna bit her lower lip. "I wanted to handle it myself."

"How did you change back?"

"I kept trying and finally I was able to."

Such terror. Solanda remembered being stuck in her cat form at the age of seven. She had had help Shifting back, but still there was a morning of fear lodged in her memory forever.

She bit back recriminations. Five years had passed. She couldn't do anything about it now. "What other limitations do you have?"

"I have to get enough rest," Arianna said. "If I don't, I'll Shift without planning to."

Like she did as a baby. All those sleepless nights where Solanda and the nurse, and sometimes Nicholas, watched Arianna, fearful that she would Shift and kill herself before anyone even noticed.

"Why didn't you come to me?" Solanda asked. "I would have helped you."

"Helped me what? Lose all this ability? Deal with it better? You taught me how to control Shifts. That was enough."

"But when you were struck—" Solanda said, and then bit it back. She hadn't meant to say that.

Arianna shrugged. "By then, I didn't want to tell anyone."

"You told Sebastian."

Arianna leaned on her elbows. She glanced at the lump. He looked at her, like a puppy would look at its human companion. "He's different," she said. "Like me. There's no one else like us. We're not Islander, and we're not Fey. And we're strange. He's really smart, but he can't talk right and he can hardly move. And I'm—" Her voice lowered. "I'm a monster."

Solanda shuddered. The kitchen staff had called Arianna that from that moment she had been born near the hearth fire. The staff had seen her Shift during birth, and didn't know what it was. But Solanda thought they had stopped calling her names when they saw what a beautiful baby she was.

"Who called you that?"

Arianna shrugged. "No one. Everyone. They always said it when I walked by. And some of them held out those religious swords. Those tiny silver ones they wear around their necks, as if it would keep me away from them."

"Did you ever tell your father?"

She shook her head. "Just Sebastian. He says they do that to him too. Only they don't call him a monster. They think he's too stupid to harm them." Arianna glared at Solanda. "You think he's stupid too."

"I don't," Solanda said, hoping the lie sounded convincing.

"You call him a lump."

"He is," Solanda said.

"He is not," Arianna said. "No more than I am a monster. We're not hideous. It's not our fault that we have parents from different races. It's not our fault we look like this. How come everyone blames us?"

"You think I treat you differently because of your parentage?"

"You worst of all," Arianna said. "You call me Fey. You teach me to act Fey. I'm not just Fey, Solanda. I'm Islander too. I'm both."

"I know that," Solanda said. She wanted to return to her cat form, to lick her paws and clean her face. She stifled the urge.

"You don't remember it," Arianna said. "You talk about how stupid the Islanders are or how backward they are. You used to call Nurse 'that woman' and you wouldn't leave me alone with her if you could help it. And you always said Dad was pretty good, for an Islander."

"He is," Solanda said.

"But don't you know what that means? How that sounds? I'm like them. I have their blood, too. So does Sebastian."

Solanda ignored the part about Sebastian. "Shape-Shifters treat everyone with contempt, even other Fey."

"Even each other?" Arianna asked.

Solanda shook her head. "I never meant to speak that way of you. You're a Shifter. You're Fey."

"And Islander."

Solanda took a deep breath. Much as she hated to admit it, Solanda knew Arianna was right. "And Islander."

Arianna smiled, the first real smile Solanda had seen from her all day. She sat up. "All right," Arianna said. "Now you can tell me who that Fey man was, and what he wanted with Sebastian."

The lump looked at Solanda. Solanda thought she saw pleading in his eyes.

She closed hers. The moment she'd been dreading had finally arrived.

FIFTEEN

NICHOLAS hurried up the stairs. His long blond hair was pulled back, but he still swiped at it with his hand. The lace fell against his wrist and made him itch.

Nervous habits.

The talk with Lord Stowe had left him unsettled.

And behind. He had wanted to check on Sebastian before now.

Over the years, he had grown to love the boy. At first, Nicholas had been extremely disappointed with Sebastian—his looks, his lack of intelligence, his physical slowness. Jewel had said that when Fey mated with non-Fey, the magick was always stronger, a counterintuitive notion that Nicholas hadn't believed then. He had hoped for it, though. He had hoped his son would combine the best of them. When it became clear, a few days after Sebastian's birth, that the boy would never be more than a placeholder, a half-wit who would take years to learn how to smile, Nicholas withdrew. It wasn't until the night of Arianna's birth that he looked at his son, his wailing, tearful son, and realized that the boy was more than a disappointment. He was a living being, a being Jewel had loved, and even though he hadn't fulfilled her hopes either, she had cared for him. Nicholas could do no less.

From that moment on, he gave the boy as much attention as he could spare. Arianna had taken some of the worries from him. When Sebastian took over the throne, Arianna would be beside him, his brains and his guide. Sebastian listened to her. Her impulsiveness wouldn't be on the throne—the boy's slowness would always give her time to reconsider her decisions—but her brilliance would.

Nicholas reached the top of the stairs. The servants said they had dressed Sebastian and told him to wait. Then Nicholas had gotten delayed. The poor boy had probably been standing near the window for most of the afternoon, trying not to soil his good clothing.

The hallway was empty. Most of the servants were below, cleaning the Great Hall or putting the finishing touches on platters of food. This would be a feast and a celebration no one would forget. They would all accept Sebastian. Nicholas would see to that.

Still, he didn't like the emptiness. In the future, he would make certain that someone guarded Sebastian at all times. The boy was heir to the throne, and an unpopular heir at that. All it would take would be one unguarded moment, and the boy would be lost for good.

Nicholas's heart twisted. He had guarded Jewel every moment of every day, and still she had been lost. Betrayed by a man of God. Since then, no Rocaanist had been allowed in the palace. Nor would one ever be allowed, as long as holy water killed the royal family.

Sometimes it felt as if he were over her death, and then the next moment, the heartache would return, as fierce as it had been the moment it happened. He had been without her longer than he had been with her, but it seemed like he could still hear her. He could still see her, more and more each passing day, as Arianna grew up. She was approaching the age Jewel was when Nicholas first saw her, wielding a sword in the palace's kitchen.

He shook the memory away and made his way toward Sebastian's suite. The door was closed, but he heard voices. Angry, female voices.

Arianna and Solanda.

They were fighting.

They never fought.

He opened the door quietly and stepped inside. Sebastian was sitting on the bed, his fine robes gathered beneath him, the smoothness of the fabric already creased. A smear of dirt ran along one side of his robe.

Arianna was sitting beside him, arms crossed, eyes fierce. She frowned when she saw him. Solanda was straddling the cane-backed chair. She stood abruptly, as if Nicholas had caught her doing something wrong.

"Are we having a meeting?" he asked.

"No, Daddy," Arianna said, and he could tell from her tone that she was upset.

Sebastian looked at him. The boy's eyes held a deep sadness, and for the first time since he'd been born, he looked guilty.

"What happened to your robe, son?" Nicholas asked gently.

Sebastian looked down at his robe. Slowly his large hands closed on the dirt stain. "Ohhhhh." The word came out as a sigh.

"Daddy," Arianna said. "There was a Fey in here."

Solanda started. Guiltily, it seemed. Nicholas had never seen her do that before.

He tried to keep it light. The room had an air of tension. No sense magnifying it because of his own disquiet. "As I see it, there are one Fey and two half-Fey in here."

"No, Daddy." Arianna's exasperation was quick and sudden. She put a hand over Sebastian's, stopping him from examining the stain on the side of his robe. "A Fey man was here. He was trying to get Sebastian to leave with him."

Nicholas's throat went dry. Arianna was fanciful, but she would never make anything like that up. "What happened?" he asked.

"I scared him off. Then I chased him. I would have got him, too, but Solanda stopped me. She knew him. She let him get away."

Nicholas felt the blood drain from his face. First a report of Fey armies in the south, and now this. "Solanda?" he said.

She was standing rigidly, her usually graceful body a single line. Her fists were clenched, and her gaze darted between Arianna and Nicholas. "You don't want to ask me this," she said.

"I do if they were trying to kidnap my son."

"They weren't trying to kidnap your son," she said.

"Then what happened?" His voice was harsher than he'd planned. He would never let anyone attack his family again. Never.

"Gift . . ." Sebastian said.

All three of them looked at him.

". . . was . . . here."

"You *know* him?" Arianna asked. Her fingers wrapped around his hand, her knuckles white. The grip looked painful, but Sebastian didn't pull away.

He nodded.

"How could you know a Fey?" she asked.

He looked at Solanda. She had backed up toward the cold fireplace. She shook her head.

"Solanda," Nicholas said, a chill running through him. Something was wrong. Something was very wrong. "It would take him too long to tell us. You explain this."

"You don't want me to," she said.

"I have asked. Twice."

Arianna was watching her, features set. Sebastian looked terrified. He hadn't looked that scared since he saved Arianna's life. How could Sebastian know something the rest of the family didn't?

"I tried to tell you. Years ago," Solanda said. "You didn't believe me."

"I'm ready to believe you now."

Solanda glanced at Sebastian, as if asking for his permission. She had hardly given him credence before.

Nicholas's mouth was dry.

"It's . . . all . . . right," Sebastian said. A tear had formed in his left eye. It hovered on his lower lid. "Bet-ter . . . now . . . than . . . to-night."

Nicholas frowned. He could feel the detachment happen as his brain separated from his body. He had learned that so that he could make decisions under extreme emotional stress. He could tell that this would be one of those times.

Solanda took a deep breath. "The Fey that was here this afternoon, Nicholas, was your son."

His son?

The tear fell off Sebastian's lower lid and landed on his cheekbone. Arianna wiped it away.

"Sebastian is my son," Nicholas said, not understanding, maybe deliberately not understanding. He couldn't have this conversation now. Not with the Coming-of-Age moments away.

"No," Solanda said. "Sebastian is not your son. He's a golem. A Changeling. Rugar stole your son five days after he was born."

"No," Nicholas said.

"Yes," Solanda said. Her voice actually had compassion in it.

Nicholas took a deep breath and turned toward the wall. The detachment wasn't working. Emotions flowed as quickly as the memories:

The laughing, bright-eyed baby who grabbed his finger in its tiny fist.

The stone-faced creature that woke from a nap one afternoon and never left.

The dream child, the boy he had imagined, brighter, better than any born on the Isle.

The real baby, so heavy that Nicholas grunted when he lifted him, whose skin was cold and whose eyes were as dull and flat as rock.

"No," he whispered.

The baby he always wanted existed. The son of his imaginings was alive—and raised by Rugar.

Nicholas shoved away from the wall. "Why didn't you tell me? Why didn't you let me know so that I could get him back?"

Sebastian winced. Arianna's skin turned gray. Solanda had her arms crossed over her chest. "I did tell you," she said, speaking slowly, as if Nicholas were the imbecile. "More than once."

Then Nicholas remembered the day Arianna was born. He had been holding her in his arms. She was still covered with afterbirth, and already the Fey were fighting over her. Nicholas was in the kitchen, Jewel's body in front of the hearth fire, the nurse and Sebastian cowering beside it. The cat that had watched the birth had just Shifted from cat to woman, the first time he'd ever seen that happen.

That was when he met Solanda. She had looked at him with contempt, even then, even when she was offering to care for his daughter.

Rugar wants this little girl, she had said. *He'll never have her. There are ways he could steal her, you know. It's been done before.*

Then she had looked at Sebastian.

He stole my son? Nicholas had asked.

Solanda had nodded.

But my son is here now, Nicholas had said.

She had made a small huffing sound, as if she couldn't believe how stupid he was. *You believe that is your son?*

What else could he be?

She had shrugged. *A bit of stone? A lump of clay?*

He hadn't believed her. How could a living, breathing child be clay?

His own son.

His real son.

His boy, and Jewel's, full-grown and raised by the Fey.

At every turn, they stole from him. Since the Fey had come, they had taken everything precious from his life.

And given him such precious things in return.

Arianna had taken a step toward Solanda. Her little hands were in fists. Sebastian reached for her—slowly, and too late.

"That's not true," Arianna said. "You lie. Sebastian is my brother."

"Is he?" Solanda asked. "Then why did that Fey boy look just like him? Only that boy could move. He could speak clearly. He was brilliant. Why?"

"What kind of magick are you talking about here?" Nicholas asked. He felt dizzy. He propped himself against the wall.

"Changeling magick. The Wisps brought in an enchanted stone. They put it in the place of your son, and it became him. Except it was empty inside. It should have disintegrated after a few weeks, but it didn't. It became a golem. I thought Jewel had infused it with life by loving it, but I was wrong. It outlived her. Someone else had given it life."

"Gift . . ." Sebastian said.

Nicholas looked at Sebastian. He loved that boy, stone or not. How could he love something that wasn't real? "Why does he keep saying that?"

"Gift is your son's name," Solanda said.

Gift.

He had a son named Gift.

A real child, as bright and quick and beautiful as Arianna. As Jewel.

Jewel, we have a son.

"Gift . . . made . . . me," Sebastian said. "Through . . . our . . . Link."

Solanda shook her head once and closed her eyes. Her features were pursed together, and she looked more like her cat self than her Fey self.

"What's he saying?" Arianna asked.

Solanda opened her eyes. "You are unbelievable children," she said.

"I still don't understand," Nicholas said. "If this Gift is my son, why did he come for Sebastian? Was he going to stand in Sebastian's place during the ceremony?"

"I don't know," Solanda said. "I didn't know he was here until I saw Arianna chase him out of the window."

"What did he want?" Nicholas asked Sebastian. The boy's entire face was a mask of sorrow.

"He kept saying he wanted Sebastian to leave with him," Arianna said. "He was trying to get him to agree. I made him run away."

"Why did he want Sebastian to leave? Did he want to take his place?"

"He wanted them to go together," Arianna said. "I thought he was kidnapping Sebastian."

"No . . ." Sebastian said.

Nicholas crouched before him and took the boy's hand. Sebastian's skin was cool as usual, something Nicholas had always found odd. The boy had never been warm enough. "Why did he come?" Nicholas asked.

Sebastian took his other hand away from Arianna's. Then he held up one finger. It meant he was going to say something which would take some time.

"Gift . . . said . . . he . . . Saw . . . death . . . here. . . .

He . . . showed . . . me . . . an . . . old . . . Fey . . . talking . . . to . . . one . . . of . . . us. . . . Some-times . . . it . . . was . . . him. . . . Some-times . . . it . . . was . . . me. . . . Then . . . an-other . . . Fey . . . killed . . . him . . . or . . . me. . . . It . . . happened . . . in . . . the . . . pa-lace. . . . He . . . was . . . afraid . . . to . . . let . . . me . . . stay. . . . But . . . I . . . didn't . . . want . . . to . . . go . . . with-out . . . tell-ing . . . you . . . or . . . Ari."

Nicholas sat down. All of this was too much for him. The boy had come to save Sebastian? Not to take his rightful place at Nicholas's side?

Solanda had focused all her intensity on Sebastian. Her cat's eyes glowed. "An old Fey?" Solanda said. "The Shaman?"

Sebastian shook his head.

"Had you ever seen Gift before?" Nicholas asked. How many times had he missed his son?

"Not . . . in . . . per-son. . . . He's . . . been . . . in . . . here"—and Sebastian slowly pointed to his head—"since . . . we . . . were . . . tiny. . . . We're . . . Linked."

"What's Linked?" Nicholas asked Solanda. His impatience came through his voice. How could Sebastian have known Gift and Nicholas not have? Why hadn't Solanda told him? Or Arianna?

What were the Fey doing by holding his son?

"We're all Linked," Solanda said. "We are Linked by blood and we are Linked by love. Most of us feel those ties but can do nothing about them. A few, Visionaries and Enchanters mostly, can travel across the Links and visit the other person inside his own head."

"So Gift," Nicholas said, "has magick."

Like Jewel had said he would.

She had been right.

She had been so right.

And her father had destroyed it all.

"Visions," Solanda said. "Gift is a powerful Visionary. The most powerful we've seen."

She was looking at Arianna as she spoke, and Nicholas knew why. Jewel had said their children would have powerful magick. Arianna had Shifted since she was in the womb. Her abilities were strong. So, apparently, were her brother's.

"And he created Sebastian? He made the Changeling?"

"No," Solanda said. "Rugar had the Changeling made. Usually that's a Domestic skill. What Gift did was breathe life into stone. Essence can be left inside a Link. If this worked in a traditional manner, little pieces of Gift were left inside Sebastian until they became their own personality."

"So Sebastian is a living person," Nicholas asked, with some relief.

"Did you doubt that?" Solanda asked.

"You did," Arianna snapped. "You called him the lump."

His personality did seem to have evolved over the years. Sebastian was a child of Nicholas and Jewel too, then. A bit of Gift living among them.

And yet . . .

"I'm asking," Nicholas said, "if Sebastian is a separate person from this Gift."

"Very much so," Solanda said. "You wouldn't have to ask if you saw Gift."

"How come you have seen my son and I haven't?" Nicholas said. He stood, faced Solanda. "You knew what we were working for. You knew how important it was for that boy to be perfect, and you did nothing."

"I don't work for the Isle," she said, eyes narrowed. "I am Fey."

"And keeping my son away from me was good for the Fey?"

"I don't know," she said. "I didn't make that decision. Rugar did."

"And you trusted his judgment? You never had before."

"It didn't matter to me," Solanda said. "I was stuck in this place no matter what he did."

"It must have mattered to you eventually. I seem to remember you with his blood on your hands."

She took one step toward him until there was no real distance between them. He could feel her warmth, smell her slightly feline scent. "He threatened Arianna."

"How was that different from Gift?"

"Arianna is mine."

Nicholas grabbed her and shoved her against the stone of the fireplace. "Arianna is my daughter. Mine and Jewel's. You are just a glorified servant."

"I am the only mother she has ever had."

They were breathing in unison. Equally angry. And she was right. She had given everything for Arianna.

Nicholas let his arm drop.

Arianna was standing by the window, her hand at her mouth. Sebastian's lower lip was trembling.

"Then you could have told me," Arianna said softly.

"To what end?" Solanda asked.

"The Black Blood," Nicholas said. "If she had attacked her brother, it could have destroyed us all."

"I never thought she would have reason to attack him." Solanda shrugged. "I thought that when she saw Gift, she would realize that he was her brother instead of the lump."

"He's not a lump," Arianna said. She still hadn't turned around.

Nicholas made himself take a deep breath. He still wasn't clear on this. His world had just shifted, and he wasn't able to put all the pieces together. "What happened to Gift after Rugar died?"

"How about before Rugar died? How about when Jewel died? He was Linked to her too." Solanda sounded angry. What right did she have to sound angry? She had known.

"What happened?" Nicholas asked.

"He nearly died when Jewel did. But he was saved by a boy in Shadowlands. And when Rugar died, Gift took his place. Gift rules the Fey now. He has for fifteen years."

"No." Nicholas crossed his arms. "Now I don't believe you. Fifteen years ago, he was just a child. A child can't rule."

"Not in your world. In ours, he had no choice. He held Shadowlands together. He held the Fey together, although I don't think he realizes it."

Arianna shook her head. She shook her head, then glanced at Sebastian. Tears lined his face. She touched his cheek, then walked between Nicholas and Solanda. She stopped in front of Solanda.

"You lie," Arianna said. She was almost as tall as Nicholas, and thinner than Solanda. Her body had the ease and power of the young. She was looking at Solanda, the contempt on her face disfiguring it. "I just figured it out. You would have told me if I really had a brother. You would have told me a long time ago. But you didn't. And you can't stand the idea of Sebastian coming of age. Sebastian's my brother, and you're in some kind of conspiracy with these Fey to make my father set Sebastian aside."

Nicholas felt as if someone had thrown cold water on him. Of course. Solanda had said she worked for the Fey. And some Fey could mask their appearance.

But that didn't explain all the conversations. It didn't explain the Shaman's comment all those years ago that a man should be able to recognize his own child.

Solanda was still leaning against the fireplace. She looked smaller than she ever had before. "What did I do to make you distrust me so?" she asked Arianna.

"You talked to those Fey out there. You stopped me from getting him."

"He's your brother," Solanda said. "You can't attack him. You don't dare. You both have Black Blood."

The chill Nicholas had felt since he came into the room had grown. "You attacked Gift?"

"I thought he was hurting Sebastian," Arianna said.

"She went after him in Shifted form," Solanda said tightly. "As a robin."

"A robin?" There were too many revelations for him. Nicholas put a hand against the tapestry frame, more to steady himself than anything. "I thought you could only Shift to cat form."

"That's what I thought," Solanda said. "It seems the girl's been holding out on us."

"Not as much as you have," Arianna said. "I see it two ways. Either you've lied about my brother all along, or you're trying to put a Fey in Sebastian's place. Either way, you haven't been honest with us at all. You didn't stay in the palace to raise me. You never even knew who I was or what I could do. You stayed so that you could spy on us."

"You could fool me and you resent that?" Solanda asked.

"Solanda didn't lie," Nicholas said. He leaned on the stone base of the window. Below birds chirped. "I remember the times she tried to tell me."

"Why are you sticking up for her?" Arianna asked. "She'll get you to depose Sebastian. The throne is his."

"No . . ." Sebastian said.

"I'm not sticking up for her," Nicholas said. "I simply know she's telling the truth."

"Gift . . . was . . . born . . . here," Sebastian said.

Arianna looked at Sebastian as if he were the one betraying her. "He seduced you, didn't he, that Fey? He made you believe what he wants you to believe."

"No . . ." Sebastian shook his head slowly. "I've . . . known . . . all . . . my . . . life."

His words echoed in the sudden silence. Arianna looked at him, then Solanda, then Nicholas. She blinked once, then looked at Sebastian again.

"Why didn't you tell me?" Arianna's voice rose to a wail. "Why didn't anyone tell me?"

"I . . . thought . . . he . . . came . . . to . . . you . . . too," Sebastian said.

Arianna made a choked sound. She put a fist against her mouth to stifle any other noises. Nicholas felt hollow. Arianna looked as if her heart had been ripped out.

She spun once, and he knew, before he could reach her, that all her anguish would explode. She couldn't stand emotional pain. She had never been able to.

She looked from Sebastian to Nicholas and then frowned at Solanda. For a moment, Arianna stood still. Then she launched herself at Solanda.

"You lied to me from the beginning. You said we were two of a kind. You said you would always be there for me." Arianna shoved her sleeve up, revealing cuts Nicholas had never seen. "Instead, you do this to me. You hurt me to let that Fey man go. You're more interested in your people than you ever were in me. I am nothing to you. I'm glad I never told you what I could do. I'm glad you didn't have all of my secrets to take to your people. Your Fey."

"They're yours too, Arianna," Solanda said softly.

"I'm Islander," Arianna said. "I'm nothing like you."

"Arianna." Nicholas reached for her. She shook him off.

"Leave me alone," she said. "I need to be alone."

She ran from the room. Sebastian stood, wobbled, and started after her. Nicholas grabbed his arm. "She's upset, Sebastian. She'll be all right."

"She . . . hates . . . me . . ." He sounded as if his heart were breaking. "She . . . knows . . . what . . . I . . . am . . . and . . . she . . . *hates* . . . me."

Nicholas looked over Sebastian's shoulder at Solanda. Solanda had her head tilted against the fireplace, eyes closed. For once, she appeared to have nothing to say.

He was trembling. He took his son—or what he had thought was his son until moments ago—and held him. Sebastian's skin had always been cold and hard. It had always felt slightly unnatural. Amazing how many things Nicholas had blamed on his union with Jewel instead of questioning.

"She doesn't hate you," Nicholas said. "She's confused right now."

Sebastian took a deep breath. "Do . . . you . . . hate . . . me?"

That was the question, then, wasn't it? Nicholas rested his head on Sebastian's shoulder. He couldn't imagine his life without this boy. Not now. Not after so many years.

"I love you, son," he said. "I've loved you since you were a little boy, and I always will."

Sebastian shuddered. Then he raised his head. He was taller than Nicholas. Nicholas wondered if his own son, his blood son, was as tall. "Do . . . I . . . have . . . to . . . leave, . . . then?"

"Who said you had to leave?"

"Gift . . ."

"He seemed to have a different agenda than the rest of us. You're my son, Sebastian. You'll stay."

"Ari?"

"Arianna will forgive you when she realizes that this isn't your fault. She's young, Sebastian. She thinks she knows a lot, but she doesn't." And that was Nicholas's fault. He had protected her, coddled her, thinking he was giving her strength. Maybe he wasn't. Maybe he had been making things harder for her.

He patted Sebastian's cheek, and pulled out of the hug. Solanda had opened her eyes slightly. Cat's eyes, alien, untrustworthy.

Cold.

He could be cold too. "What did you do to my daughter this afternoon?"

"Nothing," Solanda said. Her voice was flat.

"How did she get those marks?"

"She was going to attack Gift. She was going for his eyes. I was in my cat form. I stopped her the only way I knew how."

"She's hurt."

"Superficially. I was careful not to do any damage."

"Why did you protect the boy? He was trespassing."

Solanda sighed. "Are all you Islanders so obtuse?" She shoved herself away from the fireplace.

Nicholas grabbed her arm so tightly he knew he would leave marks. He hadn't realized how angry he was until now. "You're not going anywhere. You're going to tell me exactly what's going on. You injured my daughter."

"To save your son."

"If he is my son."

"Oh, he's yours, all right," Solanda said. She shook her arm as if she were trying to free it. Nicholas tightened his grip. "You're hurting me," she said.

"I'll hurt you worse if you're not careful."

"Ooo," she said. "Threats from the great King."

"Solanda," he cautioned.

"All right." She turned her head toward his. Her eyes had slits in them, like cat's eyes did. Arianna never had those slits. Maybe that had been a clue to her abilities. "The Shaman explained what happened when the Black Blood warred on itself. I'm sure Jewel told you too."

"Arianna didn't know."

"It doesn't matter."

"And she wasn't trying to kill him."

Solanda shook her head. "She was going to peck out his eyes. Do you think it would have stopped there?"

"My daughter wouldn't kill."

"Your daughter is Fey. She'll do whatever's necessary." She shook her arm free. "Gift is your son, by blood at least. And, surprisingly, so is the lump, in his own way. He's got Gift inside him, and that makes him—real enough, I guess." She looked at both of them, then rubbed her arm, more for show, it seemed, than anything else. "Tell Arianna that I'm leaving. She obviously doesn't need me anymore. And neither do you. You have enough servants."

Nicholas ignored the jibe. He wasn't going to apologize. He was too angry. "What about that Vision? The one in which Sebastian dies?"

"What of it?" Solanda asked. "We all die."

"Solanda," he said.

She straightened, frowned at him, then sighed. "A Vision is personal. It's up to Gift to decipher its meaning. Gift and Sebastian look alike. He might have seen his own death and decided to substitute Sebastian."

"No . . ."

She shrugged. "Or maybe not. It'll work itself out. Visions always do." Then she swiveled and shook her hands, like a cat did when it was disgusted.

"Solanda," Nicholas said softly. "You're not really leaving, are you?"

She stopped but didn't turn. "I told you I would stay until Arianna no longer needed me. It seems she hasn't needed me for some time."

"She's still young. She needs you."

Solanda shook her head. "It seems I get in her way. It seems that she can't abide my attitudes or my prejudices. Or my person." She took a deep breath. "I've done my good deed for this lifetime. I'm finally free of this place."

And then she walked out of the room.

Nicholas watched her go. He should have gone after her. He had so many questions, so much to consider. But he couldn't. She had betrayed them all by not telling him about Gift.

He didn't trust himself around her any more. He didn't know what he would do the next time she made him truly angry.

A shuddery, grating sob sounded behind him. Nicholas turned. Sebastian's face was covered with tears.

"Every-thing's . . . wrong," Sebastian said.

Nicholas took his son's hand. "Not everything," he said.

"Gift . . . is . . . gone. . . . So-lan-da . . . is . . . gone. . . . Ari . . . *hates* . . . me." The boy shuddered. "And . . . I . . . am . . . not . . . your . . . son."

"You are my son," Nicholas said. "In every way that counts."

In every way except one. The lineage of the Kingship had

been unbroken from the days of the Roca. The King had to be a firstborn son. Of the Roca's line.

Sebastian was not.

And the Coming-of-Age ceremony was that night.

Nicholas closed his eyes and wondered if he had the strength to put Sebastian on the throne.

Or the strength not to.

SIXTEEN

MATTHIAS stood on the banks of the river. The sun had set, and the air near the water was deliciously cool. Mosquitoes flourished, buzzing around him, but he merely wiped them away with one hand.

He hadn't been here in years, and never had he stood on this side of the Cardidas. He used to sit on the other side, the Tabernacle side, staring at the palace and the city surrounding it.

It had been the only place where he felt at peace.

He had found other places since. There were sites on the Cliffs of Blood that made him feel an almost religious calm, something the Tabernacle had never been able to do for him.

He took off his coat and set it down carefully, so as not to break the bottle of holy water in the side pocket. He never went anywhere without holy water. It was as much a comfort to him as it was a protection. He sat in the grass and straightened his legs before him, not caring that his pants got soiled. He pulled off his boots and stuck his bare feet in the river water, letting its coldness run through him.

Across the great bridge, past the small lights of the insignificant city dwellers, the Tabernacle rose like a beacon. Its white walls, kept that way by diligent Auds, glowed in the darkness. The tapestries over the windows were closed, but inside, the candles burned brightly. He remembered summer evenings like this. The Tabernacle was always too hot, but tradition had said that the breezes of the night brought danger.

Tradition. The Tabernacle lived by tradition. It would eventually die by it.

He leaned back. A small group of gnats swarmed his face. He moved over a few inches, and the gnats remained in their place, still swarming. In the darkness, the swords painted on the side of the Tabernacle looked like dirt stains. Some shadows moved across the tapestries. Titus and his minions. The boy who became Rocaan by default. Not a position Matthias would want to have.

Not a position Matthias had kept.

Sometimes it amazed him, the power he gave up when he left his post as Rocaan. He hadn't realized how great the power was until it became clear no one would pursue him. No one would come after him for murdering a prisoner in his cell. Not because the prisoner had been Fey, but because the killer had been an important religious leader.

The important religious leader.

He could have used the power. He could have made changes in the entire country, changes Nicholas wouldn't have been able to object to, changes Titus had been too young to make. But Matthias hadn't been prepared to do so. He had many flaws, but he wasn't a hypocrite. And he truly thought that the man who led the Rocaanists had to believe in the religion's teachings.

He had never believed.

He never would.

Although he did miss it sometimes, the comfort of routine, the consolation of ritual. It had a rhythm that his life now lacked.

But he no longer had to apologize for using his mind. And he was now followed because of his own teachings, not because of someone else's.

Yeon had already found two smiths to work on the sword. He promised more by the end of the week.

And the banquet was set for the next evening.

Matthias had high hopes for both.

His followers didn't care what happened, as long as they would be able to go about their business. And they would, soon enough.

The mosquito was back, buzzing his left ear. He brought up his hand and caught the mosquito, then crushed it, and wiped the remains in the grass.

His body had grown cooler. After the day in the smithy, he had thought he would die of the heat. He didn't know how most smiths stood it, being near that furnace all the time. Once he had his sword, he would never go back into that heat again.

His sword. The second of the Secrets. Poor Titus, guarding a hoard of information rendered useless by the very things that ensured its passage from one generation to another. Matthias would change that. The Fiftieth Rocaan had been right. The Fey were the Soldiers of the Enemy. Only the Roca had left dozens of ways to fight them. The Islanders had given up after using only one.

The Islanders hadn't really given up. They had been stunned by the loss of the Fiftieth Rocaan, but they would have rallied. Nicholas had given up. Nicholas and his father. They had sold the Isle to the Enemy without even realizing it.

The Soldiers of the Enemy had been chased off Blue Isle once before.

They would leave again.

Then voices traveled across the water. Matthias looked up. He hadn't seen anyone when he had come through the bushes, and he had been looking. Sometimes he knew that some of the unfortunates slept on this side of the river. A few got up before dawn and fished. But since the Fey invaded, the river was mostly quiet. The great seagoing trading vessels were gone. The harbor and its warehouses were empty buildings, left to decay. Most of the piers were half-rotted hunks still sitting in the river. Only a few still survived, and those were used for private vessels, the play barges of the remaining rich.

Matthias drew his knees up to his chest. He dried off his feet with his socks. His toes were like ice.

As he slipped on his boots, he heard the voices again. They were soft, but one of them had a bite.

And they were speaking Fey.

He froze. The Fey didn't come inside Jahn any more. They had their own places outside the city, at least those who no longer lived in Shadowlands. The rest remained in that invisible place, hiding, unable to show their faces because their invasion had failed.

The voices were coming from the bridge. Slowly he turned his head, careful not to make any sudden moves. If he moved quickly, they might see him. And there was no telling what Fey would do with an Islander, even in the middle of Jahn.

It took a moment for his eyes to adjust after the brightness of the Tabernacle. The darkness facing east was immense. Only the lights of the city broke it. The bridge seemed especially dark. After nightfall, the traffic on it was almost nonexistent.

Then he picked out several shapes on the bridge itself. Three Fey, talking as they crossed, as if nothing were out of the ordinary. His mouth was dry. Perhaps they were Nicholas's children and their Fey guardian.

But that didn't seem right. Nicholas had planned the Coming-of-Age ceremony for this day. His children wouldn't be on the bridge at this hour. Any royal ceremony, even an invented one, took time.

Perhaps these Fey were attending it. But they were going to the Tabernacle side of the river, away from the palace.

And they sounded young. At least the main speaker did. Too young to have any ties to Nicholas.

Besides the obvious one.

Matthias finished slipping on his boots. It was clear the three Fey didn't see him. They would leave him be. And he would leave them alone, too.

For now.

He wasn't ready to face them.

But he would have words with his own people. He had been told that the Fey rarely came to Jahn. When the Fey did come to Jahn, they worked hard at fitting in. They spoke Islander. They dressed inconspicuously. And they always had something to trade.

He had also been told that they never went on the Tabernacle side of the river.

Someone had lied to him. Or perhaps his people weren't as well informed as he thought they were.

These Fey were up to something. They had plans. And whatever the plans were, they couldn't be good.

Matthias clenched his fists. The last time he had watched the Fey from the side of the river, he had been an Elder. He had watched them take their wounded into a Shadowlands. And he had done nothing.

He would do nothing no longer.

He touched the bottle of holy water.

Those Fey would tell him what they were about.

Or they would die trying.

SEVENTEEN

ADRIAN stood outside the kitchen door, sweat trickling down his back. He had put off the baking as long as he could, but they were out of bread and breakfast rolls. He had spent most of the morning in the kitchen, and somehow, despite his best planning, morning had become evening. By then he was so hot, it no longer mattered, so he threw together some stew. The boys would appreciate solid food for dinner. He might even be able to get Scavenger to come up from his plot of land to the south.

Or, at least, that had been the plan.

But he had gotten as far as the kitchen door. He was going to call Luke and Coulter in from the fields and send one of them down to Scavenger.

But the sight of Coulter made Adrian hesitate.

Coulter sat at the edge of the tall rows of corn. His legs were crossed, his hands resting on his knees, and his head was upturned. He was staring at the night sky.

A shiver ran down Adrian's back. Coulter had done that for nearly a week. When Adrian questioned him about it, Coulter had said simply that he was feeling the sky.

Adrian didn't understand. But then Adrian never understood Coulter. He just loved the boy, and felt Coulter was his responsibility.

They had met in Shadowlands, both prisoners of the Fey. Coulter had been brought in as a baby and ignored until, as a young boy, he saved their Prince's life. Then they had experimented on Coulter to see why he, a true Islander, had such fantastic magickal powers. They didn't have time to find any answers. Adrian managed to get the boy out of there, and with the help of Scavenger, a renegade Fey, keep Coulter out of Shadowlands for good.

No one had come after them. The Fey seemed to have forgotten them.

And Adrian liked it that way.

But raising Coulter had been one strange incident after another. During a particularly wet planting season, he had stuck his hand into the ground and pulled out root worms. Most farmers never saw root worms, didn't even realize they were eating the crops until the crops were mostly dead. But Coulter found them.

And he stopped the birds from landing in the cornfields.

And one memorable afternoon, he had prevented lightning from striking the wheat.

But he had never just sat in the field like this before. He had never studied the night sky in this way.

It made Adrian nervous.

"Dad?"

Adrian didn't turn. He didn't have to. He felt Luke's presence beside him. His son, despite their encounters with the Fey, had grown into a sturdy man. He had not married, which disturbed Adrian, but Luke said it was because he feared getting close.

And after all the Fey had put Luke through, Adrian certainly understood. They had spelled the boy, used him as a weapon, and set him loose among the Islanders. He managed to survive that, but he was afraid they had tampered with more of him. He claimed it wouldn't be fair to bring a wife and children into his life only to discover another Fey booby trap, one that could cost his family their lives.

"What's he doing?" Adrian asked.

Luke leaned against the side of the building. The wood walls groaned under his weight. Luke studied Coulter. Over the years, they had developed an understanding. They weren't quite brothers, and they weren't quite friends. They were something in between. "He says something's changed in the Isle's energy."

"Whatever that means."

"He says it's not good."

Adrian sighed. "That's more than he told me."

"He says you worry too much."

"I worry? He's the one sitting in a field because the energy has changed." Adrian glanced at Luke. His hair was wet and slicked back against his sunburned head. He was muscular and strong, his hands powerful from the work in the fields. He would give Adrian good grandchildren if he only overcame that fear, the fear the Fey had given him of himself.

"He's usually right about these things," Luke said.

"I know." And that bothered Adrian. Coulter had never talked about a global change before. Only small ones. "I was going to send you for Scavenger. I have fresh bread and stew."

"No wonder it's so hot here. I can't believe you had a fire on a day like today."

"It's been this hot all week," Adrian said. "We need food."

Luke shrugged. "I guess it's no different than me picking rocks in the far field."

"I thought we weren't going to plant that."

"It's been a good summer," Luke said. "If we use that field, we can get a third corn crop."

"We can't sell that much food, Luke," Adrian said.

"I wasn't thinking of selling it," he said.

Adrian looked at him. "What else did Coulter tell you?"

Luke grimaced. "Nothing. It's just I've been talking to one of the Danites. He says they're not getting enough food down south."

"You were planning to give this away?"

"Some of it." Luke sounded diffident. He always sounded diffident when things mattered to him.

Adrian shook his head. All that work for no gain? Luke knew that Adrian hated charity. If people wanted food, they should work for it too. He had five acres that he didn't have enough resources to plant. He'd give the food to anyone who worked the land. So far no one had taken him up on it.

"How long have you been planning this?" Adrian asked.

Luke shrugged.

"When did you talk to the Danite?"

"During first planting," Luke said. "I've been looking at that field ever since."

"Who'd nurture it? Who'd harvest it? And who'd pay to get the corn down south?"

"The Danite said the Tabernacle would, if we let them know."

"Danites." Adrian crossed his arms, then when his damp skin rubbed together, uncrossed them. It was too hot even for pique.

"I know you don't like them. I know you aren't fond of the Rocaanists, but they do good things."

"Like make holy water to reveal Fey spells," Adrian said.

Luke took in a breath. Then he was silent for a long time. Adrian felt heat rise in his cheeks. He hadn't meant that. Or maybe he had. Luke hadn't been particularly religious until the Rocaan had discovered the Fey spell on him. Then Luke had embraced the religion.

Adrian had been raised in the kirk. Most people were. But he had taken it for what it was—simple rituals that kept the faithful satisfied. He had the land to satisfy him, and the warmth of the sun, and the feel of the good brown dirt beneath his fingers. He didn't need anything more than that.

"I'm sorry," he said. "That was wrong."

"Yes, it was," Luke said. "I'll do the work. It will come from my time. I own part of this land. It'll be my donation."

"And I'll pay because it will cut into your work on my time."

"You'll have nothing to say about it," Luke said. "I'm thirty-five, old enough to have my portion of this land deeded to me."

"It's deeded only when you have a family to pass it on to," Adrian said.

Then, in the darkness, Coulter stood. He raised his arms above his head. Light flashed from his fingertips, illuminating the night sky. A tiny trail, like a road carved in air, glowed purple.

Adrian pushed away from the building and hurried to Coulter's side. Luke followed.

It was cooler near the fields. A slight breeze had come up, stirring the day's heat, moving it away from the ground. Adrian stopped by Coulter and looked up.

The purple trail seemed flatter from this angle and no wider than his thumb. It jagged and veered slightly, dipped toward the barn, then rose again like a road carved in a mountainside.

"What is it?" Luke asked.

Coulter didn't answer. His fingertips flashed again and the light rose like lightning traveling from the sky to the ground. The purple trail grew brighter, littered with tiny flares and lights.

It ran south to the north, and disappeared into the darkness leading toward Jahn.

"Do you see another one?" Coulter asked.

Adrian scanned the sky. It was as if Coulter had lit a thousand candles in one small spot, giving the brightness of day. That purple trail looked as solid as a dirt road. But Adrian saw no others, at least in the lit section of the sky.

"No," he said.

"Me, either," Luke said, but his voice trailed off at the end.

"Luke?" Coulter asked.

"Not up," Luke said. "I don't see anything up."

Adrian looked at the ground. So did Coulter. It was crisscrossed with faint lines, most of them silver, and most of them leading to the house.

"No," Coulter said. "I know those."

"What are they?" Adrian asked.

"Scavenger."

All the heat from the day left Adrian's body. He understood the implication and didn't like it. "Scavenger has no magick."

"Scavenger's Fey. They all leave trails," Coulter said, as if that were the most obvious thing he'd ever said.

"You can see them?"

"Not normally. They're like a marker of where a Fey's been and when he was there. Most people can't see them."

But Coulter could. Like he could find worms from above ground and stop lightning with his bare hands.

"All Fey have them?" Luke's voice was shaking. Adrian put a hand on his son's shoulder.

"All Fey," Coulter said. "Scavenger's are silver. I thought all Fey had silver markers until tonight."

Luke and Adrian looked up. The lights that Coulter created in the sky were fading, but the purple trail blazed forward.

"What left that?" Adrian asked, not sure he wanted to know.

Coulter put down his arms. The light disappeared. The purple trail continued to glow. "There was a wind from the south today. Did you feel it?"

"Not much of one," Luke said. Discussing the weather was reflex for farmers. "It didn't do much about the heat."

"No, but it died about midday, and I felt something. I looked up and saw a firefly."

"It was daylight," Adrian said.

"And too hot. They don't come out until it cools down," Luke said.

Coulter nodded. "If I'd been thinking, I would have realized that. But it wasn't until I saw the real fireflies at twilight that I knew."

Adrian's stomach was churning, and not because he was hungry. "A Wisp?"

"I don't think it could have been anything else. There are types of Fey I've never heard of, but they usually don't duplicate magick." He ran a hand through his blond hair. Coulter had grown tall, taller than any Islander Adrian had ever known. He was whip-thin, too, and as powerful as Luke. But his skin was pale, and his eyes were bright blue, and his features were round. There wasn't any Fey blood in him. His age said that, and his body confirmed it. It was just that magick he had that seemed Fey-like and unexplained.

"Flying south to north," Luke said. "I didn't think there were Fey in the south."

"All Fey trails were silver, until now," Coulter said. "And the energy's changed. It's like the wind has come up on a summer's day, bringing a storm. There's a charge in the air. Can you feel it?"

"No," Adrian said. Sometimes he felt blind next to Coulter.

"And no one's left the Shadowlands except Gift and his guards," Coulter said, with that uncanny knowledge he seemed to have about the boy he had saved. Adrian never had a way of verifying the information, but he knew it to be true, nonetheless.

"If no one's left Shadowlands, that trail can't be Fey," Luke said. "You think an Islander did that?"

Coulter shook his head. He looked at Adrian, as he often did when he was about to make a point. Their time in Shadowlands together had left a bond that Luke could never penetrate. Coulter always thought that Luke didn't understand, that Luke couldn't understand. Luke, for his part, often didn't want to understand.

"Gift's coming," Coulter said. "With a Vision he can't explain, and a Fey in it he's never seen before. The energy's changed, and the trail is purple. And instead of two of us here, there are three."

"Of course there are three," Luke said. "You, me, and—"

"No," Coulter said before Adrian could shush his son. "It's all energy. It's like Links or trails. The energy holds things together too. I can feel it, like you can feel sunlight."

Adrian tightened his grip on Luke's shoulder. "Three what?"

"I can feel the Isle," Coulter said. "There's always been me, and someone else like me."

"Who?" Adrian said.

Coulter shrugged, his shoulders moving against the night sky. "I don't know. Someone far from here."

"And now there's a third?" Luke asked.

Coulter nodded. "To the south. Where the Wisp came from."

"What does it mean?" Luke asked.

But Adrian knew. It was all the Fey ever really talked about, all they thought about. The reinforcements had finally come, and somehow they had breached the mountains in the south.

With an Enchanter.

What had Rugar called Enchanters?

The most powerful of all Fey.

"They'll kill us now, won't they?" Adrian asked.

Luke started, but Coulter shook his head. "We're incidental," he said. "If they're here, the Isle is as good as conquered. No. They've come for Gift."

"And you had him come here?" Luke asked, the fear evident in the rigidity of his shoulders, his back.

"If he gets here, he'll be safe," Coulter said. "I can protect him."

Adrian looked up. The purple trail was no longer visible against the night sky. "If he gets here," he said.

EIGHTEEN

SHE had nowhere to go. For the first time in her life, she belonged to no one and had no responsibilities.

She was free.

Solanda veered off the road outside Jahn. She was in her Fey form. She hadn't changed since she left the palace, but she did take the time to pack her Domestic-made blankets and her clothing. She had left the palace in a blind run and had taken the only route she knew.

To Shadowlands.

But she never stayed in Shadowlands. She hated the grayness and the lack of life. And she really didn't like the Fey who lived there. Cowards, most of them, who could no longer face the real world.

She wasn't any fonder of the Fey who lived outside Shadowlands. They were less than Fey, conquered people living in a conquered land, content with the scraps the Islanders threw them.

Nicholas would have let her stay in the palace. It was the only place befitting a Shape-Shifter.

But she couldn't look at Arianna. The girl had taken her heart and shattered it.

Solanda walked across the cool grass into a clearing. The night air felt good. The air in the palace was always stifling. She liked having the stars above her.

The river wound below her. She could hear its gurgle. Sometimes, when the palace got too much for her, she went to the river in Jahn. She had to go as a cat, and it wasn't the same as being here, in the countryside. Someone always disturbed her, wanting to pet her or shoo her away.

But she could remain here as long as she liked. The Islanders seemed to hate the outdoors. Most of them avoided it. She had heard about Islanders who stayed outdoors much of the time, but they didn't live in Jahn.

Neither did she, any more.

She tossed her bag on the grass, then lay down, tucking the bag under her head like a pillow. The moon was bright, and the stars twinkled. The river was soothing. She hadn't spent a night outdoors since Arianna was born.

Arianna.

The ache in Solanda's chest grew. The Fey always said that Shape-Shifters couldn't have children, that their bodies couldn't carry a pregnancy to term, and if it did, the Shifter couldn't love. A Shifter never accepted responsibility, a Shifter always thought only of herself, a Shifter was unreliable, untrustworthy, and unwise.

Solanda had known some of those statements to be lies. She had learned early that Shifters could get pregnant. Shifters took responsibility, they just did so in ways other Fey never recognized.

But she had always believed the one about love.

She had never found anyone worthy of her love.

Until she saw that square, flat body being pulled out of Jewel's womb.

Arianna was Solanda's child, not Nicholas's. Arianna was a child of the heart, a sister under the skin, a responsibility that Solanda gladly accepted.

And one she had somehow failed.

A mother would go back. But a mother belonged. Solanda didn't, and she wouldn't beg. She was a Shifter, and Shifters never begged.

As if pride would get her anywhere. Arianna had outgrown her, simple as that.

I don't need anyone, especially you. Solanda had said that to her guardian so many years ago. And then she had gotten in trouble and was saved by Rugar, not realizing at the time that he had manipulated the whole thing to have a hold over her.

A hold that lasted until the day he died.

Solanda sighed. She scrunched up her bag and put her arms under her head. She wouldn't go back, at least right away. She would give Arianna a chance to realize how much she needed Solanda. And a chance to forgive Solanda for keeping the truth about Sebastian to herself all these years.

She wasn't sure why she hadn't told Arianna about her real brother. Fear, she supposed. Arianna already loved Sebastian beyond all bounds. Solanda didn't want to share Arianna's love with a real person.

With another Fey.

Such mistakes she had made. Mistakes she would have to unmake someday. After she had given Arianna her time alone.

But that didn't mean Solanda had to stay uninvolved. Arianna was her child, her sister under the skin. Solanda had an obligation, one that Arianna might not recognize, but Solanda did.

She had vowed to take care of the child whether anyone wanted her to or not. Before Nicholas had wanted her to. Then Arianna had.

But now Nicholas thought Arianna could take care of herself, and Arianna pretended she needed no one.

Neither of them realized that a fifteen-year-old Shape-Shifter was still a child, still capable of making those horrible errors that ruined a life forever.

Arianna had nearly made one today by attacking her own brother. Her real brother.

Who didn't belong near the palace.

Who shouldn't even have known about Arianna, but he ran from her as if he understood the terror, as if he knew what her attack would do to both of them. To the Fey. To the world.

He had known.

And he had been the one to breathe life into the Changeling.

He knew a lot more than he should have.

He apparently had lived in Shadowlands and the palace. And he had come to "save" Sebastian.

Creator saving the created? Or something more than that?

It was supposed to be Sebastian's Coming-of-Age ceremony, after all. And Gift, who had access to his golem's mind, would know that. If he had stood in for Sebastian, would that have convinced the palace that Gift needed to rule?

Was this some sort of Fey trick, as Arianna had surmised, or was it innocent as the lump had claimed?

Gift had access to Sebastian's mind, but Sebastian also had access to Gift's.

And Arianna had said Sebastian was smart, just physically unable to move quickly.

Solanda shook her head. There were too many variables. Too much to consider on her own.

And one thing bothered her: Gift had risked a lot to come into the palace. Whatever he had been after had been important.

Solanda made a satisfied grunt. She had a path now.

Arianna didn't need Solanda at the palace. But Arianna still needed Solanda.

Solanda would discover what Arianna's brother was about, and if it was no good, she would stop him.

She wasn't of the Black King's family. She had no consequences.

She had learned that before.

When she had murdered the Black King's son.

NINETEEN

SEBASTIAN had finally stopped crying. Nicholas still held him, not wanting to let him go. Sebastian rested his head against Nicholas's shoulder, and clung tightly. Nicholas had his cheek pressed against the boy's cool skin.

Not his son.

He and Jewel had had a talented child, a magick child, a gifted child, just as Jewel had said they would.

For some reason, the thought made him sad, and, beneath the sadness, he found a deep anger. Rugar, Jewel's father, had done so much to ruin all their lives. He would have done more if he'd been able to take Arianna. Nicholas wouldn't have raised any of his children.

He didn't know how he felt about Sebastian.

The love and affection was still there. He would fulfill his obligations to the boy, but something had changed in their relationship already. Not in his heart. He had always known on some deep level that Sebastian wasn't right. He just hadn't known what was wrong.

Now that he did, he felt better. He didn't feel responsible. But he didn't know what to do. He couldn't hold the

Coming-of-Age ceremony. This boy couldn't rule Blue Isle. He wasn't the hereditary heir.

The hereditary heir had been raised Fey, in the Shadow-lands. He probably thought himself Fey, the way that Arianna thought herself Islander. With no bond between the two cultures. No healing as Nicholas—and Jewel—had once hoped.

A slight breeze was coming through the window. The sun had set. The darkness was filmy; the rising moon sent soft light over the trees. Nicholas would have to go downstairs soon and cancel the ceremony. He didn't quite know how. He didn't want the Rocaan to think that he had won, that Nicholas had canceled the ceremony because of pressure from the Tabernacle. And yet he could say nothing about Gift.

Perhaps he should pretend he didn't know about Gift. Let the ceremony go on, let Sebastian rule, and have Arianna be the brains behind him.

Nicholas would go against centuries of tradition. The firstborn son, the line descended from the Roca, would be broken.

He didn't even know if Sebastian could have children. Probably not, since the boy was made of stone.

A knock on the door made him start. Sebastian slowly raised his head. His cheeks were still wet from his earlier tears. Nicholas wiped them off.

"Come," he said.

A page entered. The boy was holding a torch, and the light made Nicholas blink.

"Forgive me, Sire. I am late finding you. I did not know you were here," the boy said. He bowed, and remained down.

Nicholas ignored the excuse, wondering how long the boy had been looking. "You have news?"

The boy stood. The torch had remained level the entire time. "There is a Fey to see you, and Lord Stowe asked me to remind you that the ceremony shall begin soon."

Nicholas nodded. A Fey. Perhaps it was his son, come back the official way now that he had been discovered.

Or perhaps it was something else.

"Please tell Lord Stowe to make our guests comfortable. Sebastian and I will join them shortly."

Sebastian grabbed his hand tightly. Nicholas squeezed back, trying to offer reassurance.

"Where is the Fey?"

"In your personal Audience Chamber, Sire." The boy bowed each time he spoke. It was an annoying habit.

"Have five guards meet me there, and have four more in listening posts. Send two up here as well."

"Before I see Lord Stowe?" the boy asked.

"Before," Nicholas said.

The boy bowed and backed out of the room.

"The . . . ce-re-mo-ny," Sebastian said. "It . . . should . . . be . . . Gift's."

"It cannot be," Nicholas said. He patted the boy's hand. "We'll figure something out. Remain here. I'll come for you."

Sebastian nodded. Nicholas stood and grabbed the flint from the fireplace's mantel. He struck it, then lit several candles in the room.

Sebastian watched him from the bed, stoic and all alone. "Soon?" he asked.

"As soon as I can," Nicholas said.

Then he put the flint back and left.

The torches were lit in the hallway. The soft light was a comfort. His heart was racing. So much had happened this day already. His mind felt as soft as the light from all the revelations. Fey to the South, a Fey in the palace, an attempt to kidnap Sebastian, Arianna's Shifting ability, Solanda's departure, and a son. A real son.

And now, a Fey in the Audience Chamber.

He had to clear his mind. He had to be sharp. He had learned that the Fey never approached anything directly. If they wanted something, they attacked from all angles. Something was happening, something grander than he was, something he couldn't yet imagine, and he didn't know how it would play out.

The guards he had asked for Sebastian were coming up the stairs. Nicholas noted who they were, nodded at them, and then continued on his way.

He had beaten the Fey once before, with Jewel's help. If he was going to keep the fragile balance that Blue Isle had attained, he would need to retain that control.

Voices echoed from the main hall. Some of the guests had already arrived. Nicholas hurried down the second-floor corridor, past the portraits and the uncomfortable chairs. He took the back stairway. It was a longer trip to the Audience Chamber, but one that would keep him away from questioning nobles.

The five guards he had asked for were already outside the chamber. Nicholas nodded to them as he approached. "I need two of you inside with me," he said. "The rest must remain here."

Two guards flanked him as he opened the door and saw who waited. Then he pulled the door closed without going inside. "On second thought," he said, "stay out here. And remove the guards from the listening posts."

The guards glanced at each other. Two broke off and went for the listening posts. Nicholas waited until they had been gone a moment before going inside.

The Fey stood at the far window. She was tall even for a Fey, and her white hair fuzzed out around her head like a nimbus. Her gnarled hands were clasped behind her back. When the door closed, she turned.

"Are you going to stay this time, young Nicholas?" she asked.

He had never felt quite so relieved to see a Fey. The Shaman. He thought of her as an ally, even though he was never certain. She was powerful and powerless. She Saw things, much as Leaders did, and she had limited leadership duties. But her main role as a guide, a sounding board, the wise woman of the Fey.

He had seen her before he dismissed the guards, and he had known he was in no danger from her.

"I'm sorry. The page had said that a Fey was here to see me. He didn't say it was you." Nicholas smiled. "You've never come through official channels before."

"I have never been uncertain of my welcome before." She cocked her head. "Your men have left their secret hiding places. We can talk now."

Nicholas didn't know how she knew of the listening posts, but it didn't surprise him. Nothing about this woman surprised him. "I have told you that you're always welcome here."

She nodded, and smiled softly. The wrinkles folded on her face, nearly hiding the edge of her lips. "Things will change between us, Nicholas."

"Between you and me?"

She shook her head. "My people and yours."

"Because of this afternoon?"

Her bright eyes darkened. "Young Gift was here, then."

"You didn't know?"

"I knew he said he would come."

"He tried to take Sebastian."

"He fears for its life." The Shaman folded her hands in front of her long robe.

"Why?"

"A man's Visions are his to share or keep. I have not Seen the moment of which he speaks." She was watching Nicholas. Her gaze was so sharp that he felt as if she could see through him.

"Why didn't you tell me about Gift?" Nicholas asked.

"A man should recognize his own child, Nicholas," the Shaman said.

"You said that to me once before. I don't believe it," Nicholas said. "As if a Fey would know. Jewel didn't. She loved Sebastian."

"And that gave him life," the Shaman said. "One cannot argue with the Powers and Mysteries. They provide us with creatures like Sebastian for a reason." She peered at Nicholas sideways. "Will you keep it?"

"Sebastian? He's my son."

"It is a stone come to life, Nicholas. Not a son." Her tone chided him. He didn't like it.

He stood taller than he ever had, as if he could be her equal by increasing his height. "Solanda says Jewel did not create him. She says Gift did, and that he left pieces of himself in there. She says Sebastian was formed through a Link."

"A Link." The Shaman turned, but not before Nicholas saw her wrinkles flatten in surprise. "That is why it lives without Jewel."

Then she raised her head. "Forgive me. We are both correct. It is a son and a stone. Young Gift is right to preserve it. I had thought him mad for attempting to change the Vision. Now I see that he had cause."

Nicholas came up beside her. She smelled faintly of cinnamon and sunshine. "Please," he said. "Tell me truly. Is Gift my son?"

"He is. Rugar stole him and left your son-stone in his place. Rugar had hoped to make the child in his own image."

Nicholas felt cold. "Did he?"

"Rugar was a Blind man. He put your son with Wisps who raised him with love. Gift feared Rugar and saw him as responsible for Jewel's death."

"Rugar?" Nicholas frowned. "Matthias killed Jewel."

The Shaman shook her head. "On Nye, Jewel had her first Vision. It was of her death, only she could not know that. She saw enough to think she would survive. Death Visions are often misleading. A person never seems to See the actual passing of the spirit, only the event that causes it. She had this Vision the moment her father decided to bring her to Blue Isle. She relayed the Vision to him, and he did not check it with me, his father, or any other Visionary. She did not know to. Young Gift had the same Vision. He Saw his mother die, only he thought it to be his Wisp mother. Gift told Rugar. Rugar knew that you were in the Vision, knew that it could not be the Wisp mother, and still he did nothing. It is a Visionary's duty to prevent a death Vision. But he did not. He believed that his last Vision took precedence, the one in which he saw Jewel looking contented in your palace."

"But those Visions aren't mutually exclusive."

"I know this. Rugar should have known this. But his willingness to believe in himself over all others Blinded him, and cost his daughter her life."

Nicholas swallowed the lump in his throat. So many ways Jewel's death could have been prevented. If only he had known. He would never have asked her to be beside him at that ceremony.

"You blame yourself."

Nicholas shrugged.

"You have no Vision, Nicholas. You have no way of seeing the future."

"I should have known."

"You cannot take for yourself magick you do not have.

The magickal responsibility belonged to Rugar. If he had not taken your son, you would have known. Gift would have Seen the death while living here, and Jewel would have compared Visions with him. She would have lived."

Nicholas took a deep breath and calmed himself. He had to think. "My son has Visions?"

"Your son is a great Visionary. In our recorded history, we have not had a Visionary who Saw so young."

"Does he know about me?"

The Shaman stared at Nicholas. "I do not know. If he created your son-stone through a Link, I would guess he does. But Islanders are alien creatures to him, Nicholas. He cannot be like your Arianna, happy in this world."

Nicholas's palms were wet. He wiped them on his ceremonial robe. "Then what do I do about him?"

"I have Seen nothing. He is his own person, a man grown now, Nicholas. With responsibilities to his own people. He is their ruler, and they will need him."

"He is the eldest son, the hereditary ruler of Blue Isle. He is a descendent of our Roca. By law, by religious tradition, by all that we have ever been, I must name him my successor. He will have to rule here someday."

"If there is an Isle to rule," the Shaman said. "You do not know what will happen before you die."

The chill Nicholas had been feeling settled around his heart. "What are you saying?"

"Only what I have said before. You cannot See. It is not within your magick. You do not know what is required of your son."

"And you do?"

"Parts of it," she said. "And I am terrified, Nicholas."

He tilted his head and looked at her. She had never admitted any emotion to him before. He certainly wouldn't have expected terror. Not from the Shaman of the Fey, the wise woman. "What do you See?" he asked, afraid of the answer, but knowing he had to ask the question.

"I told Rugar when you married Jewel that your way was the way of peace. I told him the days of the warrior were over, and that he should stop fighting. He did not listen to me, and in failing to do so, he set a number of events into motion."

"Like what?" Nicholas asked.

"I do not know how long I will live, Nicholas. I must make a choice that goes to the essence of what I am. If I die, your children will have to fend for themselves. It will be difficult."

"Is there something going on among the Fey that I don't know?"

"Rugad is alive," she said. "He wants your son."

"Rugad? Rugar's father? Jewel's grandfather?" Nicholas frowned. "There are reports of Fey to the south. Is that him?"

"I do not know," she said. "But I have Seen him on the Isle. He will throw everything into chaos."

"And kill you?"

She raised her head, her eyes far away. "By law, he must. We failed, this troop. My people do not tolerate failure."

"But it wasn't your choice."

"Nonetheless," she said.

"And you let him?" Nicholas couldn't believe the casual cruelty, the way the Fey used death to solve their problems.

The Shaman smiled. "I am a warrior, Nicholas."

"You'll die for him?"

"I die for no man."

"I'll help you."

She shook her head. "You have your children. You must focus on them."

Nicholas clasped his hands behind his back. For the third time in his life, he was swimming in deep waters. One false move and he would drown.

"So you're telling me," he said slowly, "that if the Black King comes to Blue Isle, he'll be fighting a war on two fronts? He'll fight his own people and mine?"

"Three," the Shaman said softly. "If you choose to involve your children."

"Three?" Nicholas looked at her. She looked older than she had ever looked. "My children can't fight him. You've educated me about what happens when the Black King's family fights within itself."

"But you have a child who is not your child," she said. "Your son-stone seems to be of Black Blood but is not. You have a tool to fight the Black King without tainting the blood."

"Sebastian? He can't fight."

"Are you so certain?" she asked.

Nicholas frowned. Sebastian was a gentle soul. He had never harmed anything, and never would.

"Why not join with us?" Nicholas asked. "Instead of facing the Black King separately, why don't we face him together?"

The Shaman smiled and took his hand. Hers was soft and wrinkled, the hand of an old woman who had never done any physical labor. "He is not interested in killing your people," she said. "He wants them and their land."

"But we won't give it without a fight."

"That is your choice, Nicholas. But my people will not ally with yours for your sake."

"But you could use us," he said.

She shook her head. "The Black King will slaughter us and all who ally with us. We have little hope. Joining with you will gain us nothing, and lose everything for you."

"And if my children fight him?"

"If your son-stone fights him, we have a chance. We all have a chance."

"You've Seen that?"

She took her hand from his. "No," she said. "I did not even know what your Sebastian was until this afternoon. I simply know that he has life for a reason. It could be this."

Nicholas walked to a chair and put his hands on the back. "What have you Seen?" he asked. "Will the Black King conquer Blue Isle?"

"Rugad is a brilliant man, a fearless leader, and the best of the Fey," she said.

"But have you Seen him conquer Blue Isle?" Nicholas asked.

She took a deep breath, closed her eyes and bowed her head. "I have Seen little beyond his arrival. I suspect I will not live long enough to know the answer to your question."

"Perhaps you just haven't Seen what is going to come," he said, not wanting to believe her.

"Perhaps," she said, but there was no conviction in her voice.

"Ally with us," he said. "We will fight him with you."

She shook her head. "You are not all-powerful, Nicholas. Do not believe that all Fey are as easily defeated as Rugar was."

Nicholas swallowed. He did not think Rugar had been easily defeated.

"We have conquered half the world," she said. "We have defeated stronger people than yours, more battle-hardened and some with small magicks. A small island in the Infrin Sea cannot stop us forever. If you are to defeat the Black King, you must embrace your enemies and sacrifice that which you love the most."

"I've already done that," Nicholas said, thinking of Jewel and of his father.

The Shaman watched him. Her gaze held a deep compassion. "No," she said. "What you have lived through will seem simple compared with what you face. Your god asks much of you, Nicholas. You must be willing to do as he asks."

"I don't believe in God," Nicholas said.

"So you have told me," the Shaman said. "But you are a direct descendent of his representative on this land, are you not?"

"If the stories are true," Nicholas said.

"And if they are not?"

"Then I am merely a man who happens to rule, who comes from a long and unbroken line of rulers."

"Perhaps," the Shaman said. "Blue Isle is unusual in that. I know of no other country whose ruling class has had such a long reign."

"Nor of any that are confined to an island," he said, with a smile he didn't feel.

"I do not believe that is the cause," she said.

"Oh?" he asked. "What is it, then?"

"Your Roca was an unusual man," she said.

"I don't know," Nicholas said. "I think the stories were embellished."

"And if they were not?"

He frowned at her. She was trying to tell him something. "Sometimes," he said, "I am not good at subtlety."

She laughed. The sound seemed to come from deep

within her. "Your honesty is one of the things I appreciate about you," she said. "What I am trying to tell you is this: What is magick to some, Nicholas, is religion to others."

"Are you saying that the Roca was a magickal being?"

"No," she said. "I do not know enough about him. But you must consider it. Your children can do things no Fey has ever been able to do."

"The Fey have mated with non-Fey before," Nicholas said. "It's supposed to make the magick stronger."

"Stronger, yes," the Shaman said. "But not change it. Your children do not follow the normal Fey patterns. Their magick is different."

"And you think that comes from the Roca."

"I think you must consider all possibilities."

"Why are you telling me this now?" he asked. "Why not when they were born?"

"Because," she said, and her lower lip trembled, "this may be the last time I see you, Nicholas."

"Because of the Black King?" he asked. "I don't think you should protect me that way. We've been friends—"

"We've been friends a long time," she said. "I admire your courage, and your intelligence, and your flexibility. I think you have been a savior to your people, my people, and your children. I think you are one of the best individuals I have ever known, Fey or non-Fey."

"Then why leave?" he said. "I rely on you. You're one of my only friends."

"It is not my choice," she said.

"Jewel said that Visions can be changed."

"They can," the Shaman said. "But changing them must bring a better future, not a worse one."

"You're saying it is better for you to die?"

She shook her head. "I am saying it may be better that we do not meet again." She took his hands and pulled him close. "I value you, good Nicholas."

He held her tightly. She had saved Arianna's life. She had fought for Jewel. She had given him advice when no one else would. She had been his strength and his understanding.

"I value you too," he said when he could trust himself to speak.

She moved away from him, bowed her head, and started for the door.

"Find a way to come back," he said.

She smiled. "Guard your children, Nicholas," she said, "and the rest shall take care of itself."

TWENTY

GIFT wasn't sure how long the trek to Coulter's was, but he did know that they had to pass the Tabernacle at night.

The Fey hated and feared that place. It was the place where they had first died, where the Battle of Jahn had been lost. This was all before his birth, and yet he knew of it as if he had lived it. He even could recite the names of the dead.

Being on the bridge made him queasy. It was a sturdy stone bridge, wide enough for several people to walk side by side and still have room for a carriage to go through. It did not sway in any wind, and was more solid than some of the buildings that stood on dry ground.

It still made him dizzy to be on it.

He blamed some of that on the run he had made that afternoon. It had taken him a meal and more water than he cared to think about to fully recover from that. The fear stayed with him, though. His mistake had nearly been the largest made by a Fey. He hadn't counted on his sister's mis-understanding and anger. Nor had he thought she would fail to recognize him.

Cover was to his left. She had gotten the meal. He didn't

know how and he didn't ask. She watched their sides and back as if she expected something.

Leen was to his right. She walked as tall as she could, her chin jutted forward, her eyes straight ahead. She had one hand on her sword and another with a ready dagger. Her pride in being beside him was tangible.

He would have been safer with Prey.

From an outside attack, anyway. He didn't trust Prey, though. He didn't trust many Fey. They all seemed to find him lacking.

He and his companions were the only ones on the bridge. He found that odd despite Cover's reassurances. She said that Islanders rarely ventured out after dark. He didn't find it that dark. The moon cast its silver light on the bridge, making the stones glisten. It was a lovely evening. The heat of the day was receding, and near the river it was already cool.

Cover grabbed his arm. "Keep moving," she said, her voice so soft that he had to strain to hear it. "Be ready, Leen."

Leen nodded and moved closer to him. Gift's heart started to pound hard. He wanted to ask what Cover had seen, but he knew better.

She had already disappeared into the soft light. He didn't know where she hid, only that she was gone. Then he heard the sound that had alerted her. Footsteps. Quiet ones, the barely audible pressing of feet on stone.

Bare feet.

An Aud? A religious type? They could kill him. He had had enough near misses for one day.

"I can see you," a male voice said in Islander. "You don't need to hide."

Gift started. No one saw Spies.

No one.

He turned.

Leen hissed at him, grabbed his arm, tried to get him to continue moving. But he stopped.

Behind him, an Islander stood. The moonlight hit the back of his head, casting a shadow over his face, but reflecting his blond curls. The man was tall for an Islander. He wore pants and an open shirt. His feet were bare.

In his left hand, he held a vial. Gift could only guess that it contained the Islander poison.

Cover stood near the far rail, her own face indistinct so that she couldn't be recognized.

"Fey on the bridge," the man said in Islander. "Heading toward the Tabernacle. What sort of scheme do you practice now?"

"No scheme," Gift said. "We can move freely in this country."

"Anyone can move freely and risk death." The man held up the vial. "I don't like Fey."

"If you're going to kill us," Gift said, "at least let us see your face."

"Is that a Fey custom?" the man asked. He didn't move.

His voice sounded familiar. Not the sort of familiar Gift heard every day, but the familiar of dreams or Visions. Yet Gift was certain he had never Seen this moment.

"It's courtesy," Gift said.

"Why are you going to the Tabernacle?"

"We aren't," Cover said. "We're leaving Jahn."

The man moved his head slightly so that he could see her. "Going south?" he asked. "The Fey have no business south."

"We do," Leen said.

The vial had no stopper. The liquid inside reflected the moonlight.

"Are you from the Tabernacle?" Gift asked. "You seem protective of it."

"I don't need to be from it to want to preserve it," the man said.

"Only Fey with a death wish would go into that place," Cover said. She had moved closer to the man.

He turned, and the moonlight hit his face. Its features were round, but the nose was long and patrician. Gift had seen him before, in both a Vision and a dream.

The Islander was younger. He was wearing long red robes and the sword of the Islander religion. Behind him was a table with holy poison. He placed a crown on Gift's mother's head.

And she screamed.

"I thought you were dead." Gift took a step toward the

man. Gift was shaking. This man had committed murder and still he lived.

The man started, and held up his vial.

"Gift!" Cover said.

"You killed my mother," Gift said. "They told me you died for it."

"Your mother?" The man was clearly confused. He held the vial close to his heart as if to protect it.

"My mother. Fifteen years ago. You murdered her."

"Jewel?" The man sounded shocked. "Jewel is your mother? But you're Fey."

"Of course I'm Fey," Gift said. "My mother was Fey. I'm Islander too."

"You're not Sebastian," the man said. "Sebastian has no brain. You're trying to trick me."

"It's no trick," Gift said.

Leen had drawn her sword. Cover circled behind him. They obviously didn't know what Gift was about. He wasn't certain he knew either.

Except that he couldn't let this man live.

"I am not as easily fooled as you people believe," the man said. "You have nothing of Sebastian in you. He looks as if he were carved out of rock."

"Gift," Cover said, a warning in her voice.

Gift said nothing. He wasn't going to say anything. He was going to figure out a way around the vial and then kill this murderer.

"I don't like Fey," the man repeated. "And I hate Fey who lie."

He flicked his wrist, splashing the poison toward Gift. Cover hit the man in the back at the same time. Leen shoved Gift backwards. He tripped, hit the stone wall, and climbed on it. The man staggered sideways, and dropped his vial. It shattered onto the stone, spilling its dangerous contents all over the bridge.

"Cover!" Gift yelled, warning her to stay away from the poison. Leen crawled up beside Gift.

The man grabbed Cover and flung her toward the poison. She landed in it, and screamed. Gift ran along the railing, Leen yelling at him to stop. He grabbed the man by his collar, swung him around and slammed him against the wall.

The man wrapped his arms around Gift's legs, and pulled them forward. Gift lost his balance but maintained his grip.

As he fell off the bridge, the man fell with him.

The air rushing by him had the chill of river. Gift tried to twist so that he wouldn't land on his back, but the man was clinging too tightly. Gift shoved his knee into the man's jaw, breaking the man's grip slightly, then kicked the man in the chest. The man let go. Gift twisted—

—and belly-flopped into the river.

The breath left his body. He felt as if he had hit hard ground. Pain shuddered through him, from his groin to the backs of his eyes. The water was warm, and he sank. His limbs were heavy, unusable.

He would drown if he didn't force himself to move.

The man landed beside him, and sank faster. Bubbles floated around him as he lost whatever air was in his body.

Gift felt the force of the water as the man passed him, sinking deeper.

The man would drown.

Gift would not.

He forced his legs to kick, even though the effort made his eyes bulge. He didn't have enough air, and his body felt as if it would explode. His arms fluttered beside him. He made them push on the water. Black spots floated in his vision. He would pass out if he didn't get air soon.

Then he burst through and took a deep, shuddery breath. The black spots in front of his eyes grew. He thought they would go away as he was able to breathe. But they didn't. He treated water in a circle. The bridge was above him, looking impossibly high, and he was equidistant from both banks. He would have to swim.

The Tabernacle glowed from the south bank. He didn't know what he would find there, but Leen would probably try to meet him there.

And Cover, if she could.

He had raised his heavy arm in a crawl stroke when hands gripped his feet, pulling him under.

He swallowed water, coughed, and choked. He flailed his way back to the top, pulling a dead weight with him. He spat out the water and took a breath of air as the hands worked their way up his legs, yanking him down again.

The man was holding him.

The man put a hand on Gift's back and shoved, using Gift as leverage to get to the surface. The man broke through as Gift sank.

Then the water exploded around him, and he saw another pair of legs flailing. He forced himself up, and breathed.

Leen was in the water, her knife out. She was slashing at the man with one hand, holding him with the other. He was trying to protect his head, but the fall seemed to have sapped his energy. She stabbed him repeatedly, then shoved him under the water.

In the moonlight, the river looked black.

"Come on," she said.

Gift didn't have to be to told twice. The water was thick and warm around him. He kicked hard, then swam after her. When they reached the south bank, she grabbed his arm and dragged him ashore.

She was breathing hard, her hair plastered on the side of her face. Gift sat, knees against his chest, shivering despite the warmth of the night.

"I thought they were supposed to leave us alone," she said.

Gift shook his head. The Islanders were supposed to leave the Fey alone. They were supposed to be coexisting. But that didn't stop occasional retaliatory attacks for long-dead relatives killed in the war, or for just plain hatred.

It happened on both sides.

But this was a little different, and he wasn't certain he wanted to tell Leen that just yet. She had just killed the man who had murdered Gift's real mother.

Gift forced himself to his feet. His clothes were water-logged and heavy.

"What are you doing?" Leen asked.

"Cover," he said.

"She's dead."

"You can't be sure."

"Yes, I can," Leen said. She rested her forehead on her arms. "Trust me. You don't want to see her."

But he did. She had died for him. He had heard her screams as he fell.

He pulled off his soaking shirt and his pants, keeping only his boots to protect him from the poison.

"Don't touch that stuff," Leen said. "It'll kill you too."

"I won't," he said. He didn't even walk to the normal part of the bridge. Instead he climbed its side, his muscles protesting each movement. When he reached the top, he walked the wide stone railing, and stopped midway.

A mist rose from the center of the bridge and obscured the moon. The smell was overwhelming—rotted, decaying flesh. He put a hand over his mouth and continued forward.

The lump on the side of the bridge wasn't even recognizable as Fey. It was a round ball with an arm sticking out one side, fingers splayed as if reaching for help. The bottom of the ball had the hint of legs, but nothing else.

Nothing recognizable as Cover.

He had heard that death by poison was a slow agony. Often, he'd been told, it was a strangulation death because the Fey no longer had features with which to breathe. He'd never been able to envision it.

Now he'd never be able to forget it.

She'd been trying to save his life.

He turned to his left and vomited. His dinner splatted as it hit the water below. He wiped his mouth with the back of his hand. No wonder his people had stopped. No wonder they had given in to the Islanders. No wonder his mother had married his father, trying to create unity.

No one wanted to die like that. Not even his courageous, battle-strong people.

He was dizzy, exhausted, and sick to his stomach. He crawled along the bridge railing until he reached the Tabernacle side.

Leen put a hand on his back and helped him off. Then she handed him his wet clothes. She had wrung them out. He put them on and shivered.

"We can't stay here," she said. "We're near the Tabernacle. This is the most dangerous place for Fey."

"I know," he said. "We'll find somewhere to rest outside of Jahn."

But he doubted that they'd stop. He had to reach

Coulter, now more than ever. In trying to prevent a death, he had caused one.

He couldn't bring Cover back. But he could at least show that her faith in him had been justified.

"Let's get out of here," he said.

And they did.

TWENTY-ONE

TWENTY-ONE

ARIANNA huddled in the listening booth, not daring to breathe. The booth was carved into the wall, with a thin panel between it and the King's personal Audience Chamber. Usually guards hid here, prepared to emerge at the first sign of trouble.

But her father had dismissed the guards. When Arianna had come below to find her father, she found guards near the doors who described the Fey woman within.

Arianna had seen the Shaman a few times. She knew who the guards were talking about.

They didn't stop her when she went to the booth herself. They couldn't; no one could discipline her except her father.

And Solanda.

But Solanda's things were missing from her room. Arianna had discovered that when she had gone in to continue the fight. The familiar blankets and coverings were missing as well as the faintly furry odor.

Arianna had knocked over a chair, then stood above it, uncertain why she was so angry. Solanda had been in her way. She had always been in Arianna's way. Right?

Then why had Arianna felt abandoned?

She went to her father to find out, only to discover that her father was talking to the Shaman.

It had been her father's anger that had driven Solanda away, her father's anger and her own. Maybe the Shaman had come because of Solanda. Or maybe she had come because of Arianna's so-called brother, the Fey with the look of Sebastian and the bright blue eyes.

Sebastian loved that Fey, that Gift, and that terrified her. Solanda said the Fey could Spell others, Charm them, seduce them into doing what the Fey wanted. Perhaps Sebastian was Charmed.

Or perhaps he really trusted this Gift.

Sebastian had never hidden anything from her before, and that frightened her too.

She wanted to talk to her father, but the Shaman was in the way, and the guards wouldn't let Arianna go in. On that, they could countermand her. Her father had given orders that no one enter.

So she crawled inside a listening booth, and sat, knees to chest, listening.

And Arianna hadn't liked what she had heard.

The Shaman was leaving now, admonishing Arianna's father to guard his own children. Arianna hunkered deeper into the booth. She would have to wait a while now before seeing her father so that he wouldn't know she had listened. She had listened to his audiences before, but never one filled with so much information.

Information she felt wrong in having.

Her father was as confused as she was about this Gift. And he was begging the Shaman for help. The woman wouldn't help. She couldn't. And she was worried about things Arianna had never thought of.

Then the door to the listening booth opened. The Shaman stood there. Her hair was messed, as usual, but her face lacked its normal calm. She crooked her finger, indicating that Arianna should come out.

Arianna's throat was dry. She had never spoken to the Shaman alone before. Solanda had been with her a few times, and so had her father, once. The Shaman scared her, with her vague pronouncements, her obvious knowledge, and her air of personal power.

The Shaman waited.

Arianna slipped out, and the Shaman closed the door.

The hallway was cool. It was paneled with wood, a design that hid the entrances to the listening booths. Most hallways in the palace were made of stone. The hallway felt big after that little booth. Arianna hadn't realized how stifling the booth had been.

The Shaman stood alone in the hall. The guards were gone. Probably to tell Arianna's father where she was. Arianna was shaking. This day had been confusing for her as well.

The Shaman put her dry hand on Arianna's cheek. Arianna resisted the urge to pull away.

"You are a passionate girl," the Shaman said, "but you do not know where the passions come from. Solanda has taught you, but not well enough. She kept too much from you."

Arianna swallowed. "She should have told me about Gift."

"She should have told you about the responsibilities of Black Blood," the Shaman said. "You have a true brother, whom you attacked today. You have a great-grandfather, whom you must not touch. You have three uncles, and a dozen cousins, whom you may never meet. If you attack any of them, if you harm any of them, you will cause a madness the likes of which the world has never seen."

Arianna's cheeks were hot. "How do you know, if the world has never seen it?"

"It happened once," The Shaman said. "A Black family turned on itself. Three thousand people died after the Black Queen and her family slaughtered each other. *Three thousand.* Fathers turned upon sons, sons upon mothers, mothers upon daughters."

"Three thousand people is not the entire world," Arianna said, with more bravado than she felt. She didn't like being told about rules after she had broken them.

"It was then." The Shaman removed her hand from Arianna's cheek. "The madness spread throughout the entire Fey Empire. The Fey hadn't really begun their conquests. One in ten survived. That's all. The Fey Empire now covers half the world. Do you want to risk half the world for a fit of temper, Arianna?"

She wanted to argue. She wanted to say she didn't have that kind of power. But the Shaman was right. Arianna didn't know enough about herself or her Fey heritage to make that argument. And logic didn't work. Magick often defied logic.

"No," Arianna whispered. "I don't want to risk half the world."

Then she squared her shoulders. "But I didn't know I had a brother until this afternoon. Or a Fey family. I could not be blamed if something happened."

"The Powers don't care about fault," the Shaman said. "They give us our magicks and we learn how to use them. Or misuse them."

Arianna said nothing. She had no defense. She had attacked that boy. Her brother. That Fey. He had been hurting Sebastian, whom she loved.

Even if he wasn't her brother.

"What did my real brother want with Sebastian?" she asked.

"It is not my place to explain the Visions of others."

"My father might fall for that, but I don't. What did he want?"

"Gift wanted to protect your brother-stone. I did not understand why until today. But he was right in doing so. He failed because of you."

"Stop blaming me for doing what I thought was right!" Arianna's voice rose. "I thought he was going to hurt my brother—Sebastian. I thought he was going to hurt Sebastian."

"Things are not always as they appear, are they, young Arianna? You of all beings should know that. You are not a common Shape-Shifter. And Shape-Shifters are not common in the first place."

"What do you want from me?" Arianna asked.

The Shaman peered at her. "The future rests not on your brother, but on you. Choose wisely."

Arianna clenched her fists. "Tell me what to do, and I'll do it."

The Shaman smiled. "If it were that easy, I would do so.

But the Powers only let me see your importance, not your future actions."

"But I don't want to be important," Arianna said.

The Shaman tucked a strand of Arianna's hair behind her ear. "You have been important, child, from the moment you were born. You cannot walk away from it even if you try."

She nodded once to Arianna, then headed down the hall. Arianna let her go, then she pulled the strand of hair from behind her ear.

She didn't want to be important. She didn't want all that responsibility. But no one cared. And she could do nothing about it. She sighed, and slipped into the door beside the listening booth. Her father was sitting on one of the straight-backed chairs, his legs extended and crossed at the ankles. He didn't seem to hear her come in.

"Daddy?" she said.

Her father looked up. His face was wan, his eyes pale against his even paler skin. "You listened," he said without accusation.

"Only part of it."

He nodded. "I'm not strong enough for this, Ari. I lost everything the first time. My home, my father. My wife. They stole my son from me."

"But you got Sebastian."

"I did. And now that I've accepted him, they steal my son again by telling me he's not mine. He's not even human."

Arianna took a step closer to her father. She had never seen him like this. He looked defeated. She stopped on the small embroidered rug. "But you still love him, don't you?" Her heart was pounding. Somehow, that question was very important to her.

"I still love him," Nicholas said, "but I can't make him King. There are dozens of nobles waiting in the Great Hall for a ceremony that won't happen."

Arianna took his arm. "What about me?" she said, not certain what she was asking.

He closed his eyes, and shook his head slowly from side to side. "You can't rule, honey. Even if you wanted to. You're not only secondborn, you're female. My people won't accept that."

"You won't let that Fey boy rule." She tightened her grip on her father's arm. "You can't."

"I don't know what else to do," he said.

"Change it," she said. "You've changed everything else. You married a Fey. You kicked the Rocaanists out of the palace. You can make Sebastian King."

"No," her father said. "He was never right for it. You would have had to help him."

Arianna stared at him. There were deep shadows under his eyes, and hollows in his cheeks. Lines had formed near his mouth. He looked older than she had ever seen him.

"You want me to say I'll take his place," Arianna said. "I'll take Sebastian's birthright."

"It's not Sebastian's," her father said. "It belongs to Gift."

She tilted her head. The room was quiet. Except for the listening booths, this place was soundproofed. The entire palace could be falling around them and they wouldn't know.

"If I considered taking this Gift's place," she said, "would you break the rules? Would you make me rule after you die?"

He opened his eyes, and studied her. They were watery and bloodshot. "Do you know what you'd be facing?"

She shook her head.

"Islanders perceive you as Fey. You would have to convince them that you hated the Fey. If you managed that, then you would have to show them you were capable of ruling. You could never marry because they'd expect your husband to rule in your stead. And you could never have children, because it's not allowed outside of wedlock."

"So the unbroken line would die."

Her father nodded. "Unless Gift had children. Then the rule would have to be passed to them."

"What if I had children without marrying?"

"Anything you did that was unusual you would have to defend, sometimes with troops. People would accuse you of being Fey, of catering to them, of bringing their demon qualities into Blue Isle."

"They came before I was born," she said.

He nodded. "But people would blame you for it. All of it. You would rule, and you would be the most hated person on

Blue Isle. Everything you did would be unpopular, and your life would be a misery."

Arianna took a deep breath. She let go of her father's arm. She was light-headed. It had been a long time since she had eaten.

Choose wisely, the Shaman had said.

"I'm hated now, aren't I?" Arianna asked.

"No," her father said. "Of course not. The people who know you—"

"I'm not talking about them. I'm talking about all the people who don't. The people who see me as Fey. The ones my brother is supposed to rule. They hate me."

Her father dropped his gaze. He nodded.

"You once told me that a ruler doesn't have the luxury of doing the popular thing. He must do the right thing."

"Ari—"

"Didn't you?"

"Yes." Her father's head was bowed.

"Would it be right for my Fey brother to rule Blue Isle?"

"I don't know," her father said.

"Daddy." Arianna's heart was pounding. She was frightened of this conversation. "Would it be right?"

"I haven't met him. I don't know what he's like."

"He was raised Fey, wasn't he?" Arianna asked. "He probably has Fey values. Fey values shouldn't control the Isle."

"We don't know that, honey."

"All these problems you say I'll have, wouldn't he have them even more? I've seen him, Daddy. He's really Fey. He dresses like them, he looks like them. Once people know, wouldn't they treat him worse than they would treat me?"

"They wouldn't know. They'd think he was Sebastian." Her father wasn't looking at her.

"And what if the Black King comes? Wouldn't this Fey brother just give the Isle to them? Would you want that?"

"It's not that simple, Arianna."

She swallowed. "No, it's not. But it sounds like you don't want me to take Sebastian's place because it would hurt me, not because it would hurt the Isle."

Her father pushed himself out of the chair. He went to

the empty fireplace and looked in as if a fire were actually burning. He leaned his head against the stone.

"Daddy? I'm right, aren't I?"

"No." His voice sounded strangled. "It's not your place, Arianna."

"But I'll take your advice. I'll have children. I won't marry. The line will continue."

"Your line would be a bastard line. Your brother's children have the right to rule. It's the law, Arianna."

"But we are the law," she said. "We can change it any time we want."

He raised his head. A smudge ran along his eyebrows. "Why do you want this, honey? It would be divisive at best. At worst—" he choked and stopped speaking. He turned away, but not before Arianna saw his eyes fill with tears.

She went up to him and put her hand on his back. She was almost as tall as he was now. "I don't want it," she said, and knew that was true. But what the Shaman said was also true. Arianna had been born to power and to controversy. Even if she wanted to walk away, she couldn't. "But I don't think I can turn my back on it. We've always known Sebastian couldn't rule. But as long as you thought he was your child, you planned to have me stand behind him. Gradually everyone would have known that I made the decisions, but we would have kept up the fiction. You feel you can't do that now."

"I thought at least he could have children who would rule," her father said. "Even if he can, they wouldn't be from the Roca's line."

"But mine would."

"Ari—"

"Let me finish," she said. "If we let my real brother rule, we may as well give the Isle to the Fey, and all that you and my mother worked for, all that you suffered for, would go away."

"We don't know that," her father said. "We don't know what kind of person your brother is. He might be like your mother."

"And he might be like her father."

Arianna's words hung between them. Finally her father shook his head.

"I'm sorry, Arianna," he said. "I can't. Too much rides on this decision. I need to find out who your brother is first."

"He could fool you."

Her father smiled. "Not many people can fool me, Arianna, and not when I'm looking for them."

"But Mother's death—"

"Was my mistake. I knew who Matthias was. I knew what he could do."

Arianna swallowed. Time to let him know what she had been doing. "The Shaman says the Black King will come. What if he does come? And what if he manages to assassinate you? Then who will rule the Isle? Sebastian? This Gift? Or me?"

"He can't kill me, Arianna. I'm related to him."

"But not by Blood," Arianna said. "We don't know all the rules. And Solanda is gone."

Her father ran a hand through his hair. "You saw that, huh?"

"I went to her room. Her stuff is gone."

"We hurt her," her father said. "She gave up a lot for you."

"She tried to kill me this afternoon."

"She tried to save you, to save all of us."

"She lied to us."

"Yes," he said. "She did."

Arianna kept her hand on his back. He had let Solanda go. He could have stopped her and he hadn't. He was as angry with her as Arianna was.

Arianna swallowed. "My point is that we have no more resources. And we can't trust Fey help any more. The Shaman said she's going, too. We're on our own. You can't believe that they'll let you live. You can't. Not when they can put one of their own on the throne."

"You're part Fey, Arianna. It's not 'their own.' It's yours too."

"I know nothing of them," she said. "I know this place."

"And not all of that," her father said. "I kept you too sheltered."

"You haven't answered me," she said. "What happens if you die?"

He rubbed a hand over his face. The black smudge came off on his fingers. "I don't know," he said.

"If you don't know, the entire country is ripe for chaos. And if you cancel Sebastian's Coming-of-Age, people will wonder. You have no choice, Daddy. You have to appoint me."

"I have a choice, Ari," he said. "I just have to figure out what to do in the short term. I only learned of your real brother today. I can't make a decision on such short notice."

"I thought you prided yourself on your decisiveness," she said.

"I do. But I have time to consider in this instance. I can gain all the facts before I act."

"I hope you're right," she said.

A knock resounded on the door. Arianna started. No one ever knocked on the chamber door.

Her father raised his head, wiped his fingers on the chair, and then put his hand on her shoulder. "Come," he said.

The door opened. Lord Stowe was already bowing. He wore old-fashioned clothing, his long ceremonial robe tied tightly at the waist. His hair was pulled back, and as he bowed, he showed his ever-increasing bald spot. "Forgive me, Sire. I had heard that your audience was over."

"It is, Stowe," her father said.

"Your guests are here. They are waiting for the ceremony."

Something flickered and then disappeared in her father's eyes. He turned to Arianna. "Go get your brother," he said. "Sebastian. Go get him."

"But—"

"And make certain he is ready for the ceremony."

"But—"

"And make certain you are too."

She frowned. She thought her father was going to consider his decision. It seemed as if he had already made it.

"Arianna," he said, in that tone that brooked no disagreement.

She sighed. "Yes, Father," she said, and made her way past Lord Stowe.

The hallway was cool, and the guards were milling around, trying to listen. She glared at them, then hurried by. It wasn't until she reached the stairs that she realized she was shaking.

She had just tried to take her brother's rule. For the kingdom itself. And she didn't want it. Her father was right. She would be hated for the rest of her life, and she would condemn herself to a loveless future.

But she loved Blue Isle as much as her father did, maybe more, because she saw it in ways he never could. And she wasn't Fey. Even though she had Fey blood and a Fey face, she was pure Islander.

Her real brother wasn't.

Maybe her father was going to let Sebastian rule after all, with Arianna behind him. Maybe he would order Sebastian not to have children. Sebastian would listen. Then Arianna's children would rule.

The solution was convoluted, but it would work.

It simply wouldn't work well.

Then she stopped as another idea hit her.

It was the obvious, most perfect solution.

She turned around and headed back to the Audience Chamber.

She only hoped her father would think so as well.

TWENTY-TWO

AS he sank, the blood leaked out of the wounds on his face. The blood floated upward, darkening the moonlight waters.

Matthias was drowning, his energy gone. The Fey had cut his cheeks, his arms, his shoulders. He would die, whether he wanted to or not.

You have a great magick, holy man.

The face of the dead Fey, the one he had murdered fifteen years ago, the friend of Jewel's, stared at him in the black and bloody water.

You can survive anything.

He shattered the face with his fist. Blood split off like tears, floating toward the air. The movement wasn't as hard as he had thought it would be.

But his lungs were empty. He couldn't swim this wounded.

We believe because you believe.

You have a great magick, holy man.

He believed he was going to drown. So he would. Simple as that.

But he wanted to live. He needed to live.

He kicked, feebly at first, but then with more strength.

His legs were uninjured. His lungs ached, but they didn't burn. How long could a man hold his breath underwater?

He didn't know.

He kicked again, harder, the power of his legs forcing him toward the surface. The blood swirled around him, then it congealed and formed a ropy string that he could tug on.

He was delirious.

He was dying.

The string broke.

No. He needed it. The blood came together again, and braided itself, like a rope. He continued to pull, and kick, and pull. He still didn't need any air. Maybe he was already dead.

If so, he would claw his way to the Face of God. He wouldn't remain in the dark and the cold and the wet forever.

He kicked again, pulled on the string, and then his head broke the surface. He was still in the Cardidas. The moon shone silver on the water, except where his blood flowed. There the river appeared black.

The Fey splashed on the Tabernacle's banks. The woman stood, knife still in hand. The boy stripped off his clothes. Their voices carried across the water, but they were speaking Fey, and Matthias couldn't understand them.

He watched the boy toss his pants on the ground. He worried that they would do something sacrilegious on that side of the banks. Then the boy checked his boots and climbed up the bridge.

Matthias pushed himself underneath the bridge, keeping his hands underwater so that they didn't splash. He was breathing shallowly, but the sound echoed under the stone. Blood ran warm down his face, onto his neck and into the water.

If they caught him again, they would kill him.

He was exhausted and dizzy. He had to get to shore. His clothes were heavy and waterlogged. In this state, he was finding it hard to remain afloat.

He couldn't go back underwater again. He was too afraid of drowning, of tempting the Holy One too many times. He made small swirling motions with his hands, propelling himself backwards.

The woman stood on the bank, looking up at the bridge. She was tall and lean, as Jewel had been, as all Fey women seemed to be. She didn't appear to have the kind of physical power that had held him so tightly and allowed her to stab him.

But she had. If he hadn't played dead, she probably would have continued stabbing him. But he had, and she had shoved him under the water in disgust.

An odd choking sound came from above him, and then vomit streamed past, splashing into the water. The stench was incredible. He used the sound to cover his own splashes, pushing away from the vile stuff as quickly as he could.

So the boy wasn't battle-hardened. Matthias had never heard of a Fey vomiting before.

But the boy had said Jewel was his mother. He had a rounder look to his face, and his eyes were pale.

Nicholas's son?

But Nicholas's son was simple. This boy obviously was not.

Although Matthias hadn't seen the young prince in a long, long time. Perhaps his simplicity was merely slowness, due to the strange circumstances of his birth.

Perhaps.

But Matthias had not heard anything about the young Prince being smart. Nor had he heard that the young Prince traveled in the company of other Fey.

Jewel had had a daughter with Nicholas. Had she had a son before she married Nicholas? Had she had purely Fey children as well?

The woman had moved to the entrance to the bridge. Matthias was nearly to the other side. He was still in darkness, and his dizziness was growing. He was thirsty too. He'd heard that was a sign of blood loss. Yet he felt strong.

Odd the things the body did to survive.

The woman reached up and helped the boy off the bridge. Then she handed him his clothes. He put them on, shivering as he did. They spoke softly, their voices farther away now. Matthias couldn't even make out the Fey words.

The boy was hunched, shocked. Then he tossed his hair back, as Nicholas used to do, and looked toward the Tabernacle. The woman pointed and the boy nodded. They had a plan.

And Matthias was too weak to stop them.

He was near the side of the bridge. He pushed on the

water, then grabbed the stone and worked his way around to the east side. They wouldn't be able to see him from there, but they could still hear him.

The stone was slick and moss-covered. He held it as best he could and pulled himself along it, keeping his feet pointed downward. The river was deep in the center, but it shallowed quickly, otherwise the bridge could never have been built in the water itself. The Fey voices faded, but he didn't trust that they were gone.

The blood was drying on his face. It pulled against his skin. His upper arms were a mass of cuts. It was amazing that he had any strength in them at all.

He continued pulling himself along until his feet brushed mud. He forced his toes down, uncertain, afraid he was touching more of the bridge. But his toes sank into it.

Mud.

He pulled harder now. The stone was dry, and his fingers scraped against it. Soon his feet found purchase and he was able to walk up the north bank.

The palace side.

He made it to the grass before his legs collapsed from under him.

All his strength was gone.

His limbs trembled and he suddenly couldn't breathe. Black spots swam in front of his eyes. All the weakness he had expected in the water assaulted him here.

Now.

God was punishing him for leaving the Tabernacle, abandoning his post, giving the Secrets to the unworthy.

God had brought him to the water's edge to give him hope, then yanked that hope from him.

He would die.

Now.

Matthias tried to scrabble up the bank, but he couldn't. His body didn't work at all.

He closed his eyes and let the exhaustion wash over him.

The voice of Burden, the Fey he had killed, echoed in his brain, speaking to him as if Burden had never died. That Fey had haunted him for fifteen years, taunting him about magick.

He did so now.

Your magick saved you again, he said. *But you choose not to believe it. You did not drown, but you will die. The great holy magician, killed by his own beliefs.*

What would you have me do? Matthias asked. He had never expected one of his victims to watch over him, to guard him, and keep him safe.

I would have you die a longer, lingering, more painful death. This is too easy for one such as you.

And then Burden faded away as if he had never been.

Matthias stuck his hand in the mud and dragged himself forward. He wouldn't die. He would show that Fey that he could keep himself alive. The Fey hadn't been able to. Magick hadn't saved Burden.

So he lied. Magick didn't save lives. It took lives.

The Fey was trying to fool him.

Matthias would not be fooled. He would not give up, nor would he trust in something he hated, something he never really had.

He crawled to the road before he passed out.

TWENTY-THREE

LORD Stowe stood at the main doors of the Great Hall. Guards stood on all sides, hands clasped behind their back. No Fey sat at the tables. Only Islanders. Noble Islanders at that.

The Hall was an ancient room, the first part of the palace ever built. Eventually the towers were added on both sides, so many nobles believed that the Hall was built to connect them. Instead the Hall came first.

It showed its ancient roots in its design. It was long and wide and had ornate arched ceilings. The arched windows, with their precious glass, were added later.

The Hall had an impressive majesty. It easily held the hundred people the King had invited to Sebastian's Coming-of-Age ceremony. The nobles, their wives, lovers, and children wandered around the tables, specially installed for the banquet. The head table stood on a specially built platform below the arched windows. It extended from one part of the Hall to the other. The remaining tables were on the floor, so that the diners had to look up at the King and his family. Benches ran along each side, and linen covered the top, along with candles and dishes Stowe had never seen before.

The King had chosen a banquet instead of the traditional ceremony because he couldn't have another religious service in the palace.

Jewel had died in the last one.

And she had been laid out here. Stowe would have thought that would have brought bad memories for the King, but apparently it didn't. The Coronation Hall was the one he avoided. That Hall hadn't been opened since the day Jewel died.

The nobles carried on conversations with each other, speaking softly and drinking the wine the King had provided. Some wore robes, as Stowe did, but others wore Fey-inspired clothing, pants and shirts, modified to be heavy on the lace and light on the practicality. The women all wore their finest gowns, some with skirts so wide that no one could stand close to them for fear of crushing the fabric.

The scents of roast pheasant mixed with roast beef. Stowe's stomach growled. The last of the guests had arrived before dark. It wasn't like the King to keep them waiting. But they knew better than to leave. Stowe had heard snatches of the conversation. They were all blaming the wait on the King's unnatural children. Even though the nobles were here to celebrate Sebastian's right to the throne, when the day came for him to rise to that post, he would have a fight on his hands.

And the poor boy wasn't up to a fight.

Stowe suppressed a sigh. Most of the nobles stood near the inner wall, studying the swords. None of the swords were ceremonial. They dated from all periods of Blue Isle's history. Most had nicks and cuts from prolonged use. Some were almost as short as dirks, and had been used for dueling over four hundred years before. Others were long and thin and deadly. No one had put up the styles that had developed since the Fey's arrival. Apparently the King didn't want to glorify the war forced on them by his wife's people.

Lord Miller had wound his way to Stowe. Miller's second wife was on his arm. She was Lord Enford's youngest daughter, a stout, homely creature who resembled her father. But the servants swore the union was a love match. Stowe didn't see it.

"I thought we were to have a banquet," Miller said. He was a slender lord, with the long fingers of an artist. He had never wanted to run his family's lands, but he had no choice after his father died in the Fey war. Instead, he decided to make himself a work of art. His clothing was among the finest in Blue Isle. He consumed almost as much as he made. His second wife seemed to have some of it under control, but not enough. Stowe wondered if Miller's lands earned any money at all.

"We will have a banquet," Stowe said, trying to keep his voice calm. The King had been acting oddly all day. Then, with the Fey in the King's Audience Chamber, the rumors to the south, and the tension in the air, Stowe wasn't certain this banquet would happen at all.

"Well, His Highness is running behind schedule," Miller said. "Is he having second thoughts about having us live under the rule of his idiot son?"

Miller's wife squeezed his arm and whispered his name in shock. Stowe straightened. "The Prince will be a good King."

"The Prince would have been a fine King for the old Blue Isle, I'll grant you that," Miller said. "Except for the odd peasant revolt every few hundred years, the King did damn near nothing. But we need a brain behind the throne now."

"You're ahead of yourself, Miller," Stowe said. "The King is still a young man. He might live long enough to transfer rule directly to his grandson."

"The King is nearly the same age his father was when he died."

"His father was murdered."

Miller bowed his head, then rose, smiling. "My point exactly, Stowe."

"The Fey won't harm the King or his family. That was the point in marrying Jewel. It made them honorary Fey."

Miller snorted. "It simply screwed up our lineage. We'd never had imbeciles head the country before."

"That you know of," Stowe said.

Miller's wife raised an eyebrow. There was intelligence in those frosty blue eyes. She might not have looks, but she did have a personality buried within. Maybe the love match wasn't as far-fetched as he thought.

Then, behind Stowe, the heralds pounded their staffs on the stone floor. "His Majesty, King Nicholas the Fifth."

Miller stepped back from Stowe and bowed. His wife curtsied deeply and remained down. The Hall was suddenly a sea of backs and bowed heads. Stowe went down slowly, keeping an eye on the King as he entered.

He had changed into a robe. This one was a deep green, the Fey color for celebration. It had some Fey decoration on the sides. He usually wore such a thing on the anniversary of his marriage with Jewel. Stone found it odd that he had chosen to wear it now.

"And his Royal Highness, Prince Sebastian."

The King's features tightened. Stowe knew the look. It was a nervous, frightened look that Stowe hadn't seen in years. He had seen it on the day that he brought the news of the King's father's death. And not since.

Then the look vanished. Sebastian skittered in, still fidgeting with his own green robe. He smoothed his hair with one hand, then glanced at the fingers as if he didn't recognize them.

Stowe had never seen Sebastian move so quickly. Nor had he ever seen Sebastian so animated. The boy had a quirky beauty that hadn't been apparent before, and an intelligence in his eyes that had somehow remained hidden for years.

"All rise," the herald said.

The group in the Hall rose slowly. The King had his hand on his son's arm and was leading him in. Sebastian studied the room as if he had never seen it before. The sad cracks and lines on his face were gone, except for a cleft in his chin.

Stowe started to wind his way around to the King, but stopped when the King clapped his hands for attention.

"Thank you all for coming," he said. His voice was firm and sure, and he looked regal. Perhaps Stowe had imagined the nerves from earlier.

The King mounted the platform the high table rested on and stood behind his chair. He put both hands on its tall back. Sebastian lingered near his side, finally looking like the child that Stowe knew—the dull, slow-moving boy who had always been a part of their lives. The sharp child seemed to have vanished when the nobles stood.

Had Sebastian always done that?

"We are in the dawn of a new era," the King said. "I married Jewel to create peace, and we did so. There has been no war on Blue Isle in over fifteen years. When I married, I tried to maintain the royal traditions, but found—through a sad and hard lesson—that I could no longer include the Tabernacle in my plans as I would have liked. The traditional Anointing ritual is held in the Tabernacle, in the main Sanctuary. But my son is part Fey."

The King put his hand on Sebastian's shoulder. The boy started, then glanced at his father. That quick movement again. The hairs rose on the back of Stowe's neck.

"I cannot risk his life like I risked his mother's. I have decreed that all royal events involving the Tabernacle and its holy water are null. I had tried to work this out with the Rocaan, but he believes, like his predecessor did, that the Fey have no place in our world. I believe that we cannot expect our Isle to protect us forever. The Fey are with us, and part of us. We must accept them. Part of that acceptance means accepting my children. They are the future of the Isle. Part Fey and part Islander, they are both and neither at the same time. If we learn to live together, we shall have a future."

The Hall was completely silent. The nobels watched as if they had never heard the King speak before.

"The ritual I have chosen is the one that the Roca used to anoint his own son as leader of this land. There was no holy water then; holy water did not exist until the Roca's Absorption. Instead, he blessed the boy with the symbol of the future." The King looked at the wall across from him. "Lord Stowe, please bring me my great-great-grandfather's sword, the one he used in the Peasant Uprising."

Stowe started. The King hadn't said that this would be part of the ritual. It made sense, though, as a protection. That way no one could anoint the sword with holy water and hurt the heir.

Stowe made his way toward the long inner wall. He hoped he remembered which sword had belonged to the King's great-great-grandfather.

He knew the right section of the wall. It was toward the main door, with a series of swords used in the Peasant Uprising. He suspected the center sword, with its rotting tassel, was the one that belonged to the King's great-great-grandfather. It was said that the old man used the sword to kill the man who had crippled him. The story was recounted throughout Stowe's childhood as an example of great courage.

"Lord Stowe," the King said gently. "It's the big black one in front of you."

Stowe felt the warmth grow in his face. He would have grabbed the wrong sword. The one the King meant was tarnished, nicked, and stained. Stowe had forgotten that this sword had never been cleaned.

He took it gingerly in his hands. The blood flaked onto his fingers. No wonder the King wanted this one. It was obviously untouched.

The King was a smart man. Stowe, who had known the King since he was born, sometimes forgot that.

The sword was also heavy. Stowe staggered a moment under its weight, then carried it to the head table. Sebastian watched him, blue eyes shining with life. Stowe frowned. He had thought Sebastian's eyes stone gray and dull. Stowe had only seen flickers of light in them before, never this constant beam.

The King bent over the took the sword from Stowe, then held it in one hand as if it weighed nothing.

"Turn to me, child," he said softly.

Sebastian turned slowly, in traditional Sebastian fashion.

"Kneel," the King said. Again, his words were so soft that only Stowe and Sebastian could hear.

Sebastian sank to his knees. He was so tall that he still came up to his father's chest.

"Bow your head."

Sebastian lowered his head. The King gently brought the sword to rest on Sebastian's skull.

"I quote the words the Roca used with his own son," the King said. "'By the power of God, and for the future of Blue Isle, I name you my successor. Should death take me from this land, you shall stand in my place. Should anyone question you, remind them that the Roca's blood—my blood—

flows through your veins. May God grant you the wisdom, the courage, and the opportunity to create peace.'"

Stowe remembered those words from the King's Anointing. Only the King's father, Alexander, had spoken them after nearly an hour of religious ceremony capped by a Blessing done with holy water.

The King removed the sword. "You may stand."

Sebastian used a hand to brace himself, then pulled himself up. He still moved slowly, but his movements had an awkwardness Stowe had never seen in the boy. He had always had a sureness that came with his slowness. Now his hesitations seemed nervous.

The King put a hand on his son's back. "Face them," he said softly.

Sebastian turned and bowed to the nobles. As he rose, the King said, "I present to you the future ruler of Blue Isle. Anyone who refuses to accept this child as the heir apparent answers to me."

Sebastian's lower lip trembled, and his dark skin had gone gray. The King slipped an arm around his son's waist and pulled him close.

Then Stowe glanced over his shoulder. The nobles were still watching, waiting for someone to do something. Stowe raised his hands and brought them together with an audible clap. Miller followed his lead, as did the others. The applause grew, not a heartfelt sound, but an obligatory one.

If only there were another way. If only the King's son had the brilliance of his daughter.

If only Nicholas hadn't wed a Fey in the first place.

Stowe shook the thought from his head. It was treasonous. He had always been loyal to the royal family. He would continue, even if Sebastian ruled.

Two spots of color formed on Sebastian's cheeks. His eyes shone. He nodded quickly, acknowledging the applause.

As it died down, the King said, "I promised you a banquet, and a banquet we shall have. Take your seats."

Several servants scattered throughout the Hall hurried through the far doors, the doors that led into the kitchen. The King pulled his son's chair back and bade Sebastian to sit. Sebastian did, with a quick questioning glance to his father.

Then the King sat beside him. Stowe skipped a place and was about to take his seat near the King's left when the King leaned over. "The disturbances today leave me one child short," he said. "Sit beside me so that no one notices the absence."

Stowe slid over. He frowned. He had noticed, but hadn't really considered the fact that Arianna was missing. He wondered at the decision. Was it to prevent comparisons? She was so brilliant that her brother looked duller at her side. Or was it because she so favored her mother? The King didn't need any more reminders of the Fey presence within this palace.

The remaining members of the council sat at the head table. The rest of the guests sat at the long banquet tables that ran the length of the Hall. All of the people present were large landowners, but not all of them were nobility. Some of the nobility had refused to come, so the King had invited the landowners. The King felt that the large landowners, even if they had no chance of sitting on his council, needed to approve his son. The more clout Sebastian had going into his rule, the better off he would be.

The King had invited the village chiefs from the Kenni-land Marshes, but none of them had come. He had also invited Wise Leaders from the Cliffs of Blood, but none of them attended either. This disturbed Stowe. He remembered the dissent in the Marshes when he had gone down there years ago, during the visit where the King's father had died. They hated Jahn there. They might hate a half-Fey ruler even more.

The Cliffs of Blood had their own traditions. They never disturbed the cities as long as the cities never disturbed them. Still, Stowe thought it an opportunity missed.

It took a moment for the guests to sit. The conversation rose as the chairs were pushed in, and as the benches slid forward. Beside him, the King let out a long sigh. Sebastian looked at him and smiled wanly. The King smiled back.

"It's done," he said. "Are you going to be all right?"

Sebastian nodded.

Then the servants marched in. They were wearing spotless white, and carrying platters on their shoulders. Three men carried the roast beef that had smelled so good. They put that large platter on the head table. The roast pheasants were on smaller platters. They went on various sections of the long table. Potatoes, breads, mincemeat, vegetables, and fruits were set alongside each section.

Stowe hadn't seen this much food since banquets before the Fey invasion.

"Oh, my," Sebastian said, his voice high and strange. It seemed as if the solemnity of the occasion hadn't reached him until that moment.

The King put his hand on his son's and squeezed. Stowe noted the movement from the corner of his eye. If something ever did happen to the King, it would be incredibly difficult for Sebastian. Stowe had never seen quite as close a family, and he suspected it had to do with their power, their isolation, and their strange heritage.

The conversations rose around them. The Hall grew warm with the added bodies and the steam from the food. The King cut the first slice of beef, signaling the start of the dinner. Then plates clanged, and laughter rose.

The King filled his plate, followed by Sebastian. Then Stowe helped himself. This meal had been long delayed, and he was very hungry. It almost felt like the old days, when the King's father, Alexander, used to hold banquets to celebrate holy days or to reward his men for long service. Stowe hadn't realized how much he missed them.

Behind them, servants climbed on ladders and unhooked the large tapestries from their holders. Then they brought them down slowly, so that the tapestries would not put dust in the food. Night had officially settled. The candelabrums and the chandeliers were lit. The room had a soft glow.

Sebastian ate slowly, as if he weren't certain whether or not he was enjoying his meal. He watched everyone around him. The King also picked at his meal. Stowe wondered if they would tell him later what had really happened this day. He suspected something major.

Then Sebastian tilted his head up. His eyes were moving rapidly. A shiver ran down Stowe's back. He wasn't certain if he could get used to this new, improved Sebastian. Then Sebastian tapped the back of his father's hand.

The King stopped playing with his food and followed Sebastian's gaze. So did Stowe. A spark flew around them, circling as if it were looking for a place to purchase. Stowe didn't quite understand the degree of tension he felt from the King and Prince. Sparks were common in a candlelit room. One had to keep an eye on them to make certain they didn't flare, but that was it. They certainly didn't need that rapt attention.

Then, as he watched, the spark grew bigger. It came closer to the table and he saw—or thought he saw—a little man with wings. A glowing little man with blue wings.

The King wiped his mouth with the linen provided at his place setting, then put the linen on top of his food.

"Daddy," Sebastian whispered.

"What is it?" Stowe asked.

The King didn't answer either of them. The little man grew until he was the size of a bird. The conversation at the head table stopped.

The little man was definitely Fey, but Stowe didn't ever recall seeing him before. The little man flew over the head table and landed behind the King.

Sebastian whirled, moving so fast that Stowe almost couldn't see it. As Stowe turned, the little man grew to full human size. His wings grew as well, large gossamer things that folded against his back. He was fully clothed, but in material that Stowe found unfamiliar: dark blues mixed with golds that caught the flicker of the candlelight.

The Fey man studied Sebastian for a moment, then smiled. Sebastian gripped his table knife, but the King put his hand on his son's and lowered it.

"This is a private ceremony," the King said. His voice was remarkably calm. It silenced the rest of the room. Guards moved from their posts, but the King held up a hand to stop them.

"Then I shall be brief." The Fey's Islander was oddly accented. It had a trace of Nye pronunciation combined with a gruffer twang.

The Hall was completely silent now. The King stood so that he was of the same height as the new Fey. Stowe stood behind him. Then the rest of the head table stood, with the exception of Sebastian. The guests on the lower tables also stood, probably so that they could see.

The Fey's smile grew. He bowed to the others, as if he

were the guest of honor. "My name is Flurry," he said. "I am new to your Isle."

Sebastian finally stood. His face had gone gray.

"I come," Flurry said, looking at Sebastian, "in the name of the Black King."

Stowe's heart made an awkward twist within his chest. The moment had finally arrived. He made himself breathe.

"He asks me to make an announcement." Flurry seemed to be enjoying the suspense he was creating. "He says that while he is enjoying your southern climes, he believes them too small to hold his troops. He will be moving northward."

Someone moaned behind Stowe. Sebastian started to say something, but the King grabbed his arm and held it so tightly that Stowe could see the whiteness of the King's knuckles.

"He claims Blue Isle for the Fey Empire. He says it would be better for you all if you surrender now. An invasion would be unpleasant, and would cause many deaths."

"You can't beat us," a man yelled from the lower tables. "We have holy water."

Flurry nodded. "Indeed. And we have an antidote."

Other voices rose. The King held up his hand, and silence reigned again. Stowe was breathing shallowly. The reports he had heard, then, were true. The Fey had invaded. From the south.

"Let me speak with your Black King," the King said. "I'm sure we can settle this without surrender or war."

Flurry tilted his head. His wings opened and then closed, sending a small puff of air toward Stowe. "You are, of course, referring to the Black King's great-grandson." Flurry reached a hand toward Sebastian's face as if to caress it. Sebastian ducked and snarled. The King pulled his son closer. "The Black King told me to remind you that his great-grandson has Black Blood and belongs exclusively to the Black Throne. No harm will come to the boy. But he cannot promise that for the rest of you."

"This child," the King said, "also has the blood of the Islanders' royal family."

"How fortunate for you," Flurry said. "Upon your surrender, the child will be put in charge. Then your unbroken lineage will continue as it has for generations."

"I wish to speak to the Black King," the King said.

Stowe was holding his breath.

Flurry shrugged. "He does not wish to speak to you. He gives you a choice, which is more than he has ever given any nation he has conquered. You may surrender now, or surrender later. The difference is how many of your young people you care to waste in a fruitless war."

"Blue Isle will never surrender," Sebastian said. His voice was high, and it cracked.

Flurry smiled. "Is that the word, then?"

"The word is," the King said, "that there is a third option. Tell your Black King that I will meet with him on neutral ground. Any place he chooses."

"I shall tell him," Flurry said. "But in case he chooses not to meet, what shall I say? Surrender? Or will we fight?"

"He cannot fight my family," the King said.

"But he can fight your people."

"My people are my family."

Flurry's wings extended, narrowly missing a candelabrum. "I shall tell him. It will make no difference to him. Blue Isle belongs to the Fey."

Stowe glanced at the King. It was now or not at all.

"Blue Isle remains independent," the King said. "The Black King may ally with us, but he may not invade us."

"He doesn't need your permission to invade," Flurry said.

"But he needs my permission to stay."

"We shall see," Flurry said. He nodded toward the King, and then grinned at Sebastian. "Good luck to you," he said more to Sebastian than anyone else. "You do not know what you are up against."

"Neither do you," Sebastian said, but Flurry had already shrunk to his original size. The spark floated around the room, then slipped through a crack in the closed door.

"The Black King is here," Stowe said, his voice shaking.

The King stared after the tiny spark. "The wait is finally over."

TWENTY-FOUR

FLURRY flew through the crack in the main doors and into the night air. He executed a small circle in the court-yard, buzzing a dog sleeping near the stables, then rose toward the moon, chuckling as he went.

It had been easy, so easy. He hadn't expected to find the great-grandson at the King's side. And no one would have trouble recognizing Rugad's Blood in the boy. He had the look of his grandfather along his narrow chin and in his high cheekbones. He was pale for a Fey, but Islanders were pale. The odd thing was his eyes: they were a strange blue. He found them unnerving. In the right light, they seemed to disappear in the boy's face.

Flurry flew higher and followed the main road. Near the river, a rank mist rose off the bridge. He sneezed and veered away, shivering in disgust. The Nye always used their water-ways as garbage dumps; perhaps the Islanders did as well, although he had not heard of it in all his studies of them.

The night was clear, and the city appeared mostly empty. He was tired but had to continue forward. Rugad would want to know what happened here. Even though he predicted they would not surrender, he hadn't predicted that the Islander King would want a meeting.

A meeting. As if they were all bankers on Nye.

Flurry chuckled and flew on. He sneezed again. That stench had been incredible, like something off a battlefield. Rotting flesh and burning skin mixed into a fog. Garbage didn't smell like that.

He paused, wings fluttering, keeping him aloft. Then he veered back, toward the bridge.

The fog had risen like a cloud against the moon. He peered up at it, a sickly green color against the moon's brightness. The cloud was an isolated thing. It seemed to come from nowhere. The river was clear, although a slick ran down its center.

The slick looked like blood.

A battlefield? In the middle of a city that claimed to have achieved peace?

He lowered himself slowly, then saw movement in the reeds on the north side. He flew toward it, and watched as a wounded Islander crawled through the grass. The Islander was mumbling to himself about disproving magick. He was leaving a small blood trail, and his skin looked fish-white in the moonlight. Wounds gaped in his upper arms and on the side of his face.

He had been stabbed repeatedly.

Flurry floated higher and saw no one else. Some sort of Islander murder, caused by a robbery, perhaps, or a personal grievance.

Or magick.

Only those with magick had no need of knives, and Foot Soldiers, who cut the skin with their fingers, flayed it off, leaving gouges, not cuts.

Magick.

He flew back to the bridge. Only the memory of the stink remained in the moonlight. He sneezed again, knowing the sound would be so tiny as to be inaudible to full-sized ears, and slowly lowered himself.

There was a lump on the bridge, and a water trail that ran off down the south side.

He descended, feet first, wings fluttering to keep himself balanced, and landed on the stone wall. A moth landed beside him, attracted by his small light. The moth was large and ugly, its eyes empty holes in the darkness.

"Shoo," he said, and shoved the moth with both hands. Its wings flapped, nearly knocking him down, and then it flew away.

He walked to the edge of the stone and peered down. The lump was large and round. It was the source of the smell, and it still stank. He would have gone down to investigate if a moonbeam hadn't caught one detail.

An ear.

A slightly pointed, dark-skinned ear protruding from the lump.

And, on the far side, a hand clutching at nothing.

He flew upward in surprise, hands over his mouth. That had been a Fey below him. The stories he heard about the poison, then, were true. They could dissolve a Fey as if he were made of sugar. He brushed off his wings, his feet, his legs, anything that might have touched the poison—although he had been told, by the same source who had told him about the melting, that the effect was instantaneous.

If he had touched the stuff, he would have melted already.

At least he had an antidote. That poor Fey on the bridge hadn't. That Fey could not have been one of Rugad's troop. That Fey had been one of the Failures. They had no way to fight the poison.

Flurry shuddered and flew along the road. His physical exhaustion was gone now; adrenaline raced through him. Things were not as peaceful as the good Islander King made it seem. The only Fey at the banquet was his own son. And a Fey had been murdered on the main bridge.

Perhaps the Islander King was right. Perhaps these were a people to be wary of. He would mention that to Rugad. In fact, he would stress it. Rugar, the Black King's son, would never listen to reason, but Rugad would. Rugad always did.

Flurry flew on, so fast and so hard that he nearly missed the only people on the road. A couple walking side by side, heads down as they passed the Islander Tabernacle, intent, as if they didn't want to be seen.

He glanced at the Tabernacle himself. It was a large building, much as the Nye described it, more like a palace than the palace. It had ornate swords carved into its outside walls, and tapestries on every window, lights on every floor. Such extravagant waste of resources on such a meaningless pursuit.

As he flew by, though, he shuddered. The Tabernacle had an air of power. He had encountered such places before, and he learned to never underestimate them.

The couple was tall for Islanders. They wore shirts, breeches, and boots that had the softness of Fey design. He swooped low and stopped in surprise.

The King's son was here. The boy he had seen in the palace. Only this boy had a thinner face, rounder eyes, and a look of complete exhaustion. The girl beside him hadn't reached her magick yet. She wore Rugar's infantry colors, and she had a knife hilt on one side, a sword on the other.

She had stabbed the Islander climbing out of the bushes. Had the Islander murdered the Fey?

But that didn't make any sense. If the girl had stabbed the Islander after he murdered the Fey, it would have taken time. How had the boy managed to change his clothing, get down here from the palace, and accompany the girl this far?

If he had a flying magick, why was he wasting effort—and taking so much risk—in walking past the Islander Tabernacle?

Flurry licked his lips nervously. Rugad would want to know what happened here. He would chastise Flurry if he didn't discover all he could.

But Flurry wasn't certain he wanted to talk with them. The girl was clearly a Failure, and Rugad didn't want the Failures to know that he had arrived. The boy, if indeed it was the same boy, had been extremely hostile in the banquet hall. Outside of it, he might have no qualms in using his position to attack Flurry.

Flurry did not want to pit himself against anyone of Black Blood.

He would report on what he saw. If Rugad wanted a deeper understanding, he could send someone else.

Flurry hesitated above them for a moment. They weren't speaking. They were walking with purpose, even though no Islanders were near them. They were the only ones on the road.

And if the girl was raised with the Fey, she would know what Flurry was.

If he wasn't careful.

He would only have one chance. He would have to make the best of it.

He flew ahead of them and stopped near a bush. He was lucky that the moon was full; it gave him a clear vision of the two behind him. It camouflaged him well. He crouched among the leaves, trying to block his own small light. If he grew to full size, his light would wink out, but he couldn't risk that either.

Instead he watched as they approached, hoping his tiny light would be unnoticeable. He stared at them, ignoring the girl for the boy beside her.

He was tall, like most Fey, only his skin was nearly two shades lighter than the girl's. His hair was so dark that it reflected the moonlight in a single sheen. His eyes were that same electric blue. But his chin was different, rounder, without the slight cleft that Flurry had noticed on the other boy. His hair was longer, too, worn down his back in the traditional Fey military manner. His clothing looked as if it had been slept in. It was certainly still wet from an encounter with the river.

The differences were subtle, but they existed. That and the timeline meant that something was afoot.

Why would the son of the King be wandering the streets like a common criminal? Why would his only protection be a girl too young to come into her magick? And why wasn't he at the banquet?

Flurry had to take one more risk. The boy at the banquet had spoken Islander. Quickly and naturally, as if it were his tongue of preference. Flurry couldn't quiz this boy, but he could discover if the differences extended farther than the physical.

Flurry climbed out of the bush, careful to be as silent as he could. He floated upward on the wind, like a spark would do. When he was directly above the boy, he dove, heading for the boy's face. Flurry crashed into the boy's nose and kicked off it, heading upward again.

"Hey!" the boy said in Fey.

"What is it?" the girl responded in the same language.

"Something hit me in the face. It looked like a Wisp."

"Was it Wind?"

"No." The boy sounded perplexed. "He knows how much this trip means to me. He'd be beside me, not running into me."

Wind. Flurry remembered him. One of Rugar's favorite Wisps who had come along on that futile mission, thinking it was the trip of the future.

The girl looked up. She pointed. "I see it!" she said.

Flurry flew directly upward until he was out of their sight. He was trembling, but exhilarated. Apparently the boy did not have the right kind of magick to bring Flurry down.

Which was good. He had wasted enough time. He had to report to Rugad.

And his report would be interesting. Rugad had two great-grandchildren on Blue Isle. One raised by the Islander King and the other raised by Fey. There was no telling who the firstborn was, but it didn't matter.

Two mixed children of Black Blood made this trip doubly worthwhile.

Rugad would be pleased.

TWENTY-FIVE

SOLANDA stopped in the clearing and stared at the dirt circle. It had been years since she had been inside Shadowlands. She hated it so much that she often forced the Domestics to meet her outside. They had done so in exchange for food. There were still some basic items that they couldn't grow themselves.

The clearing had once been part of a forest, but over the years, the Domestics had turned it into a garden. The land sloped toward the river, and they used it to funnel water to the crops. The winters on Blue Isle were temperate enough to allow some growth all year round, if one knew what kinds of things to plant.

Solanda did not. She only ate greens when she was starving, or when her stomach was upset. If she wasn't careful, vegetables made her puke.

The neat rows stood alongside the dirt circle, a calling card to any who were looking for the Fey. But the Islanders had left them alone for over a decade now, believing that the Fey could remain in their own prison. Solanda had heard that the Outsiders were not as lucky; that they had to face the verbal assaults and physical blows of Islanders who feared them.

She had lived through none of that, except for that brief period when Alexander had banned cats. She never would live through any of it again.

A small circle of lights rotated in the air above the dirt circle. For most Shadowlands, the circle of lights was the only indication that a Shadowlands existed. There were no gardens or dirt circles. But no Fey had ever lived in a Shadowlands for longer than the duration of a single campaign before. None had ever retreated into one.

Solanda spat on the ground, showing her disgust. Rugar should be forever cursed for leading his once-proud people into a place like this.

Then she stepped into the dirt circle, reached up, and stuck her hand in the Circle Door. The lights rotated harder and grew until the circle was large enough for her to step through.

She did, and shivered as the opaque world of the Shadowlands enveloped her.

It had changed over the years. The Domicile had been rebuilt into a U-shaped building. The Domestics kept the water and food supplies on one side of the U, had the infirmary in the center, and provided room for the Domestic magicks on the other side. It had taken the place of the Meeting Block as the center to Shadowlands.

Gift and his Wisp family had taken over Rugar's quarters, the second-largest building in Shadowlands. No one had objected. Gift had saved most of their lives when he held Shadowlands together. While none of the Fey really trusted him as a leader, they knew that they owed him that much.

The other buildings were beginning to look old. They had been built as temporary homes nearly twenty years before. Even though they hadn't felt the effects of weather, they had seen the ravages of time. Some were leaning a bit. Others were missing boards.

Surprisingly, though, some were looking homey. A few Fey had painted flowers on the sides of the wood, and a few others had painted the wood themselves. Some were Domestic-spelled, looking new and clean and inviting.

They had created a small Fey community in the land of eternal grayness.

Solanda shuddered. At least the Weather Sprites had long ago stopped trying to make weather inside Shadowlands. In those days, Shadowlands always had a gray fog, because no matter what the Sprites tried, it always became a fog. She had heard that most of the Sprites had become Outsiders, which made sense, considering their penchant for being outdoors.

She smoothed her hair with one hand, and patted her clothes, the closest her Fey form came to grooming. She knew she looked a fright. Part of her didn't care. Another part, though, didn't want Gift to know the distress she was in. None of them needed to know that.

Most of the Fey were asleep. Even in Shadowlands, they kept a regular schedule: sleeping when the outside lands were dark, and awake when the lands were light. The light in Shadowlands itself never changed, but the schedule kept the Fey from going insane.

She walked past the Domicile. There were lights in the west wing, and the scent of food magick about the building. She had heard that some of the younger Domestics had taken to making sumptuous feasts for the remaining Fey, as a way of keeping life in Shadowlands from becoming too dull.

She shuddered. It already sounded dull to her.

On the far side of the Domicile, she glanced at the woodpile. Except for the cut wood, it was empty. In most campaigns, the Red Caps slept beside the Domicile or in the woodpiles. They were short, squat, magickless Fey who usually took care of the dead. They had no use in peacetime, and were probably driven out of Shadowlands. If it weren't for their Fey features, they would have had no trouble blending in with the Islander society.

As it were, they were probably pariahs to the Islanders as well.

The steps to Rugar's old place looked the same, but the porch had been fixed. Two chairs were built into the wood, chairs with no backs, perfect for Wisps and their wings.

Gift had built them. He did such things, honoring his adoptive parents. Wind and Niche had taken him in on

Rugar's request after Rugar kidnapped the boy. They raised him as their own—Wisps couldn't have children—and Niche nearly gave her life for him.

Solanda had felt that sort of devotion for Arianna, and look where it had gotten her.

She sighed, shoved the ache down, and knocked.

The sound echoed through Shadowlands, a hollow empty echo, as if it bounced off the walls of a box. She supposed it did. Shadowlands, when it came down to it, was nothing more than a box, a construct built by a Visionary to house his people during a campaign.

She knocked again.

This time, the door opened. Wind peered out, looking sleep rumpled. His eyebrows were messy, and there were fabric lines on his face. He blinked twice before he really seemed to see her.

"Solanda?" He pulled the door open. "Come in."

He didn't even ask what it was about. Such trust in Shadowlands. She mentally shook her head, and walked through the open door.

Into a main room that used to have only bare-bones furniture: a table, a few chairs, and a fireplace. This room was transformed. The walls were covered with Domestic-made quilts. Most had a simple diamond design and were Spelled for ease and relaxation. But one, the largest, had an embroidered center, depicting Gift as a boy, and strands of light running from him to all the corners of Shadowlands, and beyond.

"The Shaman did that," Wind said. His wings were folded flat against his back, indicating how soundly he had been asleep.

"The Shaman?"

Wind smiled. "We forget sometimes that hers is a Domestic magick."

Solanda had forgotten. "What does it signify?"

"It is for Gift," Wind said, "as a thank-you and as a remembrance of the service he performed as a child."

"And as a warning?" Solanda asked. She peered at the light strands. They went far beyond the walls of the embroidered Shadowlands, all the way off the edges of the quilt.

"I doubt it," Wind said. "People do not give presents as warnings."

"Even the Shaman?" Solanda asked.

"What's this talk of the Shaman?" Niche came out of one of the side bedrooms. Time had not treated her well. Her once-beautiful features had crumpled in on themselves, her face lined with pain. Wisps had hollow bones, which enabled them to change sizes and to fly, but the bones were fragile. Niche's wings had been shattered years ago, and so had one of her wrists. The Healers had been able to mend her wrist well enough for her to use it, but her wings were crumpled, useless appendages against her back. They looked more like ripped and poorly mended gauze than like wings.

Solanda had trouble looking at her. "I had never seen the quilt before."

"It's the only possession my son claims," Niche said. "The rest, he says, are simply things." She too had a deep-sleep look. Her long hair was bound around her skull, and strands fell down about the side of her face.

"I didn't mean to wake you, but it's important that I talk to Gift. Where is he?" Solanda asked.

Niche glanced at Wind.

"What happened?" Wind asked. His voice was tight.

Solanda made herself smile, as if to reassure them. "A lot has happened. It's been a long day."

"No," Wind said. "What happened to Gift? You were at the palace, weren't you? Isn't that why you're here?"

Solanda turned and put a hand on one of the upholstered chairs. Immediately she felt the urge to sit. Domestic-spelled again. She pulled her hand off.

"I'm here because I want to talk to Gift," she said.

"He's not back yet," Niche said. She came forward, hunched slightly, as if the weight of her injured wings was almost too much for her to bear. "He wasn't sure when he'd be back."

"From the palace," Solanda said. It was more a statement than a question.

"Yes," Niche said. She sank into a backless chair, still leaning forward as if afraid to brush her wings on anything. "Something went wrong, didn't it?"

"I don't know," Solanda said. "I don't know where Gift is."

"And you want us to tell you where to find him," Wind said.

"That would be helpful," Solanda said.

"Why?" Niche was frowning. "You haven't come into the Shadowlands in years. You haven't had any interest in your own people."

"Arianna is my people, more than you folks are." The words came out harshly. Solanda drew in breath, as if she could draw the words back into herself.

"So she does Shift, then," Wind said. His expression remained bland, as if her words hadn't offended him.

Solanda nodded. She felt uncomfortable, as if she had just revealed a fact someone else had wanted to remain secret. Finally she had enough. She served no one but herself. The only member of the Black Family whom she had an obligation to was Arianna, and technically Arianna had discharged Solanda of it.

Solanda was doing this for herself. And she needed to know what Gift was about. If they didn't know where Gift was, they still might be able to help him.

"Look, Arianna almost attacked her brother this afternoon. She had no idea who he was. She thought he was kidnapping the golem, and she's quite protective of that creature."

"She attacked him?" Niche closed her eyes.

"No. We stopped it in time. She didn't know. She thinks—thought—the golem was her blood kin."

"You let her think that?" Wind asked.

"I don't need your judgment," Solanda said. "You haven't lived outside of here. You've hidden for fifteen years."

"And raised the Black King's great-grandson," Wind said quietly.

"Well, I raised his great-granddaughter," Solanda said, "and for reasons that have nothing to do with you, I chose not to inform her of Gift. The golem has a life of its own, and she loves it. It saved her life more than once. That's the purpose of a golem, isn't it, to guard its main love?"

"That's one of the purposes," Wind said.

Solanda glared at him. She didn't know how he could be so calmly confident. He was facing one of his betters. Maybe raising a Black child had made him feel as if he were superior to her. In either case, she had to take the upper hand.

"I need to find out why Gift was taking the golem," she said. "Why?"

"It's not your concern," Solanda said. She wasn't going to justify herself to these people any longer. "Just tell me."

Niche glanced at Wind. He crossed his arms.

"It won't hurt," Niche said softly. "You can tell."

"If this information harms my boy in some way—" Wind began.

"You think I'm fool enough to harm an heir to the Black Throne?" Solanda asked.

"You did before," Wind said.

Niche frowned. "Wind . . ."

"All right," he said. "Gift believed that the golem's life was in danger."

"He knew about the golem?"

Niche nodded. "We were the ones who left it. I didn't think it had survived until Gift told me, about the time Jewel died."

"He was worried for its life?" Solanda asked. "Why?"

"He knew it and loved it," Niche said.

"If your golem has to choose between Gift and the girl," Wind said, "it might not choose the girl."

Solanda decided to ignore that statement. "Today Sebastian was supposed to attend a Coming-of-Age ceremony, designating him the next King of Blue Isle. If Gift had ridden a Link, he would have known about that."

Niche stood. She put a hand on the wall to keep her balance. Solanda hadn't realized how much Wisps relied on their wings.

"You believe that Gift would step in for the golem in order to rule the Isle?"

"I don't know," Solanda said. "That seems logical to me."

"You lived among the Islanders too long. Gift is Fey."

"Gift is part Fey," Solanda said, trying to ignore the irony of being on the other side of the conversation about heritage.

"He doesn't care about Islander power," Niche said. "He has never cared about power. You make him sound like Rugar."

"He's a member of the Black Family."

"Are you saying the girl would do this?"

Solanda shook her head. She had forgotten about the hatred lesser Fey felt toward her kind. "I am trying to figure out why he appeared at the palace on today of all days. He had years to show up. Why now?"

"Oh." Niche breathed the word. She looked at Wind. "Solanda is a guest," she said as if they hadn't had any discussion at all. "Make us some morning root tea, and see if any of the black bread is left, would you please, Wind?"

He frowned, but left the room as she asked. They had apparently moved the cooking area to a different room. It hardly felt like the same place it had been when Rugar lived there.

"You're worried about Arianna, aren't you?" Niche said as Wind left.

"I want to find out—"

"I know," Niche spoke softly. "I know what you want. I'm more concerned with why. You act like a mother afraid for her child."

Solanda's hands started to shake. The sympathy was almost more than she could bear.

"I sent Wind away. Sometimes he forgets that people change."

Solanda let the remark pass. She knew that Wind had never liked her, mostly because of what she was.

Niche leaned close. "Gift had a Vision which scared him. He first had it about two weeks ago, and it hasn't gone away. He went to see the Shaman and she could give him no answers, so he decided to act."

Solanda sat beside Niche. "What was the Vision?"

"He had two, actually. In one, he was talking to an older Fey, a man he didn't recognize, and several others came into the room. Everything went black. That wouldn't have alarmed him if it weren't for the companion Vision. In that, the golem is talking to the older Fey, several other Fey come into the room, and one stabs the golem, killing him. Gift believes this all happens in the palace."

"And the Shaman couldn't help?" Solanda was suddenly cold.

"She says that Gift faces a split path, and that some action will cause that path to change."

"But she didn't know what caused the Vision in the first place?" Solanda asked.

Niche shook her head. "Obviously something changed two weeks ago. Something important."

"Obviously," Solanda said. She looked up to find Wind watching her from the doorway. He was holding a tray. When she looked at him, he came in as if he hadn't been eavesdropping. "Who were the Fey in his Vision?"

Niche shook her head. "He didn't say."

"Why didn't he go to them?" Solanda asked.

"He didn't recognize them," Wind said. He set the tray on a small table near the wall. Then he handed Solanda a cup of tea as if he hadn't been angry at her earlier. "He says that happens in Visions sometimes."

"But it sounds as if he would have gotten a good look at them," Solanda said.

"The Fey didn't concern him so much as the murder," Niche said. "He wanted the golem out of the palace immediately."

"So he felt this would happen soon?"

"He said the golem looked like him, as if he were looking in a mirror," Niche said. "He thought it might happen at any moment."

"Are you sure he was trying to save Sebastian? Or to make sure the golem was still alive to take his place?"

"Gift isn't like that," Wind said.

"So you say," Solanda said. "But I have nothing to base it on."

"Except my word," Wind said.

"The word of a Wisp," she said.

Niche brought her head up. "In his own home. About his own son. You are out of line, Solanda."

"No," she said. "I'm not. I want to know all about this Vision, and I want to know why it led Gift to take such a risk. Visionaries do not often go to the site of their deaths in order to prevent that death."

"It wasn't his death he was worried about," Niche said. "He said he was prepared."

"No one is prepared," Solanda said. She remembered the

discussions she had had with Nicholas, about all the ways Jewel tried to prevent her own injury, when instead each action she took made that Vision darker, and made the injury become her death.

Niche took a cup and held it between her slender fingers. "But you thought Gift was here."

Solanda nodded.

"He left then? With the golem?"

"Arianna prevented that. She chased him, and his contingent, and we had to separate her from him. Then he left. He never came back."

"But he didn't come here either." Niche's voice rose on the last word. Wind sat beside her and took her hand in his.

Solanda waited.

"Do you think he's all right?" Niche asked.

"He was when I left him."

"Maybe he has another way to change the Vision," Wind said.

"Maybe," Solanda said. "But something bothers me. Gift knows all the Fey on the Isle, doesn't he?"

"There might be a few Outsiders . . ." Wind said.

Niche shook her head. "He knows all of them."

"So who were the Fey in the Vision? And why were they in the palace? And how would it happen soon?" Solanda stood. She hadn't touched her tea. "If it hasn't already happened."

"What do you mean?"

"Two weeks, he has had those Visions," Solanda said. "Two weeks." She looked at them. Niche appeared confused, but Wind didn't. He knew exactly what—and whom—she was talking about.

"We would have known," he said.

"We would be the last to know," she said. "We failed."

Silence filled the room. Niche's breathing, labored suddenly with fear, was the only sound. "What do we do now?" she asked.

"Go to the Shaman," Solanda said.

"But Gift already went."

"And asked the wrong questions." She stood. "it's not how to stop the Visions. He needed to know what triggered them."

Wind stood beside her. He understood. "And what if the Black King has finally arrived?"

"We evacuate Shadowlands," Solanda said, "and hope we are as good at hiding as we are at hunting."

"Better," Niche whispered. "We need to be better."

TWENTY-SIX

NICHOLAS clutched the back of his chair, still staring at the door that the spark had disappeared beneath. Arianna watched him, her blue eyes narrowed. She looked so odd, wearing Sebastian's face. She used it her way, quickly, and with animation, but it was still Sebastian's face. The only thing that marked it as hers was the slight ridge of her birthmark, its outline faint against her chin.

Her idea, to Shift and be the child honored in the Coming-of-Age. It had seemed like it would work.

Until now.

She was staring at him.

They all were staring at him, waiting for him to do something.

Then Arianna grabbed his arm and pulled him close. "I can follow him," she whispered.

Nicholas shook his head once. He knew where the Black King was. He didn't want his daughter risking her life to go to that encampment.

Conversation was rising below him. A man's voice was carrying over the din, something about the demon Fey.

Nicholas whirled. "Lord Stowe, get the Rocaan. Have him meet me in the war room."

"Yes, sir." Stowe left without a backwards glance. His departure silenced the room again.

Most of the major landowners and all of the major lords were below him. They all knew. Nicholas had to use them somehow without causing a panic.

"Daddy—" Arianna said.

"Wait, child." He faced the group. They were wearing their finery, and it was at odds with the panic on their faces. Many of them were old enough to remember the first Fey invasion. Most of them had feared this one ever since.

"You've all heard it," Nicholas said. "I will do my best to negotiate with the Black King, but it sounds as if he is not a diplomat but a warrior. If that's the case, we have a battle facing us. The worst thing we can do is panic."

"They're no match for us!" someone yelled.

"They might be," Nicholas said. "It depends on how large their force is, how well we work together, and whether or not the Fey already on the Isle will join him or us."

"What about your son?"

Nicholas glanced at Arianna. He never thought that they would question his children's loyalty. "My son was raised here. He will fight for us."

"I belong on Blue Isle," Arianna said. "It is my home."

"And you'll go over to the Black King the moment it looks like he could take the Isle."

"And betray my father?" Arianna seemed to have forgotten that she was supposed to mimic Sebastian's voice. She was speaking with her own. "I would never do that. I may look Fey to you, but I have Islander blood. I will remain here, in the palace, with my family and friends."

"This is not a time to question the heir to the throne," Nicholas said.

"It is precisely the time," Lord Miller said. "We need to have faith in our leaders."

"You have faith in me. I'm still in charge," Nicholas said.

"You married one of them," a woman shouted. Nicholas couldn't see who had spoken in the dim light.

"For peace," Nicholas said. "And we've had peace. We may still have peace if I talk to the Black King. That Fey was just an underling. He's in no position to negotiate, nor is he in any position to know his King's mind. Well, you all know mine. Blue Isle is ours. It shall remain ours. I will do everything I can to see that it remains so."

"Even denying your Fey children?"

"My children were born on this Isle. They grew up in the palace, and they shall take my place when I die. But I have no plans to die, now or in the immediate future. You all shall listen to me, and I will do the best I can to keep us safe from this new assault."

"Talking doesn't work against killers," Lord Enford said.

"That's right," Nicholas said. "Which is why I need you all to do exactly as I say. First, we shall prepare for war."

Arianna put her hand on his arm. He glanced at her. She nodded, as if in approval.

"I want the Council to meet me in the war room when this ends. The rest of you should go home, and prepare your lands for war."

"It sounds like some of our lands have already faced it."

Nicholas took a deep breath. "The Black King is in the south. None of the southern representatives are here. That was not unusual in and of itself; they rarely attend state functions. But their absence lends credence to what that Fey said."

The lords below him were silent now. None of them, apparently, had put all that information together.

"Secondly, I shall meet with the Rocaan and make certain there is enough holy water for the Isle. He was supposed to keep a supply of it, in case. Contact your Danites and Auds, make certain that they give you enough water to survive for a time."

"The Fey said that they can beat our holy water," said Lord Fesler. He sounded concerned, not contradictory.

"Let's hope he's wrong," Nicholas said. "In case he isn't, make certain that you are well armed. The Fey may have magickal powers, but they die like the rest of us. The secret is to remember that, no matter what they throw at us. A sword kills them as easily as it kills us."

Everyone was staring at him. His heart was pounding, his fingers clutching the chair back. He hadn't felt this alive in years.

"Finally, there are some Fey who have lived among us for over a decade now. Some have helped us. Some have not. React to them as individuals, not as part of an army. Some of them have knowledge—and enough fear of their own Black King—to be on our side. Remember that. And use it." He finally held the room. He finally felt in control. "Now," he said, "you have your orders. The quicker we move to safeguard our Isle, the better off we'll be. You don't have to wait for me to leave the room. You are all dismissed."

Talking began almost immediately, followed by the sound of a hundred chairs scraping against stone. Lords helped their ladies up, conversing with the people beside them. The members of the council kissed their wives, then threaded their way out the side door. The rest of the gathering grouped at the main doors, filing out in an orderly fashion.

"You should have let me go after him," Arianna said softly.

Nicholas shook his head. "Where the Black King is right now is less of a concern than what we're going to do about him."

"We've got to fight," Arianna said.

Nicholas turned. "You can't," he said quietly. "Remember what the Shaman said."

"I wasn't talking of me," she said. "I meant we, Blue Isle, us."

Nicholas knew that she couldn't lead a fight against her great-grandfather. He wasn't even sure if she could participate in one. But he knew better than to say anything in this room. "I have to get to the war room. Go take care of your sibling."

"I need to come with you," Arianna said.

"No. I need you in Sebastian's rooms." Nicholas was still choosing his words with caution. He had allowed Arianna to Shift into her brother's form, he even approved of her receiving the designation as the heir in that form, but he wasn't going to risk her. Not now, not ever.

He wasn't going to risk Sebastian either.

"You need me in the war room."

"After what happened today, I'm not going to leave either of my children alone too long. And right now, I'm worried about my other child."

Arianna sighed, but she apparently saw his point. "We'll come to the war room together, then," she said.

Nicholas's stomach lurched. This masquerade would be tougher than he thought. "You can't—"

"Don't worry," she said, smiling. "I'll dress as myself."

He felt an odd sort of relief. She did understand. She would be somewhat cautious. That was all he could hope for.

He picked up the skirts of his robe, and pushed in Lord Stowe's chair. Arianna grabbed his hand. "Daddy," she said, "what about Solanda? She's not in the palace any more."

He knew. He'd already thought of that. Solanda and the Shaman were the reasons that he mentioned handling the Isle's Fey on a case-by-case basis.

"I'm afraid she's going to have to take care of herself," he said. "She's done that for years. She'll be fine."

"I hope so," Arianna said. She remembered to turn slowly and to imitate Sebastian's gait as she stepped down from the podium. None of the guests spoke to her. A few backed away from her as she approached.

If only the Black King had waited a year. If only Nicholas had discovered earlier Arianna's uncanny abilities to Shift into many forms. Then maybe his people would have had time to accept her, and Sebastian, as the future rulers of this place.

But he knew that hope was false. His son, or the boy he thought of as his son, was eighteen years old, his daughter, fifteen. Blue Isle had had ample time to get used to part-Fey rulers. It hadn't.

He could do nothing to change that.

But he had to admit to himself that Arianna's decision to step into her brother's shoes, literally, relieved him. Ever since Sebastian's birth—or perhaps appearance was the right word—ever since, Nicholas had worried that his son wouldn't be capable of ruling. Now his son would act as a literal figurehead. Arianna would make all the decisions. His people, and his council, would simply have to believe that at times Sebastian was slow, and at others he wasn't. It would make for some discomfort, but nothing that Arianna couldn't handle.

She was like her mother. Strong, brilliant, confident.

But not invincible. He had believed that of Jewel once. Matthias had proved that wrong.

Nicholas knew what he spoke of. The Fey were as vulnerable as Islanders. The key was simply to discover the vulnerable spots.

He knew where his was. It was that beautiful daughter of his, climbing the stairs in search of her brother. Both children mattered more to him than his own life. But he had to let them free. Jewel would have told him that. She probably never would have raised them as protected as he had. She had argued from the beginning to let Sebastian go out in public. Nicholas had fought it, partly out of shame and partly out of fear.

He had been wrong.

And now, at the time Nicholas needed the Islanders to believe in him, they worried he would give the country to the Fey.

He wouldn't. He would fight the Black King if he had to.

But he was hoping he wouldn't have to.

They were family, of a sort.

But he wasn't certain what he could offer the Black King that the man would want. Nicholas wanted Blue Isle to remain the same, a small self-contained Kingdom. If it were ruled by a person with Black Blood, then the Fey could claim it as part of their Empire. But he didn't want the place overrun with the Fey any more than his people did. He wanted the Fey to leave them alone.

Yet he wasn't sure he could make the offer he knew he had to make.

The Black King wasn't interested in Blue Isle as a country. He was interested in Blue Isle as a launch point toward the Leut continent. He would have his troops stop here on their journey from Galinas as a rest, a refueling, a place to organize. Then they would continue east to Leut.

Invading it as they had invaded Blue Isle.

Nicholas had lived through that. He had seen friends die, he had lost family to it, he had watched his entire world change. He wasn't certain he could stand by and let such a crisis flow to another country in order to save his own.

But he wasn't sure he could fight the Fey back a second time. Even though he had told his people to disregard Flurry's warning about holy water, he couldn't afford to. And without holy water, the Isle was as vulnerable as a naked baby before a wolf.

He didn't like his choices. But then, he didn't have to like them.

He just had to make the best of them.

TWENTY-SEVEN

TWENTY-SEVEN

SHE took the steps quickly, uncertain about the feeling in the pit of her stomach. Her robes were long and uncomfortable. She had worn Sebastian's body before, had done so since she was a little girl, but she had never worn it inside of a robe.

It felt odd.

It also felt odd to do so with the approval of her father. He kept looking at her as if he could see *her*. In the past, he never noticed. But then she had sat very still and never said anything to him. She used it as proof, mental proof, at how dumb all the others were.

Including Solanda. Arianna wore Sebastian's form the most around Solanda to see if Solanda acted differently toward Sebastian in private.

She really didn't. She ignored him, most of the time. And somehow that hurt worse.

But Arianna couldn't shake the worry she now felt for Solanda. For the last few years, all she had felt for her substitute mother was contempt. Now, with Solanda gone, and the Black King hovering, Arianna wanted to find Solanda and hold her, like she used to do as a little girl, clinging to Solanda like a lifeboat in the middle of a choppy sea.

Of all the days for her to disappear.

Of all the days for the Black King to announce his arrival.

Of all the days for her real brother to show up.

Arianna went cold. Maybe this Gift's appearance had something to do with the Black King. But that made no sense. How would Gift know—?

Except that Solanda had said he was a Visionary. One of the best Visionaries ever in the Fey.

Ever.

Maybe he saw the Black King's arrival, and . . .

And . . .

And what? Planned to give him Sebastian as his real great-grandson? Substitute Sebastian? Take Sebastian's place?

It was all too complicated for Arianna.

But it made her take the steps even faster.

Her father had placed guards on Sebastian's door without explaining what they were guarding. Arianna had closed Sebastian's windows and locked them, ordering him to keep them closed.

Still, he trusted this Gift, and might let him in. And a spark, a Wisp, could get in anywhere.

Arianna ran the last few steps, hurried into the corridor, and forced herself to slow down. Guards were familiar with Sebastian. They had never seen him run anywhere.

For any reason.

Arianna wasn't even certain he could run.

It seemed to take forever, using Sebastian's lumbering gait, to reach his door. When she did, she nodded slowly at the guards, then turned the knob and went inside.

Candlelight caressed the walls, making the room seem cozy. But it was stifling inside, proof, she hoped, that Sebastian had kept the windows closed.

She shut the door behind her.

"Sebastian?" she asked as she rounded the corner.

He was still sitting on the bed. His hands were at his sides and there were tear streaks on his cheeks. "Ari?"

"We did it," she said. "Is that all right?"

She hadn't really discussed the change with him. All she had done was tell him the plan, ask his permission and leave.

"You . . . look . . . like . . . Gift," he said.

She stopped. The thought made her shudder. "I'm going to Shift," she said. "Open the windows, would you? And don't look."

He stood, even more slowly than she thought. Maybe she had made a mistake this evening. Maybe all of her movements were too quick. He walked to the window, his back to her, and unfastened the shutters.

She closed her eyes and Shifted. The Shift from human form to human form was always disorienting. The changes weren't as obvious. A bit of flesh disappearing here, a bit growing there. Her musculature changed, and so did the shape of her limbs, but the Shifts were tiny, nothing like the grand sweep that happened when she changed into a cat, a horse, or a bird. She couldn't feel the fur sprouting, her face lengthening or a beak forming. All she felt was some tightening here and some loosening there.

And then it was done. She was herself again.

She didn't even have to change out of the robe. She and Sebastian were of a height.

"All right," she said.

He turned, and sighed. "It's . . . you . . ."

"Who did you think it was?"

"You . . . said . . . Gift . . . might . . . come . . . back. . . . I . . . did-n't . . . want . . . to . . . see . . . him . . . with-out . . . you."

"Why not?"

"He . . . con-fus-es . . . me."

"But I thought you've always known him," she said.

"In . . . here." He reached up and touched his forehead. "But . . . out-side . . . he . . . seems . . . dif-fe-rent."

His words relieved her. She came forward, taking his hands in hers.

His eyes filled with tears again. She didn't know how he cried so easily or so well. She couldn't remember the last time she had cried. Solanda said Arianna hardly cried, even when she was a baby.

"Do . . . you . . . hate . . . me?" he asked.

"No!" She pulled away from him. "Is that why you think we did this?"

"You . . . said . . ."

"I was mad," she said. Those words would haunt her forever. That had to be why Solanda left. "I didn't mean it."

"Then . . . why . . . say . . . it?"

"Because—I don't know. Because I was mad."

"That's . . . no . . . rea-son . . . to . . . lie . . ."

She put her arms around him and pulled him close. She liked how he felt, all cool and hard and strong. She always liked it. No matter what Solanda said, no matter how much her father confirmed it, she would always think of Sebastian as her brother and Gift as the golem.

Always.

"I'm sorry," she whispered. "I didn't mean to hurt you. I never wanted to hurt you."

Even his tears were cold. They soothed her warm skin like a soft breeze on a hot day.

"Are you mad at me?"

"No . . ."

"Not even for taking your place?"

He pulled back and held her shoulders in his large hands. He had never held her like that before. It was a grown-up move, and it startled her. Despite their age difference, she had always thought of him as her little brother.

"I . . . could-n't . . . be . . . King. . . . It . . . would . . . have . . . been . . . wrong. . . . I . . . would . . . have . . . hurt . . . things . . . here. . . . Ru-ling . . . is . . . for . . . the . . . swift."

"You're not mad?" Arianna asked again. Her heart was pounding. She hadn't realized how much hurt she had caused, and she didn't want to have taken something precious from him without his permission.

"I . . . am . . . re-lie-ved." And he looked it. His face didn't seem as stiff, his eyes weren't as haunted. He also seemed relieved that she knew about Gift. Sebastian had always kept secrets, but they had never made him happy.

She had forgotten that about him.

She brushed a strand of hair out of her face. "We have to go to the war room," she said. "Something's happened."

"Is . . . it . . . bad?"

She nodded. "Daddy's expecting both of us. But you'll have to pretend like you were the one downstairs tonight. Can you do that?"

His smile was slow, but steady. "I . . . can. . . . I . . . sim-ply . . . won't . . . speak . . . to . . . any-one."

Their old method. It had always worked. She put her hands on his, then leaned forward and kissed his slightly cracked cheek. "We have to change," she said. "You need to be wearing this robe. And then on the way up, I'll brief you. Everything's changing, Sebastian."

He touched the spot where she had kissed him.

"Not . . . every-thing," he said. ". . . You . . . and . . . me, . . . we'll . . . al-ways . . . be . . . to-get-her, . . . right?"

"Right," she said, and she meant it.

Then.

TWENTY-EIGHT

ADRIAN woke abruptly, as if something had startled him awake. His heart was pounding, but the house was silent. He leaned up on his elbows.

Moonlight covered his legs, bathing the room in a silver light. The chair, with his trousers hanging over the back, looked like a live thing. His own body seemed paler than usual, the scars from his year of military service and his Fey imprisonment standing out in sharp relief against his flesh.

Then he heard it again, the sound that must have awakened him. A rustle in the corn, soft voices on the road. His window faced north, and the road was usually quiet until midday. But people were on it now.

And they were speaking Fey.

The hair rose on the nape of his neck. He grabbed his shirt and flung it on, then slid into his trousers. He buttoned them as he pulled open the door, wishing Luke still lived in the house.

But Coulter did. Adrian stopped in the hall, and pushed open Coulter's door.

The room was spotless, as usual. Coulter kept all of his things perfect, as if he were afraid that Adrian would throw him out for being messy. Not even the bed was rumpled. The coverlet was thrown back in a perfect V, and the dent in the pillow looked as if it were planned. Coulter had gone to bed, but he had gotten up.

Adrian continued down the hall. The kitchen still held the warmth of his baking frenzy earlier in the day. The back door stood open, as he had left it, and he descended silently into the yard.

The grass was covered with dew. The water reflected the moonlight, making the grass look as if it were covered in ice. The water felt good against his bare feet. He glanced behind him. His feet left dark impressions on the silvery lawn.

"This looks right." The voice, speaking Fey, was soft, musical and male.

"It better be." The other voice was female and had the sharp edge Fey women's voices often had. Part of their toughness seemed to be their ability to speak firmly. "We can't just wake up any old Islander. Not after what happened to Cover."

The male did not respond to that. Adrian walked along the edge of the grass until he could peer around the corn. The moonlight backlit the road, making it seem as if dirt path appeared out of the silvery light. Two Fey stood on it, face to face, tall and beautiful and ferocious, as Fey always were.

He couldn't see the male's face. The female's revealed her to be a girl, one of the children born just before he left. She would have no idea who he was. But the male. Something in the way he stood was familiar.

"Couldn't you find him, make sure we're in the right place?" the female asked.

The male didn't answer. He glanced toward the house. His hands were shaking.

Adrian couldn't remember the last time he had seen a frightened Fey.

"You can come out now," the male said.

Adrian let out the breath he had been holding. He stood up, pushed aside the corn, and stepped onto the road. The dirt was hard against his feet. A rock dug into his heel.

"Adrian," the male said. There was relief in his voice. He turned to the woman. "We are in the right place."

"What do you want?" Adrian asked.

"It's me, Gift." He came forward, hands outstretched.

Adrian took a step back. He never wanted to touch another Fey again. He didn't count Scavenger, who had renounced his Fey heritage and who also had no magick. But the Fey had dozens of tricks, and many of them involved touch.

"I can't see your face," he said. "I have no idea who you are."

The male turned his face toward the moonlight, illuminating his features. They were King Nicholas's features gone horribly wrong, as if an artist had taken them and forced them into a Fey mode. It didn't help that the moonlight had leached the color from his long hair.

"I haven't seen you since you were a little boy," Adrian said. "How can I be sure it's you?"

"Because I'm the one who helped you out of Shadowlands," Gift said. "I'm the one who kept my grandfather away from you as you escaped the Warders."

"Anyone could remember that."

"I'm the one who told you where Coulter was." He turned, slightly, and as he did, his features were transformed. He had some of Jewel in his high cheekbones. But he had Nicholas's eyes. They were clear in this light, ghost eyes on a Fey face.

"What do you want with us?" Adrian clasped his hands behind his back to hide his own nervousness.

"I need Coulter," Gift said. "I need his advice. I came at some risk—"

"I don't care about your risk," Adrian snapped. "You two are Linked. You didn't have to come here to see him."

"He told you that?"

"He tells me most things."

"I needed to come this time," Gift said. "Something's happened, and I can't figure it out on my own."

"Who's that?" Adrian asked, nodding toward the woman.

"Leen. She's my guard."

"The great hope of the Fey only travels with one guard?"

"I'm not the great hope," Gift said. "I'm the tolerated, untested warrior." Then he smiled. The look was completely his. What Adrian had thought at first to be an ugly combination of two mismatched faces transformed into one of the most startlingly handsome faces he had ever seen in his life.

"The other guard was murdered on the bridge in Jahn," Leen said, as if she expected Adrian to attack them as well.

He frowned. Something was happening. He didn't like having Gift here. Gift was an adult now, raised among Fey. He was, in Adrian's estimation, the most unpredictable of all of them.

"You'd better come in," he said.

"I need to find Coulter."

"I expected him to be here," Adrian said. "He wasn't in his bed."

"You can find him," Leen said.

"Yes," Adrian said. "What about your famous Link?"

Gift glared at him. "Where's the house?"

"This way." Adrian led them through the wet grass. The nerves were rippling in his back. Coulter should have been with them. And it seemed odd that Gift didn't want to Link with him.

Adrian had been around Fey for years. He knew what to expect. He would be safe enough by himself. But all the nuances of the visit bothered him.

He changed his mind; he was relieved that Luke no longer lived at home. He also helped Scavenger would choose not to show later in the day.

But he did want to know where Coulter was. Coulter didn't just know what to expect around Fey; he also knew how to handle them. Coulter had more magick abilities than most of the Fey combined, a fact that terrified them and made Adrian very curious about where Coulter got that power.

Adrian pointed to the back door. "Go on in," he said. "I'll get Coulter."

"I'll come with you," Leen said.

"And leave your charge unguarded?" Adrian shook his head. "You can bind me with some spell if you want. I promise that I won't bring anyone else here, nor will I pour holy water on you. That stuff isn't allowed in my house."

Then, without waiting for her answer, he turned and headed back toward the fields. He had an idea where Coulter was.

The woman apparently decided not to follow him. She leaned against the doorjamb and watched him go. He swerved a little, as a bit of misdirection, and then went on. The corn closed around him as if it were protecting him. But it whispered his passage all the same.

He crossed one growing field until he reached the clearing.

Coulter was sitting in the middle of the clearing. The moonlight seemed to fall directly on him, as if targeting him. He sat in the circle of light, legs crossed, hands on his knees, eyes closed. As Adrian approached, Coulter said, "Stay there, Adrian."

Adrian stopped. He had long ago learned to listen to Coulter when Coulter was in one of these moods.

"You weren't in bed," Adrian said.

"No need to play games," Coulter said. "Gift is here."

"Yes. Why haven't you greeted him?"

Coulter opened his eyes. In the odd light, they looked silver and flat. "I blocked the Link."

Adrian frowned. Once Coulter had told him the Link was his lifeline. "Why?"

"I didn't want him here."

"Why not?"

"He's not safe anymore."

"Not safe?" Adrian said. "I just let him into my house."

"Oh, he won't harm us." Coulter let his hands slide to his side, and he uncrossed his legs. "But with all the changes on the Isle, Gift is the last thing we need."

"But you wanted him here," Adrian said. "You said you'd be able to protect him."

"I said I'd be able to protect him," Coulter said. "I never said I wanted him here."

Adrian didn't understand. He had two Fey in his kitchen, and his foster son, the boy with all the Fey powers, the boy who was not Fey, didn't want them there. "Why not?"

"Because it'll distract me. I can either protect Gift or I can monitor the Other."

"The Other? The new Enchanter?"

Coulter nodded. "He is powerful, Adrian. More powerful than I am. And more in control than the one I felt before."

"Does he know you're here?" Adrian asked.

"Yes," Coulter said. "He sensed me a little while ago. He doesn't know where I am yet, and he may not look. He may not care."

"He's that much more powerful than you?"

"He's that much older, and in control. He's probably had training. I've had none."

"Then how do you know you must choose between him or Gift?"

Coulter pushed himself to his feet. He looked taller in the moonlight. "I can't choose now," he said. "I made the choice fifteen years ago, when I saved Gift's life. I have to defend him."

"I thought you already did. He owes you his life."

"And I owe him mine," Coulter said. "I Bound us. I tied us together. If one of us dies, both of us die, unless someone with my skills can break the Link."

"Why don't you?"

Coulter put a hand over his face. For the first time in a long time, he looked like the little boy he had been when Adrian first befriended him. "Because I did it wrong."

"I don't understand."

He moved his hand. His face held an anguish that Adrian had never seen. "I had never done anything like it before. I just did it by instinct. But I was wrong. There are two ways to Bind. One is subtle and delicate and can be easily asundered. The other Binds the parties heart to heart, making their life energies one. It cannot be broken. I was afraid he was dying. I only had two friends, him and you. I couldn't live without him. So I made that true. Literally."

"Then I don't understand," Adrian said. "If that's true, why don't you want to protect him?"

"Because Gift is good at protecting himself. And I need to be working on this new threat. I can't concentrate on two things at once. Not two important things."

"Then tell Gift that. Have him go on his own."

Coulter stepped out of the light. He looked like himself again. "It won't be that easy, Adrian. Gift is here because of his Vision. And I suspect that's just as important as everything else."

Adrian glanced at the sky, half expecting to see the lines he had seen before. The stars were out, visible even against the brightness of the moon. "I don't understand," he said at last. "All these important events at once. Why?"

Coulter didn't respond. Adrian looked down. Coulter was staring at him.

Adrian's heart lurched. "I meant that as a rhetorical question, but you know, don't you? You know why all of this is happening now."

"It was inevitable," Coulter said.

"And?"

Coulter sighed as if he didn't want to say any more. He came up beside Adrian. They stood side by side. Adrian could feel Coulter's warmth. "And the Islanders have put it off for fifty generations. When you put something off that long, it is cataclysmic when it happens."

"Cataclysmic." Adrian felt as if someone had thrown cold water on his face. He didn't know what Coulter was talking about. He wasn't sure he wanted to know.

Coulter nodded. He put his hand on Adrian's back. "Take me to Gift," he said.

"But you said—"

"I might be wrong." Coulter took a deep breath, glanced south, and added, "He's a Visionary, and I'm an Enchanter. If we had an army behind us, we'd be equally matched."

"To each other?"

"To the threat. We'd face it together."

And then he took off across the grass before Adrian could ask any more questions.

TWENTY-NINE

MATTHIAS swam back into consciousness. It wasn't quite like waking up. To wake up, one had to be asleep. It felt more like his brain returned. The pain beneath it all had been constant. He had been aware of it, and the closer he came to opening his eyes, the more aware he was.

The cuts on his face sent shooting pains throughout his system. The cuts on his shoulders and arms ached. His legs were heavy with exhaustion, and his arms were nearly useless. His lungs burned.

He had never felt so spent in his entire life.

Matthias opened his eyes. The room was unfamiliar. A single candle burned on the nightstand, dripping wax onto the wooden table. The mattress he lay on smelled dirty, and the floor needed to be swept. The room didn't have a window, but through the open door, he saw a kitchen with a cold hearth fire, several more candles, and a woman seated beside an open window.

She was young, in her twenties, and she leaned over a tapestry frame. Her needle worked through the top and then the bottom with the ease of practice. Her face was serene.

Her long hair had a reddish tint that suggested her family came from the Cliffs of Blood.

He coughed, to alert her that he was awake, and then he tried to sit up.

A mistake. He was dizzy. The movement caused a buzzing in his ears.

She was beside him in an instant.

"Tis not yers ta be up," she said. "Yer body's had quite a shock, it has. Ye need yer rest."

The accent was a bit narrow for the Cliffs. He frowned. She spoke more like she came from the Kenniland Marshes. "I can't stay here," he said.

"Ye must. Someone tried ta kill ye. Ye canna go back out tonight."

"You saw it?"

She shook her head. "Me brother found ye, and brought ye here. Tis thought I've healin skills, though tis not always true."

"You need someone to shake out your mattress," Matthias said, and winced at the ingratitude in his tone.

She smiled. "A lordly man like ye'd be expecting more. I dunna have the strength, and me brother, well, he disappears when tis time to work."

"And your husband?"

She gently put a hand on Matthias's chest and pushed him back. "Ye must rest."

"I can't stay," he said again.

"Ye canna leave. Ye canna walk ta that door. Ye've lost so much blood ye look like a fish too long in the sun. Tis lucky ye dinna stay there. By morning, ye'd've been a corpse."

Matthias shivered. She was probably right. The way he felt, and the things he suffered that evening, should have killed him.

But he lived on.

It takes magick to survive.

She let her hand slide along his chest. The movement was almost a caress. "I'll be gettin ye some tea. It'll restore yer spirits."

She walked into the other room, and he found himself staring after her. She wore a long red dress, embroidered with gold along the bottoms and sides. It seemed heavy for summer and warm, but she didn't seem to notice. In fact, the room, although windowless, had a coolness that spoke of fall.

His chest tingled where she had touched him. He leaned back on his pillows, letting the softness envelop him. His wounds still pained him. He had to look horrible. With his right hand, he touched the bandages on his face. They covered his cheeks and his jaw, and one went all the way above his left eye. He didn't remember getting stabbed that close to his eyes, but he barely remembered the details of the attack. It had been moments of mind-numbing terror. He had been more afraid that the Fey would drown him than he had been of being stabbed.

The woman came back and put a cup of tea on the nightstand. Then she put her arm behind his head and brought him forward.

"I can do that," he said.

"Tis my job til yer well," she said. She took the cup and held it to his lips.

The tea was warm and smelled of flowers. It had a slightly bitter taste, but soothed the back of his throat. She took the cup away, allowing him a moment to breathe.

"I don't even know you," he said. "Why are you being so nice?"

She smiled. "Me name is Marly, and I think we're kin of a sort."

"Kin?" Matthias said. "You don't even know who I am."

"I dunna need ta, ta see we gotta bond, ye and me."

He let her give him another sip of tea. It allowed him a moment to think. She couldn't know who he was. Not with all of these facial wounds. Besides, she was too young to know him from his days as Rocaan.

But she had called him "lordly." Perhaps she thought he was a lord, and by claiming a bond, she might claim him as well. As if that would do her any good. He had no land, and no holdings. Only a handful of followers, enough money put aside to finance his dreams, and one dream, a dream that would help the entire Isle, if he got a chance to pursue it.

She pulled the cup away from his mouth. "What kind of bond?" he asked reluctantly.

She smiled. "Yer from the Cliffs of Blood," she said.

He started. It wasn't obvious, like it was with her. He didn't have the telltale reddish hair, nor did he have any of the local look. "What makes you think that?"

"Ye mean aside from yer height?"

He had forgotten that. It was his turn to smile. "There are tall people born in Jahn."

"Nay," she said. "'Cepting the King's bastards."

He smiled at that. Maybe they did have a bond. He took one more sip of tea from her, then let her ease him back on the pillow. "Tell me, Marly," he said, "how bad is my face?"

She gazed down at him, her green eyes filled with compassion. "Ye were a pretty man, then?"

"Pretty?" he frowned. He had never thought of himself in that way. "You mean vain? I don't think so. I just want to know what they did to my face."

"There's no hiding the truth," she said. "Forgive me bluntness, but if'n ye made yer money off yer face, ye need ta be looking for new work."

"How bad?" he asked.

All hope of a smile was gone from hers. She touched his bandages lightly. "Seven cuts, and most are long. I had ta sew the edges together for mending. Twas good ye were gone ta the world then. I tried to keep me stitches tiny, but still ye'll have long gash scars and tiny holes beside. Wee ones won't like seeing ye in the dark."

He closed his eyes then. He had never relied on his face much, but he knew what she meant. Facial scars somehow frightened people worse than all other wounds. He had seen it over and over again, how the gaze averted when someone heavily scarred approached.

One more thing to deal with.

One more thing he had lost to the Fey.

"I dinna mean to hurt ye."

"You weren't the one who did this."

"Who did?"

He opened his eyes again. She hadn't moved. The warmth of her body felt good in the coolness of the room. Her features were classically pretty, her mouth a small bow. If he had been a lord, and wanted to take her to wife, all he would have to do was teach her how to speak correctly. No one would ever have been able to guess her humble origins from her face.

He decided to tell her the truth.

"I startled some Fey on the bridge."

"Fey? In Jahn?"

He closed his eyes, unwilling to say more. He didn't know how she stood on anything. He wasn't even really certain where he was. All he knew was that he was exhausted and he hurt worse than he ever had.

"Are there people who need ye tonight?"

He thought of Yeon and the others. They were working on their own plan. They didn't need him. Not now. And he certainly didn't want them to see him like this, weak and badly injured.

"Not tonight," he said.

"Good, then. Ye'll rest."

He could feel her get off the mattress. He opened his eyes enough to see. He caught her hand in his. "I don't want to kick you out of your bed."

She smiled. "I canna sleep this night anyway. I've got a tapestry ta finish. Tis due at Lord Miller's by week's end."

And that was all Matthias needed to know. She was one of the legion of women who made a living with their needles, sewing chair coverings, making rugs, and embroidering tapestries for the gentry.

Confiding in her would not be wise.

He would have to leave as soon as he was able.

THIRTY

"FIRST he *doesn't* want me in the palace, and now he needs me to come? The Rocaan should be equal to the King, not jump at the King's command." Titus stood by the open balcony doors in his private suite. The courtyard below was empty. Two Auds stood guard outside his door. Lord Stowe was the only other person inside.

Candles were lit all over the room, illuminating the engraved walls and the ornate furniture. The heat from the day remained inside, and the breeze, which Titus could feel on the balcony, did not seem to penetrate the interior.

Stowe stood at the edge of the balcony as well. The years had not been kind to him. He was balding, and although he hadn't gained weight as so many did, he had an agonizing thinness, the kind caused by too much worry and too little personal care. He was twisting the bottom of his hastily donned tunic with the thumb and forefinger of his left hand.

Nervous habits always annoyed Titus. They made him feel as if the person exhibiting them had lost control of his life.

Which, he supposed, Lord Stowe had.

"Besides," Titus said, "How do we know that this Fey was simply not one of the locals playing a little game?"

"We've had other indications. We had a messenger from the South earlier today—"

"As did we. How convenient. And, I suppose, the rumor that holy water is no longer effective?"

Stowe opened his mouth, closed it, and opened it again. "The Fey did say that."

"To which the King replied?"

"That he did not believe it."

Titus smiled. "Oh, how fortuitous. Then when it becomes clear that all of this was a ploy to discredit the Tabernacle, the King can claim ignorance because all of his important subjects heard him get the news." Titus narrowed his eyes. "I'm not playing this game, Stowe."

"It's not a game, Holy Sir." Stowe had wrapped the edge of the tunic around his forefinger. "The Black King is here. The King would like you to come to the war room."

"So he can humiliate me."

"So he can ask your help." Stowe's voice rose. "The King is not supposed to rule without the Rocaan. He needs you, Holy Sir."

"Now." Titus smoothed his robe. He hadn't yet changed into his nightclothes, and he was pleased he hadn't. He needed every ounce of authority from his office for this moment. "When his children were young, he didn't need me. When he believed this country was at peace, he didn't need me. He even, in his arrogance, offered to become King and Rocaan rolled into one. I believe his words were something along the lines of the fact that he was the only one who had the Roca's blood running through his veins, and that the Rocaan originally had been the Roca's second son. So therefore, shouldn't a descendent of the Roca be Rocaan? And wouldn't it be more natural for it to be him?"

Stowe frowned. "He said that to you?"

"Actually, he said it to my predecessor. But—"

"No buts," Stowe said. "Matthias was a murderer who tried to ruin this country. He had no place in the Rocaan's seat, and we all knew it. He also, we thought, had no chance of finding a worthy successor. The King told him that to get him to step down. And it worked. The threat of combining the kingship and the Rocaan into one person forced Matthias to choose you."

Titus gripped the edge of the door. The heat seemed to be growing worse. He stepped onto the balcony.

He had been a young boy when all of this was thrust on him. Too young, in his own opinion. Too young to understand all the nuances. What Stowe said made sense. Only Titus couldn't recast his memory well enough. Just because it made sense didn't mean it was true.

The courtyard below him was lit by torches. The flames reflected off the inlay, showing shadowy hints of the scenes from the Roca's life and from that of the Tabernacle. He saw no guards below, although he knew they were there. The Tabernacle had been well guarded ever since the Fey breached it over a decade before.

Stowe came out onto the balcony. He stood near the doorway, staring at the river. It was loud tonight. The gurgle of the water echoed over the silence of the city. The moon was full, and shone its bright light over the water.

"They found a body on the bridge tonight," Titus said. He had received the report shortly before Stowe arrived. "I'm surprised you didn't see the mess when you rode over."

"It was dark." Stowe sounded wary. "And I was in a hurry."

"Mmmm." Titus walked forward and put his hands on the rail. A voice cried out down the street, as if in surprise. The city was still awake. "The body was Fey. Murdered."

He turned. He had Stowe's attention. The man hadn't moved. "How?"

"Holy water. All that was recognizable was an ear, a hand, and an arm. The rest was a round lump. I am amazed the stench cleared up as quickly as it did."

"There is a breeze tonight."

"Yes," Titus said.

The silence stretched between them. Stowe clasped his hands behind his back. But he couldn't outwait Titus. His mission from his King was too strong.

"Forgive me, Holy Sir," Stowe said. "I don't see the connection."

"It's quite simple, actually." Titus leaned against the railing. It had been redone the year before, carved now from heavy wood to support his slight frame. "It's incontrovertible proof that holy water still works." He pushed away, rising to his full height. Time to remind Lord Stowe that Titus was a boy no longer. He had ruled the Tabernacle for fifteen years, as long as the Forty-Second Rocaan, longer than many others.

"Tell your King that this game won't work. Killing Auds in Southern kirks was a bad way to break faith with the Tabernacle. Replacing the holy water with normal water is a crime, Lord Stowe. Making up lies about the Black King to terrify our people into accepting our King's demented demon son as the next ruler of Blue Isle is also a bad thing to do. Don't think I haven't noticed the timing. All this occurs on the day of his son's Coming-of-Age, a ceremony, by the way, which the Tabernacle will not recognize."

"This threat is real," Stowe said. "One of your own people brought you the information. All of Blue Isle's gentry saw the Fey messenger."

Titus took one more step closer to Stowe. They were of a height, both short, stocky men. But Titus held more power. He was younger, stronger, fit. Stowe was becoming an old man.

"That messenger could have been any one of the King's Fey friends in disguise. It proves nothing, except Nicholas's own delusions. If the Black King came to Blue Isle, do you think he would announce his presence and demand a surrender? If he could do the impossible and breach our southern defenses, then he could also invade the Isle in a blink. He wouldn't need some quick meeting with Good King Nicholas to complete the deal."

"Holy Sir, please—"

Titus held up his hand for silence. "I don't know what the last act of this play was supposed to be. Perhaps I was to be goaded into attacking the royal demon spawn, so that I too could be discredited as my predecessor was. That would be another strong blow to the Tabernacle, wouldn't it? Or perhaps I was supposed to charge in like a savior, only to discover that my 'holy' water no longer worked. Perhaps I would die, like my southern Auds, and become a martyr, clearing the way for his Highness, the Great King Nicholas the Fifth, to become Rocaan."

"He doesn't want that."

"He doesn't? Good King Nicholas, the only King to banish the Tabernacle from the palace? For all his pious words, he forgets that the Roca charged his sons with two jobs: The eldest was to lead Blue Isle in the physical plane. The second son was to lead Blue Isle in the spiritual plane. *And they were to work together.*"

"He knows that," Stowe said. "He feared for his children. Matthias murdered his wife."

"The Fifty-First Rocaan," Titus corrected, "was conducting a religious ceremony, blessing the new king and his consort. God chose that moment to strike the demon down."

"That was the very attitude the King feared."

"What the King failed to recognize is that he erred in marrying a Soldier of the Enemy. What the King still fails to recognize is that those things he calls children are nothing more than blasphemies in the eyes of God."

"So you will do nothing to save your country," Stowe said.

"I will not participate in a charade that is designed as the final destruction of the Tabernacle," Titus said.

"Then may God forgive you, Holy Sir," Stowe said and turned on one foot. He headed through the main room.

"May God forgive *me*, Lord Stowe?"

Stowe stopped. He kept his back to Titus. "You are wrong, Holy Sir. And in your arrogance, your failure to step beyond your own bruised feelings, you are dooming us all."

THE ATTACK
[BEFORE DAWN, THE FOLLOWING DAY]

THIRTY-ONE

FLURRY had never flown so hard or so fast in his entire life. When he reached the Circle door, he stuck one tiny hand into the ring of lights, and then used the last of his strength to fall through.

Rugad's Shadowlands had grown since Flurry last saw it. Most of the officers must have started sleeping inside. He didn't know if that meant discontent on the part of the nearby Islanders or if it meant that Rugad needed his officers beside him.

Or both.

He collapsed on the opaque floor and willed himself to full size so that no one would step on him. He needed both sleep and food, not necessarily in that order. As his body stretched, his exhausted muscles twitched.

"I don't believe sleeping in the doorway is conducive to health," said a voice above him. Flurry twisted his head. Boteen stood above him, long face dark with intent. Boteen had a way of moving that made him seem more powerful physically than he probably was. He was also the tallest, thinnest Fey Flurry had ever seen. The lines around his wide mouth and his cheekbones were so high that they seemed, with his chin, to form a **v**. "Especially not before you report to Rugad."

Flurry pushed himself up. He was dizzy with exhaustion, his entire body aching with every movement.

"Food and water, I believe," Boteen said. He had a mocking air that grew more refined as his Enchanter's abilities improved.

Flurry frowned.

"That is what you would ask for if I were anyone else. Food and water, and you would have snapped at me about exhaustion and overexertion. You know Rugad cares nothing for these things."

Flurry smoothed his hair and pulled his wings close to his back. He made his way toward Rugad's tent.

"But I do," Boteen said. "You performed a great service this night and, I believe, may have solved an energetic mystery. All lines converge, don't they, in a small farm near Killeny's Bridge."

"I'm sorry," Flurry said. He tried not to be rude to Fey who were more powerful than he was, but sometimes the effort was beyond him. "But I don't know what you're talking about."

"I know that," Boteen said, "but I am grateful. All I needed was a path, which you provided. So I shall provide food, water, and a bed in my tent. After you report to Rugad, you may sleep all you like."

He turned and almost floated into a nearby tent. Flurry blinked once, trying to clear his eyes, but couldn't. That had been Boteen, and he actually had talked to Flurry as though they were equals. Flurry shook his head and walked across the gray floor.

Rugad's tent was large and blue. Its shade seemed vivid in here, but outside it would have been a dull color. Rugad had lived in so many Shadowlands, he knew just which colors worked against the gray and which didn't.

Learning the difference, he always said, was good for morale.

"Rugad," Flurry said as he stood outside the flap. "A report."

Wisdom was the one who pushed the flap back. His

braids swung forward, hanging almost to the opaque floor. "It's about time," he hissed.

"I got back as quickly as I could," Flurry said.

"Not quickly enough." Rugad was seated on his cot. His hair was braided down his back, and he wore his fighting boots. He stopped lacing them as Flurry came in. "Two Spies have already reported to me. The Islander King thinks he can negotiate with the leader of the Fey, does he?"

Flurry didn't question how the Spies returned so quickly. Rugad often used unconventional methods—having the Spies report to Eagle Riders, who could outfly Wisps, for example, or on one memorable occasion, having Horse Riders return with the Spies on their backs. That had caused no end of friction between the Spies and the Riders, friction that had finally ended in a fight that left two Spies and one Rider dead.

"I told him you weren't amendable to that."

"And how did you know?" Rugad said. "He is, after all, the father of my great-grandson."

"He's not Fey."

Rugad smiled and glanced at Wisdom. "See why I like this man? He has a grasp of the important."

Wisdom nodded and said nothing.

Rugad grabbed the laces of his boots. "As Flurry so accurately put it, I am not amendable to negotiation, especially with an upstart who believes that simply because he can father a child, he can be on a par with the Black King. The attack has already begun. He will be quite surprised when the answer to his request for negotiation is mass slaughter, a slaughter he chose instead of surrendering like a reasonable man."

A trickle ran up Flurry's spine. The attack had begun. The time for talk was over.

"After you rest, Flurry, you may choose which theater you would like to fight in. Wisdom has some theories about the way the various groups of Islanders will respond to an all-out Fey assault. He believes each will be interesting, and some will be more suitable to your talents than others."

Flurry bowed his head slightly. "Thank you, Rugad." He turned, and grabbed the tent flap.

"Flurry," Rugad said, his voice suddenly firm. "You aren't dismissed yet."

"I delivered your message, your Spies told you the Islander King's response, and the attack has begun. What else do you need from me?" He kept his hand on the flap.

"I understand your great need for rest," Rugad said, "but this is probably going to be our last conversation until Blue Isle is completely secured. I need to know what you saw, and your assessment of it."

Flurry turned. "You already know all the nobles were in the room. The shock was great, the palace is formidable, but we've seen worse, and there is an odd energy around the place they call the Tabernacle."

Rugad's eyes were hooded. He let his laces go. His boots hung over the sides of his legs, untied. "You haven't mentioned my great-grandson."

Flurry jolted. In his exhaustion, he had forgotten.

Rugad noted the movement. "Flurry?"

He glanced at Wisdom. Wisdom was one of Rugad's trusted advisors, but trust only went so far. "I think we need to discuss your great-grandson alone, Rugad."

"I already have heard the stories. He's feeble. For once the match didn't work."

Flurry blinked. The boys did not look feeble. If anything, their eyes glowed with the same intense intelligence as Rugad's. "It's not that," Flurry said. "Please. You'll thank me for this in a moment."

"But I won't," Wisdom said.

Rugad grinned at his advisor, then waved him away. "You'll probably hear later."

"I'd like to hear sooner."

"I'm sure you would." Rugad's smile left. "But Flurry has never requested a private audience before. I think we should grant him one, don't you? Do me a favor, Wisdom, and see how the eighth team is faring. I want them to leave shortly."

"As you wish," Wisdom said. He slipped out the tent door. Rugad got up, held the flap back, and watched until Wisdom went through the circle door, out of Shadowlands.

Rugad let the flap fall closed. "I don't grant personal audiences on a whim, Flurry."

"This is not a whim, Rugad." Flurry's muscles were trembling. His brain felt foggy. He blinked, trying to remain clear. "Your great-grandson is not feeble. The boy I saw at the King's side has your intelligence in a pair of fairly ugly blue eyes."

"My intelligence? Then how could they think he was feeble?"

"He moved oddly," Flurry said. "It might have been a game, although I didn't know what it would gain him."

"I don't understand why Wisdom couldn't hear this," Rugad said.

"Because I'm not done," Flurry said. "The boy is distinctive. Blue eyes, as I said, Fey features, and the look of Jewel about him. He also has some of his father's roundness. I've never quite seen anything like it. It will take a few generations of pure Fey mating to hide the Islander in that line."

"Strong heritage, huh?" Rugad didn't sound interested. He returned to the cot and continued lacing his boots.

"I tell you this not because of the heritage, but because of what I saw. When I left the palace, I saw two Fey across the bridge. One of them was an exact replica of the boy inside."

"A Doppelgänger?"

"No." Flurry swallowed hard. "I flew in close enough to look. No gold flecks in the eyes. In fact, his face was slightly different. A sharper angle to the chin, and a different intelligence in the eyes. As strong, but not as fierce."

Rugad patted his legs as if the words made no difference. "You're telling me that I have two great-grandchildren?"

"Yes," Flurry said.

"And you're certain?"

"Two partially Fey children couldn't have that look of Jewel in their faces. These boys weren't that dissimilar. I believe they're twins."

"Twins." This time Rugad looked up. "That's never happened in this Black line."

Flurry nodded. The only time it had happened, centuries before, the younger twin had been slaughtered shortly after birth. "That's not all," he said. "I believe they were raised separately."

"How would you know that?" Rugad's eyes narrowed. Flurry had been right. The boy in the palace did have the look of his great-grandfather in his eyes.

"Because I startled both of them. The boy in the palace responded in Islander. The boy outside spoke in Fey."

Rugad nodded. "You are a sharp observer, Flurry. That's why I sent you to speak to their King." He leaned his head back. "I don't understand how the Islanders thought the child feeble. There is a missing piece, Flurry."

"I agree," Flurry said.

"We need to discover it."

He knew what Rugad was thinking. "They both have already seen me. I don't think I could get the information you need."

"Neither do I," Rugad said. "I wasn't thinking of that, actually. I was—"

The flap flew back, and Boteen came in, carrying a tray. "Refreshments!" he called, and set them down on a side table.

Flurry stiffened, never taking his gaze from Rugad. He hadn't heard of anyone barging in on the Black King before.

Rugad's gaze went dark. "You look spent, Flurry. Take the water and some food."

Flurry did, taking a silver cup. A Domestic energy spell floated on the top of the water. He took a sip, and immediately felt refreshed. He also grabbed a sandwich, and then stood aside, waiting to be dismissed.

But Rugad wasn't looking at him. Rugad had stood. His boots were laced, his clothes were pressed, and his scabbard was at his side. He looked like the Black King.

"How much have you heard?" he said to Boteen.

Flurry's stomach twisted. He hoped the Black King never used that tone with him.

"Nothing," Boteen said. "I just came in with refreshments. When Flurry arrived, he looked so exhausted I figured I would give him a little magickal strength to get through his meeting with you. It—"

"How much have you heard?" Rugad said, his voice going lower than it had the first time.

"Really, Rugad, do you think I would stoop to listening at tent flaps?"

Rugad's gaze narrowed. He lifted his chin slightly, put one hand on the hilt of his sword and said, "For the last time, Boteen, how much have you heard?"

Boteen sighed theatrically. "It was accidental, you know. I didn't mean to listen. But your voices were raised just a bit, and I couldn't help—"

"Boteen." The word was nearly a whisper.

Boteen stopped, and swallowed. His bravado was apparently an act. "You need me," he said, as if warning Rugad not to hurt him.

"You informed me, not one day ago, that there are two other Enchanters on this Isle," Rugad said. "I do not need you."

Flurry froze. Boteen was the only Enchanter who had come on this trip, the only one born in the last century. Rugar had brought none on his unfortunate mission. Then how could there be two Enchanters on the Isle?

"On the contrary," Boteen said, all of his elaborate mannerisms gone, "without me, you'll never find them."

"Don't be so certain," Rugad said.

"Besides," Boteen said, "I know how to tell which brother is the eldest."

Rugad's expression didn't change, but he lowered his chin slightly. "That's a secondary problem," he said. "We have to find both of them first."

"If I may speak," Flurry said, not certain he wanted to, "finding them is also a secondary problem."

Rugad turned his sharp gaze on Flurry. He waited for the explanation. Flurry glanced at Boteen, who smiled at him. Flurry didn't like that smile.

"Our information about your great-grandson was wrong, and we didn't know that there were two children. Unless your Visions have given you a wider scope of knowledge about your family than I am privy to," Flurry said, choosing each word as carefully as he could, "you have to consider that there may be more children of Black Blood on this Isle."

Rugad's hand fell away from his scabbard. Boteen whistled softly. "And I thought you had wasted your time sending a Wisp," he said.

"Shut up, Boteen," Rugad said.

Boteen's smile grew. "Don't look so pale, Rugad. There's still time to inform the troops. Just don't have them touch any Fey under twenty. That should take care of the problem."

"And what if they look like an Islander?" Flurry asked.

"Fey blood tells," Boteen snapped.

"Does it?" Flurry said. "Are we so certain?"

"Your own testimony says so," Rugad said.

"But I've only seen two mixes, both from the same family."

"And that's the family we're concerned about," Boteen said.

Flurry shook his head. "Jewel married the Islander King. But her father was also of Black Blood and he lived here for several years before his death."

"Flurry has a point," Boteen said.

"Indeed he does," Rugad said. "The problem is that the first wave left here yesterday afternoon."

"I thought you waited for the Spies," Boteen said.

Rugad stared at Boteen. After a moment, Boteen flushed. He clearly understood the implication. Flurry did not.

Boteen took a deep breath. "Then we shall simply have to rely on the troops' common sense."

"They have no common sense," Rugad said. "Boteen, get me an Eagle Rider immediately. And Flurry, finish that food. I need you here. You'll tell me everything you remember about my great-grandsons. And neither of you will speak of this to anyone else. Hear me?"

Flurry nodded. Boteen did too, looking subdued. They both knew what the secret meant. Rugad had come here because he felt his grandsons—Rugar's children—weren't fit to take the Black Throne. Rugad had hoped that his great-grandson was. But until he learned which great-grandson was the elder, there would be no heir.

The Black Throne would be in dispute.

THIRTY-TWO

THE maps were old and the room smelled of dust. Even though Nicholas had been up here in the years since his father died, he always thought of the war room as his father's room. About a year after the Fey invasion, Nicholas discovered his father in this room, looking over a long scroll filled with names of the Islander dead. All those souls rested on his father's conscience and never left. When he died, he had been going to the Kenniland Marshes to see the people he had neglected.

To atone.

Nicholas stood in the door. The lords were inside. They had already taken their places around the long oak table. They looked odd in their finery; this room was made for men dressed to fight. Lord Miller's fancy cloak trailed on the floor. Lord Canter, his back hunched, examined the map Nicholas's father had tacked on the wall a generation ago. Lord Enford, who had been with his father when he died, had broadened with age, the lines on his face deep with remembered loss. He was staring at the map as well.

In the passing years, Lord Egan had become stunningly obese. He occupied the foot of the table all by himself, his body slopping over the armless chair. His robe was twice the size of the others, and the material, though expensive, was dark and plain to hide his bulk. He had once been a jovial man, but that joviality had turned into bitterness when his son died in the Fey Invasion all those years ago.

Lord Canter had apparently been speaking before Nicholas arrived. He stopped when Nicholas came in the door. Canter had never liked Nicholas, and the feeling was mutual. Canter had continued to increase his wealth over the years and to wear much of it on his back and fingers. His clothing, once imported from Nye, was now made by the finest Islander tailors, and there was talk that he even bought clothes from the Fey.

As usual, Nicholas would have to watch him.

Lord Zela sat on a stool near the back of the room. One riding boot rested on the stool's lower rung, the other on the floor. Zela nodded when he saw Nicholas. They were of an age. Zela had taken Lord Holbrook's place as the only tin-lord on the Council. Nicholas actually wished there were more spaces for tin-lords. They were self-made men whose title was a courtesy, and not passed down from generation to generation. A pity, too, since Lord Holbrook's oldest son was a fine man and would have made an excellent advisor.

Zela was a fine man too. He was short and stocky and had hands scarred in a barn fire. He'd lost most of his holdings when the Fey arrived, but shrewd business sense and an ability to seize opportunities made him into one of the richest men on the Isle in ten years. Nicholas had appointed Zela to Holbrook's seat upon Holbrook's death, fighting objections from all the other lords. But Nicholas had never regretted the decision.

Several guards were posted outside the door. Nicholas instructed them to let his children in and no one else.

Then he pulled the door closed.

"Sire," Canter said, nodding once, acknowledging Nicholas's arrival. "I don't see how the Fey could have gotten in from the south. The cliffs are too high on both sides. My father sailed around this Isle as a young man and he said that the sea side was sheer smooth rock. Nothing could find purchase."

Nicholas smiled at Canter's obvious attempt to cover the

conversation that Nicholas had walked in on. "Nonetheless," Nicholas said, "we have to take the claim seriously. I had a report earlier today that there were Fey in the south, and there are no southern landholders here tonight. The problem here is that we need to make plans and we don't know what we're up against. We don't know how they got here, we don't know how many troops they brought, and we don't know if they have magicks we're unaware of."

"You did the right thing," Zela said, "telling them we wouldn't surrender."

"I hope so," Nicholas said. "I'm still holding out for that discussion. I can't believe the Black King would attack his own family. The Fey have proscriptions against that."

"Or so you were told," Canter said.

"I was told that again this evening by the Fey's Shaman. I spoke to her before the banquet. She also believed that the Black King was here, although she hadn't been told of his arrival. And if it is him, she said that the Isle's Fey are in danger as well."

"Serves them right," Egan muttered.

Nicholas let that go. "I have sent for the Rocaan. I should have sent for Monte, and will rectify that in a few moments. My sense is that we haven't much time."

"Isn't it unusual for the Black King to warn us?"

Nicholas nodded. "I suspect he did so out of courtesy, and as a way of notifying my children that he's here. That would take care of the Blood dilemma the Fey face. My children should, under Fey rules, stay out of the fighting."

"Will they?" Canter asked.

Nicholas leaned back. He had had this argument with his father during the first Fey invasion. Then he had thought differently. Now he took his father's position. "They are heirs to the throne. They cannot endanger their lives in battle."

"It might be good for morale to see your children in the thick of things. It worked for you," Miller said.

Nicholas wasn't certain if there was sarcasm in that comment, so he let it ride.

"Sire," Canter said, "I worry about the wisdom of having your children at this meeting. They are part Fey."

Nicholas bristled. "They were raised as Islanders."

"Nonetheless—"

Nicholas slapped his hands on the table, silencing Canter. "Nonetheless," Nicholas said in his lowest, most dangerous voice, "they are my children, and the heirs to this throne. They have more right to be in this room than you do."

Canter glanced at the others. They all looked away. Nicholas was about to say more when the door opened.

Arianna came in, looking flushed. The mark on her chin was livid. Sebastian shuffled behind her, wearing the robe she had had on when she left the hall. She had thought of everything.

Her hair was down, and she wore breeches and a shirt with full sleeves. She looked more like her mother than she ever had.

"Forgive us for being late," she said. "Sebastian had trouble finding me."

"We missed you at the banquet, Princess," Lord Enford said, and he sounded sincere.

"I felt as if I were there in spirit," Arianna said, and flashed him a smile. She pulled Sebastian in and pulled the door closed. "My brother tells me he's exhausted and he would like to listen. Is that all right with you, Daddy?"

Nicholas nodded. Arianna had thought of everything. On one level he was pleased. On another he found he didn't like her talent for deception.

Lord Canter smiled at Sebastian. "It is good to see you, Your Highness. You seem quite yourself again."

Arianna frowned. She led Sebastian toward the back of the room, and Lord Zela, who had always been friendly to her. "Was he different earlier?" she asked.

"More animated, Highness, and almost personable."

Sebastian opened his mouth, but Arianna put a long slender finger over it. "You've never seen my brother, then, when he's feeling refreshed?"

Canter shrugged. "Apparently not," he said.

"I'm amazed my father never said anything." Arianna glanced at Nicholas with a look of reproach. He worked to keep the look of surprise off his face. "We discovered a long time ago that my brother isn't slow. His body just acts a little differently than the rest of ours. When he's tired, he moves slowly and talks even slower. That led people to believe he wasn't very bright. But he has had periods all his life when he can be as sharp as the rest of us." She smiled, looking beautiful and innocent. "My father certainly wouldn't trust the future of this country to someone who is dim-witted."

"Certainly not," Canter said a beat too quickly.

"I'm glad you could make it," Nicholas said, cutting the discussion off. He turned away from his daughter, from her bright face and glittering eyes, and toward the group. "We are facing a number of problems here. But we are more prepared than we were for the first invasion. Our people at least know how to defend themselves. My worry is that they'll rely too heavily on holy water."

"It should work," Zela said.

"And if it doesn't, we'll have another slaughter. We need to get word to all the provinces that the holy water may not work. We need to make sure people have arms—swords, knives, and other ways of defending themselves. Each of you needs to send word to your own sections."

The lords nodded. Canter took his seat.

Nicholas clasped his hands under the table. Finally he had control of the meeting. "Secondly, our guards are a trained fighting force. They should be able to protect the palace. We need to call our militia, and make certain that Jahn is protected as well. The word is that the Fey are in the south. We'll need to concentrate on the southern entrance to the city."

"Beg pardon, Sire, but we're discussing Fey here. They may be in the south, but they could attack from anywhere." Lord Enford spoke softly, as if he didn't want to contradict Nicholas.

"I'm aware of that, Enford," Nicholas said. "We will have to scatter troops throughout the city and the countryside. Until we actually have a sighting, we can take no direct action here."

"Sire, I have another concern," Miller said. "What if this is a hoax put on by the local Fey?"

"We would know," Arianna said.

"Ari," Nicholas said without looking at her, "You are here on my good graces. Please allow the meeting to go forward without your comments."

She sighed and said nothing else. Out of the corner of his eye, he saw Sebastian take her hand.

"That is a possibility," Nicholas said, "but it would gain them nothing."

"On the contrary," Miller said, "it would give them an advantage."

Nicholas frowned. "I see no advantage in this."

"If, as the messenger said, the Fey found a way around holy water, then this gives the Fey their might back. They know we're afraid of the Black King. They know that we're no longer afraid of them. If the Black King supposedly arrived, the Fey would be formidable again."

"Nice hypothesis," Nicholas said, "but we cannot afford to believe it, any more than we can afford to believe that the mountains to the south are impenetrable. We have seen a thousand impossible things since the Fey arrived. One more should not strain our credulity."

A knock sounded on the door. Then, in a muffled voice, a guard announced Lord Stowe's arrival.

"Send him in," Nicholas said. He stood as Stowe entered. Stowe looked windblown from his ride to the Tabernacle and back. "The Rocaan?" Nicholas said.

"He will not come," Stowe said. "Nor will he help in any way. He believes this a ploy from the palace to discredit him."

"What?" Zela asked. "How did he come to that?"

"It seems there were some attacks on the kirks in the Marshes," Stowe said. "The Danites used holy water but it had no effect. The Rocaan believes it was switched for real water. He uses as his proof a murder that occurred on the Jahn bridge tonight."

"A murder?" Egan breathed the word as if it were obscene.

"A Fey was killed with holy water on the Jahn Bridge. It appears to have happened during the banquet, maybe even during the time we were listening to that Wisp. The Rocaan believes that shows holy water still works."

"He will not even make more holy water?" Enford asked.

"He didn't say," Stowe said. "But I doubt it. This is something you need to resolve with him personally, Your Highness."

Nicholas ran a hand over his face. One more thing. He really hadn't needed one more thing on this night. "Round up all the holy water you can. Distribute it throughout the city and to the countryside. I will not allow any in the palace or near my children. I will make an appointment with the Rocaan tomorrow. In the Tabernacle. This has gone on long enough."

"Perhaps, Sire, if you had held the proper ceremonies—" Canter started.

Nicholas removed his hand from his face and glared at Canter. Canter stopped.

"I understand the desire to blame me for all the changes on Blue Isle," Nicholas said tightly. "Not everything I have done has been popular. But nothing changes the fact that I rule this Isle and will continue to do so. The Rocaan doesn't. I do. I will meet with him, but I doubt we will need him."

"You believe that messenger, don't you?" Enford asked.

Nicholas nodded. "And I believe that unless we find a way to stand our ground, we will be a part of the Fey Empire, whether we like it or not."

THIRTY-THREE

THE kitchen was warm. Gift rummaged through drawers until he found several candles and a tinderbox. He lit them. The room seemed small and confining, not at all how it had seemed when Gift first saw it, through Coulter's eyes.

Leen stood in the doorway, arms crossed. The sky was growing lighter on the eastern horizon. "I don't like it here," she said.

"You don't have to," Gift said.

"We need Cover."

He didn't answer that. He couldn't bring Cover back, even if he wanted to. And the last thing he wanted to think about was her death.

He did need a moment to get his bearings, though. He hadn't been able to reach Coulter through their Link all day. The end of the Link was blocked—Coulter's end—and that had never happened before. It was almost as if Coulter hadn't wanted to hear from him.

"Is that him?" Leen asked. She held the open door in one hand and leaned into the gray dawn. Gift stood and peered over her shoulder. He stifled a gasp.

He hadn't seen Coulter in person in a long, long time,

not since they were little boys. That was the Coulter he remembered: the boy who was too small for his age, the boy who was round in a world of angles, the boy whose hair was an unnatural yellow. This Coulter was the Coulter of Gift's childhood Vision, the Coulter who rode with him down the Cardidas, the Coulter whose eyes sparkled when they contemplated the future.

A shiver ran through Gift.

"Gift?" Leen asked.

"That's him," Gift said.

Then Adrian came out of the fields as well. Adrian had been a shock when Gift saw him earlier. Gift remembered a taller man, an older man, and one who spoke oddly. Either Adrian's mastery of Fey had improved or, through Coulter, Gift had gotten used to him.

"Let me talk to him," Gift said.

Leen moved away from the door. She went to the wooden counters and leaned on them, arms loose and near her sword. She would defend him to the last, he knew that, and he relied on it. The welcome he had expected was colder than he ever imagined it would be.

Yet when Coulter saw Gift at the door, he grinned, then ran forward, arms extended. He grabbed Gift and hugged him as he would a long-lost brother.

"You should have told me you were venturing into the real world," Coulter said. Even his voice was deeper, a man's voice, not a boy's.

"I tried," Gift said.

"You told me about the Vision, not that you'd be here."

"Things changed." Gift pulled out of the hug. "You blocked the Link."

Coulter's expression grew momentarily flat. Then he glanced at Adrian. Adrian stood a few feet back. He shrugged one shoulder, as if he had no part of this discussion.

"Something's happening to the south," Coulter said. "I've been trying to concentrate on it. I shut out all distractions."

That obviously had an element of truth, but that wasn't all. Gift could feel the nuances through their bond. "So I'm a distraction now?"

"No," Coulter said bluntly. "Now you're a diversion. Let's hope that the paths lead to the same place."

Now the bond felt clear, the Link felt open. Coulter put his arm around Gift and led him outside. Leen pulled her sword. "Wait!" she said.

"It's all right," Gift said.

"Not if something happens," Leen said.

"Nothing can happen," Coulter said. "We're Bound."

She glanced at Gift for confirmation. He nodded. Then he went with Coulter into the fields, leaving Leen and Adrian behind.

The sun was rising, touching the corn with gold. The morning air had a damp coolness that felt good against Gift's skin. That kitchen had been stifling.

Flocks of black birds of a type he had never seen flew overhead. Their caws resounded in the stillness. The dew on the grass glossed over the footprints left earlier by Adrian, Leen, and Gift.

"Why am I a diversion?" Gift asked.

Coulter looked at him. Coulter's face was still the same. His eyes were blue and clear, his features square and solid. He was the same boy, only in a larger body. He was, oddly, as tall as Gift.

"Let me show you," he said, and took Gift's hand. Then Coulter slid along their Link.

The impressions that came to Gift were fast and furious, too fast for him to process. Most weren't visual; he saw only the trails in the night sky. Most were feelings, changes, oddities in the way the earth felt, and a strange sense of surprise coming from the ground in the south.

Then, as quickly as they began, they ended. It would take Gift some time to process them.

Now let me, Gift said through the Link, and he showed Coulter what had happened at the palace. As he reviewed the images from Arianna's attack, Coulter winced and ducked.

When it was over, Coulter slid back down the Link and let go of Gift's hand. "Why is the stone boy so important?"

"We're Linked," Gift said. "Like you and me."

"You can't Link to a bit of stone."

"I didn't," Gift said. "He has a personality. It has just taken him longer to develop it. You and he are the only brothers I have, Coulter. And he can't defend himself."

Coulter sighed. "And either you'll die or he'll die if we don't do something."

Gift nodded. "We need to get him out of the palace."

"But obviously you can't bring him out. What about your sister? Could she?"

"She hates me."

"But she loves him, and will do whatever she can for him."

"I don't know," Gift said. "I don't think we have much time. If we have another failure, we could be in trouble."

Coulter stepped away from him. The sun was higher, slanting across the corn, the light hitting the center of Coulter's clothes. "Time," he said. "This is all about time."

Gift shook his head. "I don't understand."

"Your Vision happened two weeks ago. The change in energy did too. You think there will be some sort of attack against you soon, and I think they've come for you. Something else has happened. Something we don't understand."

"They finally decided to make the trip."

"After twenty years?" Coulter shook his head.

"I'm an adult now."

"Yes, but wouldn't it be better to raise a child in the manner you want instead of letting someone else do it?"

"You think that old man I saw was my great-grandfather."

"I do," Coulter said. He turned. "And if it is, will you join him?"

"In what?" Gift asked.

"In conquering the world. That's what Fey do, isn't it?"

Gift started. He had never thought of that. All his life, he had struggled to keep Shadowlands going. Traveling through the Isle itself had been an adventure. But to conquer the world—

He shook his head. "I'm not a warrior," he said.

"Only because you haven't been raised as one," Coulter said. "That's my point. If you want someone to take your place, you train him."

"You think the Black King's come to train me? Why?"

"Because I think he needs a successor," Coulter said. "And I think he needs one now."

THIRTY-FOUR

THE Shaman was not in Shadowlands. No one had seen her leave, but no one knew where she was.

Solanda stopped in the Domicile for a meal. It had been so long since she had had magicked food that she had almost forgotten how light it was. Wind was doing one more check through all the buildings. Niche waited for them at her place.

Solanda didn't like it. If the Shaman was gone, and Gift was gone, who would give the order to evacuate Shadowlands? She could. She was ranked high enough in the magick order, but no one would listen to her. She was a Shifter, and a Shifter who had lived among the Islanders at that. The Fey might think it a trap to get the them out of hiding.

She was sitting on a rug near the Domicile's main fireplace. The fire was burning low, emitting a lot of light and heat, a trick that nonmagicked fires could do only rarely. There were some things to say for Shadowlands—the constant temperature, the gathering of Fey all in one place— but they certainly weren't enough to convince her to live there ever again.

And that was the other reason she couldn't give the evacuation order. Too many Fey knew how she felt.

She sighed, finished the last of her meal, and got to her feet. She wanted to go back to cat form, but felt she didn't dare, not until she was out of Shadowlands. She wanted to be taken seriously, and that was hard for folks to do when she was feline.

Feline or not, though, she couldn't order the evacuation. The only others who could would be the Warders. And even though they had abdicated much of their power over the years, they still had Warder mystique.

The Spell Warders were the only Fey who had all the powers of the Fey. Their powers were limited, however. The magick behind them was weak, and unable to be of real use. The Warders' major skill was that they were the ones who designed the Spells for those who relied on Spells. The new Domestic spells, the ones tailored to Blue Isle, had come from the Warders. The Warders should have been the one to counteract other magick as well, but that hadn't proved too successful here. The Warders hadn't been able to counteract the Islanders' poison. In all the years on Blue Isle, the Warders had never found a spell that would act as an antidote.

Their incompetence kept the Fey trapped.

But they were Warders, and they had more talents than the others. The Fey in Shadowlands would listen to them.

Solanda wiped her mouth with one hand, then licked the grease off her palm. Some cat habits never died. She resisted the urge to then wipe her face with that palm, and instead found a pitcher of water. She splashed her face, cleaning it, and stretched.

Time to move again.

She pulled open the door to this section of the Domicile and frowned. Through the buildings, the gray walls of Shadowlands looked darker than usual. She blinked, wondering if she had stared into the fire too long, but her vision didn't clear. It was odd; she hadn't remembered the walls being that dark. But she hadn't looked at them in years.

The Domicile's long porch extended to this end of the wing. She crossed it, then hopped the steps, landing on the firm Shadowlands ground. The ground wasn't any darker than usual. She glanced up again, squinted, but she saw no magick crackling off the walls. They were as they should have been. Magickal creations, not magick themselves.

Then she walked across Shadowlands, passing through the buildings, heading toward the Warders' cabin. Several Fey passed her. She nodded at them, and they nodded in return. She rubbed her eyes once. Perhaps she needed the sleep more than she thought. Her vision was blurry, and everything looked indistinct.

The cabins surrounding her had hedges and flowers painted on their sides. One cabin had an image of the Battle for Nye. She saw the faces of most of this troop in angry assault. They had all looked younger then. They had all been younger. Some of the Foot Soldiers were too old now for a real battle. Had they succeeded in this attack on Blue Isle, they might have retired here, living in the luxury a victory provided.

How angry they must have been to find themselves in this place, in this position.

The Warders' cabin was still toward the back. It too had expanded, with a wing added onto the side for pouches and other spoils of war. Most of the pouches taken from the Second Battle for Jahn had never been touched: the Warders had almost given up in their search for an antidote to holy water. They had, instead, focused on spells to make life in Shadowlands more comfortable.

They had, in a word, become cowards.

She started up the stairs when she froze. A shiver ran down her spine. She glanced back over her shoulder, at space between buildings that the Fey loosely termed a street. It was empty.

All those Fey she had seen before were gone.

She peered through the buildings at Shadowlands' walls.

They were as gray as they had always been.

And the faces had been indistinct.

Dream Riders on the walls. Spies in the streets.

She flung open the door to the Warders' cabin and shouted, "The Black King is here!"

Four Warders sat around the square spell table, but her warning was wasted on them. Dream Riders covered the Warders' faces in shadow, their bodies twitching as the

Riders held their consciousness in thrall. Such a risk the Black King took. Magickal Fey could pull out of a Rider spell—if they discerned that it was a spell. One of the Riders lifted its head off the Warder near the door. The Rider's head was flat, like a shadow, only it had substance. It was black as night, its features completely absorbed by the magick.

But it was peering at her. She could tell from its posture.

She pulled the door closed and turned. Wind stood behind her, his hand extended. "Come back to the house," he said. "You'll be safe there."

His eyes were flecked with gold. It wasn't Wind at all. Wind was no more. This was a Doppelgänger, come to lure her to her death.

She slapped his hand away and jumped off the porch, taking off at full run. Several Spies sat near doorways. They didn't bother to wear faces; that was why they had looked so indistinct. They pointed to her as she ran. Their cries blended into a single shout, all with the same texture and indescribable quality.

When she reached the Circle Door, she found an entire squad of Foot Soldiers diving their way in. Some she recognized: they had served in the Battle of Feire, a decisive victory in the Nye campaign. Rugad's victory.

"You can't kill a Shape-Shifter," she said, holding up her hands to show she had no weapons. "We're too precious to waste."

"You're not a Shifter," Gelô said. He was as slender and dark as he had always been. His eyebrows were a thick bush that met in the middle of his face. "You're a Failure."

"I'm not a Failure," Solanda said, trying to keep the panic from her voice. "Rugar was, and he's dead."

"You cannot blame living in *this* for twenty years on Rugar," Gelô said. "He has been dead fifteen."

"By my hand," Solanda said. "And I did not live here."

Gelô extended a hand. His fingers were as long as knives. The extra set of nails at the tips of his fingers were extended. "You expect me to believe that, Failure?"

She tilted her head. "I'm a *Shifter*, Soldier. I do not stay in one place long."

"Gelô," one of the other Foot Soldiers said, "you might want to consider—"

"Sparing a life? A Failure? Are you soft, Vare?"

Vare, a slender woman with a scar running down one cheek, lowered her gaze.

"No, she's just cautious," Solanda said. She couldn't fight an entire troop of Foot Soldiers herself. "She knows that she shouldn't murder her betters."

"It's not murder when it's ordered by the Black King."

Solanda shrugged. "Then he will not learn of his great-grandchildren, will he?"

"What of his grandchildren?"

Vare brought her gaze up. "Gelô." Her word was a caution.

"There are things he doesn't know, things he needs to know."

"Jewel is dead," Gelô said. "Her brother Bridge is in Nye. None of the others will inherit. This is what I know. This is all I need to know."

"His *great*-grandchildren," Solanda said. Her heart was pounding. This was her only chance. Behind her, muffled footsteps grew. Voices shouted, their sounds dimmed by the dimensions of Shadowlands itself. But there were no sounds of war. Who knew better how to destroy the Fey than the leader of them?

"Rugad knows enough," Gelô said.

"Gelô," Vare said. "You need to listen to her."

"She is trying to save her life," he said.

"Of course I am." Solanda had had enough of him. "But I spent my years outside of Shadowlands raising one of Rugad's great-grandchildren. The least he can do is order my death himself."

"He has," Gelô said.

"Gelô." Vare took his arm. He shook her off.

"Who rules this troop?" he snarled.

She straightened. "I will, if you do not listen. She said children. Great-grandchildren. Rugad is looking for one child."

Solanda resisted the temptation to tilt her head back and smile. Rugad's Vision only went so far. The great Visionary of the Fey only saw one child, and came for that child. The question was, which one?

"He needs me," she said, "and you must tell me where he is."

"I've watched you through a dozen battles, Solanda," Gelô said. "It would have been my pleasure to kill you myself. You think you are the only Fey, that the rest of us are mere pawns to your abilities. You are wrong, and I would have loved to prove it, to flay that skin off you inch by pretty inch."

"But?" she asked sweetly.

"But you are right. The Black King needs to speak with you. And I will take you to him myself when I am finished here."

"I will go on my own," she said.

"You are a Failure," Gelô said. "You are no longer Fey. You cannot go anywhere on your own, let alone to the Black King. In staying here, you have forfeited all rights and privileges you ever enjoyed as a Shifter. Even if you live, you will be no better than a Red Cap."

Heat rushed through her, coloring her face. She didn't care. "You will soon discover that you are wrong," she said. "I killed Rugar, and I guarded the Black King's family. I kept things safe for them until Rugad could arrive. These others deserve to die, but I do not. And when the Black King realizes that you nearly killed me, he will flay *you* inch by inch."

Gelô's eyes narrowed. His jaw worked, but he said nothing.

"We need someone to watch her," Vare said. She had tucked her hands under her armpits, the sign of a Foot Soldier's rising blood lust.

Gelô nodded, and one of the Foot Soldiers broke off from the troop. Solanda watched. Her heart was pounding hard. She could beat anyone, fight any race, except her own. Death by a Foot Soldier's hands would be worse than anything, except perhaps the Islanders' poison.

The small noises had quieted behind her. The rusty stench of blood rose in the enclosed space. She knew how the attack went. It was simple, really: Dream Riders to hold consciousness at bay; Spies to find the alert Fey and to hold them back; and Doppelgängers to take them over. Once the Doppelgängers had done their work, the remaining Fey were doomed. They would trust their friends, who would lead them into a troop like this one, bloodthirsty Foot Soldiers who lived for the slaughter.

A lot of good people would die this day.

The Circle Door opened again. Gelô's troop moved aside. Another troop of Foot Soldiers entered. They passed Solanda without a second glance.

"Rugad begins his invasion by warring on his own people?" Solanda asked.

"They are the only ones that threaten him," Vare said.

"What of the Islander poison?"

"A minor inconvenience," Gelô said. "One easily defeated by competent Warders."

She couldn't argue that. She knew it to be true. A prepared troop and competent Warders would have avoided this debacle altogether.

"You worry for your friends, Solanda?" Gelô asked.

"I worry for us all," she said.

THIRTY-FIVE

THE Sanctuary was large and empty. Titus had lit all the candles, but that made the room seem even emptier. The soft light bathed the pews in gold, flickered on the blade of the large sword hanging down from the ceiling, and caught the diamond edges of the vials containing holy water.

He used to think this place the embodiment of Rocaanism. When he was a young Aud, he thought this room the most magnificent place he ever saw. It smelled of lemons and polished wood. The pews were always clean. No footprints or smudges marred the floor. The carvings on the door were made with such artistry, he knew that God's hand had been at work.

It had been years since he actually looked at this room, this center of the religion, the Great Sanctuary where all the important religious services were held, from Midnight Sacrament to the Absorption Day Service. He had been here often, but had only seen what the Auds missed: a fingerprint on the altar, a glass vial turned in the wrong direction, a candle not burning. It had been decades since he saw the room as a holy place.

He had been sitting in the front pew, staring at the altar,

most of the night. Part of him hoped for God's still small voice to come to him on the wings of the Holy One, advising him how to proceed. He had felt a disquiet ever since Stowe left, as if Titus had walked a path he should have abandoned. If Stowe had been right and the Fey were here, with their Black King and an ability to defeat holy water, Titus needed to be at Nicholas's side. They needed to put away their differences and fight together.

If they fought at all.

The Fiftieth Rocaan had thought the Fey the Soldiers of the Enemy and had tried to reenact the Roca's Absorption, thinking that in doing so, the Fey would somehow vanish from this land. The idea made a curious kind of sense. The Roca had faced an unnamed enemy, an enemy that had taken over Blue Isle. When it became clear that the Roca could not defeat that enemy in battle, he met them in a kirk and sacrificed himself. He did not die, but was Absorbed into the Hand of God, where he brought the petitions of the Islanders to God's ear. The Fiftieth Rocaan believed that he could reenact the Absorption and in so doing drive out the Fey.

He failed.

The Fifty-First Rocaan, Matthias, had no such spiritual beliefs. He thought that if the Fey were to leave, the Islanders had to drive them out. He used holy water with impunity, and he even killed Fey with his own hands.

Titus had first faced the Fey as a boy. His Charge, as a young Aud, was to take a message to the Fey leader. He had done so, refusing on pain of death to remove the small sword from his neck and somehow managing to negotiate with the Fey. The message and the subsequent meeting with the Fiftieth Rocaan and the Fey had led to the Rocaan's death. Titus had seen his enemy in two forms: in their pathetic home in the woods and in their murderous rage.

Both frightened him, but neither overwhelmed him. He did agree with Matthias that these Fey were demons. The Words Written and Unwritten said those claiming God's powers without God's consent were demons, creatures of the netherworld whose only desire was to defeat God in this land. Such a belief was considered archaic now, even though it was in the Words. No one had seen the demons,

and thought it to be a metaphor for those who would sub-
vert God's will. There were still places on the Isle, though,
where those Words held sway: In the Snow Mountains, children born with demon look, demon height, or demon
sparkle were left on the mountainside to die.

It was an old, barbarous custom, and one the Tabernacle
had never been able to prevent.

He gathered his knees to his chin like a young boy would,
and then wrapped his arms around them. In the hours of
staring, waiting, the disquiet hadn't left. Perhaps he had
been too hasty in dismissing Stowe. But Titus had trouble
accepting Nicholas. Nicholas, who had tried to take the
position of Rocaan for himself. Nicholas, who had married
demons and created more demons.

Nicholas, who loved the Fey.

How could a man who had loved Fey fight them?

Yet the position of Rocaan had been created for spiritual
leadership, not to lead warriors into battle. Even though
Matthias had thought the two related, Titus did not. In
that, he was closer to the Fiftieth Rocaan, who believed in
gentleness in all things.

A man who believed in gentleness and a man who loved
the Fey were to fight an invasion force? It could not be done.

But it had to be.

Titus swallowed. The thing he could not stomach, the
thing he had never really had to do, was make holy water as a
weapon. The fighting had been past when he became Rocaan.
He had only made holy water for Midnight Sacrament.

He wasn't certain he could make holy water and then
watch it kill. Through his nightlong reflection, that was
what he had come to. His anger against Stowe had come not
just from his dislike of Nicholas, but also from his fear that
he would be pressed into service, that he would have to use
the most holy of materials to take lives, not save them.

The Fiftieth Rocaan had done so reluctantly. The Fifty-
First had done so with gusto.

Titus would have to do so as well to save the lives of his
people.

But he could do nothing sitting here. If this wasn't a ploy
from the palace to seek power, if it had truly happened, then
he needed to take action.

And that was the conclusion he kept coming to. Perhaps the still small voice didn't speak. Perhaps it nudged. Or perhaps it kept pushing the mind in one direction, never letting the idea pass.

Titus looked up. The sword was a weapon and a symbol of the most holy moment in all of Rocaanism. It symbolized the Roca's sacrifice. When faced with the Soldiers of the Enemy, he had asked his own soldiers to lay down their arms. Then he cleared his sword with holy water. The Soldiers of the Enemy took his sword and ran him through, and he was Absorbed into the Hand of God, where he sat now, watching over his people.

A weapon and a symbol.

Just like holy water was.

Titus had no choice. He was Rocaan. He had to guard his people's spiritual well-being, and sometimes that meant guarding their life. He couldn't trust Nicholas to do it. Nicholas had already shown that he did not understand the importance of the spiritual realm.

Titus had to guard that on his own.

And God had given him a particularly difficult task in doing so. Titus did not see the world as either evil or good. He did not take the extremes of either of his predecessors. He had to work with Nicholas because, at the moment, Nicholas was the best the Roca's line had to offer. Then Titus had to either convince Nicholas to set his children aside, or Titus had to train them. They were part Fey and part Islander. He had been concentrating on the Fey. He needed to concentrate on the Islander, bring out the blood of the Roca within them, and let them fight the spiritual battles within themselves. If the good rose to the surface in just one of Nicholas's children, that would be enough to save the Isle.

The task of bringing that good forth, though, belonged to Titus.

He stood and sighed. For too long, he had been using his youth as an excuse, his odd entrance into the Rocaan's position as a way out of the difficult decisions. At times he had followed the path created by the Fiftieth Rocaan, and at times he had followed the path created by the Fifty-First. He had never really blazed his own trail.

He had never needed to until now.

He picked up the candle snuffer, and starting with the candles near the altar, he put out the flames. Tiny wisps of black smoke rose, filling the air with the scent of wax and singed string. He was stalling, he knew, trying to find a way around going to the palace. An Aud could put out the candles, and Titus could leave immediately. But he really didn't want to enter Nicholas's territory so quickly after the decision. He wanted a moment to change his mind, a chance to rethink things.

As if he hadn't thought of them enough already.

When he finished with the candles, he hung the snuffer on its peg in the back of the Sanctuary and let himself out. He blinked once as he stepped into the corridor. The corridor was dusky dark, as if someone hadn't lit the evening torches yet. But the torches were out. The dawn had come some time ago.

Something was blocking the light.

His two Aud guards stood by the door. They nodded when they saw him. He didn't nod back. Instead, he stepped farther into the hall.

Half a dozen Danites crowded around one window. The windows were narrow slits in this part of the Tabernacle, and the Danites had to pile on top of each other to see. At the next window, another group of Danites stood, and another all the way along.

"Is there a problem?" he asked, and the Danites closest to him jumped. One held his finger to his lips.

"Look, Holy Sir," he said. "A miracle."

"A miracle," Titus said softly, "and no one thought to get me?"

The Danite flushed. The others stepped silently away from the window. Titus walked forward and peered through the slit.

Animals sat in the courtyard. Hundreds of animals. They lined themselves in neat rows: small cats formed the first row. They sat, their paws neatly before them, and stared at the Tabernacle. Behind the cats, a row of dogs. They also sat at attention, heads forward, paws down. Behind them, wolves, and behind them, even larger cats, larger than any Titus had ever seen. It was the creatures in the back that startled him, though. Black, gray, brown, they towered over the others, and stood on their hind legs like men. They had massive front paws, with long sharp claws. Their faces seemed dog-like, with a long snout and tiny eyes, only they didn't look like dogs. They didn't look like any creatures he had ever seen. They too were silent, staring at the Tabernacle, as if waiting.

"How long has this been going on?" Titus asked.

"Since dawn," the Danite said.

"And no one thought to get me?"

"At first no one could find you, Holy Sir, and when they did locate you, you were in meditation, and you had asked not to be disturbed."

Titus's heart was pounding hard against his chest. *They could be right,* he told himself. *It could be a miracle.*

He picked up the skirts of his robe and hurried up the stairs, taking them two at a time. It was as if he rose in the ranks of the Tabernacle as he did so: Auds and Danites stared out the windows on the first three levels, and Officiates crowded the windows on the fourth.

The corridors on the fifth were empty. The Elders had their own rooms. Titus hurried to his. He pulled open the double doors, crossed the living area, and went onto the balcony.

There he stopped.

The animals formed a barrier between the Tabernacle and the road, the Tabernacle and the river, the Tabernacle and the rest of Jahn. The streets were empty, the bridge was empty, even this early in the morning.

A group of horses were galloping along one of the side roads. The riders on their backs wore no uniforms. In fact, they wore no shirts at all. They were male and female.

And Fey.

Titus's mouth was dry.

He glanced down at the animals below and realized that from the ground level, he had missed something.

All of them had riders on their backs. Tiny Fey on the backs of the cats, and large Fey on the backs of the giant hairy creatures.

Fey everywhere.

Fey staring at the Tabernacle.

Fey waiting.

For what? A command?

He glanced at the river, and saw creatures coming out the other side. Long flat creatures that looked like snakes with legs, with snouts big enough to eat a man. Their tails thrashed as they moved into the city.

Fey sat on their backs as well.

"My God," he whispered, understanding now his own feeling of disquiet.

He had been wrong. The Fey were here, and this time they were determined to win.

THIRTY-SIX

MATTHIAS started awake, wincing at the pain in his chest and shoulders. His eyes were gummed together, and his mouth tasted of cotton. He blinked the sleep out, then frowned, trying to pinpoint what had awakened him.

Something was different.

The candle had burned down to the end of its wick. The light was flickering. The room was dark because it had no windows. He peered through the open door. The candle still burned beside the tapestry frame, but Marly wasn't in her chair.

He leaned up on one elbow, frowning as the skin pulled on his wounds. With his right hand, he rubbed the sleep out of his eyes. His fingers came away gummy. He should have bathed after falling in the river. Who knew what sort of debris had been floating in there?

A rustle in the other room caught his attention. He pushed the blankets back. He was naked except for the bandages. His thin legs looked spindly in the dim light. Bruises ran along his thighs and calves. The Fey had kicked him when she tried to drown him.

He was lucky to be alive.

A panel moved beside the fireplace. Matthias pulled the blanket to his waist and looked for his pants. He couldn't see them. His heart was pounding. He didn't know how much energy he would have.

He didn't know how much he would need.

With a slight grinding sound, the panel slid open. Marly stepped out. He must have heard her go in. That had to be what had awakened him.

But that didn't feel right.

When she saw him, she put a finger to her lips. He nodded. Then she propped the door open with a brick and grabbed a basket from beside the fireplace.

"There are men's clothes beside the bed," she whispered. "I had hoped ta clean yers, but there isna time."

What kind of woman kept men's clothes beside her bed? He wasn't certain he wanted to know. He tried to slide off the bed, still holding the blanket in place.

"We dunna have time for modesty," she said. "Hurry."

He didn't have the energy for it, either. He let the blanket fall away. He crouched, his weak legs trembling with the effort. If he had wondered how close to death he had been, he had an answer now. Simply getting out of bed and crouching was too much for him.

"Hurry," she said again.

There were several wooden chests between the bed and the wall. The chests were lying on their sides. He pulled one open and took a soft blue shirt and tan breeches that tied at the waist. Then he grabbed a pair of fabric shoes, which were beside the bed.

"Hurry!"

He was hurrying. He stood, swayed and almost fell.

"Ye dunna have time ta dress," she said. "Get in here."

He carried the clothes across the room, ignoring his own dizziness. Then he put a hand on the mantel and nearly toppled through the open panel. She caught him, kicked the brick aside and let the panel swing shut.

The darkness was complete. He had never been anywhere that dark.

She took his hand. "Ye'll need ta be quiet," she said. "When we're past the main section of tunnel, I'll light a lantern. Til then, we have ta go in the darkness."

"Can I dress?" he asked, not certain he could carry the clothes and walk at the same time.

"Hurry," she said.

Her hand left his. He missed the warmth. He leaned against the hot wall, the one that was part of the fireplace, and pulled on his breeches. Then he slid the shirt over his head. He had never felt material so soft.

The shoes were also soft, but they covered his feet, and the hard soles protected him from whatever he was going to walk on. When he finished, he groped in the darkness for her. His fingers brushed the rich fabric of her dress. She caught his hand with her own.

Her fingers were warm and dry. Their grip was sound. She led him through the darkness, slow step by slow step, supporting him once or twice as he swayed.

Since he couldn't see and he couldn't talk, he focused on the moment that he had awakened. The odd sense that something was wrong. The sense hadn't come from anything in the room, even if the panel had grated. It had come from outside.

Outside.

The feeling of outside had changed.

He had noticed that before years ago, when he was still in the Tabernacle. He had felt it in Jahn as well. The feeling that someone had come into his home, that a person who didn't belong had touched his things. He had shrugged the feeling off. He no longer had a home, and he really didn't have things. He had been without possessions or a place to lay his head since he left the Tabernacle fifteen years before.

But the feeling was stronger now.

It resembled the feeling he had in that dream, the one the Dream Rider had given him when the Fey had tried to kill him. The feeling of something horribly, horribly out of place.

His heartbeat increased. He really didn't know this woman. She said she had saved him, but how could he know that for certain? And why would she have a tunnel beside her house?

Yet the feelings he was getting didn't come from her. They came from outside.

She wasn't Fey. He would have known it. The Fey had a

distinctive sense to them, one he had become attuned to long ago.

But she was different. He had met a lot of those women who embroidered for the court. They had squinty eyes and pinched mouths and an air of bitterness about them. They never looked like Marly, and they never had her air of self-assurance.

The path they were on sloped downhill. Matthias put his free hand out and touched the wall. It was made of stone. Damp stone. Someone had put a lot of work into this tunnel.

Then it veered sharply to the right. Marly slowed as she walked, holding him back. The path's steepness grew even sharper. Matthias was growing lightheaded. He felt odd. His wounds ached, and his bruises made him stiff. Yet his body didn't feel like his own. He felt detached from it, as far away as he could get.

He supposed that was a way of holding off pain, of keeping himself upright and moving.

They rounded another sharp corner. A light glowed at the far end of the tunnel, and he heard voices. The voices sounded ringing and hollow. He was hearing echoes.

". . . column fifteen across. Dunno how deep . . ."

". . . past Killeny's Bridge . . ."

". . . some come outta the woods on the west side a town as if they was waitin there."

". . . from that Shadowlands? . . ."

". . . Dunno. Dunno how many was in there. . . ."

". . . never seemed like this many, though. . . ."

The voices were all male. As he got closer, the wall was covered with a slimy moss, and the smell of the river grew. The light got brighter, and the tunnel widened.

Marly had a firm grip on his arm. Her brows were furrowed with concentration. She stepped gingerly along the path, as if she were looking out for puddles.

Then they went through an arch, and Matthias found himself in a large underground cavern. It seemed, at first, to be a natural structure, but he had never heard of caves near the rivers. The ground was too flat for it. There were caves all along the rim of Blue Isle, but none in the middle. Then, as he peered closer, he realized that the walls and the ceiling were lined with stone. It was old and moss-covered, making it look natural. Water dripped not too far from here, and he wondered how stable the cavern was.

The space was a larger version of the catacombs beneath the Tabernacle and, from the looks of it, had been built around the same time.

A dozen men sat on crates in the middle of the cavern. Lanterns were spaced around the crates and near the ceiling on the far end, torches flared in holders. The stone above them was blackened.

"Marly." The man on the right stood. He was stocky, his face soot-darkened, his hair plastered in mud. "Bout time, girl. We was about ta get ye."

"Sure ye were," she said. "N pigs swim."

She pulled Matthias into the light.

"Couldn't just leave yer lordly charge," she said.

This man who had spoken rolled his eyes. "If'n I knew twas ta be this kinda night, I'da never brung him to ye."

"Too late." Her tone had a false cheerfulness to it.

"Ye shoulda left him above, Marly." The man who spoke was leaning against the wall, a blade of river grass between his teeth.

"Aye, Marls." A third man spoke. He was trim and lanky, his blond hair shining in the lantern light. "Ye know what ye brung us, mmm? Certain death, he is."

Matthias's dizziness was overpowering. He swayed. Marly grabbed him tighter. "Help me get him ta the blankets," she said.

Two of the men who hadn't spoken grabbed his arms and carried him forward, pulling his feet off the ground, and then setting him on a pile of blankets.

"N where're we ta sleep, Marly?" the first man asked.

"Here, Jakib," she said. "Just like we planned."

"I don't need anything special," Matthias said. His voice quivered.

"Let's kill him now n be done with it," the third man said.

"Stop," Marly said. "He's hurt and he's na threat to ye."

"Aye, but he is, Marls," the third man said. "Ye dunno what ye have there."

"N what do I have here, Yasep? Besides a man who needs me help?"

"The Fifty-First Rocaan." Yasep crossed his arms and leaned back against a crate. "The man what killed most of the Fey. The man what killed the Fey prisoner fifteen years back. The man what killed the Demon Queen."

Matthias looked up at the man. Yasep had squarish features and round eyes a cold ice blue. His clothes were as tattered as the others' but not as filthy. His shirt still had traces of white.

Matthias didn't recognize him, but that meant nothing. This Yasep could have attended services. Or he could simply have been one of those people who paid close attention to the world around him.

Of that, actually, Matthias had no doubt.

"Naw," Jakib was saying. "The Fifty-First Rocaan is dead. Murdered in the Tabernacle he was by the Fifty-Second Rocaan."

Matthias took a deep breath. If he was going to die tonight, it might as well be now. "Actually," he said, "Titus would never kill anyone. It was my own hesitation in appointing him my successor."

"Lor." Marly breathed the word. She crouched beside him and took his injured face gently in her hands. Then she turned it from side to side and touched his graying curls. "I seen ye in all yer finery years ago, Holy Sir, and ye was never this thin or this finely edged."

"Don't call me Holy Sir," Matthias said. "I'm not Rocaan any more."

"I dinna know a man could stop bein Beloved a God," the second man said.

"Shush, Denl," Jakib said.

Denl shrugged. "Tis what the Auds taught me."

"Dunna matter," Yasep said. "We need ta kill him."

"No," Marly said. "I do what ye all wan when ye wan it, but I tol ye years ago na help ye kill and I will na use me talents ta harm. Tis again what I am."

"Ye dunna have ta do it, Marls, but we canna let him stay here." Yasep sounded quite certain of himself. "And we canna let him go, knowin where we are."

Matthias had no more energy to defend himself. In a hand-to-hand fight, he would lose quickly and easily. His heart was pounding, though.

Marly leaned against him, protecting him with her body. "Ye'll na kill him. Ye have no reason."

"I got plenty reason," Yasep said. "The Fey hate him. They hate him more'n any other man. Tis one a their best he killed and they willna forget it."

"Maybe we can use him," Denl said. He glanced at Matthias, his face pale. "Ye know, trade him."

"Tis well known the Fey dunna keep their bargains," one of the other men said.

"I dunna see why ye have ta kill him," Marly said. "Tis serious wounded he is. He'll do ye no harm."

"Ha ye na been listening, woman?" Yasep said. "He's the hated enemy a all Fey. And who is it we be hidin from, huh? Tweren't for this place, we'd be fightin fer our lives as we speak."

"They willna find him here."

"Can ye be sure a that?" Yasep said. "They got powers, they do."

Matthias swallowed. He wasn't following all of this. But he had an idea. And it sent chills down his back. "They've got powers," he said, forcing himself to sit up. He swayed with dizziness. He gripped the edge of the blankets to steady himself. "But they've wanted me for fifteen years, and never found me. Their powers don't extend to finding someone who wants to be hidden."

"See?" Marly said. She put a hand on his shoulder, and stopped his swaying.

"I would think that instead of killing me you would want my help," he said. "I don't know the situation—Marly hasn't told me—but I've killed Fey, as you know, and I've hidden from them successfully. I would think that I'm someone you'd want beside you in a battle against the Fey instead of one you'd want to get rid of."

"I dunno about the others," Denl said, "but I dunna like ta be in the presence a someone who's abandoned God. Beg pardon, Holy Sir."

Jakib snorted. Yasep shook his head. One of the other men stifled a giggle.

"Tis not a laughin matter," Marly said. "Denl believes. Ye can respect that."

The men stopped, heads down as if they were suppressing their mirth.

Matthias's grip on the blankets tightened. He had to stay conscious, and he had to argue for himself. It was the only chance he saw of staying alive.

"I did not abandon God," Matthias said. "I stepped down from a position I should never have held in the first place. The Fiftieth Rocaan was murdered. He never expected that, nor did he expect me to truly become Rocaan. My presence would have destroyed Rocaanism. I left because I love God and the Church, not because I abandoned it."

"Lor." The man who spoke sat in half darkness toward the back of the crates. His face was lined with fatigue and his hair was stringy. His clothes were so filthy that Matthias could smell them. "The Fifty-First Rocaan telling us why he dinna stay in his post. Tis odd things these days bring."

"Aye, tis," Yasep said. "But tis truly none a our concern. We canna care for ye, religious one, nor can we ha ye here. Them Fey'll—"

"What about the Fey?" Matthias asked. "What's changed?"

The men glanced at each other. Marly's hand tightened on his shoulder.

"I dinna tell him," she said. "Twas na time."

"Latse," Yasep said, nodding toward the filthy man in the back, "twas near Killeny's Bridge just afore dawn. He seen—"

"I seen," Latse said loudly, obviously determined to tell it himself, "Fey coming out a the side roads as if they'n been there a while. They joined up on the south end a the Bridge n marched across, fifteen to a row, rows n rows deep. Me n the horse twas under a bridge—"

"You have a horse?" Matthias asked. Very few Islanders had horses. Most of the ones who did were gentry.

"Aye," Latse said. He glanced at the others. Yasep crossed his arm and waited for Latse to continue. "They dinna see me. But it took em a good long time ta march across. I took the horse, and went along a path I know—tis the old Aud's path what winds—"

"I know it," Matthias said. He'd walked it enough in his youth, during his own years as an Aud.

"Well," Latse said. "I come inta Jahn ahead of em, but

they's already Fey here. Tiny ones riding other animals. And more coming, from the skies and outta hiding places. Some're on the streets and at first they have faces, and then the faces shimmer and become nothing. Twas scary."

"He came to me," Yasep said. "But—"

"I'd already come," Denl said. "I seen Fey comin in from the woods on the west side a town. Them big Fey, the ones what can pull skin off with their fingers."

"Jakib sent word ta me," Marly said, "n that's when I brung ye here."

Matthias blinked, trying to absorb the information. Fey, invading Jahn again, not from the river this time, nor really from the Shadowlands, but from the south.

The feeling he'd had for weeks.

Somehow the Fey had arrived from the south. The question was, who were these Fey? The reinforcements so long feared? Or the Fey who'd always been on the Isle?

Not that it mattered. What mattered first was saving his own life.

He sighed. He only had one thing to bargain with. He had to use it. "I know how to make holy water," he said.

"Ye make it?" Denl asked. "I thought twas the Rocaan's blessing twas what made it holy."

Matthias shook his head. "There's a procedure. I can do it."

"Twoud be blasphemy," Denl said.

"Aye," Latse said. "but twould save our hides."

"He's evil, that one," Denl said. "He's only tryin ta save his own hide."

"Yes, I am," Matthias said. "Wouldn't you in my shoes?"

"A man a God should be trustin God," Denl said.

"A man of God," Matthias said in a voice he hadn't used since he was Rocaan, "shouldn't take God for granted."

The cavern was silent. One of the men shifted slightly, rocking back and forth on his feet. Marly eased her arm around Matthias, supporting his back. His entire body hurt. Black spots danced in front of his eyes, but he wouldn't let himself pass out.

He couldn't.

Finally Yasep turned away. "Still n all," he said, "I dunna think ye can stay with us. Ye'll have ta take him back up, Marly."

"She will na," Jakib said. "Tain't safe up there."

"Yer sister dunna ha ta go in," Yasep said. "She just has ta open the panel."

"And show em where we're at."

"They willna come in a empty building," Yasep said. "They dinna afore."

"Afore they dinna ha so many soldiers," Denl said. "They'll use empty buildings."

"And they'll know someone was in that un," Marly said. "I dinna hide the fact that we just left."

"She canna go," Jakib said.

Matthias had had enough. His body would quit on him soon whether he wanted it to or not. He had to do something.

He took a deep breath, and used the last of his strength. "Why are you afraid of me, Yasep?"

"I'm afraid a no man," Yasep said.

"I can help you. I can make holy water. I can save all our lives. I have defeated more Fey than you've seen, and you still want me out of your life. Why?" Matthias put all his strength in his voice. He sounded authoritarian, even to his own ears.

Yasep licked his lips. He glanced at the others. They all watched him, eyes glowing in the latern light. "Yer tall," he said.

"So?" Matthias said, hating the charge.

"Tis said only a demon can defeat a demon."

"Lor," Marly said. "He's from the Cliffs a Blood. It dinna make him a demon."

"He's tall," Yasep said again.

Marly opened her mouth, but Matthias brought up a hand and covered hers, hoping to silence her. "I am not a demon," he said. "I cannot control how I'm built or the circumstances of my birth. But you may believe what you want. If you take me for a demon, so be it."

"Dunna say that," Marly hissed.

He ignored her. "The point is, I'm a demon who is offering to help you."

"At the price a yer own life," Yasep said. He had his arms crossed, but the fingers of his right hand drummed on his upper arm.

"I believe the Fey do not belong on Blue Isle," Matthias

said. "I believe they are the Soldiers of the Enemy mentioned in the Words Written and Unwritten."

He looked at Denl as he said that. Denl looked away.

"I believe that we, like the Roca, must do all within our power to drive them out of Jahn and off the Isle. I tried to do that as Rocaan, but discovered too much opposition. I'm doing the work now, in my own way. The Fey did this to me." He ran a hand over his bandaged face. "I have fought them and will continue to fight them until I can no longer take a breath."

His voice resembled through the cavern. Marly had turned so that she could see him. This time no one else moved at all.

"You know who I am, but I do not know who any of you are. I suspect you do not want me to know. That's fine. I know about the ring of thieves operating through Jahn, appearing and disappearing at a whim, never getting caught. These caverns would make a nice escape tunnel."

Marly tensed beside him.

"It's a brilliant scheme, but it's one that doesn't matter any more if what you say about the Fey is true. It doesn't matter anyway. I haven't been particular about my friends since I left the Tabernacle. I don't care who you are or what you do as long as you fight Fey."

"If ye stay, ye'll not lead us," Yasep said.

Finally, he gave voice to his real fear. Matthias smiled. The movement of his lips pulled the skin on his face, and he winced. "I can barely sit up," he said. "I certainly cannot lead a group of people I've never met before."

Yasep nodded. "Tis settled, then."

"How's it settled?" Marly asked. "Ye'll na kill him as he sleeps."

"Na," Yasep said. "He'll stay here, with us, until the fightin ends or the Fey finds us. N when our holy water is gone, he'll make us more."

"How much holy water do you have?" Matthias asked.

"Yer lookin at it," Jakib said, sweeping his hands toward the crates.

Matthias stifled his whistle of amazement. If he'd had suspicions of this troop's illegal activities before, he had confir-

mation of it now. There should never be this much holy
water outside of the Tabernacle.

It was odd to steal holy water.

Unless you were afraid of the Fey and afraid that no one
would defend you.

"It'll be a while before you need me, then," Matthias said.

"Aye," Yasep said.

"Good." Matthias let himself sway. "In that case, I hope
don't mind if I pass out."

And then, before they had a chance to reply, he leaned
into Marly and let the darkness take him.

THIRTY-SEVEN

TITUS whirled away from the window. He hurried back through his chamber, nearly tripping over the ornate furniture, his heart pounding.

Fey, surrounding the Tabernacle, coming into the city. It was the invasion all over again. Only this time he was Rocaan. This time, he was in charge of holy water.

Of the only thing that could help the Islanders survive.

He burst through the doors of his apartments and looked for an Aud in the hallway. Anyone. But the hallway was empty. The night's torches still burned.

He knew where he would find people. Near the windows. Thinking they were looking at a miracle.

He hurried down the corridor and took the steps at the end two at a time. The effort jolted his knees. He was horribly out of shape, which surprised him. In his mind, he wasn't much older than the nineteen-year-old who had become Rocaan.

At the window on the landing, five Officiates stood. Titus grabbed the arm of Lindo. His plush black robe flared as he turned. Lindo was an older Officiate, one who had never made the cut to Elder, but served well in this capacity. His narrow eyes widened when he saw Titus.

"It's a miracle, Holy Sir," he said.

Titus didn't have time to argue with him. "Get the Elders in my suite immediately. Then I want everyone away from the windows, and I want the doors sealed. Double-check the supply of holy water, and then report to me."

"Holy Sir—"

"Oh," Titus said, "Open the catacombs below and stock them with as many supplies as you can find. Including holy water."

"Holy Sir, what?"

"That's not a miracle," Titus said. "That's the Fey. Now get busy."

The other Officiates turned at that news. They looked confused. Rusel was among them. His portly frame shook. "Holy Sir, if that's the Fey—"

"Then we don't have much time," Titus said.

"Shouldn't we just pour holy water on them? Stop them before they do anything?"

"Have they threatened us?" Titus asked. "From my understanding, they've just been sitting there most of the morning."

"Yes, Holy Sir."

"Well, then, we can't really attack. We are supposed to have a truce with them, remember?"

Without waiting for a response, he hurried back up the stairs. The door to his apartments stood open, as he had left it. He went inside, heart pounding. Rusel had a good suggestion. Just attack. But Titus couldn't. Matthias would have been able to. But Titus knew God's strictures and abided by them. *A man is only as good as his word,* said the Words Written and Unwritten in one section. Then, in another, they said, *A promise broken is a trust forsaken.* And then, again, it said, *A promise is a man's solemn oath between himself, another, and God.*

Matthias might have been able to break his promises and sever his relationship with God. Titus could not.

When he reached the inside of his apartments, he made himself stop and catch his breath. He leaned on one of the velvet couches, and it slid. He caught it, and held on. His life had suddenly become impossible. He had to prepare for an attack without allowing his people to attack. And he had to protect them. He also had to listen to whatever the Fey had to say.

He suspected they had something to tell him. Otherwise, why surround the Tabernacle? Why not just invade?

He went to the balcony, gripped the wooden railing, and looked out. None of the creatures had moved. He went back inside, grabbed the double doors, and pulled them closed.

Sunlight seeped in around the edges of the doors. And still came in through the windows. He grabbed each tapestry and let it roll down. The Fey would know that something had changed. Instead of being watched, they would see that the doors were being locked, the windows shuttered.

He needed to get a message to Nicholas. If there was trouble here, there would be some at the palace as well. He peeked his head out the door. Rusel stood beside it, a silent sentinel.

"You're my guard?" Titus asked. Titus would do better guarding himself. Rusel couldn't fight. He could barely run.

Rusel shrugged. "Until we can clear the windows," he said. "It is an Officiate's job to fill in."

"Well," Titus said, "you'll need to fill in elsewhere. I need an Aud and I need him quickly."

Rusel nodded. "At once, Holy Sir." He spun and headed down the hall, his black robe swirling behind him.

The mood had shifted in the Tabernacle. He could feel it. No longer did they see this as a miracle, but as a crisis. His own attitude had changed it. Now he had to prevent a panic.

He went back into his rooms. He had a store of holy water in a cabinet built into the wall between his bedroom and his main living quarters. Matthias had ordered that during his tenure as Rocaan. The Auds kept it stocked. Titus pulled it open. Row after row of green vials glittered. There was enough here to keep him and the Elders supplied for a while at least. He knew that the Elders had similar cabinets in their rooms. The dormitories were stocked, as was the Servant's Chapel, the rooms behind it, and the Sanctuary.

A drop of holy water could kill a Fey.

The Tabernacle was protected. At least for the moment.

A knock sounded on the door. Titus pulled it open. Porciluna stood outside. His girth had increased over the years. Now he couldn't walk the steps without breaking into a sweat. His black robe hung on his stomach as if it were a table. He wore his red sash around his neck because it slipped from his waist.

"The animals have Fey on them," Porciluna said, mopping his brow with a white cloth.

"When did you notice?"

"I didn't even know they were outside until Lindo appeared at my door." Porciluna's small eyes darted back and forth. "I was in my studies."

Or sleeping or indulging in something that Titus didn't want to think about. When Titus became Rocaan, Porciluna lost all interest in the religious aspects of the Tabernacle. Some of the other Elders suspected that Porciluna had only done his duties for show anyway, while he waited to be appointed Rocaan. He had been bitterly disappointed when the Fiftieth Rocaan had appointed Matthias. Porciluna had been angry when Matthias left the Secrets with Titus, and when Titus decided to hold them himself.

Titus stepped away from his door. "The others will be here momentarily."

"I don't think now is the time to hold a meeting," Porciluna said. He breathed heavily as if each word were an effort.

"Nonetheless," Titus said. He left the door open and resisted the urge to peer down the hallway to see if anyone else was coming.

Rusel approached, an Aud in tow. The Aud looked no more than thirteen. His face was filthy and his feet were dark with dirt. Titus wondered if he had looked like that when the Fiftieth Rocaan had given him his Charge.

"Thank you," Titus said to Rusel, dismissing him by tone.

Rusel nodded, then backed away. As he started to leave, Porciluna peeked his head out the door. "I believe we should have Auds up here. With holy water."

Titus bit back annoyance. Rusel, to his credit, looked at Titus. Titus nodded. Porciluna went back inside.

Titus took the Aud's arm and brought him in as well.

The fabric of his robe was coarse, and he smelled faintly of sweat. "What's your name, son?" Titus asked.

"Constantine," the boy whispered. He kept his head down. "After that old King."

So the boy came from an upper-class family. His accent showed it, and his name confirmed it.

"I prefer Con." The boy said in the face of Titus's silence.

"Con it is, then," Titus said. "Listen, Con, I have a Charge for you. But it is risky, and it might cost you your life."

Con kept his head down. The back of his skull was a mass of dirty blond curls.

"He's giving you an out, boy," Porciluna said. "A way to save yourself."

"It's an Aud's duty to do what his Rocaan asks," Con said, looking at Porciluna sideways.

Score one for the educated young man. Titus suppressed a smile. He put a hand on the boy's shoulder. "Are you familiar with the catacombs beneath the Tabernacle?"

The boy finally raised his head. His eyes were the clearest blue Titus had ever seen. His skin was rosy and unblemished. He was beautiful, the kind of beauty that made breath stop in the throat.

"No, Holy Sir," Con said.

"Porciluna," Titus said, "would you get the map? It's in the drawer in my bedside table."

"You can explain—"

"We'll need it for the meeting you don't want, as well," Titus said.

Porciluna sighed heavily and made his way into the bedroom. His breathing was stentorian and, this time, Titus suspected, mostly faked.

Titus led the boy deeper into the room. "There are ancient catacombs under the Tabernacle," he said. "In fact, they go under most of Jahn. They link the Tabernacle and the palace—or at least, that is what they were designed for, in the days of the Thirteenth Rocaan."

"Beg pardon, Holy Sir, but I don't see how that's possible, what with the river between." The boy managed to look solemn and frightened at the same time.

"It is a marvel of engineering," Porciluna said as he

emerged from the bedroom. The map was rolled up in his right hand. "They built a secret passage through Jahn Bridge."

"I'd send you above ground," Titus said, "but I have a bad feeling about these Fey below. They've never liked us. They may be gathered outside the Tabernacle for a perfectly innocent reason, and then again, they may not. We have no real way of knowing what else is going on in the city. We might be the only ones in this situation. We cannot wait for the King to get word. We must send it ourselves."

"You want me to speak to the King, Holy Sir?" The boy's voice squeaked.

"Yes, Con, I do. You need to warn him about what's happening here, and you need to do it quickly."

Another Elder, Reece, came to the door. Reece was thin and nervous, accenting the long lines of his face. Titus waved him in. Reece glanced at Con, frowned, and walked around him.

Porciluna spread the map on one of Titus's end tables. He used votive candle holders to keep the ends in place. "Here, son," Porciluna said, his voice soft. Titus couldn't believe Porciluna was helping. The vision of the Fey on the backs of those creatures must have spooked him as well. "This map is old, but it does show the path."

Con glanced at Titus. Titus led the boy to the table. Reece followed, looking confused.

The map was brittle. The catacombs were painted with a thin brush as a single black line. The ground above was marked with an ink pen, and the river was painted as well. Most of the building landmarks, with the exception of the palace, the Tabernacle, and the bridge, were gone.

"He'll need to take this with him," Porciluna said. "The catacombs branch. The last thing we want is for him to get lost."

"I heard," a voice said from the door, "that when you are heading toward the bridge, you should always walk toward the sound of the water."

Titus turned. Linus stood there. He was one of the older Elders, a man who had been in the Tabernacle for a very long time. His blond hair was cut in a bowl shape, which had the effect of making his round face seem even rounder.

"Have you been below?" Titus asked.

Linus shook his head. "I know only one person who has been in the catacombs, and I don't think we can ask him about them."

From his tone, Titus knew who he was talking about. Matthias.

"Take water of your own, boy," Reece said. "It'll be thirsty work going through that dust."

"And food," Porciluna added.

"And holy water," Titus said softly.

Porciluna rolled up the map and handed it to the boy. "The entrance to the catacombs is on the first floor where the old kirk connects to the newer Tabernacle."

"Near the Servant's Chapel," Titus said, "across from the damaged portrait of the Tenth Rocaan." He untied his keys from his sash and removed a long one with a heart-shaped head. "The door is small and wooden. This key will open it."

"Have him take mine," Reece said. "You might need yours, Holy Sir."

Titus smiled his gratitude, and put the key back on the ring. With a shaking hand, Con took Reece's key, then tucked the map under his arm.

"After I've spoken to the King, Holy Sir, what do you want me to do?"

"Return if you can," Titus said.

The boy nodded. He turned and bowed his head as he walked to the door.

"Con," Titus said, "God will be with you."

The boy looked up, smiled, and for a moment, the entire world seemed to bask in his beauty. Then he slipped out the door as Elder Vaughn slipped in. Vaughn stared after the boy as if he didn't understand what he saw.

He probably didn't.

"He may not make it," Reece said. "No one's been in those tunnels in generations."

Titus shrugged. "We do what we can. His trip might be moot."

Two other Elders, Timothy and Ilim, entered. These Elders were all serving the church when Matthias was Rocaan. They had all been in contention when Matthias left. Titus hadn't trusted any of them in this post.

He still didn't.

Fedo was the only other Elder remaining from that period. Elder Eirman died of apoplexy four years before.

Fedo entered, followed by Catton, Ury, and Hume, the Elders that Titus had chosen. Catton was older than the others, an Officiate who had long assumed he would never become Elder. In some ways, he reminded Titus of the Fiftieth Rocaan, especially in his short balding build, his balding head, and his reliance on the spiritual side of the Tabernacle.

Ury was younger than Titus, still in his twenties, and his progression through the Tabernacle ranks had been swift. He was slender and strong, with a young man's body and intelligent eyes. He was cunning and had few beliefs, but he was supportive of Titus. Titus needed him to balance Porciluna—or so he had thought when Eirman died.

Hume was the deserving one. He was small, hunched and about Titus's age, which made him one of the younger men in the room. He was bald except for some curls on the base of his skull, curls that one Elder in a moment of unkindness had called fringe. Hume had served the Tabernacle with distinction. He was a scholar who understood the Words and who took Eirman's place in recording the oral histories, but he was also a believer who rose before dawn every morning to find a quiet time with the Holy One and with God.

"I need to send one of you down to speak to these Fey," Titus said without preamble. "It's dangerous. There is a possibility they could kill the messenger. For that reason, I can't go—no one else knows the secrets—and I can't send an Aud. The Fey have been on the Isle long enough to know the Tabernacle's hierarchies. I cannot insult them by sending the wrong person. It has to be an Elder, and it has to be one who is not afraid of them. He has to go without holy water. They can't think he's armed."

"That's suicide," Porciluna muttered.

"Perhaps," Titus said. "I hope it is simply a first phase in a negotiation."

The Elders glanced at each other. No one stepped forward.

"I do not have much time. They haven't made any moves, but I don't know what they're waiting for."

"Whatever it is, it can't be pretty," Linus said. "They've got us surrounded."

Titus clasped his hands behind his back. Still none of his Elders said anything.

"That young Aud," Titus said, "accepted his Charge without argument. None of you have his courage? The courage of a boy of thirteen?"

"I'll go," Reece said. "I can talk with them, and I have a physical reaction to holy water. It's not as severe as theirs, but it could be seen as a bond."

"I don't want you to discover their life's story," Titus said. "Just find out why they've gathered below."

"All right, Holy Sir." Reece bowed, then backed out of the room. As he did, Lindo entered.

"You asked about the holy water supply, Holy Sir?" Lindo said.

Titus nodded. They needed that information before continuing.

"We have two thousand bottles scattered throughout the Tabernacle, and five barrels in the storeroom."

"We'll need more," Porciluna said.

Titus ignored him. "Thank you, Lindo," he said. "And what of the other matters?"

"We are moving supplies into the catacombs, but it is slow going, Holy Sir. The stairs have rotted away. One of the Danites constructed a rope ladder, but it is difficult to get things down it."

"I'm certain that you will prevail," Titus said, not caring about the difficulties. "Thank you for your report."

Lindo nodded at the acknowledgment, then bowed and left. Porciluna waited until he was out of the room before speaking. "You're filling the catacombs? Who is going to go below?"

"No one, I hope," Titus said.

"But what are you thinking?"

"I'm thinking that the Fey may have a legitimate reason for being here. That's why I sent Reece to them. If they don't want to see us on peaceful terms, then we are in trouble. They will try to destroy us."

"Hence the holy water supplies," Linus said.

Titus didn't acknowledge that. He didn't really want to think about it.

"But there are a lot of animals below," Titus said. "More than I could count. And I am afraid that they might overpower us no matter what we do. Then we use the catacombs."

"If we do that, the Fey will follow," Linus said.

Titus shrugged. "That's a risk we'll have to take. The catacombs are our last resort."

Porciluna placed his hands across his stomach. "If that's the case, it seems odd to me that you're preparing for it now."

Titus glared at him. He'd never be able to convince Porciluna. Never. "That's it," he said. "You're dismissed. Make sure that everyone under you is well supplied with holy water, and keep away from the windows."

The Elders glanced at him, as if they couldn't believe his sudden burst of temper. He wasn't certain he could believe it either. But after a rocky start, he'd finally reached an equilibrium with his office, an equilibrium that had lasted nearly a decade. Now he felt as if he were tossed into a murky area, an area he never wanted to walk again.

"Hume, stay, please," Titus said.

The other Elders slowly made their way out the door. Porciluna paused at it, as if he had more to say, but Titus just glared at him. Porciluna left.

Titus went to the door and pushed it closed. Then he leaned on it, feeling the ridged surface of the designs against his back. "We have finally come to it," he said.

Hume sat on the arm of a plush chair. He still hunched, as if he were trying to see the ground. "Holy water."

Titus nodded. "We have enough to start an attack if we need to, but not to sustain it, not with those numbers out there. But this time I know if I make it, I make it as a weapon and not as an instrument of the religion."

"There is precedent," Hume said, "The Fiftieth Rocaan did so in the first Fey invasion."

"Under Matthias's guidance."

"Nonetheless," Hume said. "The Fiftieth Rocaan was his own man. He would not have made the choice if he had not believed in it."

Titus sighed. "I don't believe in it," he said. "I don't

believe that our place in this religion is to kill people. The Roca showed that by setting down his sword."

"He didn't set down his sword, Holy Sir. He cleaned it and gave it to the Soldiers of the Enemy. That could be interpreted as an act which showed that sometimes killing is necessary."

Titus smiled. "You're not making this easier."

"I didn't know I was supposed to," Hume said. Then he leaned back. "My point is, Holy Sir, that I am a scholar. I can find something in the Words to defend any belief you hold."

"You also believe," Titus said. "I didn't ask you to stay for your knowledge. I wanted to know what your heart tells you."

Hume looked at his hands. They were crabbed and bent, stained with ink, and filthy.

"Hume," Titus said.

"My heart says two things," Hume spoke slowly. "When I am faced with the Soldiers of the Enemy, when I am faced with my own death, I could not encourage it as the Roca did. I would fight back, using anything at my disposal."

"But?" Titus asked.

"But when there is peace and a moment of calm, I believe that man should not take a life."

"We do so all the time. The food we eat—"

"An intelligent life. The Fey, no matter what they may represent to us, are beings as we are. They live, they think, they love. I cannot condone killing them."

"Even in war?" Titus asked.

"War." Hume rubbed his hands on his robe. The ink smudges disappeared from part of his fingers, but the blackness of the robe hid any dirt. "I do not, nor have I ever, believed in war, Holy Sir."

"Although they make it on us?"

"They have not for a generation. We do not know what their intentions are. My advice to you, if that is what you are seeking, Holy Sir, is to wait until Reece has spoken with them. Then make your decision."

"And fight them if they fight?"

Hume took a deep breath and released it. "Replace any

holy water that gets used, as you usually do. Assume that you are making it for religious reasons."

"But I won't be," Titus said.

Hume stood. "That is where we run into the scholarly difficulties, Holy Sir. An act of war just might be a holy thing."

"What are you saying, Hume?" Titus asked.

Hume licked his lips. "I'm saying, Holy Sir, that the last few years of the Roca's life were spent fighting invaders, Soldiers of the Enemy. We assume he defeated them because we worship him, not them. And we believe that his act of self-sacrifice was the defining moment in that defeat."

"Yes?" Titus said, not sure he liked how this was going.

"Our great religious leader, the man we call Beloved of God, the man we have raised to the level of God, waged war, Holy Sir. He led men into battle. You might have to as well."

Hume's words hung between them. Titus stepped away from the door. He felt numb. "You may go," he said.

Hume nodded, then let himself out.

The religious leader as warrior prince. The sword as weapon and symbol. Holy water as purifier and killer.

It all added up.

Which made Titus hate it even more.

THIRTY-EIGHT

THE fingers on his face were cool, light. Nicholas started awake. Sebastian bent over him, the skin around his gray eyes crinkled with worry.

"Pa . . ." Sebastian said softly.

Nicholas stretched. He hadn't meant to fall asleep. He was sitting in the chair beside the fireplace in Sebastian's room. He had sat down only for a moment, after posting several guards on his children, and watched Sebastian sleep, wondering how a child who had been so much a part of his life could be anything but his flesh and blood. The fact that Sebastian wasn't really human but made of stone made even less sense.

The room was full of early morning light, the soft kind that crept across floors and took the darkness away. It was still pink with the dawn. Sebastian was wearing his night robe. He was crouched beside Nicholas's chair.

His fingers brushed Nicholas's face again.

"Pa?"

Nicholas caught Sebastian's hand in his own, and squeezed the boy's hard, smooth palm before letting it go. "I'm awake, son," he said. The word "son" sent a shiver through him. It was accurate and inaccurate at the same time.

"Pa . . ." Sebastian said, then swept his left hand toward the open window. He seemed agitated. His lower lip was trembling and he could not remain still.

Nicholas ran a hand through his son's strawlike hair, then stood up. He was still wearing the ceremonial robe from the night before. He hadn't been asleep long. It hadn't quite been dawn when the group left the war room, and Nicholas had come down here to make certain his children were well guarded. He had planned, at dawn, to send a message to the Rocaan. Enough divisiveness. They had to work together.

His boots hurt his feet, and his clothing felt sticky. Sebastian stepped aside as Nicholas made his way to the window.

The dawn was pink, as he had expected. Clouds streaked across the sky in various hues of red, mixing with some solid yellows. The air smelled of roses and fresh grass. It would be a beautiful day.

Sebastian came to his side, and pointed downward. Nicholas leaned his hands on the stone ledge and peered out.

The gardens were strangely silent. Usually at this time of day, the birds chirruped and made a raucous song. This morning, though, they covered the trees, the shrubs, and the grass. Hundreds upon hundreds of starlings, robins, and gulls stared at the palace. Nicholas couldn't recognize all of the species. He recognized eagles, but not the large birds that sat beside them. Birds with long multicolored beaks sat on the topmost branches. They were larger than many cats, and their beaks looked as if they could break smaller animals in half.

Nicholas glanced to his left. Birds, in a circle around the palace. He glanced to his right. More birds. Then he backed out of the window, crossed the room, and looked out the other window. The far side of the garden was also filled with birds, and even more sat on the stone wall protecting the palace. As he peered toward the kitchens, he saw birds spread like a carpet across the courtyard.

"Pa . . ." Sebastian said softly. He pointed again. Nicholas squinted.

A tiny Fey sat above the wings of every bird.

Nicholas backed away from the window, nearly tripping on the other chair in the room. Sebastian caught it before it fell, a fast move for the boy.

"What is it?" Nicholas whispered. "What are they doing?"

"I . . . don't . . . know," Sebastian said.

"How did you know they were there?"

"Magick," Sebastian said.

Nicholas nodded. That didn't surprise him. Sebastian had sensed magick before, most notably the day Arianna's grandfather arrived to steal her. Sebastian had been three then, and more terrified than any living being had a right to be, at least according to Solanda.

But Sebastian didn't always sense magick. Something was different.

"Is this dangerous?" Nicholas asked.

Sebastian brought his head up once, then down again. The boy seemed distracted, as if part of him were concentrating on the birds and not on Nicholas.

The door to Sebastian's room opened, and Arianna came in. Her hair was down, her feet were bare, and she wore her thin night robe. Half a dozen guards trailed her.

"Daddy?" she asked, worry in her voice. She let out a sigh when she saw him.

"I know, Ari," he said.

"They've all got tiny Fey on them."

He knew that too. He also knew what it meant.

It meant the Black King wasn't going to negotiate.

"You," Nicholas said to one of the guards, "I want you to get all the servants to close the tapestries and bolt the doors. I want guards posted on each window. If there aren't enough guards, post male servants. I want the most experienced guards on my children, and make certain they are armed."

"Holy water, Sire?" the guard asked, his gaze darting to Arianna before he looked directly at the King.

Nicholas hesitated, and as he did, he remembered seeing Fey die, even when the holy water didn't hit them directly. "No," he said. "Swords will have to do."

"Aye, Sire," the guards said. He bowed, turned and left.

"We'll be all right, Daddy," Arianna said. "I can protect Sebastian."

"You have no idea what you're up against," Nicholas said. He wasn't even certain he did. He raised the tapestry and peered out the window again. The birds blacked the area around the palace for a long distance. He didn't even try to count them; he suspected there were more birds around the palace than had been in the entire first invasion force.

Then he raised his chin, looked beyond the beautiful sunrise, and stared into his city. He couldn't see movement from this distance, but smoke was coming from an area west of the river. A lot of smoke.

He had to think. The Black King had come for his great-grandchildren. Nicholas had to hide them until he knew the Black King's intentions.

Jewel had known of the war room and some of the tunnels. She had seen them long before she and Nicholas were married. She might have reported their existence to the other Fey who now might be part of the Black King's force.

The only place he could think of were the dungeons. Jewel had never seen them, and Nicholas had never used them. His father had only once, when the Fey invaded the first time, and that hadn't really worked either. The Fey hadn't made it that deep. The prisoner had killed his guard in the tunnels before they reached the dungeons.

He took Sebastian by the hand. "You're both going to have to come with me," Nicholas said.

Arianna planted her feet. "What are you doing?"

"I'm taking you somewhere safe."

"You're hiding us."

Nicholas suppressed a sigh. He didn't have time to fight with her now. "That's exactly what I'm doing."

"I won't hide," she said. "You need me."

He had said those same words to his father during the first invasion. He suspected now that it had something to do with being young and thinking oneself immortal.

"I need you alive, Arianna," he said, "and I need you to guard Sebastian."

"You can't hide us just because—"

"I can and I will," Nicholas said. "The Shaman told me to keep you safe."

"But I can hide in plain sight," Arianna said.

He grabbed his daughter and pulled her away from the guards. Then he lowered his voice. "First of all, I need you to protect your brother. But secondly, you've never faced Fey. Real Fey. They're used to your magick. The people here are not. You might think you can hide in plain sight, but not from them."

"I could hide from Solanda. She was a real Fey. She was the same as me."

"It's not the same," Nicholas said.

"It is," Arianna said.

Nicholas's stomach turned. She was his daughter, Jewel's daughter. She wasn't going to hide. He wouldn't have hidden at her age. He had yelled at his father for trying to make him hide. Arianna had an even greater imperative.

She had the blood of two warriors running through her.

"You can be smart and fight," she said.

He crossed his arms. "Is that what you did when you nearly killed your real brother?"

"That isn't the same," she said. "He was trying to get Sebastian."

"What do you think these Fey want?" Nicholas said. He put his hands on the window. The birds below looked up at him. Their Fey counterparts did as well. He grabbed the tapestry and pulled it over the window. "If they had wanted to slaughter us, they would have done so already. Look how many there are, Arianna. More than we have. And those are just Beast Riders. There have to be Infantry and Foot Soldiers and all other kinds of Fey on this Isle. There are fires in the west. What do you think caused that?"

She swallowed. "You're saying they're guarding us?"

"I'm saying they're being cautious. They know that there is Black Blood in this palace, and they're going to wait until they know who it belongs to before slaughtering everyone else."

"Sebastian isn't flesh and blood," she said.

"They don't know that."

"They might." She glanced at her brother. His head was tilted, his eyes empty. It was almost as if he were listening to faraway music.

"It doesn't matter. You have Black Blood."

She touched her brother's cheek. He started, looked at

her, and frowned. "Then hiding us will make no difference," she said.

Nicholas watched her. It didn't matter to her that Sebastian wasn't her blood kin. It didn't change her behavior at all. She loved him with a fierceness that Nicholas had never seen in anyone.

"If they know we're here—and they do—then they'll hunt for us until they find us. They'll look everywhere. Putting us in the dungeon or down in the tunnels will just prolong the search."

She sounded like he had when he was young. And she was right. The Fey were ruthless. Once they started to fight, they wouldn't stop. Once they started searching the palace, they would look until they found Arianna and Sebastian.

He took a deep breath. He didn't want to risk his daughter or his son, his Sebastian. His children were everything to him.

The problem was they had been at risk from the moment they were born.

"So what do you suggest?" he asked.

"I don't know yet," Arianna said.

He didn't know either. Beast Riders outside, the city on fire, and he couldn't use holy water for fear of hurting his own children.

He was surrounded and outnumbered.

But he had assets. He just had to find them.

"You won't put yourself in jeopardy," he said.

Arianna laughed. "I can't promise that, Daddy."

"You're the future of Blue Isle, Ari. You."

She shook her head, her eyes sad. "You have two children, Daddy. If something happens to me, you'll have to trust Sebastian."

"Three," Sebastian said.

They both turned to him. Nicholas hadn't expected his son to speak.

"You ... have ... three ... child-ren," Sebastian said. "Ari, ... me, ... and ... Gift."

"Gift was raised by Fey. He'll help the Black King," Arianna said.

Nicholas grabbed her arm. He wasn't so certain that his

son-by-blood would help the Fey. The boy had come here to save Sebastian, or so he claimed.

The boy was Jewel's son. Jewel's and his. That had to count for something.

"No," Sebastian said. "Re-mem-ber . . . the . . . Link."

"The Link?" Arianna asked. "You're Linked with him now?"

"Al-ways," Sebastian said.

Nicholas frowned. Sebastian knew what Gift was doing? "Has he joined up with his great-grandfather?"

Sebastian disappeared from his eyes. So that was what it looked like when he checked his Link. When his life force returned, his eyes filled with tears. "Gift . . . is . . . a-lone. . . . No . . . Black . . . King . . . but . . . some-thing . . . is . . . wrong. . . . Gift . . . hurts." Sebastian sank to his knees. "He . . . hurts."

THIRTY-NINE

HE did not consider himself a courageous man. In fact, as he walked down the steps from the Rocaan's suite, Reece thought himself one of the greatest cowards he had ever known. His hands were shaking and his mouth was dry. He wasn't certain he could get two words out at one time.

But the Rocaan, as a boy of fourteen, had faced the Fey alone. He hadn't even had holy water with him when he went into the Fey's magick circle.

Reece could match a boy of thirteen.

He hoped.

An Aud had offered him a vial of holy water, but Reece had refused. He would go out to speak with the tiny Fey unarmed. He would show them that the Tabernacle wasn't afraid of them. He would show them that the Tabernacle would speak to them in good faith.

That was why he had chosen to go, why he had spoken up before the Rocaan appointed someone else. Reece was frightened, yes, but he knew that his duty to the Tabernacle was greater than his duty to himself. He also knew that many of the other Elders had yet to make that realization.

The Tabernacle seemed oddly dark with all the tapestries

drawn over the windows. Someone had lit the candles and the torches on the main level. It looked as if a storm had hit midday, and the Tabernacle itself was preparing for an eternal darkness.

He clenched his fists to stop his hands from shaking, but he knew it would do no good. They would smell the fear on him, all those animals. He could only hope their Fey masters were able to keep the animals reigned in.

"Respected Sir?" one of the Danites bobbed beside him. Reece, who normally remembered everyone's name, couldn't recall this Danite's, even though he knew the man. Reece's mind was so focused on those Fey, there wasn't room for anything else.

"Not now," Reece said softly.

"You need holy water, Respected Sir," the Danite said.

Reece shook his head. He would get that offer all the way to the door if he didn't stop it now. "I choose to go out empty-handed."

"Respected Sir—"

Reece patted the Danite on the shoulder and continued forward. Several Danites stood near the main doors. They watched him, their eyes wide. He nodded to them, wishing they weren't taking this with such solemnity.

It made him even more nervous.

Then he gripped the golden handles and pulled both doors open.

Sunlight flooded the room, nearly blinding him. The Danites stood back. Reece stepped into the brightness, closing the doors behind him.

The only Islander among hundreds of Fey.

The stench hit him first. Overpowering, wild, the musky scent of fur mixed with that of particular animals: the sharp smell of male cats; the furry body odor of dogs; the pungent odor of wolves. His stomach turned, and bile rose in his throat. He had never smelled so many wild things so very close.

He swallowed, willing his stomach to remain calm. They were only a few yards from him. Most of the tiles on the courtyard were uncovered, the scenes from the Roca's life glistening in the sunlight. The animals surrounded the Tabernacle like a wall of fur. Their eyes were hollow, intense, focused on him. One wolf directly across from him opened its muzzle, revealing sharp, yellowed teeth.

A small cat drooled.

He made himself take a step closer to them. Even this close, he couldn't see the Fey on the animals' backs. It looked as if he were alone in a forest, with wild creatures and nowhere to go.

"I would like to speak to the head of your troop," he said in Nye. His Fey was poor—he knew only a few words.

"You're not the head of yours." The voice that responded was female. She spoke Islander.

"No, I am not the Rocaan," Reece said. "I am an Elder, one of the next in line."

"We only speak to the leader."

It wouldn't work. Reece wouldn't see the Rocaan down here, not for anything. "Forgive me, ma'am," he said in Islander, "but you are not the leader of all Fey either. I am the best you can do."

A dog growled to his left. Reece refused to look at it.

"Good point," the woman said. "So speak."

"I cannot see you, ma'am." He had to speak slowly to keep from stuttering. He concentrated even harder, controlling his voice as well as his body. "Please let me see whom I am addressing."

One of the dogs came forward. It was larger than any dog he had ever seen. It had short brown fur and muscles that ran along its forelegs. Its head came up to Reece's shoulders. The Fey woman sat on the flat place where the dog's neck met its back. She was tiny, about the size of Reece's hand. Her hands clutched the dog's fur, and her legs—

She didn't have any legs. She seemed to be a part of the dog, her torso sliding into its body.

"You are addressing me," she said. "I am Onha. I head this troop."

"Onha." Reece bowed slightly. The Fey's practice of allowing women to lead, even though he had been familiar with it for nearly two decades, still startled him. "I am Reece, an Elder in the Tabernacle."

"Well," she said, her voice amazingly strong for her size. "Now that we have completed the pleasantries, how about some lunch?"

The laughter behind him told him that she had made a joke, presumably at his expense. He didn't like the implication.

"The Rocaan wishes to welcome you and to ask you the purpose of your visit."

"He could have done that himself from his balcony." She looked up, and then she waved.

Reece looked up as well. Titus stood on his balcony, Hume beside him. The other balconies were empty.

"The circumstance is a bit unusual, ma'am," Reece said. "We thought it best—"

"To spare your Rocaan in case we decided to eat his messenger?"

A shiver ran down Reece's spine. Another reference to food. He didn't like this.

Reece swallowed before replying. "It—is our custom, ma'am, to have any guest brought to the Rocaan."

The little Fey smiled. "We are not any guests."

"Indeed," Reece said. "We have never had a grouping quite like this one."

"I would think not."

Another growl sounded from behind Onha. This one made Reece's head come up in alarm. He had never heard such a large sound from an animal before.

"Ah, the Bear Riders," Onha said, her voice as calm as it had been a moment before. "They are so hard to control."

"Bear?" Reece asked, then wished he hadn't.

The little Fey's smile grew. "That's right. You have no large predators on Blue Isle, do you?"

"Predators?" Reece was repeating after her, but he couldn't help himself.

"Predators," Onha said. She leaned back, revealing small breasts. All the little Fey were nude. "Bears. Tigers. Lions. Creatures whose prey includes man."

Another shiver ran through Reece. He had to break out of this. He wouldn't be helping the Tabernacle, the Isle, if he lost control now. Even though the Fey were trying to make him do just that.

"The Rocaan will see you," Reece said, standing as straight as he could. He let his voice rise just a little. "But he would prefer to see you one at a time."

"He will see us, will he?" Onha said. "Why do that when he can make a speech from his balcony?"

"It would be his last," a male voice growled behind Reece.

Reece drew in breath, held it, and slowly released it before responding. "You came to see us," he said, feeling helpless.

"No." Onha took one hand off the dog's ruff and wiped her own hair out of her face. "We did not come to *see* you."

"Then why are you here?"

"You are the famed Black Robes, are you not?" she asked.

Black Robes was the Fey's term for the Tabernacle. It was a derogatory term, and one they had used from the beginning. Reece did not answer.

"You are the ones so powerful that you can stop Fey."

"We have a truce," Reece said. "We live together on the Isle now."

"You have a truce." Onha's voice was mocking. "A truce enforced by your magick water and our people's cowardice."

Reece held out his hands. "I am unarmed. I came to see you in good faith."

"Good faith. Such a religious term," Onha said. "Of course your faith is good, Black Robe. You have controlled this situation from the beginning."

Reece licked his lips, then looked at all the animals. They were still watching him, their bodies perfectly still. One of the large upright animals (bears?) had its snout open, its stubby teeth visible.

"If you were going to attack us, I assume you would have done so the Fey way," Reece said. "You would have done so with surprise. So you want something else. What is it?"

The dog sat down, its tail wrapping around its haunches. The Fey on its back leaned forward, as if she had legs to slide along the dog's side, to make her balance even better.

"You assume incorrectly, Black Robe," she said. "My orders were to wait until you noticed us and, failing that, to wait until midday, when the Foot Soldiers were due to arrive."

Reece frowned. He didn't understand. Or maybe he was afraid he did.

"We're willing to talk with you. The Rocaan will see you all," Reece said. "I don't understand—"

"You need to know what kills you, Black Robe," Onha said. "You need to know that your puny powers are no match for the Black King."

"The Black King?" Reece swallowed. "But we have a truce."

"You have a truce with Failures," Onha said.

The growling behind her grew.

The animals surged forward.

Reece had barely time to ask the Roca's forgiveness before he died.

FORTY

THE screaming brought Adrian into the clearing. Male screaming, low and pain-filled. Adrian ran as quickly as he could, the Fey woman at his side, each thinking the opposite of the other: Adrian was afraid that Gift had finally attacked Coulter, and the Fey woman was obviously afraid that Coulter had hurt Gift.

But they both stopped when they reached Coulter's usual place. Both young men were enveloped in light. Gift had his hands around his head. He was screaming, and Adrian could finally make out the words.

The Fey word for "no."

Coulter's face had an expression of complete panic. His hands were moving quickly, weaving, mending, reforming the strings of light that bound them both together. The strings were shattering. Each time Coulter sent out a new one, it broke as if it were brittle.

"Stop it!" the Fey woman yelled. She started forward, but Adrian grabbed her arm. She shook at him. "That Islander will kill him."

"Coulter saved his life once," Adrian said. "He'll do it again if he has to."

She pulled her arm from Adrian's grip but didn't try to go forward again.

The two boys were locked in light. The strings binding them glowed. Each time the strings snapped, sparks would fly out of the circle and land on the ground around them. The sparks left tiny burn marks in the grass.

"No!" Gift was screaming in Fey.

Coulter wasn't saying anything. He was moving closer to Gift, repairing the strings as he went, creating new ones that would then snap. Adrian's heart was pounding. He had seen them both wrapped in light before—the day he and Coulter left Shadowlands. Then Gift had cried "no" too, but years later, Coulter had told Adrian that Gift had done so because he hadn't wanted Coulter to leave.

Now something different was happening.

"We can't just let this continue," the woman said.

Adrian tightened the grip on her arm. He had learned to trust Coulter despite his strange powers. He knew that Coulter could handle this.

He had to. Adrian certainly didn't have the skills to do so, and neither did the woman. From the look of her, she was Infantry, too young to have come into her magick.

Coulter stepped closer to Gift, reached out, and grabbed his shoulder. The light around them flared so brightly that Adrian and the woman covered their eyes. Gift's screaming stopped.

All sound stopped.

Adrian uncovered his eyes, blinked and frowned. Before him, someone had cut a hole in the air. Through that hole, he could see the Cardidas River and Jahn on the other side, looking empty and abandoned. The Tabernacle was barely within his sight, the white walls singed. Coulter and Gift stood on a barge. Coulter was pointing toward the Tabernacle, but Gift was looking straight ahead, at the bridge.

He looked frightened.

Then the image faded, as did all the lights. Coulter was holding Gift, and Gift was sobbing.

"Did you see that?" the Fey woman asked.

Adrian nodded, not certain what to make of it.

"I don't like the looks of it," said a voice from behind

him. Adrian turned. Scavenger stood there, with Luke at his side. Scavenger was a Red Cap, the lowest of all Fey. He was short and squat, and the only things that identified him as Fey were his dark skin, dark hair, and upswept features.

Luke looked sheepish. "He made me bring him here. I know Coulter won't like it."

Adrian shrugged. What Coulter did and didn't like was of no concern at the moment. He was still tending Gift, who was trying to shove him away.

The Fey woman had her arms crossed. "You're an Outsider," she said.

"I, my dear," Scavenger said, "am the original Outsider. And you are too tall to be my friend."

"Don't judge on appearances," Luke said. His relationship with Scavenger had somehow developed into this chiding warmth. He wasn't really looking at Scavenger, though. He was looking at the Fey woman with interest. He had never looked at any of the local women with interest.

Adrian didn't like that. "You saw that image too?" he asked Scavenger.

"Open Vision," Scavenger said. "It's an Open Vision. They're extremely rare. They occur with firm destinies, when the parties are tied together by an event of such importance the fate of the world rests on it."

"The world?" The Fey woman asked. Her sarcasm grew.

"The world," Scavenger said. He wasn't looking at her. He was watching Coulter and Gift. Gift had leaned into Coulter's embrace, and his entire body was shaking, as if he were sobbing.

"You Outsiders make the most interesting things up," she said.

"I'm not making this up," Scavenger said. "You're a child, raised improperly. You know nothing of Fey magick. You probably won't even know when you come into your own powers."

"Scavenger," Adrian warned. He wasn't certain he wanted to anger this young woman.

"You are just a deformed Red Cap," the woman said. "It doesn't matter how clean you are. The stink of your pitiful life follows you everywhere."

Adrian tightened his grip on her arm. "He's my friend," Adrian said. "You'll not say such things to him on my land."

"Oh, let her," Scavenger said. "It's no worse than what they'd say behind my back. That's why I left you people, because of the way you treat us."

Gift was sitting up now, wiping his face with the back of his hand.

"You didn't tell me Coutler was Bound to the Black King's great-grandson," Scavenger said to Adrian, voice low. "You never told me."

"I didn't see how it would matter."

"It matters," Scavenger's voice was low. "That's a powerful Binding. It's a Life Binding. One of them would not be alive without the other."

"Coulter saved Gift's life."

Scavenger closed his eyes.

The Fey woman wrenched her arm from Adrian. "Why do you listen to him? Red Caps don't know anything."

"People who deny other people's knowledge often don't know anything either," Adrian said.

"Pa," Luke said. "She's entitled to her opinion."

"It's not based on fact," Adrian said. "Scavenger made a study of Fey magicks to see why he didn't have any. He probably knows more about them than most magickal Fey. I listen to him, and more than once, his knowledge has saved my life."

Gift was wiping his face with the back of his hand. His skin was ashen, and he was shaking. Coulter was speaking softly to him. Adrian couldn't make out the words.

"I don't like this," Scavenger said. "A Life Binding and an Open Vision."

"It can't be all that bad," Luke said.

Scavenger frowned at him. "You have no idea what bad really is," he said. "The Fey were easy on Blue Isle. You should have seen what happened to the Nyeians."

He shuddered. He had been in the position to know, of course. He'd been the one to dispose of the bodies.

"Things change," the woman said.

"Who *are* you?" Scavenger asked.

"My name is Leen," she said.

"Born to whom?"

"Dello and Frill," she said.

Scavenger rolled his eyes. "A Domestic and a Spy. What hope have you of real magick?"

Leen opened her mouth, but at the moment, Coulter said, "Adrian, could you come here? Alone?"

Adrian put a hand on Scavenger's shoulder, hoping that would calm him for a moment, then went to Coulter. Coulter's eyes had deep circles under them, and his mouth was pinched together. He looked as if he had aged years in a matter of moments.

Coulter waved him down. Adrian sat in the dew-damp grass.

"You can trust him," Coulter said to Gift.

Gift's eyes, which had been clear a few moments before, were clouded and red with tears. His lower lip trembled. "I— can't," he said.

Coulter nodded. "Mind if I do?"

Gift shook his head. He averted his gaze from Adrian's. The power of Gift's emotions filled the air. Adrian could almost see them. He had never felt turmoil that strong, not even in himself.

"Shadowlands is gone," Coulter said.

"What?" Adrian asked. Shadowlands was tied to its maker. Gift had reconstructed Shadowlands after Rugar's death caused it to explode. Coulter had once said it would work the same in reverse. If the Shadowlands were destroyed, its maker would be too. Adrian glanced at Gift, who, aside from his gray features, looked fine. "How is that possible?"

"The walls are still standing," Coulter said. "But everyone inside is dead."

"Everyone?" Adrian felt as if the bottom of his stomach had fallen out. He had lived there for a long time and, although he had made few friends, he had known the Fey who lived inside.

It was Gift who answered him. "Everyone," he said. "My parents, too."

By that, he meant his adoptive parents, Niche and Wind. They had raised him from his fifth day of life. No wonder he had gone so crazy. No wonder he was barely hanging on.

Without thinking, Adrian took Gift's hand. He knew what it was like to lose family. He had lost a lot during the invasion, and then he had lost Luke for several years.

Gift looked down at the touch, but didn't take his hand away. "I should have been there," he said.

Adrian ignored that. If Gift had been there, he would have died. "What happened?" he asked.

"The Black King," Coulter said. "He decided to get rid of the Fey first."

Adrian shook his head. Even after decades of knowing them, he found the Fey a mystery. "Why? Wouldn't they—?"

"Failures," Gift said, his voice thick. "He considered them Failures. He could have come in—they thought he was going to come in—and use them as an advance team. But I guess he didn't want any of their help. I guess he didn't think they were worth saving. I guess . . ."

His voice broke on the last word and then he rubbed his hand with his face. "They're dead," he said. "And I was sworn to protect them."

"You couldn't have stopped it," Adrian said. Then he noted Coulter glaring at him.

"Platitudes aren't the answer," Coulter said.

"But it's true," Adrian said.

"It's not true." Gift spoke softly. "I am the Black King's great-grandson. He could not have fought me. If I had been there to defend Shadowlands, he would not have killed everyone inside."

His words hung in the morning air. Adrian felt the truth of them. His heart ached. He remembered that feeling. If he had not said yes that morning when Luke had wanted to accompany him on the attack on Shadowlands, they would never have been captured. Adrian wouldn't have lost all those years, and Luke would never have been Charmed by the Fey.

"But he knew," Gift said. "He knew I wasn't there. He kept Shadowlands intact so that I wouldn't die. He wouldn't have attacked—"

"Enough," Adrian said. "This will get you nowhere."

"Besides," Coulter said. "We have a more serious problem."

Gift raised empty eyes to him. "Niche and Wind were my parents, Coulter. There is no more serious problem."

"To me there is," Coulter said. "If the Black King knew you weren't in Shadowlands, does he know where you are now?"

"How could he?"

Adrian knew where Coulter was going with this. "How could he get on this Isle without coming down the Cardidas? I suspect your great-grandfather is a better man than your grandfather was."

"I don't care," Gift said. "He murdered my family. I never even Saw it."

"But you Saw your own death."

"Or Sebastian's." Gift brought his free hand to his mouth. "The old Fey I saw. Was that my great-grandfather?"

The thought seemed to sober Coulter. He put a hand on Gift's back. "When did you first have the Vision?"

"Two weeks ago."

"That's when you said the energy changed," Adrian said.

Coulter nodded. "And Visions are brought into play when something happens to inspire them."

"It was my great-grandfather."

"But he didn't kill you," Coulter said.

Gift shook his head. "He seemed surprised."

Adrian rubbed his nose with his thumb and forefinger. "This seems like a muddle to me. Why would he destroy everything associated with you?"

"He could destroy the entire Isle as long as he doesn't touch me or my blood family," Gift said. He sounded weary now. Resigned. "And that doesn't include Sebastian."

"It might," Coulter said. "He has a part of you inside."

"We have to get Sebastian," Gift said.

"I don't think we can now. The Black King will look for you at the palace. We need to hide you."

"We can't let Sebastian face him alone."

"He won't be alone," Coulter said. "He has his father and sister."

Gift shook his head. "But what if he and I are Bound like you and me? What if I die when he does?"

"He isn't real," Coulter said.

"He's real." Gift's voice had a quiet strength.

Coulter looked at Adrian over Gift's head. "We'll worry about that later. First we have to find a safe place for you."

"I won't hide," Gift said. "What's there to hide from? The Black King can't kill me. He won't hurt me. He probably came for me. That's the only reason he would come to the Isle now. Hiding me will make no difference. The worst has already happened." His eyes teared as he spoke that last, but no tears fell. "Help me up," he said, extending a hand to Coulter, sounding kinglike himself.

Coulter helped Gift to his feet. Adrian stood also.

"What are we going to do now?" Coulter asked. Adrian finally understood why Coulter had felt so trapped by Gift's arrival. The events were spiraling too fast to follow. Coulter had to stay at Gift's side because they were Bound.

"We're going to find Sebastian," Gift said. "And we're going to find my great-grandfather."

Adrian's mouth went dry. "Coulter, do you know what kind of a risk you're facing? You were just a boy with Rugar. He was bad enough. His father has ruled the Fey for generations. He'll be—"

"Even worse, I know," Coulter said. "You've made that point." He never took his attention off Gift. He leaned closer and said, softly, "You can't kill him, Gift, any more than he can kill you."

Adrian glanced at Gift. The set line of his mouth, the narrowness of his eyes. He didn't seem like someone who wanted to kill, except for that tingling turmoil around him, that anger as repressed as the tears.

"That's right, I can't," Gift said. "But I don't need him like he needs me. I don't have to live in his shadow my whole life."

"What are you thinking?" Coulter asked.

"I'm not going to kill him," Gift said. "But I'm not going to stand in the way if anyone else does." Then he smiled, eased away from Coulter's hands, and walked forward.

"Leen," he said in a voice that made chills run down Adrian's back. "Something's happened."

Her family was dead too, and she didn't know. Gift told her in that same chilly voice. And Adrian watched as her expression went from puzzled to complete and total fury.

"I don't like this," he said softly to Coulter.

"You don't have to like it," Coulter said. "You just have to survive it."

And this time, Adrian wondered if he would.

FORTY-ONE

TITUS watched, horrified, as the animals surged around Reece. For a moment, Reece disappeared beneath a pile of brown and black fur. He screamed, once, and then the sound was cut off midthrum. The animals pulled back, as if getting their bearings, giving Titus a clear picture of the scene below.

A wolf had Reece by the throat, and although he thrashed, he screamed no more. Blood spattered all over the tiles, hiding the scenes from the Roca's life. A cat at the edge of the animal group broke away and began licking the blood off the ceramic.

Titus reached for his holy water vial. He had killed with it before. Only once, when the Fey were going after the Fiftieth Rocaan. His hands were shaking. But before he could grab his own vial, Hume was pouring holy water over the balcony's rail.

The animals were growling below, and there was a horrible smacking sound. Reece's feet slammed against the tile, once, twice, three times before becoming still. Several animals ripped flesh, pulling it away. A big cat ripped off Reece's arm and dragged it to the side of the courtyard, growling at any creature that got too close. One of the large creatures, the ones that Onha had called bears, swept others aside with its huge paws and wrapped its forearms around Reece's body, dragging him back toward the gate. Reece's head lolled, his neck a gaping wound.

He was dead.

The holy water splattered onto the tile, mixing with the blood and diluting it. The Fey animals didn't even look up. Nothing happened. Hume ran off the balcony and went inside to get to Titus's stash of holy water vials. So much for the intellectual arguments. When it came down to war, Hume fought as he had said he would.

There were shouts and growls from the road. More Fey were showing up, tall Fey, two-legged normal Fey, their faces sleek and dark, their hands tucked under their arms. They were wearing tunics and leggings of a kind Titus had never seen. They were marching in a line that seemed to go on forever.

A bear opened the gate to them, and they came in.

More shouts and a long, whipping cry. Then the animals surged forward, toward the Tabernacle.

Hume was back on the balcony, holding up the skirt of his robe. It contained vials. He grabbed one and tossed it to Titus. Titus caught it with one hand. The cut-glass diamonds were sharp against his palm, the glass itself cool.

It had come to this.

There were more Fey outside than religious folk inside. Hume reached the edge of the balcony and, with a wave of his skirt, tossed the vials over the railing. They glistened in the sun as they spun their way down, sending bits of colored light, like signals, back to Titus.

Then they shattered around a dozen Fey.

The Fey growled and looked up. Some wiped the glass off their fur. A piece of glass sliced off a tiny Fey's head, and the entire creature stopped, jolted, and fell over, dead. They were tied together somehow.

But the water did nothing.

"Is this holy water?" Hume asked him.

Titus nodded. He had made some of it, Matthias had made some, and the Fiftieth Rocaan had made the rest. He couldn't even blame the fact that it didn't work on his own error.

The normal Fey pushed their way through the animals and tried to open the doors below. The Auds had it barricaded. The pounding resounded through the morning air as the Fey tried to break in.

Hume grabbed Titus's arm. "We need to get you to the catacombs," he said.

The holy water wasn't working. The warnings had been right, and he hadn't listened to them. In his arrogance, he had blamed Nicholas.

"Come on," Hume said, dragging him.

If the holy water didn't work, then they were all in danger.

"I can make it," Titus said. "Evacuate the entire Tabernacle into the catacombs. We have to do it before the Fey break in."

Hume nodded once and was out the door. Titus held the holy water vial, turned it over in his hand, and stared at it. They had no protections now.

He glanced below. The animals were surging forward, surrounding the Tabernacle, the normal Fey mixed in with them. The shouts and growls and cries were overwhelming.

Titus set the bottle on the rail and then ran to the door. He pulled it open to find Auds running through the hallways. "Go to the catacombs!" he yelled. "Quickly! Warn everyone!'

There was more yelling below. Lots of yelling. Screams and cries and warnings that the Fey were about to break in. He could feel the fear, like a presence in the Tabernacle.

And he couldn't feel God.

His sandals slapped against the stairs. A Danite nearly ran him down as he passed, without an apology to the Holy Sir. They already knew what was going to happen. It was hopeless. The only way they could save themselves was to get to the catacombs, several stories down.

On the third floor, Porciluna was standing on the landing, holding a hand to his chest and breathing hard. Several Danites and an Officiate passed him.

Titus stopped.

"Come, my friend," Titus said. "We have to get below."

Porciluna's face was flushed. Sweat dripped off his chin. "I—can't—" He was taking shallow breaths between each word. "Go—"

"No." Titus put an arm around Porciluna and pulled him away from the wall. Porciluna's robe was soaked in sweat. "I'm not going without you."

"They'll—kill—you. You—can't—die—"

"They won't kill me," Titus said. "Now come on."

"I—can't—"

Titus wasn't listening. He helped Porciluna to the steps. "You're coming. We're going together."

"No—" He said, but he went down the steps anyway, speeding up as he went along. His face grew redder, and the sweat ran off him like water. "There's—a—rope—ladder—"

Titus understood his fear. "We'll get you down it," Titus said.

They reached the second landing, and Porciluna grabbed an Aud. "Help—me,—boy,—so—the—Rocaan—can—go—"

The Aud looked at Titus. The boy was maybe eleven. Maybe.

"I can do this," Titus said.

"You—have—the—Secrets," Porciluna said.

"I have him, Holy Sir." The Aud shoved himself under Porciluna's arm and took the brunt of the older man's weight.

"Thank you," Titus said.

The pounding below was growing louder. It would only be a matter of moments before the Fey broke in. Fortunately, they hadn't realized that the windows would have been easier to break through: they were blocked only by the tapestries.

Titus hurried down the steps, his arm soaked from Porciluna's sweat. The older man's fear stink clung to him and made his own heart pound faster.

He reached the first floor as the Fey broke through the main doors. The animals ran in, the little Fey on their backs shouting gleefully. Cats, bears, wolves all ran through the corridor of the Tabernacle. A large cat with a wild mane knocked over a candelabrum, and the burning candles scattered.

Danites screamed, and Auds were running down the hall,

cats of all sizes behind them. The dogs had cornered an Officiate near the portrait of the Eighth Rocaan, and were
snarling at him, drooling as they did. The stench was horrible.

The worst was the large bear creatures. One of them had
an Aud by the throat and was shoving him against the wall.
Most of the other Fey remained outside the open door,
catching those Rocaanists who ran from the building. Titus
could see from his position on the steps. The Fey caught the
Auds, the Danites, the runners, and one Fey would hold the
victim while the others skinned him alive. Skinned him with
a single touch.

Titus's stomach churned. The Danites were throwing
holy water as if it were rain. It did no good. One of the Auds
had grabbed the sword from the wall of the Servant's Chapel
and was wielding it like a real weapon. The Fey animals
stayed away from him.

No one had seen Titus on the stairs. Others ran past him,
stopped when they saw the confusion below, and ran back
up. Porciluna and his helpful Aud finally reached Titus.

"We're not going to get out this way, are we?" Porciluna
asked. His breath had obviously come back, although his
face was a mottled purple and his robe was soaking wet.

Titus shook his head. "Even if we tried, we'd just lead
them to the catacombs. Those who are inside need a chance
to escape."

"And what of you, Holy Sir?" the young Aud asked.

What of him indeed? He was the key to it all, and the
one the Fey would most like dead.

"Get him an Aud's robe," Porciluna said. "Quickly."

"I'll get it myself," Titus said. The Fey hadn't come to
the stairways yet, but they would, and then Porciluna and
the young Aud would be on their own.

The idea was a good one, though. It might give Titus a
chance to escape.

He pushed his way back up the stairs, warning the others
to do the same. Perhaps they could find places to hide, or
perhaps they could get out through the windows. The Fey
might no longer be guarding the outside. They might all be
coming in.

The tide on the stairs turned, and moved him along with
it. He grabbed the door to one of the Danite closets on the

second floor and managed to yank it open. Half a dozen soiled robes littered the floor. The Auds were supposed to clean them.

More screaming echoed from below. Titus grabbed a robe and pulled it over his. It fit loosely and was dreadfully hot, but it would work.

It had to.

Then he hurried to the windows. The sight below was not encouraging. A dozen Auds were being flayed alive, their heads intact, screaming as each strip of flesh was removed. The tiles were drenched in blood. Several smaller animals had joined the cat, licking the red river as it flowed by.

He couldn't save these people. He could do nothing. He hurried across the hall, to another room, went inside and looked out the window. The same scene replayed on the other side.

The Fey had the Tabernacle surrounded.

There was no escape.

Except perhaps they would move on after they killed. He went back to the stairs, and stopped. The stench had grown, and mixed in it were the smells of smoke, burning fur, and burning flesh. The heat he felt had nothing to do with the robes.

The Tabernacle was on fire.

FORTY-TWO

THE tunnels were dark. And damp. And filled with bugs. Con was hunched over as he went. He suspected he was near the river, because the tunnel's walls dripped water. He could also see, several feet ahead, that the tunnel grew so narrow he would have to crawl.

It was good that the Rocaan had sent a boy of Con's size and weight. Anyone larger would not have been able to get through.

Con had had the foresight to tie several torches to his rope belt. He had already used one up and lit the second, but it was becoming a liability. The tunnel he was in was narrowing, and there seemed to be an odd current of air flowing through it, moving the smoke back at him.

He didn't want to put out the torch, but he needed to breathe.

He waited until he got to the crawl space. The path was going uphill here, and it felt as if he were inside a building. From the map, he thought it looked as if the tunnel was built into the foundation level of the old warehouses, the ones that his father had told him about. The foundations remained, but the warehouses were long gone, except for some stonework near the river bed.

He figured the tunnel would go through the foundation, then uphill and into the bridge itself. The bridge was a large stone structure with a lot of arches. He had always thought there was more stones there than needed, even to support the roadway itself.

Now he knew why.

He reached the crawl space, climbed in, and held his torch outside it. The fit was narrow and cramped, and the stone floor was damp beneath his knees. He couldn't crawl with the torch in front of him; the smoke would grow even worse. Besides, he needed both hands.

He pulled the map out from inside his robe and looked at it. The tunnel through the bridge was clearly marked, and there were no branches. If he traveled anywhere without a light, it would be through here.

Then he rolled up the map and stuck it back inside his robe. He carried a lot of extra weight. His pockets were full of bread and he wore a water pouch around his neck. He hated small spaces, absolutely hated them, had since he was a child (which, if he were honest, wasn't that long ago). But he had a Charge.

He would see it through.

Finally he patted the pocket of his Aud's robe for his flint, begged his own forgiveness, and put out the torch.

The darkness was complete and total. He had never been a place so black. He couldn't see his hand when it touched his face. He would have to go by feel now, entirely.

And he didn't like that.

But the Rocaan was counting on him.

The Rocaan, the Roca, and God. Con had his Charge. He would complete it with honor.

Once the smoke cleared, the air had a musty odor. Musty and dank. He could smell the mud of the river somewhere nearby, a rank odor that had a bit of decay mixed in it. The stone floor was overgrown with moss. Some of the stone had crumbled, leaving pebbles in the soft mushy surface. They dug into his palms and knees. He winced as he went, but didn't stop.

The faster he got out of here, the quicker he would see

the King. The quicker he saw the King, the sooner the nightmare would end.

The tunnel narrowed even more. He didn't notice it at first, then he realized his back was scraping on the ceiling. He grabbed the water pouch and slung it around to the front. His robe was damp and heavy as if he had been crawling through water. It dragged from his knees down. The moss was cold and slimy under his bare toes. A shudder ran through him as something soft brushed his left cheek. Immediately he was crawly, as if he were covered in bugs. But he couldn't move to slap them off, and he knew it was all a figment of his imagination. There were bugs, but because he had felt one, it seemed as if he were coated in them.

Amazing the tricks the mind played.

Through the cracks in the stone, he could hear the river gurgling as it passed. The sound was exceptionally loud above. It sounded like a faint murmur in here. He crawled with his hands as far forward as they went; in his active imagination, he saw holes in the tunnel, holes that would send him plunging into the river below.

But the only cave-ins he noted were tiny ones done by time. He suspected it wasn't even the stones that he was feeling, but the mortar used to hold the stones together. If indeed they had used mortar. He hadn't noticed when he crawled inside.

The darkness was still complete. His eyes hadn't adjusted at all. He had heard somewhere that the Cardidas was a mile across at its narrowest point—the place at which the bridge had been built. He had no idea how far he crawled or how long it would take to crawl a mile. He was also afraid the tunnel would narrow even more. Then he wouldn't be able to get through at all. He would get stuck, all by himself, in this place where no one had been in generations. Only the Rocaan and a few Elders knew where he was. If he never returned, would they consider him a failed Charge? Or would they send someone after him?

He crawled even faster, scraping his hands on the marshy, pebbly surface. Water dripped somewhere ahead. He could hear it over the faint gurgle. He didn't know how water could drip in here, how it even got in, unless it built up.

He didn't want to think about what was below his hands, what was growing in the moss.

Most of all, he didn't want to think about all those Fey animals, sitting outside the Tabernacle, waiting for something, watching, a serious enough threat that the Rocaan seemed nervous. Con had never seen so many Fey. He hadn't even known there were that many Fey, although it made sense. He had heard that the Fey had conquered half the world. That had simply been a saying to him, an abstraction. But when he thought about it, it would take a lot of people to conquer that much space.

And now they might be on Blue Isle.

He didn't know what would happen to him when he reached the palace. He didn't know what he'd do after he informed the King.

Con hadn't brought holy water, even though the Rocaan had told him to. There wasn't room for that with the torches, the map, and the bit of bread he'd been able to bring. Despite his thirst, he hadn't had a drink of water yet. That was for emergencies.

He suspected he might have some under here.

The air was stifling hot. The odd breeze he had felt before was gone. The only room inside this tunnel was on the sides. His back brushed the ceiling, and his hands and knees were scraping. The briny, mucky, stale odor was growing.

Something landed in his hair. He brought his head down, and brushed his head, heard something plop, and then he continued forward. He was shaking.

Maybe if he lay down for just a moment, lit a torch and saw where he was. Maybe then it would help.

But he knew it wouldn't. It would just smoke up his air and discourage him. He suspected he couldn't see a beginning or an end to the tunnel yet.

The bridge was the longest in all of Blue Isle, and he was inside it.

He heard a faint rumble, a growl almost. Then the ground beneath him started to shake. He stopped, breathing hard. The shaking was growing. Tiny rocks shook off the ceiling and sprinkled him.

The rumble grew, and through it, he could make out individual sounds. Someone was marching overhead.

A number of someones.

A large number of someones, all in step, and together. Islanders never crossed the bridge like that.

He was beneath the Fey.

They were heading from the Tabernacle to the other side of Jahn.

To the palace.

He had to beat them.

He started crossing faster, keeping pace with their footsteps, almost slithering across the damp ground. All the while he moved, he prayed softly under his breath, hoping the Holy One would take his message to God's Ear.

"Let me get there first," he whispered. "Please. Let me get there first."

FORTY-THREE

TITUS tried to go down the stairs, but the smoke was inky black and putrid. The fire had to be moving fast. He backed up, turned, and caught two Auds with his arms.

"You can't go down there," he said.

"But the catacombs—"

He shook his head. He didn't want to think about the catacombs. He brought the boys back up the stairs. Fey were coming down the corridor, the normal Fey, their faces streaked with smoke and blood. They didn't seem to care about the fire. They caught Danites, and the remaining Auds, and shoved them against the wall.

Titus took his two charges and pulled them into the nearest room, bolting the door. They were in a Danite cell. A single bed stood near the window, and two chairs were beside a small table. He passed them, and pulled the tapestry back.

The entire southern part of the city appeared to be under attack. Fey were going in and out of all the buildings. The animals were still there below, some feeding on dead bodies. A large cat had his paw on one of the Officiates and was gnawing at the man's innards.

Smoke billowed out of the lower windows. The spilled

candles must have lit the rugs on fire, and the wood trim throughout the Tabernacle caught. The entire building would be unsafe in a matter of moments.

Something thudded at the door. The smallest Aud cringed. The other one looked at Titus, and then recognized him.

"Holy Sir," he breathed.

Titus felt ridiculous in his poor disguise. Still, he raised a hand to his lips to shush the boy.

"What do we do?" the boy asked.

They had no choice. If they remained in the room, it was certain death. The animals below, on the other hand, looked busy. And perhaps they were seated. He couldn't tell and he didn't want to speculate.

He just knew they had to get out.

He peered out the window again. The drop was too steep for him. "Tie the blankets together," he said.

The boys looked at him as if he were crazy. Perhaps he was. But he could do nothing for his staff now, nothing for the Tabernacle. Porciluna was right. Titus had to save himself. He had the Secrets.

The Auds yanked the blankets off the bed. Titus leaned over it to see if it was built into the wall.

It was.

He grabbed one end of a blanket and tied it onto the bed's wooden frame. There were only two blankets. The boys had tied them together. The make-shift ladder wouldn't be long enough to reach the bottom, but it would do.

The thud at the door sounded again. Soon whatever it was outside would break in. Titus glanced at the boys. They looked terrified. He didn't know if it was better to send them down first or to go down first himself.

He didn't even know if the blanket ladder would work. It might catch fire near the lower windows.

The door thudded again, and then splintered.

His decision was made. He grabbed the other end of the blanket and tossed it out the window.

"Climb out," he said, "and hide as best you can. Don't call attention to yourself."

"C-c-climb, Holy Sir?" the first Aud asked.

The splinters in the door grew wider. "Now!" he said.

The boys scrambled onto the blanket. The Aud who

hadn't hid, the one who looked older, climbed down first. The second Aud had just gone over the side of the window when the door shattered.

"Holy Sir!" the Aud said.

"Go!" Titus yelled.

A Fey burst in. She was female, with a long, lean face, her eyes bright. She had her hands out. They actually had a second set of fingernails.

Titus reached behind him and untied the blanket. It slid out the window. He prayed he hadn't hurt the boys, but he knew if he had left it, the Fey would have followed the trail.

It was the boys' only chance.

But it destroyed his. He glanced out the window. The blanket was pooled at the bottom, but the boys were gone. The animals appeared to be eating nearby, and he saw no sign of chase.

Then someone tapped him on the shoulder. He turned. The woman was smiling at him. She had a drying drop of blood on the side of her nose. Several more Fey, men and women, had come into the room.

"Do you know what I can do?" she asked in Islander, as she ran her finger down the side of his Aud's robe. "I can remove your skin, one layer at a time."

A thin slice of the robe came off, curling onto the floor. The other Fey were watching, their eyes bright.

They would hold him and kill him, and he would have no chance at all.

Titus glanced up at her, letting all the fear he felt fill his face. Let her think he was going to give in. Let her relax for one moment.

She laughed, and raised a come-hither glance to the other Fey.

And Titus took advantage of that brief instant to launch himself backwards through the open window.

It was his only chance.

His feet hit the window ledge and thumped him against the stone side of the building, knocking the air from him. He was falling straight down, head first, and as he passed the lower level windows, he knew he didn't have time to right himself.

The blanket was looming, but it wouldn't break his fall.

Nothing would break his fall. He put his hands on top of his head, but it would do no good.

In his last moments of life, he knew a horror so profound he couldn't even scream.

He had not shared the Secrets.

He would die, and Rocaanism would die with him.

THE SEARCH

FORTY-FOUR

RUGAD stepped through the open Circle Door. The smell of smoke had been strong in the clearing; it was even stronger here. Shadowlands' porous walls absorbed the smoke as they were designed to do, but they couldn't remove such a vast stench—at least not so quickly.

Most of his troops were gone. Those that remained were Infantry, Red Caps, and a few Foot Soldiers. The rest had gone up Daisy Stream, to secure the villages along the stream bed. He counted on the Dream Riders to do most of that. After a few long nightmares, the Islanders upstream would awaken to an invasion force already in place. If they tried to fight, they would die.

Wisdom predicted they would lose half the villages. Rugad thought that they would lose an eighth at most. Islanders were not warriors. If they held true to the behavior of their cousins to the south, a few would make a token resistance, and once they learned their precious holy water no longer worked, they would give in.

Rugad would have his land and people to tend it.

But first he had to deal with this place.

He had seen only one devastated Shadowlands. When he

was a boy, one of the Leaders, a kin to the Black Family, had
made a Shadowlands in the middle of a Histle battlefield.
The Histle were fierce fighters; despite their small nation—
or perhaps because of it—the Histle had warriors equal to
the Fey's Infantry. The battles, which should have taken a
few days, had taken a few weeks. And a Histle commander
had seen the Fey disappear into Shadowlands one night. He
waited until they left in the morning, and then laid waste
the tents inside.

The devastation had been minor compared with this.

Ruined buildings still smoldered. The largest, a pile of ash
near the Circle Door, had obviously taken the brunt of the
attack. In all his years, Rugad had never seen a Shadowlands
this big. But then, they were always built as temporary
housing during a campaign. Never as permanent homes for a
Fey troop.

Until his son's failure. Until Rugar failed to take Blue Isle.

Even then, with Jewel's marriage and the Fey royal children, these Fey should have left Shadowlands and made
homes outside. Their vast fear of the Islanders' poison was
what made them failures in Rugad's eyes, not their thwarted
invasion. In some ways, the invasion had been successful.
The Black King's blood had mixed with royal Islander blood,
and the Islanders themselves had no idea how to fight Fey
without their poison.

But Rugad couldn't have as part of his troop Fey who had
lived in fear for twenty years. He would never know if he
could trust them, whether or not they would flee again.

Besides, Fey did not live in peace unless ordered to by
their ruler. Rugad had ordered the Fey on Galinas to live in
peace. They needed to have children, needed to raise a new
group of Infantry and magick users. And the oldest generation needed to retire. Fey had to learn calm as well as fury.

And they had.

But on Blue Isle, the Fey should have fought. They
should have fought until their last dying breath. If they
didn't have enough people to win a war, they should have
fought a guerrilla campaign. They could have scared the
Islanders into capitulation.

Instead, the Fey gave up.

Partly he blamed his son. Rugar was a great warrior

whose Visions were always precise. His interpretations of them were often difficult. His last Vision had been of Jewel on this Isle. When he had told Rugad about it, Rugad had said that the Fey would not win until the Black King arrived.

Rugar, his son, had refused to believe him.

All the failures resulted from that moment, from Rugar's decision to dismiss his father.

Rugad blinked. His eyes were raw from the smoky smell. He took a step in deeper, away from the smoldering ruins. Near the far wall of the Shadowlands, Red Caps were stacking bodies. Most of the Failures had no skin left—the Foot Soldiers had already gotten to them—but Rugad's Domestics could use the bones, and some of the Beast Riders might like the internal organs. Their animal hosts found such things delicacies.

The Red Caps were already going to work. A dozen of them crowded the body stack, pouches beside them. The short, squat Caps were anathema to most Fey, but Rugad had a fondness for them. He had seen Fey armies without Red Caps, bodies rotting in the sun, all that blood and flesh gone to waste. Ever since then, he always made certain he had an abundance of Red Caps on his campaigns.

Rugad clasped his hands behind his back and stepped deeper in the Shadowlands. He had left the Shadowlands standing because he believed his great-grandson had designed it. But standing inside it startled Rugad. The design bore his son's mark, Rugar's mark, in the perfect box-like shape, the unimaginative air, the additional space. Rugar rarely liked to make anything small.

But he had been dead a long time. And still the Shadowlands stood. Perhaps his great-grandson had designed the Shadowlands on Rugar's model. Or perhaps the boy had found a way to save the Shadowlands when Rugar died. That had been tried several times, but never accomplished.

If Rugad's great-grandson had achieved that, he was more powerful than Rugad had initially thought.

The details didn't matter, though. What did matter was that this Shadowlands was somehow tied to his great-grandson. For that reason, Rugad had ordered his troop to leave the Shadowlands standing. Otherwise he would have had a Shaman with the troop and she would have shattered the Shadowlands from within.

He was afraid, though, that if he did that, he would destroy the very person he had come to get.

His great-grandson.

And now, they told him, he had two. Odd that he had never Seen it. When the invasion was over, he would call his Shamans together, and see if their Visions matched his or if they could add information to that story of two children.

If so, he had to modify his plans.

His plans were elaborate. He had deliberately waited until his great-grandson had reached full adulthood, the full extent of his powers, before coming to the Isle. The boy had been corrupted from birth; training him then or training him now would make no difference. Rugad made better use of the time consolidating his hold on Nye and the entire Galinas continent. That way, when he left, he was assured that, despite his grandsons' incompetence, the Fey would continue to rule Galinas.

Rugad always knew he would conquer Blue Isle, and he knew the boy would be his. He had simply waited for the best time to come, the time when the Islanders had forgotten how to fight, when the Warders had discovered the best antidote to the poison, and when the boy had reached his maturity.

When the boy realized that Rugad controlled the Isle, the boy would work with his great-grandfather. The boy was brilliant. He would understand that he had no choice.

Fey passed Rugad, some salvaging magick items. The Infantry were carrying out pouches that appeared to date from Rugar's invasion. A pile of pouches stood in one of the other corners of Shadowlands—ruined pouches. Several other Infantry were carrying Domestic tools, needles, cloth, and spinning wheels. He was glad they had had the foresight to remove the items for salvage before the destruction was complete.

Only one building remained standing in Shadowlands. It was a small shack with no windows in the very center of the devastation. Four Foot Soldiers stood guard around it.

They had a prisoner.

He had ordered that only one person be taken prisoner—

his great-grandson. Yet he couldn't feel the presence of another Visionary here. It was odd, and he wasn't certain he liked odd.

Odd always made him nervous.

He strode toward the Foot Soldiers. The man in front of the door surprised him. Gelô led the Foot Soldier troop. He should have been with his soldiers on the trip up Daisy Stream. He certainly shouldn't have been guarding a small building in the center of Shadowlands.

"Gelô," Rugad said. He kept his tone wary but courteous, so that Gelô knew he wasn't in trouble yet, but he could be.

"We have a situation," Gelô said.

"I am beginning to understand that," Rugad said.

Gelô nodded to other Foot Soldiers, then grabbed Rugad's arm and stepped away from his post. "I have Solanda inside."

"Solanda!" Rugad had forgotten about her. She was Rugar's pet Shape-Shifter. Rugad had sent her along on the trip to Blue Isle without a second thought.

He did, however, expect her to be dead.

He waited.

Gelô swallowed. "She claims she raised your family on Blue Isle."

"And you believe her? She's a Shifter. They don't raise children."

"No." Gelô lowered his voice. "But Double confirms her story."

"How would Double know?" Rugad asked softly.

"Double took over one of the Wisps who raised your great-grandson in Shadowlands. He took over the male Wisp, Wind. The female was badly injured." Gelô shuddered. "Her wings were ruined."

"Where is Double?"

"Heading back to your encampment as you ordered," Gelô said. "All four of the Doppelgängers made successful transitions, although two of them say the information from their hosts is useless."

"Which two can we use?"

"Double, who became Wind, and Ghost, who became Touched."

"Touched?" Rugad did not remember anyone named Touched sent on this journey.

"A Spell Warder. He was a boy when he came here."

Then Rugad remembered. He had thought the boy would come to nothing.

"Ghost says he needs to see you as soon as you are done here. He says you'll need to know what that Warder knew."

"All right. Then we should hurry. Tell me why you let the Shifter live."

Gelô swallowed. He obviously knew that he had disobeyed a direct order, and he clearly hoped that his reasons were good enough. "The Doppelgängers were used up," he said, "and she had information. I thought it was better if you got it from her. Then you could make the decision to kill her or to let her live."

"You don't think this was a ploy for survival?"

"I'm sure it is," Gelô said, "but I think there's more. And with Double's confirmation, I am convinced of it."

Rugad took a deep breath and considered. The killing of a Shifter was a major event, not taken lightly in most circumstances. To kill a Shifter who might have valuable information would be more of a breach than not to do so.

He nodded. "Take her to my headquarters. Use a large guard. She has been here for twenty years, and most without guidance. We don't know where her loyalties are."

Gelô clicked his heels together. "Yes, sir." He went back to his post, then sent one of his men to get Infantry. They would take Solanda to Rugad's new Shadowlands under heavy guard.

But she was a peripheral issue. He had come into this gruesome place to find his great-grandson or to find the Shaman. Whoever had held this Shadowlands together had to answer to him.

He walked toward the far wall. Several Red Caps were working behind the remains of a building. A dozen bodies had been brought out. They had bruises on the sides of their faces, peaceful expressions on their features, and holes through their hearts. Dream Riders had held them in sweet dreams while Infantry had stabbed them through.

Amazing how even Fey could fall prey to such an easy death.

The Caps were lifting the bodies to move them to the cleaning site. The female Cap nearest Rugad staggered under the weight of the body she was carrying. Another Cap slung a dead child over his shoulder. There were a number of children among the bodies. Apparently the troop had felt safe enough here to raise families.

The idea made Rugad shudder. He had always thought the Fey were above becoming prisoners of the mind. Always. The fact that these weren't, that his own son's handpicked troops had decided not to fight for their own freedom, disgusted him.

Disturbed him.

He had to make certain that this large group of Failures did not demoralize his own troops. Somehow he had to make them realize that this group, picked by Rugar, were inferior to other Fey. He would have to do it subtly, since some of his troop had known people here. He would have to be careful.

Bits of shredded skin littered the gray floor of Shadowlands. Apparently a number of Failures had died in this spot, so many that the Foot Soldiers hadn't picked up all the pieces—or the Red Caps had been too busy to do so.

He brushed the skin aside with his boot. No blood on the floor, though. The Caps and the Soldiers both had been efficient about that. Which was good, since Fey blood would help his Warders more than anything else taken from these Failures. Fey blood conducted magick well, and the Warders needed it for their experiments.

His nostrils had apparently grown used to the smoky stench. It seemed less than it had only a few moments earlier. The smells were all leaching out of Shadowlands to float away in the outside air. He crossed the last pile of rubble, and stood beside the opaque wall.

His hand trembled.

He rubbed his thumbs over his forefingers, clearing them of any debris. Then he glanced around once, to make certain all the live Fey inside this Shadowlands were his. They were. Then he closed his eyes and put his fingertips on the wall.

The surface was cool and porous, almost like a hardened mist. His fingers sank in partway, confirming his hopes.

This was a Black Family Shadowlands. The Shaman hadn't tinkered at all.

Then he shoved his fingers deeper into the material, feeling it for the Links. He found it and his body shook with Remembered Vision—

Large thunderous cracks resounded through Shadowlands. The ground was shaking. Bits of the sky were falling, revealing a startling blueness above. Fey were screaming.

Screaming.

The Warders' cabin collapsed as the Warders ran outside. The porch that he was standing on was coming apart. Domestics poured out the door, running toward the Circle Door.

The buildings were collapsing. The Domicile was one of the few that remained upright, but it wouldn't last long. Already Fey were dying near the Circle Door. Fey were dying under falling pieces of sky. Fey were dying as they fell through the ground.

Shadowlands had to stay together.

He reached out with his mind and grabbed the corners of his world. He held them up with all the strength he could find. His father was still shouting, people were still screaming, but the smacking thuds had stopped.

He closed his eyes and imagined Shadowlands as it was. He rebuilt the holes in the walls, replaced pieces in the sky, and patched the chasms in the ground. In his mind, he walked around and tested each part of the Shadowlands, making it stronger than it had ever been.

The screaming stopped.

He opened his eyes.

There was carnage all around him. People lying under slabs of gray matter or large boards. Bodies flattened. Wounded moaning. But the ground had stopped trembling. The blue holes were gone from the sky, and a mist was rising.

It was his Shadowlands now.

—His.

Rugad shook himself out of the Remembrance. That had been a long time ago. The hands he saw through the Remembered Vision were tiny, a child's hands.

Despite himself, excitement built. His great-grandson had repaired Shadowlands when Rugar died. No wonder it had the look of Rugar but not the sense of him.

But it wasn't enough of Rugad's great-grandson's Shadowlands to have a sense of him as well. For that, Rugad would have to hunt the Links.

He removed his hand for a moment and flexed the fingers. They were already sore from their contact with an unfamiliar Shadowlands.

The Foot Soldiers had left the small building in the center of Shadowlands, and many of the Infantry were gone. Most of those who remained were Red Caps. Two were still staggering under the weight of bodies. A few were removing bodies from the rubble, charred bodies that obviously hadn't been rescued quickly enough to be useful. The rest of the Caps were across Shadowlands from him, absorbed in their work.

They weren't watching, which was good. It was one thing to know that your Leader had Vision. It was another to watch it.

He took a deep breath and shoved his finger back inside the wall. This time, he kept his eyes open, but his vision turned inside. The walls of Shadowlands had a dozen Links in them. Most came from the care the place had received from other Fey, Domestics now dead. Those Links were still bright, but their endings were gray, as if they were dying, slowly.

Then there was a black Link that ran all around Shadowlands, weaving through it like a thread. The Link was flat and decayed, an empty husk of itself.

Rugar's Link, long dead, but not properly severed. Apparently the boy, the great-grandson, had been too young.

A blue Link traveled through the middle of Shadowlands. It was bright and strong and vibrant. Rugad touched it ever so lightly with his index finger and then jerked back.

The Shaman.

She was alive.

And she had built a protection around her ties to Shadowlands. He couldn't get inside her Link. He couldn't find her.

A fury ran through him, but he knew better than to try to beat a Protection. She was supposed to have died. He had trained an entire team especially to kill her. It took an elite squad to kill a Shaman, not because it was difficult, but because it was taboo.

They had failed.

But not because they lacked the courage to kill her.

They apparently hadn't found her yet. She had known Rugad was coming.

And if she had known, his great-grandson had probably known.

He couldn't imagine what these Failures had told his great-grandson. That was, in fact, his greatest worry about the boy. He wasn't certain if the boy could trust him, if the boy could work for any Fey goals because he had been raised among Failures.

It had been a trade-off, one Rugad had pondered long and hard. But he had to trust his Visions, and his Visions told him to wait until the boy was through his childhood years. And those Visions were slowly being confirmed, one by one, as the days on Blue Isle went on.

He still held the Vision of that valley and the subsequent victories before him like a beacon. Blue Isle would be his. Then he would find his great-grandson, and together they would go to Leut. Together they would conquer the next few nations, and when Rugad was ready to retire, his great-grandson would go on to conquer the continent.

That last was a mere hope. But he did see the boy, in his mind's eye, on a ship for Leut. And he did see his own victory on Blue Isle.

Everything else was speculation. He wasn't even certain if he had seen his own death yet. Perhaps it hadn't been determined. Perhaps the defining moment was still waiting to happen.

But none of this mattered if he didn't find the boy. His grandsons couldn't rule, and there was no other family.

Except the other boy.

But an Islander, no matter what his bloodline, couldn't run the Fey. It took someone raised in Fey warrior traditions, someone with the battlefield in his heart.

Jewel had had that.

Her brothers had not.

Rugad took a deep breath. Going through the last Link would be a risk. He would find his great-grandson, but his great-grandson would also find him. And he didn't know yet how well that would sit with the boy.

This time Rugad closed his eyes. He didn't want the boy

to see the devastation of Shadowlands, at least not yet. He wanted to be able to explain it to him, to let him know how necessary it was. He would let the boy know the true meaning of Failure before explaining how it got punished and why it was not allowed.

Rugad stuck his fingers back in the wall. The material seemed to have cooled even more. A shudder ran through him. The last Link was bright, golden, and laced through everything like stitches on a hastily mended shirt. The Link vibrated with life.

Rugad touched it gently. It hummed. Then he thrust his consciousness into it and traveled along the Link, his mind sliding along the pathway as if it had been designed for him.

He landed inside a mass of anguish and loss, the body exhausted with tears and grief. The eyes opened onto a field and an Islander looking at it with some concern.

"Gift?" the Islander said, and in that moment, Rugad learned his great-grandson's name.

FORTY-FIVE

HIS whole body was shaking. Gift stood next to Leen, letting her rage wash over him. She had lost her family too, and if she had been in Shadowlands, she would have died.

Died.

Everyone he knew was dead.

Everyone.

Except Leen, Coulter, and Sebastian.

It had been like the time Shadowlands exploded.

Only this time, he couldn't stop it. He hadn't even known it was happening. Wasn't he a Visionary? Shouldn't he have known?

Coulter was talking to Leen, calming the rage that Gift had let her build. It didn't matter. It would fester in her now. He would get his revenge.

What he didn't like was the way Adrian was watching him and the way that clean Red Cap was looking at him. As if they expected something from him. Something he didn't like.

The sun had risen. The morning's warmth was burning off the dew. Steam was rising from the ground, and the corn still glistened in the bright air. Amazing how such an unspeakable thing could happen on such a gorgeous day.

He would never look at sunlight the same way again.

His mother was dead. Both of his mothers. His real mother died when he was three, and now Niche . . .

He swallowed hard and rubbed the bridge of his nose. He had saved Shadowlands to save her life. His grandfather had beaten her up so badly, she hadn't been able to escape when Shadowlands shattered. Rather than let her die, Gift had repaired Shadowlands.

But it had done no good. Now his great-grandfather had shown up and instead of rewarding her for raising his great-grandson, he murdered her.

And Gift's adoptive father.

And all the others whom he had lived with his entire life.

Coulter was still talking to Leen, but he was watching Gift. Gift turned. It was time to get Coulter away from her. He didn't understand, Coulter didn't, what it meant. He didn't know the depth of Gift's anger, the things they had to fight.

Then he felt something, a tendril of something, as if someone had opened a door in a long-empty room. Breeze came in, stirring up dust. Gift shuddered.

The feeling was inside him, and he didn't know where the door was. He turned his attention inward. Coulter came over to Gift, but Gift didn't look at him.

Then Gift felt another presence, whole and complete, crossing a Link Gift hadn't known he had. A powerful presence, old and complex, and strong. Stronger than Gift was. Maybe stronger than he would ever be.

The presence shoved Gift aside and peered out of Gift's eyes. Now—finally—Gift knew how Sebastian had felt all those years before Gift knew Sebastian existed, when Gift would come into Sebastian's body.

The presence stood where Gift usually stood, saw what Gift usually saw, felt what Gift usually felt. Gift felt as if he were stuffed into a corner of his own body and held there by an unseen hand.

Dimly, he heard Coulter say, "Gift?"

But Gift's body didn't answer. The presence filled it, startled and pleased at its discovery, studying the area around it.

Gift pushed at the presence, trying to move it aside, but it wouldn't budge.

The presence felt familiar and alien at the same time. It was male, a man, an old presence, but it had a young Image. In his youth, the man had looked like Gift, only with dark skin and dark eyes. Dark, dark, dark. There were choices inside this presence, choices that made Gift quake. Son or granddaughter? Mother or brother?

Gift didn't know what the question meant, and he wasn't certain he wanted to find out.

All he knew was that he couldn't budge the presence. It wouldn't move.

It wanted him.

Then a second presence appeared inside Gift. It had traveled across a different Link, and this presence Gift recognized. It was Coulter, bathed in white light. Coulter saw the dark presence and wrapped it in light, then shoved it back through its Link and slammed the door. Then Coulter moved through Gift's self, closing doors, locking them, and wrapping them with Coulter's light.

—What are you doing? Gift asked.

—Protecting you, Coulter said, and then he disappeared back down his Link.

Gift stepped back into his own place within himself. The dark presence had left a residue, but it wasn't of evil or threat as Gift had expected.

It was of curiosity and a longing that Gift couldn't identify. Gift gathered the threads of the remaining presence and held them for a moment, feeling an odd sort of sympathy at the loneliness that fed them.

Then he dropped them as if they burned him.

That had been his great-grandfather. The man who had killed his adoptive parents and all his friends. The man who had successfully destroyed Gift's home.

Gift kicked the threads, and they disappeared into a darkness within him. He never wanted to see them again.

Then he felt a hand on his shoulder.

He looked out of his own eyes, and felt himself come back to his body. Coulter was holding his shoulder. The Red Cap was standing in front of him and Leen was standing alone, arms crossed, a look of terror on her face.

"I said," Coulter asked slowly, "are you all right?"

Gift nodded. He felt odd, not quite himself. There was a residue of another person inside of him, and . . . emptiness. When Coulter had put guards on Gift's interior doors, he had closed things that had never been closed before.

"Who was that?" Coulter asked.

"You don't know?" Gift was startled. He thought Coulter would know everything. He had, after all, touched the presence.

Coulter shook his head. "I was too busy blocking you off."

"It was Rugad," the Red Cap said.

Gift looked at the little man. So did everyone else. "How did you know?"

"I recognized him," the Red Cap said. "No one else has that force in his personality. No one."

Gift shuddered. He had felt that, that presence so much stronger than his own.

"So he found you," Adrian said. "That was easy."

"But it won't be from now on," Coulter said. "I shut him out."

"For good?" Gift asked.

"Let's hope so," Coulter said.

FORTY-SIX

RUGAD slowly withdrew his hand from the wall of Shadowlands. His fingers burned and his eyes ached, even though he hadn't used them at all. The grayness of Shadowlands looked even duller after the brightness that had chased him out of his Link. He was dizzy. He sat on a pile of cut logs near the wall and rubbed his eyes with his uninjured fist.

He had never felt anything like that. The force that had come into his great-grandson and literally chased Rugad out. That force had not been part of his grandson. Visionaries did not have light and binding abilities. That had been an Enchanter.

A powerful one.

One Rugad didn't recognize.

His body was tingling. It felt its age. He had forgotten how a young body felt, all vibrant and full of life. His had aches, aches he had grown accustomed to, but aches all the same.

An Enchanter.

He had purposely not sent an Enchanter with Rugar on his invasion of Blue Isle. Rugad's excuse had been that there weren't enough Enchanters—which was true—but if he had thought the mission had any chance of succeeding, he would have sent one.

What had Boteen said? That he had felt others like him in this place?

Others.

One might have died in the destruction of Shadowlands. But one hadn't. Rugad knew that for sure.

And the one that hadn't had enough power to dislodge an old and powerful Visionary from his post. And then lock him out.

"Are you all right, sir?" The voice was young. Rugad opened his eyes. An Infantryman stood before him, tall enough for magick, but still with the slenderness of extreme youth. The boy hadn't come into his power yet.

Rugad didn't feel all right. He felt shaken, startled, and slightly ill from the touch of all that light. "What's your name, boy?"

"Percival, sir."

Percival. The name clearly gave his age. Percival. A Nyeian name. While Rugad respected the Fey tradition of taking names from the conquered countries, he rather regretted it for the last generation. Nyeian names were flowery and fanciful. They didn't belong to soldiers.

"Well, Percival," Rugad said, making certain his voice sounded strong, "how did you cross country to get to this place?"

"We came up through the marshes and back country, sir, shortly after we came down those mountains."

He sounded a bit shaky when he mentioned the mountains. Rugad couldn't blame him. The trip over the mountains had been very difficult for the magickless Infantry. They had had to climb up the ocean side, using Domestic ropes held in place at the top by spelled spikes, and then they had had to climb down the other side. Only one rope had snapped, and Gull Riders had managed to shore it up before it took too many lives.

"Did you cross farmland?" Rugad asked.

"Yes, sir," Percival said. "In the center of the country. There was a vast amount of it. Well tended. The harvest looked good."

Rugad smiled. His soldiers were well trained. Even

though they had learned the art of battle, they knew what good land looked like. They had to. They were under strict orders not to destroy good land or healthy crops.

"How far is it from here?"

"Several days' fast walk," Percival said.

Rugad nodded. Several days. By that time, his great-grandson would be gone. It wouldn't do to go himself. He would have to try to Link one more time, and if that failed, then he would have to send someone after the boy, someone who would be able to get the information out of those Islander farmers.

Someone he could trust.

He would have to think on that. He would have an idea by the time he reached his own Shadowlands.

"Thank you," he said to Percival. "How much longer before the work finishes in here?"

"We're nearly done, sir, getting all the salvaged magick items. Then we leave it to the Caps. They seem to have good hauling, sir."

Rugad nodded. Good hauling. Lots of blood and flesh and bones for the Warders. He had brought quite a few Warders with him, not certain how many he would need. The poison and its effect on Fey might be an unhappy accident.

Then again, it might not.

He worked on the theory that it was not, that the Islanders had other tricks, other ways of defeating the Fey, ways he had not heard of yet.

His son, Rugar, had come to this Isle with the idea that it would be easy to conquer. Rugad had come with the idea that it would be difficult. Rugad had not only Rugar's experiences to reply on, but also Fey history. The Fey seemed to work hardest to capture the smaller countries. Somehow the larger ones toppled in quick disarray.

If Blue Isle toppled quickly, wonderful.

If it did not, then Rugad was prepared.

But before Blue Isle fell completely, Rugad had to find his great-grandsons. It wouldn't do any good to win the Isle and create chaos by accidentally killing someone of Black Blood.

"You've done well," he said to Percival.

Percival smiled, clicked his heels together, bowed slightly, and left. Rugad watched him go. The troops were doing very well. The entire Isle would be secure in a short period of time.

The key to success, though, would be that Fey Visionary Rugad had met just briefly.

The one who had repaired Shadowlands at the age of three.

Gift.

FORTY-SEVEN

FORTY-SEVEN

IT took a moment for Sebastian's words to penetrate. Gift was hurt. Nicholas's blood son. The son he had never known. The son stolen from him.

The happy, chubby newborn with the alert eyes.

Gift.

"How is he hurt?" Nicholas asked.

Arianna had crossed her arms and turned her back and was peeking through the tapestry at the birds below. She was pretending not to listen. She had, apparently, decided to hate her real brother.

Sebastian didn't answer. His mouth was open and his eyes were empty again. A tiny line of drool ran between his upper lip and his tongue.

"Sebastian!" Nicholas snapped.

Something in his tone made Arianna whirl. The tapestry flopped against the window. She grabbed Sebastian's arm. He tilted his head and moaned.

Nicholas had never seen Sebastian like this. He had always thought the boy's eyes were dull, devoid of intelligence, but he had never really seen it until now. The eyes were empty.

Completely empty.

"Sebastian!" Arianna shook him. His head flopped back and forth. It creaked as it did so.

Nicholas moved closer, grabbed Sebastian's other arm, and led him toward the chair. Sebastian's legs moved, but as if he were a doll. He had little control over them.

"Sebastian!" Arianna's voice was full of panic now. She looked up at Nicholas, as if Nicholas could make it all better. He had no idea what to do.

"Have you ever seen him like this?" Nicholas asked.

She pursed her lips together and helped her brother into the chair. She had. She obviously had, but she didn't want to admit when.

He didn't have time to fight his strong-willed daughter.

He knelt in front of his son. "Sebastian? Sebastian, come back."

Sebastian blinked and then was present in his eyes again. They filled with tears.

"Sebastian?" Nicholas asked.

"Gift . . . is . . . gone," Sebastian whispered.

Nicholas felt a chill run through him. Sebastian had wailed when Jewel died. Sebastian had felt his grandfather's magick once, long ago. Sebastian had felt the magick of the birds outside.

Now this.

"What do you mean he's gone?" Arianna asked. Her lower jaw was set. She didn't like talking about her real brother. Something in that expression bothered Nicholas, but he didn't have time to focus on it right now.

"He's . . . u-sual-ly . . . some-where," Sebastian said. The tears fell as he spoke, running like water down his cheek.

"Everyone's usually somewhere." Arianna's words were clipped as if she were angry with Sebastian for having a relationship with Gift. Any kind of relationship.

Nicholas brushed the tears from Sebastian's cheek. The boy was trembling.

"In-side . . . me," Sebastian said. "The . . . Link . . ."

"Oh." Arianna turned away again, going back to the window. She acted as if the conversation were over.

Nicholas smoothed back a strand of Sebastian's coarse hair. "The Link is gone?" he asked.

Sebastian nodded. He brought his free hand up and wiped the water from the underside of his jaw.

"But how can that be?" Nicholas asked. Unless Gift was dead. Wouldn't Sebastian know if Gift died? Wouldn't that have traveled across the Link?

"It . . . snapped," Sebastian said.

The chill grew inside Nicholas. A sudden ending. But Sebastian spoke slowly. Maybe he meant something else.

"It's broken?" Nicholas asked.

"Some-one . . . else . . . cut . . . it . . . off."

Nicholas rocked back on his heels. He had not expected that answer.

Apparently Arianna hadn't either. She crossed her arms and leaned against the window frame. "You mean like someone killed him?" she asked.

Sebastian shook his head, the movement even and methodical. "Like . . . a . . . thread . . . cut . . . with . . . scis-sors."

"Is Gift alive?" Nicholas asked.

"I . . . don't . . . know," Sebastian said. His voice rose in a wail. Arianna came back to him, wrapped her arms around his shoulders, and frowned at Nicholas.

"Don't upset him."

"I'm not," Nicholas said. He didn't want to fight his daughter too. "Think, Sebastian. Was he alive when the thread was cut?"

"Yes . . ."

"I thought Links were stronger than threads," Nicholas said.

"What does it matter if he's dead?" Arianna asked.

Sebastian threw himself forward, toward Nicholas, out of Arianna's arms. He moved faster than he had ever moved. "It . . . mat-ters. . . . I . . . love . . . him."

Arianna held up her hands. "Sorry," she said.

"Wouldn't it be different if he died?" Nicholas asked. "Wouldn't the Link remain?"

He hated magick he didn't understand. Hated it. If only Solanda were still here.

But she wasn't. They had to figure this out on their own. And quickly.

Sebastian frowned. The tears had stopped, but his eyes were still wet, as if more tears threatened. "I . . . don't . . .

know," he said. But he looked uncertain, as if he hadn't thought of Nicholas's question before.

"Can you find him?" Arianna asked. "Reestablish the Link?"

Sebastian blinked and disappeared from his eyes again. Nicholas hated that. This Sebastian was truly an empty shell. He didn't want this boy to go away. Nicholas couldn't bear it if he did. It shook him deeply, made him wonder if he shouldn't have sent his two children below despite Arianna's arguments.

Then Sebastian blinked. He was back, and so were the tears. "I . . . can't . . . find . . . him."

"Well, we'll find out what happened soon enough," Arianna said. She went back to the tapestry and peered through the side. She was right not to forget those birds. Nicholas needed to get back to that matter, but he couldn't. Not yet.

Gift was his blood son. His firstborn. The one that the Black King would want.

"Stop . . ." Sebastian said. He had turned toward Arianna. "Stop . . ."

"Stop what?" Nicholas asked.

Sebastian's lower lip trembled. More tears ran down his cheeks, making them black and shiny.

Like water on stone.

"Gift . . . is . . . im-por-tant. . . ." Sebastian said.

"Not to us," Arianna said. "Whatever happens to him happens."

Nicholas squeezed Sebastian's hand. "No," he said. "Sebastian's right. Gift is important. Like it or not, he's family. And Sebastian seems to be the only one who recognizes it. If Gift is dead, we need to know by whose hand. And if someone cut the Link between Sebastian and Gift, we need to know who did and why."

"Did you ever think that Gift did?" Arianna asked.

"Why?" Sebastian asked.

"So you wouldn't know what he was doing," Arianna said. "So you wouldn't know what he was planning."

"Or," Nicholas said, "so that someone else wouldn't know about Sebastian. You said there was a third party involved?"

"Four . . ." Sebastian said. "For . . . a . . . mo-ment, . . . I . . . felt . . . four."

"Four what?" Arianna sounded bored. She still wasn't watching, but her back was rigid. She cared more than she wanted to admit.

"Me, . . . Gift, . . . and . . . two . . . others," Sebastian said. "A . . . big . . . pres-ence . . . and . . . then . . . the . . . snipper."

"The snipper?" Arianna said.

"The one who cut the Link," Nicholas said.

"See?" Arianna said. "He's trying to hide something from us."

"No!" Sebastian pushed himself out of the chair. Then he swayed for a moment. "Gift . . . would-n't . . . hurt . . . me."

"Don't be so sure," Arianna said.

"I . . . know . . . him," Sebastian said. Nicholas sat back and watched the boy. He had never seen him so animated, so intent.

"Why . . . don't . . . you . . . be-lieve . . . me, . . . Ari?"

"Because she's jealous," Nicholas said. He needed to interrupt, needed to get this back on track.

"Of that Fey?" Arianna whirled, fists tight. "I am not!"

"It doesn't matter," Nicholas said. "I thought Solanda said your Link sustained both of you."

"That's . . . Bound," Sebastian said. "Link . . . is . . . like . . . talk-ing. . . . He's . . . quiet . . . now. . . . May-be . . . gone."

Maybe gone. The phrase chilled Nicholas. But he could do nothing about it. Neither could Arianna. If he understood Linking right, it wasn't part of her magick.

"So he's gone," Nicholas said, "and I, for one, want to know why." He stood, brushed off his wrinkled robe, and sighed. "But it will have to wait. Those birds are our focus now."

"No . . ." Sebastian said. His voice was soft, but plaintive.

"No, what?" Nicholas said. He spoke gently, not wanting to upset the boy.

"I . . . need . . . Gift," Sebastian said.

"Why?" Arianna asked. Her face was a small thundercloud. She looked like Jewel for a moment, all angles and strength.

"I'm ... all ... by ... my-self," he said in a very small voice.

They had had that Link from the moment Sebastian was formed. Even if Nicholas thought of Sebastian as his son, Sebastian really wasn't. He was a creation, a creation of Gift's.

And now Gift was gone, severed from him.

"You're not alone," Arianna said, wrapping her arms around him. "I'm with you."

"But ... not ... in-side," he said.

"No," she said, smoothing his coarse hair away from his face. "Not inside. But you're inside. Most of us are all alone in there. You'll be all right, once you get used to it."

He sighed and leaned his head against her. He was still trembling. His gaze met Nicholas's. Nicholas couldn't entirely understand the feeling. Nicholas had always been alone in his body. But if Solanda were correct, Sebastian had never been. He had been created when Gift left parts of himself inside the stone.

"We'll find him," Nicholas said, knowing instinctively that the sanity of his son—maybe of both his sons—depended on it. "And we'll find out what happened."

"Sebastian doesn't need him," Arianna said. "He has us."

"Sebastian isn't like us," Nicholas said. "We don't know what he needs." He took his son's hand. "Can you get along alone, Sebastian?"

Sebastian bit his lower lip. More tears fell. He swallowed, clearly trying to get control of himself. "Can ... we ... find ... Gift?"

"As soon as possible," Nicholas said.

"Can ... we ... send ... Ari?"

Nicholas glanced at his daughter. She had her eyes closed. She didn't want to help with this.

"I think we can," Nicholas said. "But first we have to deal with the birds below. The Fey are all over the city. I can't send her into that. We don't want something to happen to her, too."

"You'll have to send me into that eventually," Arianna said. She still had her eyes closed. Her face was half-buried in Sebastian's hair. "I'm the only one who can tell you how many birds there are. I'm the only one who can get out of here."

"We don't know that," Nicholas said. He didn't want her outside. He didn't want her anywhere near those Fey.

"I can fly out one of the small windows on the North Tower. I can see the whole city and be back here in a very short time. No one else in this palace can."

"No . . ." Sebastian whispered.

"Do you want me to find Gift or not?' Arianna asked.

"Don't . . . leave . . . me," Sebastian said.

"I have to, if you want me to find him. But first we have to save ourselves."

"No . . ." Sebastian said.

"I'll be here," Nicholas said. "One of us will always be with you."

Sebastian raised his shiny face to his father. ". . . Pro-mise?"

"Yes," Nicholas said.

Sebastian turned in Arianna's arms. "You . . . have . . . to . . . come . . . back. . . . Pro-mise . . . you'll . . . come . . . back."

"I promise," Arianna said. She kissed his cheek, then stepped back.

Nicholas swallowed. She was really going to leave. And he needed her to.

She was one of his assets.

The problem was that she was the most valuable. He couldn't bear to lose her.

"Arianna," he said, not letting any of those emotions into his voice. "If you see Fey, you cannot attack them."

"The Shaman explained it to me."

"No matter who you see," Nicholas said. "Demand, if they catch you, to see the Black King. He will want to see you."

"He won't," Arianna said. "They'll never figure out who I am. Trust me, Daddy."

He did trust her. But he had also learned that life was rarely simple, that the world would change in the space of a heartbeat, that all that was precious could disappear in a moment.

"I love you, honey," he said.

She nodded and smiled. "I'll take that with me," she said. "Take care of Sebastian."

"I will."

"I'll be back before you miss me," she said as she ran to the door.

He held his stone son, watching her go, hearing her footsteps echo in the hallway. She was wrong. She wouldn't be back soon enough.

He missed her already.

FORTY-EIGHT

"WE got holy water but na food. A man canna drink holy water, and he canna eat it."

Matthias did not open his eyes. The band he had allied with were still talking. He didn't know how long he had been out, but his head ached and his throat was dry. His back hurt too. He had passed out leaning against Marly, but she had obviously moved, leaving him on the blanket someone had spread across the cavern's stone floor.

He was warm, though, warmer than he probably should have been given that he was in a damp cavern. Someone had placed a blanket over him too. He was using their resources. No wonder they had complained.

"We need ta send someone back for that food," the voice said.

"We canna. Ye heard Ubur. They're burning Jahn."

"It dunna make sense, burning Jahn."

"I seen it. And the Tabernacle too."

Matthias opened his eyes, and sat up on his elbows. The movement made him dizzy and pulled on the wounds along his shoulders, but he didn't care. "The Fey are burning the Tabernacle?"

Yasep smiled with one side of his mouth. "Tis a shame, holy man. If ye'd been there, ye'd be dead."

There were two more men in the group, neither of whom he recognized. They sat near the crates, their faces covered with soot, their clothes old and torn. One of the men held a knife in his right hand. It still bore fresh blood.

"They be burning all a Jahn," the man without the knife said.

"But why?" Matthias said.

"How should we know? We just got down here with our lives."

"Ye sure ye weren't followed?" Denl asked.

"Ubur killed the Fey what was closest," said the man without the knife. The man with the knife, Ubur, nodded.

"I hear they can turn invisible," said Jakib.

"They can do more than that," Matthias said. "They can take over a man's body, and make him do their bidding. They can even become that man."

"Yer lyin," Yasep said.

Matthias pushed himself all the way into a sitting position. Some of the dizziness was fading. He shoved the blanket down, and let the cavern's coolness overwhelm him. It felt good. "If you want to take that kind of risk with these two new men, fine," Matthias said. "You're the leader."

"How can ye tell they're not human?" Jakib asked.

"Holy water, ye fool," said one of the other men. "A babe'd know that."

"Yer willin to touch holy water?" Yasep asked the two new men.

"Aye," Ubur said.

"Twould na do harm, if'n it makes his lordship happy," the other said.

"Taint no lord," Denl said. "Tis the Fifty-First Rocaan."

"Naw," Ubur said. "He's dead."

"Did ye test him with holy water?" the second newcomer asked.

"I did," Marly spoke from behind Matthias. She was sitting cross-legged near one of the crates, her skirt tugged taunt over her knees. "I cleaned his wounds with it."

"Ye willin to take a woman's word?" Ubur asked.

"She's my sister," Jakib said, his voice low.

The newcomers looked at each other. Finally Ubur lowered his head in acknowledgment. "Tis sorry I am. I dinna know."

"Get holy water," Yasep said to one of the men behind him. He opened a crate and pulled out a vial. These had come from the Tabernacle or one of the kirks. Matthias recognized the type of vial. They were specially made for the church by glass craftsmen near the Slides of Death.

The man pulled out the stopped and approached the other two.

"Wait," Matthias said. "Let me make sure that is holy water."

"Oh, n how can ye do that, holy man?"

"It has an odor," Matthias said, "a distinct odor."

The man handed Matthias the bottle. The man's hands left slimy prints on the bottle's side. Matthias sniffed. The water smelled faintly bitter, as it was supposed to.

"This is all right," he said.

The two newcomers held out their hands. The man poured some water on them. Nothing happened.

"Ye worry fer nothin," Yasep said.

"I worry for good reason. The Fey infiltrated the Tabernacle in the early years, a number of times. If they saw someone come down here, they would come too." Matthias rubbed his face with his clean hand. His fingernail caught a bandage and pulled on the healing skin, making him wince.

"Dunna do that," Marly said, catching his hand in her own. "Ye'll hurt yerself. Takes time ta heal."

"If they're burning Jahn, we don't have time. Where does the air down here come from?"

The men shrugged.

"There's a number a openings," Yasep said. "N parts a the tunnels are gone."

"That's what I'm worried about," Matthias said. "If water can get in, air can get in. Smoke can get in. We might suffocate down here."

"Tis na a small place," Yasep said. "Ye saw only a tiny passage. These tunnels run all under the palace side a the city. A man could live down here for years n no one'd ever find him."

"Is that what you've done?" Matthias asked.

Denl grinned at him. "Makes our business easy."

Matthias had promised himself he wouldn't ask what their business was. He didn't want to know. "What's this about food? Do you have any here?"

"A course we do," Yasep said.

"But na enough fer this many fer verra long," Denl said.

Yasep glared at him.

"Would ye be likin something?" Marly asked.

Matthias nodded, then clutched the side of his head. Even that simple move made him dizzy. He might want to heal, but willing himself well would only work so far.

"Water at least," he said.

"N tak?" she asked.

He suppressed a grimace. He had lived on tak in those horrible days just after he left the Tabernacle. Tak was dried bread preserved in fish oils. It tasted both stale and spoiled, and yet somehow was neither. Travelers often kept plenty of it on hand.

"Sounds fine," he said.

"So yer holiness knows tak," Yasep said.

Matthias sighed. "Of course I do, Yasep. I am not the kind of protected lord you think I am. I lived outside for five years, and have been without a home for fifteen. I've eaten more tak than I care to think about."

"Na need ta get testy," Yasep said.

"Then stop baitin him," Marly said. "We all know yer jealous, him being a great man n all, but ye lead this troop and will until ye become stupid, which it seems, yer on the edge of."

"Shut up, woman."

"Dunna talk ta me sister that way," Jakib said.

"I can talk ta her anyway I like," Yasep said.

"See?" she said, pulling a tube of tak from one of the crates. "Stupid."

"Woman—"

"Leave her alone," Matthias said. "You've got enough problems without dividing the troop."

"N how do ye know that?" Yasep said.

"I heard," he said. He took the tak that Marly offered, ripped off a quarter of it, and handed three-quarters back to her. She frowned at him. He smiled at her. He wouldn't eat all their food. He didn't need to. He had proven to himself a long time ago that he could survive on very little.

He took a bite. Tak tasted as bad as he remembered. "If there are fires all over Jahn and Fey everywhere, food is going to become scarce quickly. You'll have to make some decisions about what to do. If the Fey don't discover these tunnels, you could stay down here indefinitely. Provided, of course, that you have enough food."

"Ye think ye know everything," Yasep said.

"No," Matthias said. "I just know that right now my fate is tied to yours. If these things are taken care of, I'll survive."

"We could take care a ye," Yasep said. His tone was not pleasant.

"I suppose you could," Matthias said. "Then I would be dead and you would be in the same situation."

"Yer petty jealousy'll kill us all," Marly said. "Canna ye see he's right? Listen ta him, like ye'd listen ta the others."

"I believe," Matthias said softly, "he is listening to me like he listens to the others."

"And ye, yer here causa me. Dunna abuse that. I willna defend ye if I think ye'll hurt us all." She was all fire when she spoke to him, fire and fury. He liked that. It put color in her cheeks.

"Water?" he asked. The tak was going down hard.

"Oh, aye." She was back to her old self. Meeker, less angry. And it happened in the space of a heartbeat.

That seemed like a good thing to know, her ability to change so quickly, although he didn't know quite why.

"Ye'll na take the leadership from me," Yasep said.

"I already said I wouldn't." Matthias took the water from Marly, and drank. It was cool and fresh and tasted wonderful. It got rid of the last pieces of tak from his mouth.

"But ye are," Yasep said.

Matthias sighed and handed the cup back to Marly. "No, I'm not," he said. "Most leaders have advisors who say what they think the leader should do. The leader chooses to listen or not—"

"Then I willna listen."

"—depending, of course, on how sound the leader thinks the advice is, not on whether or not he likes the advisor."

Yasep stared at him for a moment, then turned away.

"He's gotta point," Jakib said.

"Shut up," Yasep said.

"Twould be good ta listen," Denl said. "He knows things we dunna."

Yasep sighed.

"N twould be right ta keep him with Fey all around. He knows holy water."

"All right then," Yasep said, "yer the leader, as ye wanted."

"I did not want," Matthias said. "And I will not accept the position. I don't even know what your business is."

"Tis survival now," Marly said softly.

"Still n all," Yasep said, "yer gonna lead."

Matthias took another bite of tak and nearly choked. He forced himself to swallow it. This was how it always happened. Four times now, ever since he had left the Tabernacle, he had been given the leadership of a group.

The others looked relieved. They wanted him in charge, and he knew it. He attracted followers, and he didn't like it. In his first months away from the Tabernacle, he had a small group of people going everywhere with him, and he never spoke to them. Not once.

Then he went to the Cliffs of Blood and whole towns would come out whenever he appeared. Finally he found Yeon, who asked him why he was fighting his ability to attract people, why he wasn't using it.

Matthias had said he wasn't used to it, that no one had followed him in the Tabernacle.

Funny, isn't it? Yeon had said, *How God gives us gifts when we don't need them, and takes them away when we do?*

Sometimes Matthias wondered if that's what really happened, or if God had given him the gift after he left to show him that he had to do something different with his life. What that different thing was, he didn't know.

"Do ye have nothin ta say?"

"I don't want to lead," Matthias said.

"I dunna care what ye want!"

Matthias tilted his head so that he could see Yasep clearly in the torch light. "First you're jealous of me leading your people, then you try to force me to do it? Make up your mind, Yasep."

But Yasep didn't look at him. He stopped beside Ubur instead. "Tis true, bout the Fey? They be all over Jahn, killin n burnin?"

"Aye," Ubur said. He appeared to be watching this interaction with great interest.

"N ye think they'll stop?"

"Not till nothin's left."

"Nicholas wouldn't let them do that," Matthias said. Whatever he thought of Nicholas, the boy wouldn't allow his city to burn away.

"I dinna see our guards," Ubur said.

"Nicholas," Denl breathed. "Ye mean King Nicholas?"

Matthias shrugged. "If that's how you want to call him."

"Ye dunna believe he should be king?"

"He's got the legal right to the title," Matthias said. "I just wonder where his loyalties are."

Jakib smiled and crouched beside Matthias. "I knew twas fated I save ye. Tis as we believe. No Fey lovers."

"Jakib!" Marly snapped.

"It's all right," Matthias said. "I'm not a Fey lover, and I certainly opposed Nicholas with his marriage to that Fey from the beginning. He didn't listen to me, which ultimately caused my exile here."

"I canna do this," Yasep said. He sat down heavily.

"Do what?" Marly asked.

"Give up me post ta this man."

"Then don't," Matthias said. "I don't want to lead anyone. I'm not good at it."

"See?" Marly asked.

"But ye dunna ken," Yasep said to Matthias, finally talking to him on an equal basis. "I dunna unnerstand Fey. I wouldna ha checked Ubur and Dalis if'n ye hadna reminded me. I wouldna ha thought anyone would come down here who dinna belong. If I lead, I'll kill us all."

"And that's where your jealousy came from? This fear?"

"Aye," Yasep said softly. "Ye know. Ye know what ta do ta the Fey."

"I suppose," Matthias said, "but not in this instance. In this instance you're right. Hide. It sounds as if there's too many of them to fight."

"Aye," said Dalis. He wiped his hand over his sooty face.

It only smeared the soot. "I never seen so many Fey. More'n the people a Jahn, seemed ta me."

"So do it tagether like he said," Marly said, exasperation in her voice. "Ye give orders well n fine, Yasep. Let the Holy Sir have the ideas."

"I'm not the Holy Sir," Matthias said.

"Twould be that best. He knows what ta do, n ye know us. Twould work out fine," Jakib said.

"And you know the tunnels and the amounts of food and holy water that you have," Matthias said. "Besides, I'm too weak to do much leading."

Yasep nodded, once. "I willna talk a this again," he said to Matthias.

"Good," Matthias said. "I find it wearying."

He took another sip of the water, then bit some more tak. The nourishment was helping him feel a little better. Now with this leadership matter clearly decided, he might be able to get a bit more rest.

Denl held up a hand. "Hear that?" he whispered, his voice almost inaudible.

"No," Jakib said.

"Shhh," Denl said. The entire troop leaned forward. Matthias stopped chewing.

A slithery sound.

A footstep.

A curse.

"Tis Fey!" Ubur whispered. "They followed us."

"We don't know that," Matthias whispered. "Others might know of this place."

"N our food," Dalis whispered.

Yasep put a hand to his lips. He nodded at Jakib and Latse. They hurried to the side of the tunnel. Then he nodded at Ubur and Dalis. Dalis pulled his knife. Ubur's was still out. They went to the other side of the tunnel. The rest of the men blended into the darkness of the walls. Yasep put a hand on Marly's shoulder, forcing her on the blanket beside Matthias.

"No," she whispered.

"Tis best," Yasep whispered back.

"I agree," Matthias whispered. He understood the plan. Leave Marly and Matthias among the supplies as if this were their hiding place, a couple escaping the Fey, and then attack if need be. "But give me a knife."

Yasep studied him for a moment, then pulled a knife from his boot. "Only if tis Fey."

Marly crawled across the floor, grabbed the vial of holy water, and grinned. "Nay. If tis Fey, we'll use this."

Yasep disappeared into the darkness. Matthias took Marly's hand. He didn't have the heart to tell her that if their intruder was Fey, they would have to use the holy water, the knife, and anything else they could find.

And even then, they might not survive.

FORTY-NINE

"COME on," Coulter said. He took Gift's hand and tugged. Gift didn't move. He felt disoriented, alone, more alone than he'd ever been. It was as if his body were a house, and someone had just removed all the furniture. He echoed in there.

Alone.

Adrian was watching him. The Red Cap had his little arms crossed, a frown on his square face. He didn't trust Gift anymore, if he ever had. The taint of his great-grandfather was too much. The Red Cap had killed once before, Coulter had told him that a long time ago. Maybe the Red Cap would kill again.

Leen's skin was ashen. The anger seemed to have drained out of her. Gift had never seen her like that before.

And Adrian's son stood to the side, as if he didn't want to get close to any real Fey.

"Where are we going to go?" Gift asked. "If he could find me here, he can find me anywhere."

Coulter shook his head. "I shut him out. He won't be able to find you again. But we don't know what he's seen. We don't know how soon he'll find us. We have to go somewhere else."

"There is nowhere," Gift said. His great-grandfather had already been inside Shadowlands, and was probably in Jahn now.

"There are a lot of places on the Isle," Adrian said. "There are mountain caves near the Slides of Death."

"The villages to the north are very remote," Adrian's son said. "No one would find you there."

"You could build a Shadowlands of your own," Leen said.

The sun had come up completely now. The dew had dried, and the heat was rising. It was truly summer, a season that Gift usually liked.

That Coulter usually liked.

A season that Sebastian loved.

Suddenly Gift felt a little frisson of fear. He went back inside himself, slid toward his oldest and most favorite Link—

—and slammed into a door. His consciousness staggered and nearly winked out, but he forced himself to remain present. The door was covered with light. The light Coulter had wrapped around it.

Gift touched the light and felt a shivery charge run through him, a charge that went from his consciousness to his real body. The door was locked, inside and out. He reached again, stuck his imaginary hand in as far as it would go, but the charge grew too great.

His Link was closed. He was cut off from Sebastian, and Sebastian needed him.

Sebastian might face the Black King, and he might have to do so alone. Gift wouldn't allow that.

He raced back to his own eyes, and felt as if he nearly burst through them, as an angry child would run through a room.

Adrian took a startled step backwards. Even Leen looked surprised. Gift wondered idly how long he'd been gone.

"You cut my Links," he said to Coulter.

"I didn't cut them. I just closed them."

"Open them," Gift said.

"If I do, your great-grandfather can use them to find you.

He didn't come directly the first time. He came through Shadowlands."

"Open my Links."

Coulter held out his hands. "They're not all closed. Our Link is still open."

"Can't my great-grandfather use that one too?" Gift's voice was mocking. "Or can he only use the ones that threaten you?"

"It's not that way, Gift." Coulter's voice sounded too smooth, too confident.

"Open my Link to Sebastian."

"No," Coulter said.

"Open it."

"Why don't you do it yourself?" Adrian asked, his voice soft, as if he didn't really want to be in this fight but felt no way around it.

"I tried. Coulter locked me out."

"Coulter?"

Coulter shrugged. "Sebastian is hollow. It would be easy for the Black King to fill him and then get you."

"Sebastian is not hollow," Gift said. "He's part of me. And he'll die without me."

"Like you'll die without me?" Coulter asked.

The words hung between them. Coulter had rescued Gift. He had saved Gift's life when they were boys. Gift owed him for that. Gift would always owe him for that.

"No," Gift said softly. "Sebastian needs me to survive."

"There's a difference between Linking and Binding," Coulter said.

"I know that," Gift said. "But Sebastian relies on me. That Vision—without me, he won't survive."

"Do you know that for sure?" Coulter asked. "Do you really know that?"

Gift swallowed. He didn't know it. He didn't know if anyone did. But he wasn't going to risk Sebastian's life to find out. "Open it. I won't let him die."

"He's not really alive anyway."

"I came to you to help save him!" Gift said. "That's why I'm here, for Sebastian."

"No," Coulter said. "You're here so that I can protect you

from the Black King. He's already murdered your adoptive family. What do you think he'll do to you?"

"He can't kill me," Gift said. "He's come for me. You know that. Don't make something up to justify what you did."

"I'm saving you from him."

"Open that Link," Gift said.

"No." Coulter crossed his arms.

"Open it." Gift said.

"No. He'll find you through the Link. Don't you know that? Maybe that's what your Vision means. That he'll find you and shatter Sebastian as he does so."

"Visions are never metaphors," Gift said. "They're always pieces of the actual happening."

"I don't think we should stand here arguing any more," Adrian said. "If the Black King knows where Gift is, then Gift should move."

"And we might want to leave too," Adrian's son said.

They looked at each other across the Red Cap's head.

"He can't harm us unless we let him," Gift said.

"It seems to me that he can do a lot of harm," Leen said.

"If he gets close, I'll make a Shadowlands," Gift said.

"He'll be able to come in," Coulter said. "He's got the magick."

"If he can find the Shadowlands," Gift said.

"It shouldn't be hard," Coulter said.

Gift smiled. "Most Shadowlands are not as big as the one my grandfather made. Most Shadowlands are designed to hide small groups."

"Can you do that?" Leen asked.

Gift didn't answer her. He kept his gaze on Coulter's face. Coulter's blue eyes were pale, paler than any other blue eyes that Gift had seen. "I don't need you," Gift said.

"I just saved your life," Coulter said.

"Did you?" Gift asked. "Or did you just sentence someone I love to death?"

"Sebastian isn't a living being."

"Sebastian is alive," Gift said.

"He's a magickal creation, not a real one," Coulter said.

"Tell me the difference." Gift crossed his arms. "Sebastian thinks. He feels. He eats and sleeps and breathes like the rest of us. Tell me the difference."

"He has no soul."

Gift started. He had never heard Coulter use that word before. "Yes, he does. I've seen it. I've spoken to it."

"That's a part of yourself," Coulter said.

"That's Sebastian. Open the Link."

"No."

Gift swallowed, remembering the odd pain he had felt when he tried. Somehow Coulter had made a lock that affected his consciousness as well as his body. Coulter's powerful magick, which Gift had always taken for granted, was finally turning against him.

"Then tell me how," Gift said. "I want the Link open with Sebastian."

"You can't open it," Coulter said. "I control your Links. I have since that day your mother died."

"Liar."

Coulter shrugged. "It's true. How else did I keep you alive?"

Gift didn't know the answer to that. He really didn't know how Coulter had kept him alive, only that Coulter had done it and that they had been close ever since.

"You won't help, then," Gift said.

"I believe you need the Link closed. Otherwise the Black King can find you. I'm protecting you, Gift."

"I won't let you," Gift said, "Not at the price of Sebastian's life."

"Then that's why I'm protecting you," Coulter said. "Because I know what's best."

That was the final blow. Gift couldn't take any more. He had lost his adoptive parents, his friends, and everything he knew. He had come to Coulter for help, and got cut off from the one other person he considered family.

"You don't know what's best," Gift said.

"In this case I do."

Gift looked at Leen. She had bitten her lower lip so hard that blood was running down her chin. Gift wiped the blood away with the thumb of his left hand. Then, with his other hand, he smoothed her hair back.

"I'm going to Jahn," he said to her. "Will you come with me?"

She wiped her lip with the back of her sleeve. Her hand was shaking. She had never experienced this kind of loss either. "Why?" she asked.

"Because," he said, "I need you beside me."

"The Fey won't harm you," she said. "They can't."

"But the Islanders might try. Will you come?"

She tried to smile, but winced as her lip stretched. "I have nowhere else to go."

"Don't go to Jahn," Coulter said. "That's where the Fey soldiers will be searching."

"I thought you said they'd be coming here," Gift said.

"And here."

Gift shrugged. "Open my Link, and I'll do whatever you want."

"And if I don't?"

"I'll go to Jahn and protect Sebastian by myself."

"You'd risk everything for a hunk of stone?"

"I'd risk everything for Sebastian," Gift said. "Just like I would have risked everything for you."

"Would have?"

Gift nodded. "Would have."

Coulter took a step back. His eyes were wide and shocked. "I did it for you," he said.

"No," Gift said. "You're doing it for you. I'm old enough and strong enough to decide my own fate. I don't need you to do so."

"What happens if I don't open the Link?"

"Then I close ours," Gift said. "And we cease being friends."

"You can't sever ours. You don't know what it will do." There was panic in Coulter's voice.

"Close it, as you closed mine with Sebastian."

Coulter swallowed so hard his adam's apple bobbed. For a moment, he looked like the lonely, abandoned boy that Gift had known when they were young. "I can't open that Link. It's too dangerous."

"Fine," Gift said. He went inside himself and slammed shut the final door, the one Linking him and Coulter. Around it he envisioned Shadowlands after Shadowlands, a locked series of mazes that would entrap or repel anyone who tried to break through.

When Gift returned to himself, Coulter was still watching him. "Don't do that," Coulter whispered. "You need me."

The plea didn't move Gift as it once would have. "No," he said. "I don't need you. I don't need anyone."

He looked at Leen. Her eyes were big, her skin blotchy, and her lip bruised. "Are you going to come?"

She nodded.

"All right then." Gift turned and walked out of the field. He didn't wait to see if Leen followed.

"Gift!" Coulter was calling after him. "Gift, wait!"

The terror in Coulter's voice made the hair on the back of Gift's neck rise. But he didn't stop. He didn't wait. If he had to meet with his great-grandfather, so be it. But he wouldn't let anything happen to Sebastian.

Sebastian was all he had left.

FIFTY

ARIANNA hopped on the tiny ledge, her wings clasped against her body. The ledge was filthy. Dust and bird droppings littered the sill, just as they littered the crawl space under the roof. This part of the North Tower hadn't been touched for a long time. She wasn't certain if anyone else knew about the crawl space.

She had found it as a young girl. Birds nested in the roof itself. Mice had made their home on the floor. The whole area smelled musty. But she didn't care. She left an old robe on the floor, and Shifted.

The ledge was a small hole in the stonework. It was hidden by the edge of the roof. More than once she had escaped other birds by flying here. The hole wasn't visible unless one was right near it. Most birds didn't have the intelligence to look for such a place.

These birds would.

She was facing a different sort of foe now.

She was back in her robin guise. There were a few Fey robins below, not enough to notice her. She hoped the Fey would think she really was a bird. That required a bit of planning on her part. If she flew directly out of the palace, someone might suspect—not that she was a Shifter, necessarily, but that she was somehow tied to the palace. Solanda had told her that some cultures used birds as couriers, training them to fly to certain places with messages wrapped around one thin leg.

If Solanda believed such things happened, the other Fey would too.

Arianna peered below. She was too high to determine where the other birds were looking. She knew better than to assume that just because she couldn't see them, they couldn't see her.

The city stretched out before her. From the west, large clouds of black smoke stained the sky. Tendrils of smoke rose from the south. She was afraid that smoke was coming from the area of the Tabernacle. People were moving in the street, but the city was oddly silent. She could hear no shouting or screaming or even the clanging of weapons.

She didn't like it. Somehow she had imagined war to be noisy.

She eased toward the center of the tiny ledge. The key was to fly straight, as if she were flying over the palace, instead of coming out of it. She had done this only a few times. It required her to be at top speed the moment she hit the air, and to maintain that speed as if nothing bothered her.

There were no real birds. That fact bothered her. She didn't know if they were staying away because of the Fey or if the Fey had chased them away.

She unfolded her wings. A slight breeze swirled around the side of the building, ruffling her feathers. The breeze would make this takeoff even more difficult. She would have to give one hundred percent right at the very start. No faltering, no failing.

She waited until the wind eased, then leaped off the ledge and flapped her wings languidly. She dipped a little, and turned to the left, flying away from the smoke and away from the Fey. She knew birds well enough to know that none of them would willingly fly into danger.

It took all her strength to keep herself from glancing at the Fey. She would know soon enough if they followed her. She also knew what she would do. She would partially Shift, and explain who she was. If they wanted to capture her, they would have to catch her, and she even figured she knew ways around that.

She was alone in this part of the sky.

She flew higher. The Beast Riders surrounded the palace, and they were all birds. They also sat in lines twenty deep.

They were the only Fey not fighting.

Fey were dragging Islanders out of houses on the east side of Jahn. They were killing the Islanders slowly, peeling off their skin. The screaming that Arianna hadn't heard at the palace was horrible here. She couldn't tell the sound of one voice from another. They all mingled into one great cry of pain.

She turned right and headed toward the Cardidas. The river was empty. No ships. The Fey had come some other way. The bridges across the river were empty as well.

And so were the streets.

Except near the Tabernacle. Another large concentration of Fey forces surrounded, enveloped, and combed the Tabernacle. The wisps of white smoke she had seen rose from the Tabernacle's lower levels. The fire had apparently grown more serious, because the smoke from below was no longer white. It was inky black and smelled of human flesh.

Her stomach churned. Auds were running outside, being chased by Fey. All manner of animals filled the courtyard. They were ripping and clawing and eating the bodies of the dead Islanders. People were scattered all over the holy ground, and so were their parts: half-eaten heads, severed hands, and mangled limbs.

Bile rose in her throat. She swallowed it down. She had never vomited through her beak before. She wasn't going to start, no matter what she saw.

There was no silence here either. The Beast Fey were growling and yowling and grunting. The Islanders were screaming, and the flames crackled. She flew past it, back across the river, and headed west, where the worst of the smoke rose.

When she got close, she gasped in horror. Row after row of houses had been leveled. They were gaping, smoking ruins; charred bodies were lying on the streets. No Fey were around—they had already moved on. No Islanders were either, at least not alive. A few animals fled the rubble, confused, as if they didn't know how to get out of the streets.

She had never seen so many dead in her life.

How did this happen so quickly? The Fey had only announced their presence the night before. How could so many have appeared without anyone realizing it?

She swooped down as close as she could get to the still smoldering remains. It looked as if people had run out of their homes, as if the fires had started before they were awake. What had Solanda told her? The secret to wars was to take the victim by complete surprise.

Complete surprise.

While she and her father argued in Sebastian's room, while her father met with his nobles, while she fussed over Solanda's absence, the Fey were attacking. Quietly. Just as they had surrounded the palace.

The birds had been silent. Birds were never silent. She knew that, but she hadn't thought of it. Birds in repose sang and cooed and chirruped. These sat and waited.

As if waiting for an order.

The stench of burning flesh was so strong that it seeped inside her, through her nose and her throat and into her stomach. She doubted she would ever get it out.

Her city would never be the same.

Her home would never be the same.

Just a few days before, she had worried about her birthmark and her looks and the fact that people stared at her. Now none of that mattered. Many of the people who had stared were probably dead. And her birthmark, the sign of her Shifting, might save the rest, if she let it.

If she didn't hide as her father wanted her to.

Entire columns of Fey moved from the near west side toward the Jahn Bridge. They were going to the Tabernacle. Smart, her great-grandfather. Very smart. The Tabernacle had destroyed the first force, so he would neutralize the Tabernacle's threat before the Islanders even realized he had arrived.

The Fey didn't negotiate, as her father had wanted. They would only take. They meant to conquer.

Which meant that her family had to fight back, somehow. They were suddenly the weaker force, with no holy water and no surprise. They had to retake the advantage for themselves.

She swung back north, to the palace. Another column of troops were marching through the streets of Jahn rousting people from their homes. She swooped again, then caught herself. She couldn't fight that troop. She was one person, and she couldn't save all the others below. All she could do was report to her father and not give up.

She had promised the Shaman that she wouldn't touch her great-grandfather—and she wouldn't.

But she had no such promise about his troops.

This was her island, and he had no right to demolish it.

No right at all.

FIFTY-ONE

RUGAD strode into his own Shadowlands. This was the second largest Shadowlands he had built on Blue Isle. He had built it between his son's old Shadowlands and the city of Jahn, the perfect place for a bivouac. He hadn't realized how uncomfortable he had been in the ruined Shadowlands until he came into this one.

This was how a military Shadowlands should be. Tents were pitched along the walls. Several more were pitched in the center, forming long, straight rows. There was space to walk between them, but that was all. The tents were for privacy only. They were made of special material he discovered in Nye, material that fought back the grays of Shadowlands and brought color to the drab interior. Reds still showed as faint rose, bright green as a faint gray-green, but the colors spruced up the place and added to the morale.

Each warrior was responsible for his own food and his own care. The population of Shadowlands shifted as the battles shifted. Sometimes Leaders slept here. Sometimes Infantry.

But no one hid. Despite his son's treatment of Shadowlands, that wasn't what they were for.

At the moment, most of the warriors who had destroyed Rugar's Shadowlands were in Rugad's. They were resting before they went on to join the fighting in Jahn. The Fey had learned, long ago, that winning wars meant having enough manpower to allow for some to be attacking while others were resting. Well-rested troops made no mistakes. Well-rested troops killed only the enemy, never themselves.

Rugad couldn't remember how many times he had seen exhausted troops on the enemy line see movement, fire, and accidentally kill one of their own.

The folks who had fought that last battle looked exhausted. It was, he knew, an exhaustion of the spirit as well as of the body. It took a lot of discipline to kill other Fey, and that discipline never prevented the thought: What if it had been me?

He scanned the muted color tents for Gelô. The Foot Soldier wasn't visible, but in the search, Rugad found the prison tent. It had several Infantry guards around it as well as a few Foot Soldiers. Very few prisoners were kept in Shadowlands—usually only the important ones, or the ones who would have some bearing on the campaign itself.

As Rugad walked through the tents, he saw Wisdom. Wisdom wore a military tunic that left his arms bare, showing their scarification. His braids ran down his back, brushing the edges of his dark pants. He had seen Rugad and was watching him approach.

Without preamble, Rugad said, "I need a small troop to go back to the farmlands in the center of the Isle. I have reason to believe my great-grandson is hiding there."

"Perhaps a large troop would be better then," Wisdom said.

Rugad shook his head. "I don't want our people seen. I want to surprise the boy, if I can. He may be expecting me."

"Very well," Wisdom said.

"And Wisdom, let the troop know who they're looking for. I want no mistakes, and I want him taken alive and unharmed."

"Yes, sir," Wisdom said.

"The quicker we can do this, the better," Rugad said. "I would recommend sending a Bird Rider to the nearest garrison."

"Many of those troops have gone onto Jahn."

"But not all," Rugad said. Then his gaze met Wisdom's. "Right?"

"Yes, sir. I will take care of this, sir." He bowed his head slightly, then added, "Ghost needs to see you."

"Have him wait in my tent. I have one other piece of business to attend to first."

Wisdom looked over his shoulder toward the prison tent. "She's angry at her treatment."

"She'll be angrier if she doesn't cooperate. She's only alive because we ran out of Doppelgängers."

Wisdom smiled, a little. "Don't underestimate her, sir."

"She's a Shifter," Rugad said. "I never underestimate them."

"She also, according to reports, murdered your son."

Rugad nodded as the information went in. It wasn't as detrimental as the other Fey thought. If she had killed Rugar, then she had done Rugad a favor.

He made his way to the prison tent. The flap was pulled across and tied with a spelled rope. This tent was gray, and its interior dark. A Foot Soldier handed Rugad a Fey lamp before he went in.

He peered at it. The lamp was bright. The souls inside were shining with a brilliance he hadn't seen in a long time.

"Fey?" he asked.

The Foot Soldier shook his head. "Too dangerous," he said. "We've been taking only Islander souls."

"Good," Rugad said. He didn't want any Failure Fey, not even those without bodies, anywhere near his people.

He took the lamp inside. Four guards stood at the door of the tent, and three more sat on the rug inside. Rugad snapped his fingers, and they all left.

Solanda stood in the center of the tent. She wore a blouse and pants, both stained with blood. Her tawny hair fell free. She hadn't aged a day in those twenty years. She still looked like a teenager, even though she was at least as old as Rugar had been, maybe older.

"I was told you murdered my son," Rugad said.

She lifted her chin. Her birthmark was dark against her golden skin. "He was disobeying the Shaman."

"Visionaries do not need to listen to Shamans."

"Liar," Solanda said. "Visionaries need Shamans. Even more so when they are Blind."

"Are you making my son's Blindness up as a justification of your actions?"

"Don't pretend with me, Rugad. I have little to lose here. I know you can extract information from me and kill me quite easily."

"So you should be kinder to me."

She snorted through her nose. "Kindness has nothing to do with what's between us. I have lived on this desolate place because you banished me here, because your son bound me to him, and because I had no way of returning home and regaining my honor. I am tarnished with the same brush as all those Fey you slaughtered today, through no fault of my own."

"So tell me why you live."

She crossed her arms. "Because you ran out of Doppelgängers."

"I have more here, in Shadowlands."

She nodded. "But you want to hear me out first, to see what it is that I know and you don't."

"I suspect you know a lot that I don't."

"Stop playing games with me, Rugad. You want your great-grandson."

"I understand I have two of them."

She paused, tilted her head as if she were listening to a faraway sound, and then she said, "Two great-grandsons?"

"Yes."

She laughed. The sound was fluted, pleasant, and completely inappropriate.

Rugad pulled the flap behind him tighter. The tent was theirs. The light from the Fey lamp made everything golden. Solanda's shadow fell on the tent's far wall, his on one of the sides. They looked frozen there, trapped by her laugh and the knowledge it held.

He wasn't certain he was going to like what she had to say next. Something in his assumptions was wrong, and he rarely made wrong assumptions.

"You have a great-grandson and his golem, Rugad," Solanda said. "Your son stole your great-grandson and left a

Changeling in his place, and your talented granddaughter never even suspected."

"She embodied the Changeling with life?"

Solanda shook her head. "Your great-grandson did."

"I would have discovered the golem," he said. "They shatter under pressure."

"It's not the golem that concerns me," Solanda said. "It will take care of itself, or die trying."

"And my great-grandson?"

"Is a talented Visionary, but I'm sure you already know that. I'm sure that's why you're here."

"All of these certainties, Solanda, and none of them really wrong. But you're not offering me anything new."

"Then let me," she said. She put her hands on her hips and watched him as if he were the prisoner. "There's a wild magick here."

"We've already discovered that, and we neutralized their poison."

"The poison is only one manifestation of it. Your great-grandson is another. He bred true, and had his first Vision by the age of three. He built a Shadowlands that same year. But he is not a warrior."

"How could he be, growing up here?"

"Already you make excuses for him, Rugad," Solanda said. "Jewel's brothers must be hopeless."

"I would rather have let my son rule," he said.

Solanda smiled. "Desperate and growing old. Not a good pattern for a Black King. Are you Blind?"

He didn't take offense at the question. Her life already hung by a thread. She was right; she had nothing to lose by being honest with him.

"No," he said.

"You lie. Rugar was Blind. You must be."

Rugad shook his head. "I have had Visions, even on this Isle. I have Seen my great-grandson, sailing for Leut. I have Seen our victory, and I have Seen the death of their Rocaan. I have Seen many things, Solanda, and I expect to continue for sometime to come."

"But you have not Seen the most important thing of all," she said. "You have two great-grandchildren, Rugad."

"But you said one is a golem."

"I said you have one great-grandson."

He set the Fey lamp down so that she couldn't see the surprise on his face. He *had* missed that. But that was the nature of Visions. Only partial answers, partial surprises, partial revelations.

Still, he would have thought that he would have Seen something as important as a great-granddaughter.

"A great-granddaughter," he said as he rose. "How do you know this?"

"I was there when she was born. I raised her."

He laughed. It snuck out of him, a bark, almost. He made no attempt to hide it.

"You almost had me, Shifter," he said. "But it is well known that Shifters do not raise children."

"That's right, they don't," Solanda said. "except in one instance."

He froze. Her voice had the ring of truth. Besides, he knew that Jewel had died in childbirth shortly before Rugar had died. But since Rugad never Saw the baby, he assumed it had died.

"She Shifts?" he asked. "That's not possible. Her mother was a Visionary, and her father has no magick."

"You forget." Solanda smiled. "This Isle has wild magick. Her father is the direct descendent of the founder of their religion, and the religion developed the poison."

"She Shifts," he said, mostly to himself.

"Oh, but there is more," Solanda said. She was bouncing on her toes, as if she couldn't contain her excitement. "She has several Forms."

"How many?"

"I've seen two. She claims more than that. She doesn't know how many. She says any time she practices a Form, she can Shift to it."

"That's not possible."

"Not to average Fey," Solanda said. "But then neither is having a Vision at three. Wild magick, Rugad."

He took a deep breath. His heart was pounding. "She's the younger?"

Solanda nodded.

"Why are you telling me about her? To bargain for your own life?"

"In part. And also because you need to know, Rugad. She is your destiny."

"I have Seen her brother sailing to Leut."

"Don't let your Vision cloud your Sight. Rugar did that too much. You need her, Rugad."

"She grew up in Shadowlands?"

"She grew up in the Islander palace. She knows everything about Blue Isle."

"Then she is loyal to it."

"Of course," Solanda said. "You can use that."

Rugad laughed. His great-granddaughter, raised by the soft Islanders. As if she were something he could use. "She won't listen to me."

"She will if I tell her to."

"Another ploy, Solanda?"

Solanda looked at him. Her gaze was flat, measuring. The stare of a cat that knew it was superior. "I am the closest thing she has to a mother, Rugad. She'll listen to me."

"A mother who betrays her daughter to the enemy?" Rugad asked.

"You are not the enemy," Solanda said. "You are the Black King."

"And you killed my son," Rugad said. "That can be construed as treason."

Solanda smiled. " 'Construed' is such a good word. Yes, it can be construed as treason. Or it can be construed as patriotism. Perhaps I did you the favor you couldn't do yourself, Rugad."

"Perhaps," he said. "But why would you give up the girl to me?"

"Because she is so much more than an Islander Princess. She is more Fey than any Fey I have ever met. She deserves the life that she was born into."

Rugad crossed his arms and smiled. "You are fond of the girl. I admire fondness, especially from a Shifter, but it does not sway me."

"It should," Solanda said. She brushed her tawny hair from her face. "You were angry at Rugar for taking Jewel. You thought Jewel was the future of the Fey. And you were right. She was. But she was the future because of the child she bore. Not her son. Her son has Vision, yes, but he cannot Shift. The wild magick isn't as powerful in him."

"Flurry saw two boys. One spoke Islander and the other Fey. Both, he said, were intelligent."

"The golem has elements of your great-grandson. It is your great-grandson who gives him life."

"So Flurry saw the golem and my great-grandson."

"It would seem so."

"And if my great-grandson gave a golem life, kept a Shadowlands together, and had a Vision at age three, then he has wild magick."

"But it isn't as powerful as Arianna's."

"The girl's?"

Solanda nodded.

"Does the girl have Vision?"

"Not yet," Solanda said. "But she is fifteen. She came into her Shifting young. She will have Vision, though. She is the daughter of a Visionary."

"Her brother had Vision at three."

"Her brother has only that power. She has two powers."

"You can't be certain," Rugad said. He wasn't certain he wanted to believe in this girl, this all-powerful child who carried his blood.

"You said that about Jewel," Solanda said. "She hadn't come into her Visions yet when you sent her with Rugar. You thought she never would. She was eighteen. Three years older than Arianna. You were wrong."

He let his arms fall. He had been wrong. That, he felt, had been the greatest mistake of his life. The only moment when Rugar had the upper hand. Rugar had taken Jewel, the future of the Fey, to prevent his own father from turning on him.

It had failed. Jewel had not helped Rugar conquer the Isle, at least not the way he wanted, and Rugad had remained in Nye, Watching from afar, hoping that his granddaughter would save them all. When she did not, when she died, he had turned to his grandsons, the hopeless Bridge and the others, thinking that maybe they could evolve into something better. Their Visions were tiny, and their intelligence even tinier. He could do nothing to change that. He could do nothing to make them great leaders.

Only the Vision of his great-grandson sustained him.

His great-grandson had brought him here. Solanda was right. Rugad was a desperate man. For his entire life, he had looked toward the future, and until he had a successor, the future looked bleak.

"I'm right, aren't I?" Solanda asked.

He let go of the lamp, but didn't turn to face her. He couldn't. Not yet.

"You said the Isle has a wild magick. She might never come into her Vision."

"That's right, she might not," Solanda said. "I don't think it matters."

This time he did turn. The tent had grown hot. It wasn't designed for the flap to be down so hard, so long. She had her hands on her hips, a debater's stance.

"Because you have two great-grandchildren, one with Vision and one that Shifts. Think if they shared power."

"They can't share power," Rugad said. "The Black Throne has room for one."

Solanda shook her head. "You don't know that. There have never been two worthy candidates born into a Black Family before."

"Yes, there has," Rugad said. "In Ycyno, the Black Queen took power because she was the eldest. But when she died childless, her brother took the throne. There have been other instances of that, but never of anyone sharing."

Solanda smiled. "If there are two worthy candidates, let them battle it out."

"I don't like it when you smile, Solanda."

She shrugged. "Young Gift was raised by Failures. He is no match for Arianna."

"They cannot fight. You know that."

"Just like you couldn't kill your unworthy son," Solanda said.

Rugad took a deep breath. He didn't like this woman's intelligence. It was rare he met a mind as powerful as his. He didn't like being on the other side of that.

"Your charge was raised by a Failure too," he said. "And she lived among the enemy."

"I am a warrior, Rugad, not a Failure," Solanda said.

"And Arianna knows more about the Fey than her brother does. She is the warrior. He is not. She'll do as I tell her."

"Will she?" Rugad asked. He moved the light a little closer, setting it on the floor between them. "Then why were you in Shadowlands without her?"

Solanda's gaze flickered away, then back to him, the movement so small that most wouldn't have noticed. But Rugad did. It was all he needed to know.

"I am not tied to the palace," Solanda said. "I am free to go where I please."

"Were," Rugad said softly. "You were free to go where you pleased."

Her mouth dropped open, and her eyes went momentarily blank before they filled with panic. He liked intelligence. It made explanations unnecessary.

"You need me, Rugad."

"Do I?" he asked. Her panic, carefully masked now, made him cold inside. She should have known better. Her fear for her own life covered her intelligence, made her lose the edge she had had a moment before.

"She'll listen to me."

"I'm sure she'll listen to a Doppelgänger too. If she was raised among the Islanders, she's probably never seen one."

"Don't do that," Solanda said. She stood very still. "Two Shifters on your side could be very valuable."

"I didn't know I had a side," Rugad said. "By tomorrow, I will own this Isle, and then my great-grandchildren and I will move on to Leut."

"She won't leave."

Rugad shrugged. "I have two great-grandchildren. I don't need them both."

Solanda licked her lips. "You're making a mistake, Rugad."

"No," he said quietly. "You're making the mistake, Solanda. The girl will be useful, but she does nothing to negate your Failure."

"I have not Failed," Solanda said. "I killed Rugar for you. I raised your great-granddaughter. Surely you owe me for both those things."

"For the slaughter of a member of the Black King's family, I owe you a long, painful death," Rugad said. "For the help you gave my great-granddaughter, I can guarantee that the death will be an easy one. That is all I can do."

"Rugad." She took a step forward.

He held up his hand. She stopped. "The girl is fifteen," he said. "She no longer needs you. She can survive on her own. You claim to care about the Fey. If that is so, then you understand why I cannot let any of the Failures live."

"Rugad—"

"You have had a long life, Solanda, and now you have someone to mourn you. Surely that is enough."

Her eyes glistened. "When you face this moment, Rugad, remember me. You will not think your time has been enough either."

"If you expect sympathy, you have come to the wrong man."

To his surprise, she smiled. "I have already faced the worst from your family," she said. She squared her shoulders. "Send in your Doppelgänger. I am ready for him."

Rugad nodded at her, grabbed the Fey lamp, and left the tent. The air in Shadowlands was cooler, an odd contrast he had never really felt before.

He took a deep breath, clearing the sense of her failure from his lungs. She would have been a powerful ally, but he never would have been able to trust her. Her murder of his son gave her the ability to disobey Black Blood. Her love for his great-granddaughter might jeopardize his great-grandson.

Too much risk for too little gain.

A pity, though. She was strong, and brilliant, and magnificent. Shifters truly were the finest of the Fey.

The guards at the door watched him. Rugad nodded to them, then headed through the maze of tents until he saw Gelô.

"Take ten of your best people," Rugad said, "and kill the prisoner."

Gelô blinked. "I thought you would use a Doppelgänger," he said.

"So does she." Rugad smiled. "But why should I give my son's murderer such an easy death?"

Gelô clicked his heels together and nodded. Then he went past Rugad to round up his killing squad.

Solanda would be prepared for a Doppelgänger. That strong intelligence might even have figured out a way around the death and a way to escape. But she wouldn't expect an execution, especially an execution for a traitor.

It would serve as a lesson to her and to the others. The Black King's family was untouchable. He hadn't taught that lesson in twenty years. But he needed it now.

He had great-grandchildren.

A boy and a girl.

A Visionary and a Shifter.

The Isle's wild magick was paying off. Rugar's haste in conquering Blue Isle might have given the Fey the last bit of magick they needed to conquer the Isle and move to the remaining continents. Rugad would live to see the conquering of Leut. He knew that much. And his great-grandchildren would do the rest.

Wild magick.

It was the advantage he needed.

FIFTY-TWO

CON slid down a moss-covered incline, hands and face first. He wasn't able to stop himself. The tunnel had gotten suddenly wider and higher, and the air fresher. He could smell the tang of the river mixed with the faint overripe scents of rot.

He had reached the other side.

The rocks below the moss were worn smooth by some ancient water leakage. He slid down it, unable to find purchase, grasping and straining with his fingers and his toes. He had dropped his torch when the slide began. It had slithered ahead of him and disappeared into the murky darkness.

He didn't hear it clatter to the bottom of any shaft.

He could no longer hear it at all, and that worried him. He could envision himself sliding until the floor broke away, and then he would fall the rest of the way, breaking bones. He wouldn't be able to climb out, and no one would ever find him again.

No one even knew he was here.

Gradually he slowed. He lay at the bottom of the incline, his heart pounding. The area was silent, except for the ragged sound of his own breathing. The silence was eerie after the pounding march of the Fey.

He sat up, caught his breath, and felt for his flint. His supplies were flattened and moss-covered, but he didn't seem to be missing anything. He grabbed another torch from his belt, lit it with a spark from the flint, and blinked as the flame caught.

The walls were black with moss. The tunnel opened even wider, into a corridor large enough for several people to walk through. The ceiling was high and old. Some of the stones had fallen and shattered on the walkway below.

He stood. His robe was sodden and hung on him unevenly. His face was caked with grime. His hands were black, and he supposed his feet were too. It didn't matter. He just had to get to the palace.

The map had shown the tunnel splitting here into several others. He must have slid into one of the side passages. There were many ways to get to the palace from here. All he had to do was to take a tunnel north from this tunnel.

If he could figure out where north was.

It was away from the river, that much he did know and would be able to determine.

He took a deep breath and started forward. His feet hurt. He must have bruised them in the slide. The silence made him nervous. The hair was rising on the back of his neck. He had never felt like this before, as if someone were watching him, someone unseen.

The Fey couldn't have discovered this place.

Could they?

The corridor snaked around unseen barriers and went deeper into the ground. He suspected that the warehouses were above him, but he had no way to know if that were true.

He picked up his pace, holding his torch ahead of him, swearing softly as he stubbed his toe on a fallen stone. Then he begged the Holy One's forgiveness for his blasphemy. He had never been through anything like this, not in all his thirteen years.

He rounded a corner and saw movement ahead of him. A man, a woman, and a pile of crates. He stopped. The woman glanced at the man, and then someone hit Con from behind.

Someone else yanked his torch away, and hands gripped his arms, pulling them back.

He didn't say anything. He couldn't tell if they were Fey.

The hands pulled his arms so tight the skin stretched over his chest. He didn't struggle. He couldn't. There seemed to be too many of them.

His torch was behind him now. All he could see was the man and the woman. She was sitting in torchlight by herself. It caught her golden hair and red dress. She was older, but she still had a prettiness to her.

The man was tall, and Con couldn't see his face. The height frightened him, though. The Fey were tall. Islanders weren't.

"I thought you respected the religious, Denl," the tall man said. His voice reverberated through the cavern. It had a power that Con had never heard in any voice before.

"Dunna make fun a him," the woman said.

"I'm not making fun of anyone. I was just wondering why Denl wouldn't let an Aud go through."

"Could be Fey," said a male voice behind Con.

Con didn't say anything. This could be a ruse. He didn't know yet.

More men came out of the shadows. Ten of them at least. They settled on and around the crates. "I told him ta grab him," a man said. He was also behind Con. Con resisted the urge to turn his head. "I figured he was one a yers, holy man."

This time, Con did raise his head. Who was before him? Who would they call holy man?

"I haven't been near an Aud in fifteen years," the first man said.

Con shuddered. What kind of Islander avoided the church? Or maybe this was all an act, designed to get him to relax before they slaughtered him.

The torch circled around him. The man holding it was short, like Con, and had blue eyes that reflected the light. His face was covered with dirt, but his light skin showed through. "Tis just a boy," he said with some surprise.

"Auds usually are children," the first man said. "Especially Auds on a Charge."

"I seen old Auds," the one called Denl said.

"Of course you have, but rarely have you seen them in the Tabernacle."

Con bit his lower lip. The Fey didn't know that much about Rocaanism, did they?

"Maybe this ain't no Aud," said another male voice, also from behind.

"Sure is a quiet one," said one of the men on the crates.

"He dunna look like no Fey," said the man with the torch.

"Some Fey can mask themselves as Islanders," said the first man.

The woman got up and came closer. Her dress was dirty at the hem, but she wore shoes. Strands of hair were escaping from the bun she kept it in. She shoved her way through the men and stopped in front of Con. Her face was clean, her eyes compassionate. She took his chin in one hand, and wiped the dirt from his skin.

"How old are ye?" she asked.

"Thirteen," he said, and his voice cracked as if to prove it.

The man behind him laughed. Con kept his gaze on her face.

"Did ye come here lookin fer ana one?" she asked.

He shook his head.

"He's on a Charge," said the first man.

"N how do ye know that, holy one?" asked the man behind Con.

"Because he's got supplies," the first man said.

"Or because ye sent him yerself."

Con couldn't take this any more. "Please let me go," he said. "Please. You can take everything from me, just let me go."

"See?" said the first man. "A Charge. You're getting in the way of a religious mission, Yasep."

"I'll be gettin in the way a anathin if it might take me life," said Yasep, the unseen man in the back.

"I'm not going to take your life," Con said. "Please, let me go. People will die if I stay here."

"Yer so important, are ye?" Yasep asked. He shook Con just a little.

"He might be," the first man said. "What's your Charge, son?"

Con swallowed. He didn't know if he should tell these people or not. What if they were Fey? He would have no way of telling.

"Go on, ye can tell him," Yasep said. "He's a holy man like ye are."

The first man wasn't wearing robes. He was wearing pants and a ripped blouse. His hair was pulled back, and he was old, older than the Rocaan. Con had never seen him before. He had bandages on his face.

"Are you Fey?" Con asked.

The men around laughed. The woman stepped in front of him slightly as if she knew the question might put him in jeopardy.

"No more than you are," the first man said.

"He's the Rocaan, boy," said Denl. "Do ye na recognize him?"

"How could he recognize me?" the first man said. "He wasn't even born when I left Jahn."

"The Rocaan's at the Tabernacle," Con whispered.

"Aye, and a good thing that is," Denl said. "The Fey are about."

Con couldn't take it any more. "No, it's not good. The Fey have the place surrounded. They're going to attack. I'm supposed to warn the palace, and if you don't let me go, I won't be able to help."

"Warn the palace, eh?" Yasep said.

"Dunna," the woman said.

"I always wondered awhere these tunnels led."

"No," the woman said. "The boy's right. The Fey're all over. They'll be at the palace, ye can bet on it."

"Let him go," the first man said.

"Why, holy one? What's he ta you?"

"He's a boy with a Charge and a good one, too. If Nicholas isn't warned, then the Fey might get an advantage."

"Seems they already got one," Yasep said.

"Then why give them more?"

"Yer fightin hard for a boy ye dunna know."

"I know what he is and what he's doing. Don't stand in the way of it."

"Yer gonna stop me?"

"On this I am."

"Ye canna even stand by yerself, holy man. How're you gonna stop me?"

"Don't push me," the first man said. "You don't know what I can do."

"Let him go," the woman said. "he's na worth fightin over."

The pressure on Con's arm eased. He brought them forward, rubbed his wrists and turned. His captor was not much taller than he was, just as filthy, and much older. His captor's jaw was set.

"Go on," he said. "Warn the King. He canna do nothin anaway. There's too many Fey."

"He can try," Con said.

"Go, boy," the first man said. "Finish your Charge."

Con went over to him. The first man wasn't Fey, despite his height. He had blond curls and deep-set blue eyes barely visible around his bandages. He was badly injured, and he looked exhausted.

Con knelt in front of him. "Who are you that they think I might recognize you?"

The man smiled. One of his bandages moved up his cheek. He winced and put a hand on it. "No one you have to concern yourself with. Just an old Aud gone bad. Now go. You don't want the Fey to get there before you do."

"No, sir."

Denl came up beside him, and handed him his torch. "Godspeed," Denl said softly. Then he glanced over his shoulder at Yasep. Yasep was watching it all, arms crossed, scowling.

"Thank you," Con said. He took the torch and looked around, hoping to see an opening.

"The nearest passage is on yer right," Denl said, "just ahead there."

Con nodded, and hurried to the passage. When he reached it, he stopped and caught his breath. He didn't know what they were doing there. He didn't want to know. He just wanted to get to the palace before the Fey, and then return to the Tabernacle where everything would eventually be all right.

FIFTY-THREE

ASSETS. The word had remained on Nicholas's mind since Arianna left. He had assets. He just had to figure out how to use them.

He had taken Sebastian with him to the North Tower. The palace really didn't have towers, not the way the Tabernacle did, but it had ancient square anchors on three corners. The fourth had been torn down when one of his ancestors expanded the kitchen. The towers, as they were called, rose an extra story above the highest parts of the palace. Jewel had wondered at them. She had thought that the palace was built like an ancient Hervish fortress, and she often wondered whether seafaring peoples from the Galinas Continent had settled Blue Isle.

She used the Hervish design as a point in her argument.

Nicholas had always disagreed. He thought the palace design made sense to any warrior peoples. And he knew that his people had fought some kind of battle in their early years just from the clues in the Words Written and Unwritten. The Roca had been fighting the Soldiers of the Enemy. The Islanders had developed weapons, like swords, that had only military uses. The religious uses came later.

A lot of good it did him now. Until the Fey arrived, Blue Isle had been at peace throughout its recorded history. Even though he had insisted on training his people to fight after their first victory over the Fey, very few had done serious, diligent work.

They had expected holy water to save them.

And, from his vantage, it didn't appear to be working.

He and Sebastian were in the Uprising Room. The room was square and took up the entire top of the North Tower. For centuries, it had had no glass, but his great-great-grandfather had glassed in the room during the Peasant Uprising. He had said he wanted to watch his armies defeat the Uprising and not get cold.

The old man had been nothing if not pragmatic.

Nicholas could use some of that pragmatism now.

There were chairs on all the stone walls and a square stone table built into the center of the room. It was a larger version of the war room, and one he needed at the moment.

Sebastian was standing in the center of the room, as still as one of the pillars. He had his hands clasped behind his back, his chin out. He was watching Nicholas as if he were afraid his father would disappear. Given the loss of Gift and Arianna's flight, Sebastian had reason for the fear.

Assets. Sebastian was one. He looked like Gift. He might stall the Black King if necessary, although Nicholas didn't see how. There were few others.

The birds still surrounded the palace. They were in all shapes and sizes, watching from the gate, from trees, and from the ground. The tiny Fey on their backs, male and female, were nude. Nicholas had looked at them through a crude spyglass. The hair on their heads was feathered. They were part bird.

None of the Fey had ventured onto the palace itself, even though they had been staring at it all morning.

But they didn't interest him as much any more. What interested him was the smoke cluttering the horizon, smoke all over the city of Jahn. Black tendrils climbing from the

southwest, others from the southeast. Jewel had told him
that the Fey never laid waste to useful land.

Perhaps they didn't think these parts of the Isle useful.

New smoke was rising, thick and oily, from the other side
of the Cardidas River.

And it looked as if the smoke were coming from the
Tabernacle.

Arianna would tell him what was burning.

If she returned.

He whirled, unable to bear the thought. Sebastian's eyes
tracked him. Nicholas went over to his son, touched him,
found reassurance in the stony flesh.

"How . . . long . . . till . . . she . . . comes . . . back?" he
whispered.

"I wish I knew," Nicholas said. She was on her own, more
alone than she had ever been. If only he sent them down to
the dungeons when he had had the chance.

If only she had gone.

The dungeons.

They were his other asset.

If he used them right.

He patted Sebastian's shoulder, then turned and went to
the door. He pulled the door open. Five guards stood on the
stairwell, arms crossed. They were his handpicked body-
guards, men he recognized. Still, before he spoke to them,
he looked closely at their eyes. Jewel had taught him
that Fey Doppelgängers, who literally took over a victim's
body, were recognizable only through the gold flecks in
their eyes.

His guards were clear. No Fey had made it up these stairs.
Yet.

All five of the guards looked at him expectantly. They
were young men, in their early twenties at the most, and
muscular. He had picked them because of their proficiency
in swordplay and at hand-to-hand combat.

"Trey," he said to the young blond at his immediate left.
"Find Monte. Bring him to me. Quickly."

Trey nodded, then hurried down the steps. Nicholas
watched him disappear into the bowels of the palace, then
he closed the door. They both knew where Monte was. He

was on the lower level, making certain the doorways and windows were secure. He was the only one of Nicholas's trusted advisors who had been in the palace when the Fey appeared. So far as Nicholas could reconstruct, the Fey had all arrived at the same time, a great horde of them darkening the early dawn sky. The kitchen crew had seen them and had thought it odd, so many birds arriving all at once. But they hadn't realized they were Fey until it was too late.

Sebastian still stood, stiff and unnatural, in the center of the room. He had an uncanny ability to blend in, to look like nearby stone structures. He had had that ability since babyhood, and it had been that ability that had saved both him and Arianna from her grandfather's wrath all those years ago.

Nicholas put his arm around Sebastian and led him to a chair. Sebastian shook his head slowly. "Want . . . to . . . see . . . Ari . . . when . . . she . . . comes."

"She'll come back to me," Nicholas said. "You'll see her."

"Wish . . . she . . . were . . . here," Sebastian said.

"Me, too," Nicholas said. He eased his son into the chair and noted with satisfaction that it was near one of the pillars. Sebastian looked like a carving built into the wall.

Sunlight was streaming in the windows, highlighting the embroidery on the chairs. There were no tapestries on these windows. They were open all the time. The windows in the East and West towers were the same, but didn't quite give him as good a view of the city. The towers got in each other's way, which was not a problem here. There was no South Tower.

The smoke was thicker. He hoped Arianna hadn't gotten caught in it.

He hoped she still lived.

He didn't know what he would do without her.

Then he closed his eyes. He had once thought that way about Jewel. What he had done without her was go on. One day at a time. Every morning he somehow got up, faced the day, and thought about Jewel. Then, over time, rising became easier. But he never stopped thinking about her. Even now, especially now, she was in his thoughts.

He should have foreseen the attack on the Tabernacle. She had warned him. He had once asked Jewel what she would have done if she had known about Blue Isle's holy water before she attacked, instead of learning about it later.

Destroy all the Back Robes, she said.

Apparently she had thought like her grandfather.

Nicholas would have to do that too. He would have to think like the Fey's Black King.

What had Jewel told him? She had explained strategy to him more than once. She had felt that he was deficient in that area. *There's more to a soldier than good swordsmanship*, she had said. *Strategy is the most important. A good strategist turns his opponent's expectations to his own advantage.*

What did the Black King expect?

He expected Nicholas to wait for a meeting.

He also expected Nicholas to attempt an escape.

Maybe he even expected Nicholas to mount an attack from within the palace.

There were fires all over the city. And Fey soldiers on the streets. The Black King wasn't going to negotiate. He was going to take Blue Isle and his great-grandchildren.

He's ruthless, Jewel had said. The Shaman had said the same. Even Rugar, Jewel's father, had mentioned it.

Ruthless.

He wouldn't expect Nicholas to be ruthless, too.

Nicholas swallowed. He could be ruthless. He hadn't been ruthless in a long long time, but it wasn't something a man could forget.

Matthias had taught him how, all those years ago. By killing Jewel.

By trying to destroy everything Nicholas cared about.

There was a triple knock on the door. Sebastian started. Nicholas turned.

"It is Trey, Sire." The voice, speaking through the door, sounded like Trey. Nicholas hoped it was.

Nicholas crossed the room. His heart was beating hard. He had no protection against the Fey in this palace. If they sent a Doppelgänger, who would know the codes, Nicholas had no recourse. He could only trust that they weren't going to attack him first, not without word from the Black King.

He pulled the door open. His guards remained. Trey stood there, his blue eyes clear, and Monte stood beside him. His eyes had no gold in them either, although they were shot with red. Monte was getting too old for this sort of thing.

But he had to make it through this last battle.

They all did.

"Thank you," Nicholas said to Trey. Monte came in, and Nicholas closed the door.

Monte glanced around the room, his gaze skimming right over Sebastian as if the boy weren't there. Nicholas decided not to draw the Captain of the Guard's attention to the boy.

"Are you familiar with the tunnels beyond the dungeons?" Nicholas asked.

Monte snapped to attention. He clearly hadn't expected the question. "Yes, Sire. But I haven't been in them since your father was alive."

"Where do they come out?"

"All over the city, Sire.

"Any near the palace?"

"No, Sire, not outside the walls. Inside, they come up through the barracks."

"And the birds are blocking the barracks right now, aren't they?" Nicholas asked.

"They're blocking everything." Monte sounded resigned. "There's thousands of them, Sire. And only a few hundred of us."

Nicholas nodded. "But they're birds, Monte."

"With Fey riders."

"Still," Nicholas said, "Jewel told me that Beast Riders still have the instincts of the creatures they share. We can use that."

"I don't see how, Sire. The numbers—"

"Are overwhelming." Nicholas crossed the room and leaned out the windows. The birds hadn't moved. The Fey on their backs held the neck feathers as if they were reins. The Fey were holding them in, keeping them in check.

Birds were violent, but they startled easily.

"All right," Nicholas said. "Here's what I want you to do." He pushed away from the window, turned and faced

Monte. "It's a gamble, but I think we have no choice. If we don't act now, we'll never get another chance."

"Do you think we have a chance now?" Monte asked, looking over Nicholas's shoulder.

"Yes," Nicholas said. "I think we do."

FIFTY-FOUR

COULTER took two steps after Gift, then stopped. Coulter's shoulders fell, and his mouth was slightly open. The corn surrounded him, embraced him, held him as if he were a part of it.

This was the Coulter who had lived in Shadowlands. The one the Fey had rejected. The one who had spent his entire life as a pariah.

Adrian walked over to him and put his hand on Coulter's arm. Coulter started. He was rigid. The boy who wouldn't take affection—who couldn't take affection because it was never given—was back.

"Why didn't you just open the Link?" Adrian asked, trying to give Coulter a way to solve the problem, a way out, a way to get his best—and oldest—friend back.

Coulter turned slowly. He licked his lips, blinked once, and frowned. The adult mask fell over his face, but the little wounded boy still peeked through his eyes.

"I couldn't," he said.

"Because you were jealous?" Adrian asked.

Coulter shook his head. He sighed, and as he did, his eyes filled with tears. He brushed at them angrily. "If I were so jealous, I would have cut the Link a long time ago, without Gift knowing."

"Why didn't you tell him that?"

"I tried." Coulter's voice rose, a little-boy sound. He cleared his throat and repeated in a softer, more controlled way, "I tried."

He swallowed, glanced after Gift, then leaned against Adrian. Not quite a hug—they were too adult for that now—but a reassuring touch.

"It's the Black King," he said quietly. "I felt the Black King."

Adrian waited. He had been with Coulter a long time now and had raised the boy as his own. He had learned to give Coulter time, and then Coulter would give back. Coulter always did. Despite what Gift said, Coulter was a good man.

"I'd never felt anything like him before, Adrian." Coulter's voice became even lower, as if he were afraid the Black King would overhear. "He's evil."

"Evil?" Adrian hadn't heard Coulter use that word. He wasn't even sure it was in Coulter's vocabulary.

Until now.

Coulter nodded. He was still staring at the road, at the path Gift had taken. "I felt him when he found Gift. He's strong, Adrian, and ruthless. He's old and smart, and he has twenty times, maybe a hundred times, the power of Rugar. The only reason I was able to force him out of Gift was because I surprised him. He didn't know what I was."

Coulter was trembling, small, thin shudders that ran through all of his muscles. He hadn't been this frightened since his first day outside of Shadowlands, when he didn't know what smells or colors were.

"What makes you think he would have harmed Gift? Gift is his family, after all."

Coulter shook his head. "He doesn't understand family. Not like you do. Gift is a tool, and the Black King would have used that tool right from the start. He would have changed Gift."

"Through the Link?"

"Just touching him, letting his mind brush Gift's, changed him."

"You think that was it? Or do you think it might have been the shock? Gift has never really experienced this kind of loss before."

Coulter brought a hand to his face. "He shut me out, Adrian. He's never done that. If he had made a mistake and severed the Link, he might have died."

"But he didn't."

"Not yet," Coulter said.

"I think Gift knows better than to do that. He loves that stoney boy, though. Can't you hook them back up?"

Coulter shook his head. "Sebastian is the perfect Link. When the Black King finds him, and all that nothingness, he'll invade him, and Sebastian will be gone. And if that had happened when Gift's Link was open, Gift would have been conquered next."

Adrian didn't like the sound of any of this. He trusted Coulter, had watched the boy work his own magick for years, and knew that Coulter's senses were usually right.

"Can Gift reopen the Link himself?"

Coulter shook his head. "Not with the kind of Lock I put on it."

"Can the Black King open it from the other side?"

"From Sebastian?"

Adrian nodded.

"No," Coulter said.

"Then Gift is safe."

"Gift is not safe. Links aren't the only way to conquer a person. You know that," Coulter said.

Adrian did know that. Jewel had conquered him by threatening his son. It had been an easy acquiescence, because Luke's life was so much more important to Adrian than his own.

"You're afraid the Black King will be like Jewel, then," Adrian said.

"No." Coulter turned around. "The Black King isn't like Jewel. She had his mind, all right, but she was young and lacked his experience. She was like a baby compared with him. There's a reason he rules over half the world. He has the most incredible presence that I've encountered."

"And Gift didn't inherit it?"

"Gift is no match for him. I'm no match for him. I doubt anyone on the Isle is."

"But he can't kill Gift."

"No, he can't," Coulter said. "But I'm afraid what he will do is worse."

The words hung between them. Adrian swallowed. He had seen what the Fey did to their own kind. Scavenger had shown him how the Fey treated those they considered lesser. And Adrian had seen the subtleties, the coercion, the ways the Fey had of keeping each other in line.

He couldn't imagine it being directed from the inside, from within the brain.

"He made a mistake, then, blocking his Link with you."

Coulter shook his head sadly. "No, he was right. Any Link to him is dangerous now. I just didn't have the strength to block that one."

"He's all by himself, then," Adrian said. "More so than he's ever been in his life."

Coulter glanced over the corn. "I know."

"He'll need protection. Leen's not up for it."

Coulter looked at Adrian. The boy's eyes were dulled from sadness, his shoulders slumping from the energy he had used protecting Gift. "What are you saying?"

"I'm saying that we should go after him. He needs you, Coulter, now more than ever."

Coulter sighed. "He won't accept me."

"He won't have a choice."

Coulter brushed his hair off his face. Adrian had not seen him look this indecisive in years. He was still vulnerable beneath all that power. Rejection hurt him more than others, probably because he had faced so much of it in his short life.

"You don't have to come," Coulter said.

"Oh, but I do," Adrian said. "Someone needs to look out for you."

"I'm an adult now, Adrian. I can look after myself."

Adrian suppressed a fond smile. Coulter was an adult, but that didn't mean he could do everything on his own. Even if he didn't want to admit that, Adrian knew it. And he knew how to get Coulter to allow him to go along.

"I know that," Adrian said. "But the Fey are going to

come here, looking for Gift. And when they don't find him, they'll go after me and Luke and Scavenger. I don't want to face that again. I'd rather know you're safe."

Coulter smiled. It was a small smile, slightly distracted, but a smile nonetheless. "You're not very good at manipulation."

"I know," Adrian said.

"You know it means you'd have to go directly into the Fey."

"I know," Adrian said.

"You'll probably be in more danger there," Coulter said.

"So will you," Adrian said.

"You're not going to let me go alone, are you?" Coulter asked.

"No," Adrian said.

Coulter took a deep breath, as if with it, he could steel himself for the next few days. "All right," he said. "Let's gather up supplies. I suspect we don't have much time until the Fey find us."

Adrian suspected the same thing. He took one more glance at his land, the farm he had tended since he was a boy, the corn rising high in the sun, the buildings his grand-father had built. He hoped he would be able to see it again.

But he doubted that he would.

And that was a price he was willing to pay to keep Coulter safe.

FIFTY-FIVE

SOLANDA paced the tent. It felt smaller and more confining than any other tent she had been in.

Prisoner.

How humiliating.

How wrong.

But there was nothing she could do. She was in Rugad's Shadowlands, being guarded by his people. She was among Fey, and if she Shifted and ran through the camp, they would know what she was.

They would know who she was.

Besides, the door was spelled, and she didn't have time to finesse her way under the tent.

The air was stuffy in here, and still smelled of Rugad's leathers. That meeting had gone poorly. He had believed her about Arianna, but he hadn't seen Solanda's point about her own usefulness. Rugad's problem—and he did have a problem—was that he assumed his great-grandchildren would think like Fey.

Neither of them did.

Gift was too soft and Arianna, although she had her great-grandfather's fierceness and intelligence, considered herself an Islander. Nothing Solanda had done could change that. The only way to make Arianna part of the Fey Empire was through loyalty, and Solanda was the Black King's only hope for that.

But she had slipped. She had let him see the rupture between her and Arianna.

If she wasn't careful, that rupture would cost her her life.

She stopped pacing and swallowed. Rugad wouldn't be back. She had sent him away, taunting him to kill her, and he would. She couldn't escape the tent.

But he had forgotten one thing—or perhaps he had never known. Doppelgängers could not use magick that wasn't theirs. They could overtake a Spy or an Enchanter, but they couldn't use Spy or Enchanter magick.

They could take over a Shifter in her natural Fey form, but they couldn't Shift once they'd done so. And they couldn't use a Shifter's magick.

Which meant they couldn't use a Shifter's magick form.

Solanda blinked, gripped her fists, and took a deep breath. Shifting was her last and only hope. When the Doppelgänger came in the tent, she would have to flee. She would have to run with all her feline swiftness for the Circle door. When she reached it, she would have to leap through it and head for the river. They would never think of following her into the river. They probably didn't even know she could swim.

Then she would go to Arianna and convince the girl to bargain with her great-grandfather. It was Arianna's only hope. Rugad was focused on Gift. He wouldn't think a second powerful Fey great-grandchild necessary.

Solanda closed her eyes and Shifted. Her body compacted downward, her nose and mouth extended, and her limbs became paws. The hair absorbed into her skull and fur grew on her body. Her clothing piled on her, and she stepped out of it, one dainty foot at a time.

She had Shifted.

Now the secret was to surprise the Doppelgänger before he surprised her. An attack on the face might do it. The natural reaction to an animal attack on the eyes was to fling the animal away. Or she could run through his legs—

Voices reverberated outside the tent. Her mouth was dry. She ran her rough tongue over her lips, a nervous habit that she kept from her full Fey form. She slipped to the back of the tent, and waited, poised, in the shadows.

The tent flap opened. She launched herself forward, leaping at the Doppelgänger's face. Midway through the air, she realized she had made a mistake.

Several people had come into the tent, not one, and they weren't Doppelgängers. They were Foot Soldiers. Instead of leaping her way out of danger, she had flung herself into the hands of the enemy.

Literally.

Her limbs pinwheeled in an attempt to stop her leap, but Gelô caught her. She could feel his extra set of fingernails extended into her stomach.

"A pity you Shifted," he said. "Such a small mass of skin. It won't take as much time as we'd hope."

She hissed and spat and clawed at his face, and knew it was too late. Rugad had won. Despite all she was, all she had done for him, he was treating her like a common murderer.

He was executing her.

And there was nothing she could do to stop it.

FIFTY-SIX

RUGAD'S tent was large. It was actually three tents, with openings built between them. They were pushed together into a triangle, which allowed him two meeting areas and a place to sleep. This was the configuration he preferred in Shadowlands, rather than the single tent he had had down south.

Ghost waited for him in one tent. As Rugad approached, Wisdom stopped him.

"Winglet is in your secondary meeting room," Wisdom said. "She has word of the palace."

"Make certain the flaps are closed between tents," Rugad said.

Wisdom nodded and went into the first tent. Rugad gave him a moment before going into the second.

The second tent was smaller than the main tent. It had canvas chairs made by Domestics on Nye and soothing blankets covering the floor and the ceiling. They were slightly spelled so that their colors seeped into Shadowlands. His personal servants had a series of possessions they set up in all of his Shadowlands to make him feel more comfortable. Being surrounded by the familiar made him feel powerful, gave him a sense of community he otherwise would forget during a campaign.

Winglet sat on one of the canvas chairs, her feet curled beneath her. She leaned forward in the manner of most Beast Riders, protecting both the small creature in her belly and assuming the comfortable posture that she usually had after her transformation. Winglet was a Sparrow Rider. Her beakish nose and brownish feathered hair reflected that. She was tall, like most Fey, but so slender that Rugad could circle her waist with one hand.

"What news?" he asked.

"The Riders are in place," she said, "the Infantry is on its way, and the Islanders have tried nothing."

"They haven't even tried to see if they can get out?"

She shook her head. "I believe their King is waiting for his meeting with you."

"Then he will continue to wait. What else?"

"The Tabernacle is burning. Most of the inhabitants are dead. I suspect the rest will be dead by nightfall. Some of the city is on fire as well." She said this last as if she expected him to yell at her.

He shrugged. Cities did not interest him unless they were commercial centers. Jahn hadn't been a commercial center for twenty years.

"All right," he said. "Go back, and tell Flock not to do anything until I arrive. I should be there by morning."

Winglet nodded. She pushed herself out of the chair. "This should be an easy one, shouldn't it?"

Rugad shook his head. "Don't underestimate these people," he said. "That was my son's mistake. You can tell Flock that too. Warn him to remain alert."

"I will," Winglet said. Then she let herself out of the tent. As she pulled back the tent flap, a cat's yowl of pain and terror resounded through Shadowlands. A shudder ran down Rugad's back. Smart one, that Solanda. She had known that a Doppelgänger couldn't become an animal. She had protected herself from her assassin, not knowing that Rugad had been ahead of her.

The yowl sounded again, followed by loud hissing and screeching. He pulled the tent flap closed. It blocked much of the sound. Even though she had chosen a smaller form, her death would still take a while. The Foot Soldiers would see to that. He had promised them a death execution-style, and they would take advantage of that.

He swallowed. His throat was dry. He crossed the room, and took a pouch of water, sipped from it. The pouch was Domestic-spelled, making the water within cool and fresh. He tied the pouch to his hip, trying twice before finishing the move.

His hands were shaking.

He wiped them on his breeches. Killing did not always come easily to him. Sometimes it took more out of him than he showed. He took a deep breath. No one needed to know that detail. No one needed to see it.

He took a moment to let the calm flow through him like the cool water. Then he pushed back the inside flap and went into the first tent.

Its decor was the same as the second tent except for a large wooden table in the center. He had brought three of them, battle-scarred and ancient, to place in all of his important Shadowlands. He had used those tables since he became Black King, planning his strategy on them, writing orders, and learning his statecraft. The tables had served him well.

This one was the oldest. Its wood came from L'Nacin, its scars from many of the battles in Nye. Rugar and Jewel had both carved their names in the surface, as had his other children and grandchildren. He stared at those signatures sometimes, wondering at the price he paid for ruling the Fey.

As if on cue, another screaming howl echoed through the camp. The tent muted it, but the sound was still loud.

The other Fey in the tent flinched. He was wearing clothing too small for his frame. He appeared to be in his midthirties, but his eyes were much older. And they were stained with gold.

"Ghost?" Rugad asked, more to confirm the Doppelgänger's presence than his identity.

He nodded and licked his lips. Then he stood. "I took a Spell Warder," he said, his voice trembling. He kept his eyes downcast, and Rugad could feel the shame coming from him. The death of Fey, even Failure Fey, fell hard on those who heard it, saw it, or caused it.

"So I understand," Rugad said. "You should be out of Shadowlands by now. I'm sure there are other places that can use your services."

"I needed to speak to you first," Ghost said. He put his hands on his knees and pushed himself to his feet. He obviously wasn't used to the new body yet. "This Warder had found the holy water antidote."

"And he didn't use it?"

"It required an Enchanter."

"Ah." Rugad sighed. He had forbidden the Enchanters to go with Rugar. So they might have conquered the Isle after all, if he hadn't made that decree. Was that what Ghost was bringing to him? Knowledge of Rugad's own culpability in the death of his son?

"That's not all," Ghost said. "They found an Enchanter."

Rugad looked at him. Ghost's eyes were dark in his victim's face. "Who?" Rugad asked, not daring to hope it was one of his great-grandchildren.

"He was an Islander child."

Rugad nodded. That made sense. The mixture of Fey blood and Islander blood had produced a strong Visionary and a strong Shifter. There was no reason why it wouldn't produce an Enchanter. "Born how long after the Invasion?"

"Before."

Rugad blinked. He had expected Ghost to say many years after the Invasion, the child being too young to use its magick yet and the Fey biding their time. But this, this made no sense. "There were no babies on that Force."

"I know. The child was Islander." Ghost said that with the precision of someone who was repeating himself.

"Pure Islander?"

"Short, blue-eyed, round-faced, blond-haired, born several months before the first invasion fleet arrived. Solanda found him."

Solanda. Despite himself, Rugad looked toward the prisoner tent. She had withheld even more information from him. To what purpose? He almost felt like stopping the death.

But he couldn't. It was too late.

"How long ago?"

"Nineteen years ago."

The Enchanter was an adult, then. "What happened to him?" Rugad asked.

"He lived in Shadowlands for years before anyone realized what he was. When they did, they approached him wrong and terrified him. He escaped Shadowlands with another Islander prisoner, and even though the Failures searched, they never found him."

"His name?"

"Coulter."

Through the entire explanation, Ghost hadn't raised his head. He knew even more.

"What else?" Rugad asked.

"He saved your great-grandson's life. He remained close to Gift. And Gift never let the Failures know where he was."

"Gift kept them imprisoned in here."

Ghost nodded. "He knew that the Enchanter could give them the antidote to holy water, and he did nothing."

Rugad clenched his fists. But he had Seen his great-grandson leading the way to Leut. Seen it clearly. Yet the boy had acted in the interest of the Isle, not the Fey.

It made no sense.

"You're certain of this?"

"Positive," Ghost said. "This Warder that I inhabit, Touched, was the one who discovered the Enchanter, and the one who tried to talk Gift into bringing him back."

"And he refused?"

"Gift claimed they were going to hurt this Coulter, and he wouldn't let them do that." Ghost licked his lips. "In all fairness, Touched was afraid the experiments the Warders planned would hurt or kill the Enchanter. Coulter was only five years old at the time."

Rugad clenched his fists, then unclenched them. Solanda had warned him. Gift was raised by Failures, she had said. She had had no hopes for him.

But she had had hopes for his sister.

"What happened to the Enchanter?"

"As of this morning, he was still alive," Ghost said. "Touched could feel him. But since I only have an echo of Touched's powers instead of the actual powers, I can't tell you more than that."

"Protecting Gift?"

"One could assume so."

Rugad nodded. So he had met this Enchanter already, the furious presence that had interrupted the Link, then closed and locked the doors.

A powerful Enchanter. Of Islander blood.

He had always assumed the Enchanters Boteen had felt were born to Fey on the Isle. He had thought they would die with the Failures.

He was wrong about one.

Had he been wrong about the other?

FIFTY-SEVEN

NICHOLAS paced the Uprising Room. He was alone except for Sebastian. Monte had gone to lead the troops within the palace. Arianna still wasn't back.

Nicholas didn't want to think about that.

The sunlight had grown thinner. Smoke from all over the city blocked some of the light. Below, on the birds, the sunlight was still bright.

Sebastian was watching him, eyes wide. The boy didn't say much, but he knew what was happening.

So did Nicholas. The moment of leadership had truly arrived. He had just sent men to their deaths. He knew it, Monte knew it, and Sebastian knew it.

The men probably knew it.

But he had learned once before that one life meant nothing compared with hundreds of lives.

Unless that life had Black Blood. Somehow the Fey had even turned that one simple rule around. Nicholas's children, his real children, meant more than everyone in the palace put together.

He wondered if Sebastian understood that.

He stopped pacing near Sebastian. Sebastian took a deep, slow breath.

"Will . . . Ari . . . be . . . able . . . to . . . come . . . back?"

Sebastian meant would she be able to come back after the battle started. Could she get in? Would she be safe?

"I hope so," Nicholas said.

Sebastian peeled himself away from the wall and linked his arm through Nicholas's. Together they walked to the windows overlooking the courtyard.

"So . . . many," Sebastian said.

Nicholas nodded. So many birds. The glass felt like thin protection, and the height felt like no protection at all.

Birds.

They could be at his level in a heartbeat, and their Fey riders could shatter the glass in no time.

Then Sebastian squeezed his arm. Two guards emerged in the courtyard below. They wore no hats, and their hair shone like spun gold in the sun. They walked with their backs straight and their shoulders squared, and never once did they look at the birds around them.

Only at the birds on the gate.

Nicholas looked at those as well. Hawks, ravens, eagles, along with smaller birds, robins, wren, and sparrow. There were several birds he didn't recognize in the mix, birds larger than ten-year-old children, with brightly colored plumage and beaks that were as long as his hand and as thick as his arm.

He held his breath. Sebastian's grip grew tighter.

The men walked side by side. Wings rose and then settled again. Feathers ruffled as if a wind blew through them. But leaves didn't move. There was no wind. The guards made the birds uneasy.

Tiny bubbles were imbedded in the glass, making his view imperfect. He leaned as close as he could get, his fists resting on the sill beneath his waist.

The guards had crossed the courtyard. They had nearly reached the first layer of birds.

Then, as if by an unseen command, a flock of birds rose from the right side and attacked the guard nearest them. They covered him, pecking and cawing, ripping at his skin with their talons. His blood flew everywhere.

Sebastian moaned and turned away.

Nicholas couldn't.

Another flock, almost at the same time, surrounded the second guard, but did not touch him. Blood spattered him, but he stared straight ahead as if it did not matter to him.

Maybe Nicholas had been wrong. Maybe the training he had ordered had worked for some of the guards.

The attack was oddly silent. The guard did not scream, and the birds didn't make a sound. The guard raised a bird-covered hand. Bits of skin flew in all directions. A dove rose from the melee below and flew to Nicholas's window, the Fey on its back holding something the size of an egg.

It was an eyeball.

As the Fey passed Nicholas, it held up the eye and grinned. The eye was nearly as big as the Fey was.

The Fey was female. Blood covered her bare breasts. Nicholas had to force himself to keep watching, force himself to keep his expression impassive.

When she got no reaction from him, she tossed the eyeball at the window with such force that the eyeball spattered when it hit.

In spite of himself, Nicholas took a step backwards.

Sebastian cringed at the sound, covering his face with his hands.

The Fey woman laughed.

The dove dipped below the window, flying out of his sight.

He stepped to another window and looked down.

The left guard was still surrounded by birds. His companion was sprawled on the courtyard, clearly dead. His face was pecked raw, a bloody mass of tissue and bones, not recognizable as human any more. His uniform hung in tatters around him, and the center of his body, from his intestines to his heart, was gone.

Nicholas swallowed. He had seen worse, but only once.

When Jewel died.

And that was worse only because he loved her.

The birds were all staring up at him. So were the Fey on their backs. The second flock herded the second guard back to the palace's door, then sat outside until he went in.

The message was clear.

Too clear.

The birds would only attack anyone trying to leave the palace. They were all to remain inside, for reasons that Nicholas didn't know yet.

He wasn't going to wait to find out.

Sebastian raised his head. He stared at the blood streaking the window. "Oh, ... Pa-pa ..." he said, and shuddered.

Nicholas touched the stained glass. It was cool, smooth, and dry against his fingertips. The blood didn't touch him yet.

But it would.

It would.

"This is only the beginning, Sebastian," Nicholas said, and wished it weren't true.

FIFTY-EIGHT

FLURRY had forgotten how tiring war could be.

He had been flying consistently since he had given Rugad's message to the palace. After he had reported to Rugad, he had been allowed one half day's rest before flying back north.

And now they were sending him south again.

Only this time he knew where to go. Rugad believed one of his great-grandsons was on farmland. Flurry had flown over more farmland than he cared to think about. All of it was in the center of Blue Isle, and it stretched forever.

But he had an advantage over the other Wisps who were searching. He had actually seen the great-grandson and had known which road the boy was on. The farm couldn't have been too far off the main road, not with the time involved.

Flurry swooped low. He had flown quickly since he received the instructions, going around Jahn, over the river, and cutting across the nobles' lands on the south side of the Cardidas. Then he reached farm country quicker than the others.

His companion, Cinder, was having trouble keeping up with him. She had only flown across Blue Isle as part of a

Wisp unit, going from south to north. She hadn't flown freely like he had.

They were of an age, but Flurry had risen in the Fey ranks until he worked as messenger for Rugad on occasion. Cinder only took low-ranking assignments, and had tried, so she told him, to get out of the trip to Blue Isle altogether. She preferred Nye. But Rugad had needed all the Wisps, all the Beast Riders, and all the Doppelgängers he had. He hadn't let any stay behind.

Rugad was leaving nothing to chance on this trip. It was almost as if he were afraid of Blue Isle but unwilling to admit it.

The road finally appeared, wide and brown, like a river frozen below him. Flurry swerved until he was over it, then he glanced over his tiny shoulder and looked for Cinder. She was far enough behind him that he had to stare before he saw her, a black dot against the blueness of the sky. She was having trouble keeping up, as he expected her to. He bit back irritation. Epo, the Wisp leader, had insisted that they fly in pairs. That way, if the great-grandson were spotted, one member of the pair would stay with the boy and the other would report back as quickly as possible. Epo had also paired the Wisps strong to weak, which annoyed Flurry. He would have to stay with the great-grandson, and hope that Cinder would make it back to Rugad in record speed.

She wouldn't, of course, but there wasn't much Flurry could do about that.

Farms started dotting the sides of the road, like black spots on the face of a quilt. Flurry swooped lower, then cursed under his breath.

It was midday. Islanders were out, working on land. On every farm, he saw three, four, sometimes five Islanders bent over the crops, occasionally using a horse to pull equipment or carrying buckets from their water pumps toward the fields.

If the great-grandson made a Shadowlands, the Circle Door would be difficult to see in this light. Just as Flurry was difficult to see.

This would take longer than he thought.

He hovered, waiting for Cinder. She arrived beside him, her wings fluttering like a hummingbird's, sweat beading her face. She was breathing hard.

"Was it necessary to go that fast?" she asked.

"It'll be necessary to go even faster when we find him," Flurry said.

"We won't find him, not in all of this." She swept a tiny arm across the panorama before her. Fields everywhere, farmers, Islanders. She was right. It would be a lot of work.

"We will," Flurry said. Her negative response angered him. It was as if she hated working for her Black King, as if she hated her life. He didn't. He was proud to be on the Black King's team and at his side. "He's part Fey. I've seen him. He's tall and darker than the others. He looks Fey. He should stand out."

Cinder grunted. She looked down. The farms stretched before them as far as the eye could see. "We don't even know he's still here," she said. "If the Black King were coming after me, I would move as quickly as I could."

"How would he know—?" Flurry stopped himself. The great-grandson was a Visionary too. He might know. He might know a lot.

The other Wisps would be looking on farms for the very signs that Flurry was talking about.

"How would he know what?" Cinder asked.

Flurry held up his hand. Hovering was making him thirsty. He wanted to land and have something to drink, but he wasn't ready yet. He needed to think.

If he were Visionary, and knew that the Black King was lookng for him, he might also know that Shadowlands was gone. He might make his own Shadowlands, but that was feeble protection against other Fey. In fact, it was no protection at all. The Fey merely had to find the door and open it. Such a strange situation, Fey fighting Fey. Usually Fey fought nonmagickal beings, and those beings couldn't open a Shadowlands.

The boy that Flurry had seen looked smart. He also spoke Fey. Rugad had said the boy who spoke Fey was the great-grandson, the other merely an excellent golem. It would have to have been a near-perfect golem, but Flurry did not argue with his leader. A Fey speaker, raised among Fey, would know a Shadowlands was a poor hiding place in this circumstance.

And if the boy knew his old Shadowlands was gone, he

wouldn't go west, he wouldn't go back home. He had just come from the city, so he wouldn't go back there.

Or would he?

That would be the very opposite of the farmland. And since he had been on the farmland when the Black King saw him, he couldn't have been there long. A night at most. So he couldn't have gone too far south in the first place. Traveling south or west would mean remaining on farmland.

But traveling north would probably take him out of the Black King's reach.

"We're wrong," Flurry said.

Cinder wiped her face with the back of her arm. She left a smear of dirt along her forehead. "Wrong?"

"Everyone else will be checking the farms. Let's go north."

"But our orders are to—"

"Our orders are to find him," Flurry said, "whatever that takes. The farmland is just a place to start. Come on. Let's follow the road north."

"If I were hiding, I wouldn't take a road," Cinder said.

"You would if you knew people were looking for you in farmland," Flurry said.

She shook her head, her close-cropped hair blowing into her eyes. She brushed it away. "I would find a hidey-hole and stay there."

She would, too. Flurry looked at her. A lot of people would. But the great-grandson of the Black King? Rugad wouldn't stay, nor would his son, Rugar. Jewel wouldn't have stayed either, or her brother Bridge. As for the others? Maybe. But Flurry doubted it. They were taught from birth to lead, and part of leadership meant movement. It didn't mean hiding.

But he had no idea what this Fey had been taught. He did know, though, that he was searching for the great-grandson raised by the Fey, not the one raised by the Islander. If any great-grandson had the possibility of leadership, this one did.

Which was probably why Rugad was looking for him.

"That's a good point," Flurry said, "but such a search would take days. It would be difficult, and we have little chance of success. Let the others try that. You and I will search the road."

"After we stop and have some nourishment." She crossed her little arms, her frown severe.

He stared at her for a moment. He needed her. He had to keep reminding himself of that. He needed her. He wouldn't let her run this, but he would have to take her wishes into account sometimes.

"All right," he said. "We'll stop. But only for a very short time."

She smiled, flattened her arms against her side, and dove for the ground. He sighed and dove after her.

She had better get a good rest here. Once they got back in the air, he intended to find Rugad's great-grandson.

No matter what it took.

FIFTY-NINE

THE acrid taste of smoke filled her mouth. Arianna felt as if the stench covered her, as if she would never be the same. The flight over the city had left her discouraged and angry, and terrified that her family—her people—would be helpless against the Fey.

She had promised the Shaman that she wouldn't attack her great-grandfather, but the same promise had to hold for him. He couldn't go after her either. That should give her some leeway. What kind, she didn't know yet.

Her wings felt heavy. She had used these muscles a lot in the past two days, when she hadn't flown much before that. She should have kept herself in better condition, should have been preparing for something like this, anything like this.

As if an invasion, anticipated for twenty years but never really believed in, could be prepared for.

The scrapes from her encounter with Solanda still ached. They showed in the thin feather covering on her right wing. That encounter seemed so long ago.

Arianna sighed. In all her searching, she had seen no sign of that Gift. She had a lot to report, but nothing her brother Sebastian wanted to hear.

Fey were scattered all over the city below her. But for the most part, they stayed away from the palace area. That both pleased and worried her. The Black King had a plan for those birds.

She suspected that she wouldn't like it.

The palace grew closer. At least it was still standing. She had a fear, after seeing the Tabernacle, that she would return to see the palace on fire as well.

But it wasn't. It still stood, its three towers tall in the sunlight, the flags flying off its turrets. The windows were shuttered, though, the tapestries down, and that looked odd in the middle of the day.

The birds remained below, but some had shifted position. They had backed up from before.

The feathers on her back rose, and she let out an involuntary warble. The sound was small, and carried away by the wind. She barely heard it herself.

She clamped her beak closed then and flew as low as she could without appearing like she was looking.

A body lay in the courtyard.

At least she thought it was a body. It had bones and some skin and the remains of clothing. Blood was spattered everywhere. Some of the birds were still coated.

She resisted the urge to fly even lower. She would be seen. They would realize she wasn't a robin after all, but had Fey blood just like they did.

Although she didn't want to claim that blood any longer. No matter what Solanda said, Arianna was Islander. Pure Islander. She would never be part of this savagery, the savagery below her.

Her heart was pounding hard. Bile rose again in her throat. Someone had died down there. Maybe even someone she knew.

Her father?

She hoped not.

The only thing she could be certain of was that it wasn't Sebastian. She had no idea what was inside his body, only that it wouldn't be that easy to peck apart.

Then she saw the guard huddled near the kitchen door, his uniform splattered with blood, and she knew what had happened. A guard had gone out there, and had died.

A guard.

She was relieved it wasn't her father, and ashamed of that feeling at the same time. A life was a life was a life.

Except when it belonged to someone she loved.

She swept upward on an air current and let herself drift toward the North Tower. Then she landed on her ledge and slipped behind it, as she had done before. She resisted the urge to look behind her, to peek her small robin's head around the barrier and see if any other birds had followed her.

She hopped off the ledge inside the room. It hadn't changed. No birds had come in here since she left. She moved away from the window and Shifted. Her bird's body elongated, her bones filled, and her feathers slipped inside her skin. Her fragile wings remolded into arms, and her spiky legs into human legs. Her beak flattened, her nose returned, and she had a mouth again.

The taste of smoke was so strong it lay like a layer of filth on her tongue. She swallowed, and the bile she had been holding back rose up. She put a hand on the dirty wall and vomited, once, twice, three times, until her stomach was empty.

Her mouth tasted foul, but at least the stench of smoke was gone. She ripped a corner off her robe and wiped her face. Never before had she had such a reaction to Shifting. But she suspected it hadn't been caused by the Shift, but by all the death around her.

Her body had merely waited until it was safe before allowing a reaction.

She took a deep breath, and blinked. Her eyes burned, and nothing she did seemed to make them feel any better.

It was real now.

It was war.

And it wouldn't get any better.

Her parents had met in conditions like this. Her father had hoped to spare her. But it wasn't possible. Not with her heritage. Not with Blue Isle between Leut and Galinas.

Not with the possibility of Fey failure, a failure that would be known worldwide.

Solanda had warned her this day might come, but Arianna hadn't known what it would mean. It meant bodies and the smell of burning flesh. It meant smoke all over the city and being a prisoner in her own home. It meant fear so deep that it was like another power inside her.

She pulled on her robe and staggered back to the window. It was open and would remain so, unless she did something.

No birds had followed her, but she had found this place. They might too.

She put boards and hay across it, building a barrier as quickly as she could. It could be knocked away easily, but the birds might not even try. They would go for more obvious places.

She hoped.

Then she tightened the belt on her robe and let herself out of the small room.

The tower was dark. The lack of window light made it seem like night in the stairwell. The sound of her feet slapping against stone echoed. That feeling of being alone, the one she had had earlier, was back. She resisted the urge to cry out. No one would be here. She had specifically requested that her guards be called off. No one knew about her Shifts except her father, the nurse, Sebastian, and Solanda. No one else could know. The Islanders wouldn't accept it.

She made it down to the Uprising Room, where her father said he would wait for her. Then she stopped.

The stairwell was still empty. If her father was inside, there should have been guards outside.

There were none.

Was that body below the last remnants of a fight? Had there been a defection? A kidnapping?

Had the Black King come and taken her family away?

She bit back the fear. She had been taught, in a situation like this, to go away from the place in question, to find help. But that teaching had supposed a normal world and normal events. She gripped her side of the door and eased it open, preparing to run if she saw something unusual.

What she saw was her father, standing alone in the center of the room, his face pale. She slipped around the door and came in, remembering Solanda's teachings. Fey could take over a person's body and become that person. The only way to tell was to look in the eyes.

"Daddy?" she asked.

He turned quickly and joy filled her face. Sebastian peeled himself away from the far wall—she hadn't even seen him—and shouted, "Ari!" in a tone that matched her father's look.

Nicholas hurried across the room, but when he came close, she held out her arm. Her sleeve fell away, leaving her skin exposed to the air. She felt as if her entire self were exposed.

"I'm sorry," she said, her voice trembling. "Let me see your eyes."

"Arianna," he said.

"Please."

He opened his eyes wide. They were blue and bloodshot, the whites nearly red from strain. But there was no gold in them.

"It's . . . him," Sebastian said, and she trusted that more than she trusted Solanda's description of a phenomenon Arianna had never seen. Sebastian always recognized dangerous magick, and Sebastian was impossible to duplicate. Solanda had told her that Doppelgängers couldn't become a magick construct. They couldn't even use someone else's magick, only someone else's appearance.

"Daddy," she said, and fell forward into his arms. He wrapped them around her and pulled her tight. For a moment she felt like a little girl again, safe and secure in her father's arms, as if he could make it all better, as if he were the most powerful person in the entire world.

No.

That was her great-grandfather.

The thought made her pull back, but her father continued to hold her. He buried his face in her hair. He was trembling. For the first time, she felt how frail he was. How deeply terrified he had been.

She brought a hand up and stroked his head. "Daddy," she said. "It's all right. I'm back."

He nodded into her hair, but didn't let her go yet.

"I'm safe."

"I . . . thought . . . you . . . would . . . die," Sebastian said, and his voice held so much sadness that both Arianna and her father turned to him. They opened their embrace to him, and clung, the small family, backs to the world.

"I won't die," she said. Although she wasn't as certain of that as she had been just a few hours ago. She had seen more in that time than she had seen in her entire life.

Finally her father took a deep breath and pulled out of the hug. He caressed Arianna's cheek with one hand, a gesture he had never used before, and then smiled, just a little. "Don't take too many more risks, honey," he said.

She squeezed Sebastian's side, then let him go. "I can't make that promise," she said. "The Fey are all over the city. They're burning it. People are—" the bile rose again, and she swallowed it back. "People are dead."

Her father nodded, as if he weren't surprised. Then he turned, clasped his hands behind his back, and walked to the window. The sky was black with purple markings. The sun, coming through the smoke, had turned hazy white.

She turned to Sebastian. His cracked face was full of hope. "I didn't see him," she said.

The change in his features was slow. His mouth dropped open, his cracks grew deeper, and tears filled his eyes. She took his hand. "But that doesn't mean anything. He could be anywhere. He's probably hiding from the Fey."

Her father hadn't turned, but he had obviously heard that too. She couldn't tell how he was feeling about Gift. She wasn't sure she wanted to know.

He took a deep breath. "What of the Tabernacle?" he asked.

"It's burning," she said.

A shudder ran through him, but she didn't know what it meant. Her father had hated the Tabernacle, had hated it for a long time. And yet he had ties to it. He was part of it, even though he didn't want to admit it.

"Your great-grandfather is smart," her father said.

She nodded, even though he couldn't see her. "Why isn't anyone guarding this room?" she asked.

"No one's left in the palace except us," her father said.

She frowned. She had only seen one body below. Had the others escaped? Was it just her family being held? "Where is everyone else?"

"Monte and I have a plan," her father said, and then added no more.

"You sent them away?" She wasn't understanding this.

"You sent guards away, and staff, and people who would protect you and Sebastian? Are you crazy?"

Her father's shoulders rose and fell as he sighed. "Look at all the birds," he said.

"I've seen them. There's thousands, and more Fey reinforcements coming. It's an army, Daddy, an army like we've never seen before. And you're not protected."

"An army gives an illusion of safety," her father said. "I was no safer with the guards here than without. It was just a few more lives as a barrier to the Fey, more people to slaughter before those butchers got to me."

"I don't understand," she said. "You need protection."

He shook his head. "I've been thinking like my own father lately, and that's wrong. I was in the middle of the fighting when I met your mother. I was fighting hand-to-hand with Fey, stepping over bodies to do so."

"It was a different war," Arianna said.

"That's right." Her father turned. He looked old and exhausted. His face had sunken in on itself. "It was an easier war. If we lose now, we lose everything. So we have to risk everything. The Fey are already doing that for us. We may as well take the veneer off of it and look at it for what it is."

"Where are the others, Daddy?" she asked.

"Monte's leading them into a counterattack."

"But there's more of them than us. That can't work. It's—"

"It works. And has worked in the past. I spent years studying military techniques after your mother died. Lord Stowe has a lot of books on the matters. The peasants lost the Uprising even though they had a superior force, did you know that?"

"Of course I know that. We need better weapons."

Her father shook his head. "We had the same weapons, and we had, at first, less desire. We had a smaller force, but a smarter commander. He knew how to turn the advantage to us. That's what Monte and I are trying to do now."

"Why won't you tell me what's going to happen?"

"Because you'll see it in a moment," her father said.

Arianna wiped her hand over her face. Sebastian touched her arm. She glanced at him. He was frowning, exposing all the cracks in his skin. "It . . . is . . . a . . . good . . . plan."

Arianna sighed. She couldn't get the flames and the images of all those bodies out of her mind. "What happens if it fails?" she asked. "We're unprotected up here."

Her father turned. "We're not unprotected," he said. He tucked a strand of her hair behind her ear. "We have the best protection of all. Your mother's protection."

"My mother is dead."

"Your mother gave us the protection of her family."

"But the Shaman says you might not be able to claim it."

"But you can," her father said. "The events of this day have shown me, Arianna, that saving Blue Isle might be entirely up to you."

She bowed her head. "I can't—"

"You can," he said. "You might have to. This is what you were arguing for last night. You're stronger than all of us. You'll do what's right."

"I hope so," she whispered. She didn't feel stronger. She felt as if she had lost her whole world. Everything except the two men with her. She couldn't bear to lose them.

She took Sebastian's hand. He put his arm around her. "It . . . will . . . be . . . all . . . right," he said, trying to comfort her. "I . . . will . . . al-ways . . . be . . . be-side . . . you."

"Promise?" she asked, suddenly needing his reassurance as much as he had once needed hers.

"Pro-mise . . ." he said. "By . . . all . . . I . . . am, . . . I . . . pro-mise."

SIXTY

HE only had to check the map once.

It seemed all passageways ultimately ended at the palace.

Con ran through the darkness, torch before him, heart pounding. Those dirty strangers in the large cavern, and the former Aud, had terrified him. He had been afraid that they were part Fey and would stop him, or worse, even though he couldn't quite imagine what worse would be. All he knew was that they left him with the feeling he was late, too late to do anything, that his crawl through the bridge had been for nothing.

The passages through here were as dirty and cobwebby as the bridge tunnel had been. No one had been through this area in a long, long time. That reassured him a little, but didn't allow him to slow his pace. He kept glancing over his shoulder, afraid that the others were following him.

Afraid of what they would do when they caught him.

The former Aud terrified him the most. He was an obviously learned man, injured, and living like a rat beneath the river. Was this how the sacrilegious ended up? Shells of people, strewn like dirt, in the abandoned tunnels of society?

Was this how he would end up if he failed his Charge?

He didn't know and wasn't certain he wanted to. He hurried forward, spurred by the vision of his own failure more than anything else. He was concentrating so hard and moving so quickly that at first he didn't even notice the sounds.

Footsteps on stone.

Many footsteps.

Not above him, but ahead of him.

They sounded in unison, those footsteps, as if a group were walking in step.

Like the Fey had done.

But how had they gotten into the tunnels? Had they found one of the side entrances?

The thought made his mouth go dry. He was dirty, exhausted, and terrified, and for what? For an encounter with the Fey that would leave him dead?

But he had a Charge, and he had the Roca's protection. The Rocaan had walked into the Fey secret camp when he was an Aud on a Charge. The Roca had watched over him, and brought him out alive.

The Roca would bring Con out alive too.

He stopped running, though, and walked forward, his torch close to him now. When he reached a fork in the tunnel, he would stop and listen before moving on.

The footsteps grew louder, and with them, the whisper of clothing, the soft murmur of an occasional voice.

It took three crossroads before he realized that the voices were not speaking Fey.

They were speaking Islander.

Relief flowed over him like a cool breeze. Islander. They were his people.

But what were they doing here?

He started running again. His legs were tired, and it felt as if his feet were bleeding, but he no longer cared. He was nearly to the palace, and there were people below, walking in lockstep, Islanders, not a bunch of thieves hiding near the river.

And then he rounded a corner, and found them: a sea of men in the uniforms of the King's guards, looking serious, looking terrified, looking serene. They had swords strapped to their hips and dagger hilts peeking out of their boots.

They were going to fight.

The King already knew.

Still, Con had his Charge. He waited until he saw a man who wasn't in step, one of the leaders, probably, and walked up to him.

"Excuse me," he said.

The man drew his dagger. "Get away from me, boy."

"I'm an Aud, sir. I come from the Tabernacle, with the Rocaan's message for the King."

"No one sees the King." The man had stopped. He held his knife near Con's throat. A few of the others stopped behind him, watching.

"Sir, it's a Charge." Con said, careful not to move. "I need to see him."

"How do we know you're not Fey?" the man said.

"Beg pardon, milord, tis obvious," said one of the men in the back. "Tis holy water vials he carries in his pockets. Ye can see the glass."

"It would be a good disguise, to come here dressed as an Aud," the leader said.

"Aye," the second man said, "but na with holy water, and na looking like Constantine, the Baby Aud."

Con raised his head at the nickname. The barracks guards had called him that after a particularly disastrous Blessing he attempted to deliver a year ago.

"Servis?" he asked.

"Aye, n who'd ye think else'd remember who ye are, eh?" the guard stepped into the light. It was Servis, a guard who was only a few years older than Con and who had given him grief ever since that difficult day.

"You know this Aud?" the leader asked.

"Aye, milord. Tis a good boy, he is."

"Please, sirs, let me see the King."

The leader shook his head. "I can't let you do that," he said.

"But my Charge—"

"Is?"

"To let the King know of the Fey."

"He knows, lad."

"Tis Respected Sir, milord. He is n Aud."

"That he is, Servis." The leader nodded. "Forgive me,

Respected Sir. The palace has been surrounded by Fey all morning. We're going to take care of that now."

He snapped his fingers. The guards kept moving forward. There were more of them than Con had imagined.

He blinked. He wasn't certain what to do now. "The Tabernacle's surrounded too," he said. "The Rocaan wanted me to warn you, wanted me to talk to the King. He says they need to work together."

"I'm sure they do," the leader said, "but they need to survive the afternoon first. Wait here for us. When the battle's over, I'll take you with me."

"No, milord," Con said. "I'm sorry not to listen, but I have a Charge. I need to get to the King."

"And I can't let you go alone. There's no telling who you are."

Con understood that. Even so, it didn't make things much easier. But he felt that his message had lost its urgency. Now all that mattered was surviving the next few hours.

"Then I'll come with you," Con said, "and watch."

"Nay, Baby Aud," Servis said. He had stopped beside the leader. The rest of the troop continued to march behind him, weaving through the tunnels and disappearing into the darkness. "Tis na place fer an innocent above. Ye'll wait here, and I'll see to it that we get ye to the King."

"Stay with him, Servis," the leader said.

"Beg pardon, milord, but ye need me ta face the Fey."

"I need you to protect the King," the leader said, with a strange emphasis on the word "protect."

"It's all right," Con said. "I'll wait alone. I don't mind."

"Of course not, Respected Sir, but I can't guarantee that you won't go to the palace the moment the troops leave here."

"I'd give you my word."

"And your word means nothing in the face of a Charge."

The leader was right, and Con knew it. The moment they left, he would go on to the palace. He had to.

It was his Charge.

Servis sighed. "I'll stay, milord."

"Good," the leader said. "When I get back, I'll take you to the King."

"Yes, sir," Con said. He was failing. And Servis, a casual friend, would have to guard him to prevent him from doing what his Rocaan, and his God, required him to do.

That was at the center of a Charge. How far would an Aud go to do his duty? How many laws would he break, if he broke any?

Con hoped he wouldn't have to find out.

SIXTY-ONE

MONTE led his troop up the last few stairs and into the barracks. His mouth was dry, and he felt older than he ever had before. He'd been in difficult situations, but never one where he believed it would take God's Hand to help him survive the day. He'd faced Fey a hundred times before, but never like this.

Never like this.

To their credit, his men said nothing. They had simply accepted the orders, trusting in him and in Nicholas.

The bird-Fey outnumbered them five to one. Long odds, even with a surprise attack.

Monte hunched as he crossed the wooden floor. He walked as quietly as he could. So did the men behind him, but he could still hear the rap-rap-rap of boots. He hoped it wouldn't be too audible in that strange silence outside.

The boy bothered him too, the one Servis had called Baby Aud. The boy bothered him in two ways. If he were Fey, then this whole surprise attack wouldn't work. They already knew about the tunnels. If he wasn't Fey, if he truly was an Aud, then that meant that the Rocaan had been willing to work with them, and it was too late.

It already felt too late. The Fey had been ahead of them on everything. Like the first time, only much larger. He had never imagined there were so many Fey in the world. Never.

What he wouldn't do for a vial of holy water. But Nicholas had forbidden it on the palace grounds. A few of the troop had vials—Monte had seen them. He didn't want to know how the guards had gotten them or why. They were going against the King's direct order. But a man couldn't stop others from protecting themselves when they were terrified.

These men were terrified. Monte could feel it. He could feel it in the jerkiness of their movements, in the uncertainty of their looks. They all knew when this latest Fey troop arrived that this strange period of peace was over. The end of the invasion, begun when Rugar came twenty years before, was finally here.

Monte reached the barracks door. The important thing on this entire plan was noise and timing. He took a deep breath, held it, then sent the signal back through his troop.

It traveled from man to man quickly until it reached the tunnels. There the men would relay it to the other barracks, to the other commanders waiting. Monte was counting. He had it timed to the instant, and hoped his guess was right.

"All right," he said softly. "Draw your swords."

His men did. The sound of metal against sheath sounded loud in the large room. He turned slightly. They were watching him, eyes narrowed, faces blank in an attempt to hide their emotions.

He put his hand on the doorknob and turned it slowly.

"Now!" he said.

He yanked open the door and jumped down the steps. Men surged past him, running toward the birds. When they reached a bird, they would grab its Fey head and slice it off. A single, quick movement, like wringing the neck of a chicken.

Monte was in the middle of it, sword drawn, running for the birds. The tiny Fey heads turned, but the bird heads squawked and wings fluttered. Birds rose in the air like a real flock, surging away in terrified surprise.

At first the attack happened in silence, but then the men

started to yell. Nicholas had thought of that: the guards doing the Fey battle cry, startling the birds even more.

The movement on the end of the bird line startled the birds on the front of the line. They flew forward too, slamming into each other in midair. Feathers fell around them. Some of the guards moved fast, catching birds with their swords, slicing the feathered bodies in half.

The cries were deafening, the roar of wings exhilarating. Monte surged into the middle of the group, swinging his sword above his head like a mace, chopping and slashing and cutting at birds. The sky was black with them.

And the ground was empty.

The ground was empty.

A few of the guards were spilling holy water on the bird bodies, but it did nothing. The Fey hadn't lied. They had found an antidote.

Some of the birds had swung around and were coming back. The guards were ready. They stabbed and fought and smashed. The birds stood no chance.

The rout was working.

It would buy time.

Monte only hoped it would be enough.

SIXTY-TWO

RUGAD gripped the strings of his harness, careful not to pull on them. He swung in the afternoon air, his feet dangling over the road below. The twenty-five Hawk Riders flapped their wings above him, hawk faces intent on the city ahead of them, the tiny Fey Riders clinging to their backs. There was no laughter this time, no soft conversation back and forth. Before they had been invading, investigating, and now they were fighting.

And they had the most precious cargo of all.

The Black King.

Rugad hadn't expected to use his harness this much in the Blue Isle campaign. He had thought that he would use it only to get onto the Isle proper. But so far he had used it twice over the ocean, once to get to his great-grandson's Shadowlands, and now to get to Jahn quickly.

Normally he would have marched with his troops, but he had a sense that time was of the essence in this campaign. He was worried that the Islanders, given enough warning, would find another method of defeating the Fey. Even though he might believe their holy poison a fluke, he couldn't act upon it.

The news of the Islander Enchanter worried him. Solanda's passion for her ward worried him as well. He had gone to see her body after the Foot Soldiers were through with her. Only the bones were left, tiny bones, the bones of a cat.

She had tried to bargain for the girl, claiming wild magick.

If Rugad's great-grandchildren were examples of wild magick, and the holy water was an example of wild magick, perhaps the Islander Enchanter was too. Perhaps there would be others.

He had to plan for more surprises. And the only way he could do that was to subdue the Islanders so quickly, so effectively, that they wouldn't know what hit them until it was too late.

The sky was gray with smoke. He had made the decision to burn Jahn after he had arrived on the Isle and seen the poverty in the outlying areas. The fields and farms had the wealth he sought. They simple funneled it into the city, where that wealth was used to maintain the lords and the merchants. Without international trade, the outlying villages had stagnated.

But Jahn hadn't.

Rugad had no need for a small city's wealth. As soon as he owned Blue Isle, he could reestablish international trade, and the wealth would reappear. He needed the farms, the millers, and the Islander bodies. Workers to turn the entire Isle into one big grain basket for the rest of the world.

The city was merely taking up valuable farmland. By burning it, he was doing several things: he was taking out the wealthy class, he was destroying morale, and he was preparing the land for the next spring's planting.

Simple, effective, and swift. The watchwords of any successful campaign.

The very next thing he had to do was take the palace. He needed the Islander King for his children and for his ability to control the morale of the country. The man had an arrogance that Rugad didn't like. Rugad would probably have to kill him, but before he did so, he wanted to see if the man could be broken and molded.

He suspected the secret to that was to go after the

children. Rugad could not kill them, but he didn't have to. Some things, such as loss of loyalty, could be a lot more devastating than a child's death. He simply had to play it right.

He still hadn't figured out what he would do with the golem. The creature's existence both excited him and worried him. It excited him because it meant that Gift had extraordinary powers. It worried him because he did not know why the Changeling had lasted so long, what purpose it served.

Constructed magick, with long life, often had hidden powers of its own. It was said, by the older Shamans, that such constructs were actually tools of the Powers themselves. The Shamans always refused to study the constructs as well, saying they were part of the Mysteries and were not meant to be understood.

Rugad had seen enough of the Mysteries to know how dangerous they could be. And all his life he had been at the mercy of the Powers. He believed them to be the source of the Black Family's Visions. The Powers were capricious guardians of the future. If they controlled the golem, they held more than its fate in their imaginary hands.

He shivered, even though it was warm. The heat of the day rose from below, mixing with the heat of the fires now burning out of control in the row houses on the edge of Jahn. Bits of ash floated around him, and sparks mingled with the debris. The air felt thin, and his heart beat hard to compensate for the shallow breaths he took. He raised one arm and signaled the lead Hawk Rider to go faster.

The sooner he reached the palace, the happier he would be.

The heat was intense. Some of the fires were dangerously close to out of control. He needed to send Red Caps to quench those fires. He made a mental note to do so when he landed.

The palace was ahead, an island of calm in the middle of Fey fury. From this distance, and with the clarity of height, he could see his Bird Riders surrounding the place. Apparently King Nicholas had been smart. There was no sign of attack, no sign of battle.

Only the birds, waiting.

Nicholas was such a fool. For all his pretense, and despite his Fey marriage, he did not gain Fey wisdom. He still waited for Rugad to negotiate with him. Rugad had thought this would happen; he had hoped that Nicholas would think the Bird Riders were there to guard the palace until Rugad arrived. But he had hoped that Nicolas had been worthy of Jewel, that he hadn't fallen for this trick, and that he would be harder to defeat than the rulers on Galinas.

Cowards all.

Rugad had hated fighting them, had hated the way they had stuck their soldiers into battle and fled when it was time to fight themselves. He had slaughtered a number of those rulers with his bare hands, not because he had to assert his own leadership, but because he was so disgusted with theirs.

Wisdom had always warned him against that, citing how dangerous it was for a Visionary to go into battle. Rugad usually agreed, but in those cases, he felt it necessary. They needed to learn, even if it was in their dying moments, what true leadership meant.

He was nearly above his Bird Riders when movement behind them caught his eye.

Islanders, dressed in tan and black, swarmed out of buildings and over the fence, hundreds of them, swords drawn. They seemed to move with an incredible silence. When they reached the first of the Bird Riders, they sliced off the Fey's heads, then ripped the Fey off the backs. Then they yelled, a horrible imitation of the Fey warrior cry. The sound of it rose all over the city.

The smaller birds rippled and flew away—instinct kicking in on the bird selves, the Fey on their backs shouting and trying to force their bird bodies down. When the smaller birds flew, they startled the larger birds and they took off too—black dots against the grayish yellow sky.

Suddenly the battle on the ground was more evenly matched. The birds that remained were the large ones, the macaws and the parrots, pecking and stabbing, and screaming and honking.

The terrified birds, rising, brushed against Rugad's perch. He held on, trying not to tug on the strings, as the Riders shouted apologies into the air. The Hawk Riders took Rugad up with the breeze, away from the panicked birds gathering around them.

He could no longer see below. He leaned forward, shouting, "Go back! Go back! I order you to go back!"

The Fey were shouting back at him, screaming that they were trying. But this was the hazard of Beast Riders: Sometimes the beast took over. And the birds, terrified, were acting like birds and flying away.

The air was full of flapping wings, feathers, and ash. He could hear screaming below, mixed with cawing. The Hawk Riders were taking him even higher, trying to protect him—he thought—until he looked up. Then he saw the bird faces, straining forward, terror in the black eyes. The Fey on the hawk's backs were yelling and beating on the side of the hawks' necks.

The hawks were panicked and out of control. So were the other birds. His harness tilted precariously. He was in more danger than he had ever been, and he was more vulnerable than he had been in a long, long time.

He shouted—

—and the world tilted. He was sinking into a Vision.

"No!" he cried, but he couldn't stop it. He was trapped within the Mystery of the Powers and they had him and suddenly—

—He was in a room in the Islander palace, looking at his great-grandson. The boy had lighter skin and more rounded features, but his eyebrows swooped upward properly and his ears were pointed. He had the look of Jewel to him, despite his pale eyes. He was about to speak when another Fey ran into the room and stabbed the boy in the back. He gargled, blood gushing from his mouth, and then he fell forward. Rugad got up—

—and nearly tilted the boat. They were on the open sea, and his great-grandson was in the water. Arms flapping, head dipping below the surface, no one to save him but Rugad. Rugad leaned forward, reaching out with an oar, but the boy didn't see it. He slipped below the surface and—

—then he stood in the burned-out ruin of their holy building, a girl protectively behind his back. She clung to him. He held a sword out, its tip against Rugad's stomach. *I will kill you,* the boy said. *You can't,* Rugad said. *Oh,* the boy said, smiling, *but I can.*

—Rugad started to speak, but other images swirled

around him, faster and faster, too fast for him to make much sense of. All of them included the boy. In some of them, he was quick and lithe, and in others he looked fragile. He died in some, Rugad died in others, and a blond boy watched from the back, his eyes narrowed. A girl stood to the side, and a blond man held a knife—or was it a sword? Then a blade came out of nowhere, and Rugad felt a jolt of impact against his neck that became excruciating pain as the blade went deeper. How long did it take a man to die after his head had been cut off? He didn't know.

Then suddenly, he was surrounded by birds and bird wings. Drool covered his chin and chest. Sparrow Riders held him upright, their claws hooked in his shirt. They smelled of musty bird and smoke. The Hawk Riders were still out of control, flapping him away from the palace instead of toward it. Hundreds of Bird Riders surrounded him. He couldn't see the ground below.

It was a rout.

It was a rout.

Nicholas had somehow routed his Riders, and there was nothing Rugad could do about it.

At least, not yet.

SIXTY-THREE

THE rising flock of birds startled her. Arianna stepped back from the windows only to collide with her father. He put his arms around her and held her as they watched. Sebastian breathed a sigh of awe.

The birds rose quickly, filling the sky with their wings and feathers and panic. The Fey on their backs were shouting, their little mouths opening and closing, their arms flapping as if they could counteract their bird selves.

Arianna could understand their feelings. Many times, after she had Shifted, her animal nature took over, and she did things her human self was ashamed of. Even now she didn't want to think about them.

There were remarkably few cries from below. Her father had apparently ordered the guards to attack in silence, and they had. Most of the noise came from the Bird Riders— birds squawking and cawing and whistling their fears, the stupendous snapping sounds of a thousand wings flapping at once. Her heart rose with them. What had seemed so hopeless only a moment before now seemed to turn toward them. They could survive this. They could.

Then a shout started below. A shout she'd never heard

before. A warbling cry that seemed to come from one mouth and a hundred mouths all at once.

"It's the guards," her father said. He sounded pleased.

Some of the birds flapped against the windows, their claws tapping the warped glass. The Riders on the backs were looking in, trying to control their birds and getting nowhere. Sebastian had stepped away from the window. Arianna's father's grip tightened. She was about to tell him to move back when—

—everything shifted. She felt dizzy, like she sometimes did when she Shifted from a small body to a large one. She blinked once, twice, three times—

—and found herself standing in a room, holding a sword at her side. An elderly Fey man sat in a chair. He was talking to Sebastian—or was it Gift?—who looked very distressed. They were so engrossed in their conversation that they didn't see another Fey man approach, knife out. She shouted a warning and—

—Sebastian shattered—

—Gift bled—

—Her great-grandfather fell to the ground, knife in his heart—

—all at the same time, and all at separate times. She reached for Sebastian/Gift and that dizzy feeling returned—

—everything spun and she was on the riverbank beside a handsome blond man only a few years older than she was. He held her hands, his blue eyes gazing into hers. He leaned to kiss her—

—he was kissing her—

—he had kissed her—

—when Sebastian (Gift?) reached around the blond man's head and put a knife to his throat. She screamed—

—and there was a third shift. She was small, too small to be human, and below her, her great-grandfather and Gift were in a long boat. Her arms were tired—were they wings?—and she watched them approach land. Then a giant fish came out of the water and hit the edge of the boat, knocking Gift out. Her great-grandfather screamed, and reached for him, threatening to capsize the boat. She watched for a moment, until Gift's head disappeared, then flew on, away—

Then the shifts happened faster and faster. Her size varied, and so did her place. But she saw either Gift or her great-grandfather or Sebastian in all of the images, and in every other one, Sebastian shattered.

She kept reaching for him, but stone cut her hand.

Sebastian shattered.

Sebastian.

Shattered.

She screamed, and then felt herself on the ground, her father's arms around her, Sebastian leaning over her, the lines in his face prominent as he brushed the hair off her forehead.

"Visions . . ." he said.

"I thought she Shifted," her father said, his voice shaky from behind her. She was resting on his lap, and he was holding her tightly. The birds still flew outside the windows, droppings and feathers and ash filling the air.

"She . . . can . . . do . . . both," Sebastian said.

"Lucky me," Arianna said, and was surprised at the way her voice croaked out of her. She was covered in sweat. Her robe was wet, her forehead was wet, her back was wet. She had never felt so filthy in her life.

"Arianna," her father said, "are you all right?"

"I don't know," she said. "I'm dizzy."

Then she put a hand on the floor to feel its solidness. The stone was cool against her palm. She glanced down. Her fingers weren't bleeding. Sebastian was whole. He hadn't shattered yet.

"Sebastian," she said, but her voice broke before she could say more.

"What did you see?" her father asked. He sounded frightened. The birds outside the window kept rising, as if they were floating on air currents. Their cawing and squawking sounded faraway.

"Too much," she said. "If this is Vision, I don't like it." She sat up, and wiped the sweat off her forehead. Her brain was still swirling with images. A bird slammed into the window and fell back, its Fey rider looking terrified as they headed toward the ground.

"By the Roca," her father said, showing the depth of his alarm. He never used religious sayings around her. He caressed the back of her head as he stood and looked out. "We scared over half the birds. The odds are good now."

He sounded like he didn't care. He sounded like he was talking to calm himself.

"Ari . . ." Sebastian said.

"I Saw you die," she said to him. "I Saw you die a hundred times."

Her father turned. "Someone can die only once," he said.

She shook her head. "It wasn't like that. It was like I Saw alternate deaths. No matter what I saw, Sebastian ended up dead."

She choked on the word "dead," and put her face in her hands.

Sebastian put his hand on her shoulder. She recognized it from the weight and strength of it. "Ari," he said, "I . . . don't . . . live. . . . How . . . could . . . I . . . die?"

A rage rose within her. She wanted to whirl on him, to let him know that he had no right to disparage himself so. But she couldn't move. "You live," she said. "And I saw you shatter."

"Shatter . . ." he whispered, as if contemplating it.

Her father crouched beside her. She could feel the warmth of his body, the heat it gave off. "Arianna," he said, touching her arm. "The Shaman once said she had several Visions about an event. She said that meant the time was in flux, that it was an important event, and only one of those Visions could come true."

She peeked out of her hands, feeling hope. A few scraggly birds still flew by the window, but she could see the sky again. It was a sickly greenish gray from the fires.

"Did he die in all of them?" her father asked.

"Almost," she said.

He nodded. "Then we have to separate those Visions out, figure out what they mean, and prevent the ones that cause Sebastian's death. Are you up for that?"

"Now?" she asked. "They're fighting below."

"How soon do these Visions happen?" he asked.

"I don't know," she said.

"Then," he said, "we'd better do it soon. We don't want one of your Visions to come true by accident because we weren't paying enough attention. If we had fought them before, your mother would still be alive."

"But would I?" Arianna whispered.

Her father cupped her face in his hand. "You're here now," he said, "you and Sebastian. And as far as I'm concerned, that matters the most."

"More than Blue Isle?" she asked.

He stared at her a moment, his features suddenly somber. "I hope I never have to find out."

SIXTY-FOUR

HE had never felt like this before: hollow and empty and yet so full of rage that a stone in his boot could send him into a fury. Leen apparently felt the same way. She kept her distance from him, and they walked toward Jahn in silence.

Gift had decided to walk along the road. His great-grandfather probably knew he had been on a farm. If the Fey were searching for him, they would look on various farms. Besides, if they found him, they couldn't harm him. He didn't want them to catch him; that would prevent him from helping Sebastian. But he wasn't concerned if they did. He knew that he would be in that room with his great-grandfather, and by letting the Fey catch him, it might save Sebastian's life.

Gift wasn't going to hide. His days of hiding in a Shadowlands were over.

The road was empty in the heat of the day. A few farmers were working their fields, but most had gone inside to wait until the cooler night air to finish their tasks. He regretted not bringing extra food and water. He hadn't thought this return trip through. He was moving on adrenaline only, adrenaline and anger. He hadn't slept in almost two days.

This road looked different in the daylight than it had at night. Friendlier somehow, as if the worst hadn't happened. Betrayal after betrayal, the worst being Coulter shutting Gift off from Sebastian and refusing to reopen the Link. Gift had tried a number of times to reopen it himself, and so far he had failed.

But he would find a way.

He felt so lonely, all alone within himself. He had been alone inside himself before—that was his normal state—but never before had he lacked the option of traveling across a Link. Before, he had always known he could turn to someone else.

And that didn't even count the loss of his parents. He couldn't think about life without Niche and Wind. And how he hadn't been there to protect them.

The sound of his boots crunching on the dirt matched the sound of Leen's. They were alone out there, in the sunshine, in the heat, a day he would normally have enjoyed because they had been so rare in his life. Yet everything felt hollow and had an unreal air, as if he weren't really experiencing it, as if he were watching someone else experience it. He felt distant, almost detached, although that wasn't quite accurate, since the rage felt real enough. And the sadness, when he allowed himself to feel it.

The walk felt as if it would take forever. He wasn't really certain what he would do when he arrived. He would have to make his way through his great-grandfather's army to the palace. And he would have to do so without the rage overtaking him.

He wasn't sure if that was possible.

He turned to Leen. Her face was set in a hard line, her features pointing downward. Her skin was gray, and she looked older than she ever had before. This day had aged her as well. They would never be the same after this. He knew that. He wondered if she did.

Maybe if they talked. Maybe if they pooled their thoughts, they could come up with a way to get through Jahn without approaching the Black King's army. He opened his mouth—

—and the world swirled. A Vision. He cursed it without speaking even as it sucked him in—

—Again, he was in that palace room, talking to an old Fey. The man had the look of Gift through the face, only the old Fey's was hardened and looked more like stone than Sebastian's did. He reached out. Gift backed away from the hand. The old Fey looked up, terrified, and Gift felt a sharp pain in his back. He reached for it, feeling pain, feeling blood, the world going black—

—Then he was above it, Sebastian shattering in his place, a Fey guard across from them stepping forward, spear in hand. The knife-wielder started to run from the room, but Gift went after him, jumping over the shards of his heart-brother, the old Fey shouting—

The swirls grew faster.

—Gift was on his back, a gleaming silver-white sword at his neck. The Islander he had seen on the bridge held it to his skin. His father, his real father, was shouting in the background—

—He was in the water, thrashing, an undertow pulling him down. Water filled his mouth, tasting of brine and salt. The old Fey was above him in a boat, reaching for him, but if he grabbed the old Fey's hand, he would pull the old Fey in. He didn't want to do that. He—

—watched Coulter kiss a Fey girl, then grabbed the back of Coulter's hair, and put a knife to his throat. He was—

—standing beside Coulter on the Cardidas, heading toward the Tabernacle. It looked burned—

—His real father—

—Sebastian, shattering—

—The old Fey—

—Sebastian, shattering—

—The Fey girl, pounding his chest with her fists, tears running down her cheeks—

—Sebastian—

Gift was on the ground. He had drooled out of the left side of his mouth, and he had gotten dirt in his teeth, on his tongue. Leen was crouched beside him, a hand on his side. The sun felt hotter then it ever had, and he was drained.

"You all right?" she asked.

He couldn't answer her at first. The images were too powerful. They still swirled through his mind. He had never had a Vision like that—a series of Visions, actually, none of them making real sense.

Except for the one that he had Seen before, the one that had led him to Sebastian and the palace in the first place.

The Fey girl, the one Coulter kissed, was Gift's sister, the witch who didn't want him near Sebastian. She had been crying in one of the Visions. She didn't strike Gift as someone who cried.

"Gift." Leen's voice was trembling. "You're scaring me."

"Sorry." He lisped the word. He pushed himself up and wiped the dirt off his cheek with his sleeve. Then he spat the grit out of his mouth. It was hard. His mouth was dry. "Water?"

"We don't have a lot," she said as she handed him their pouch. He drank some. It was warm, and it loosened more dirt. He couldn't swallow, at least not yet. He spat the water out, and mumbled an apology to Leen.

She handed him the pouch again. This time, he swallowed. The water seemed to revive him, a little.

"What happened?" she asked.

"Vision," he said, not willing to say any more until he knew what all the images meant.

"I've never seen you act like that with a Vision before."

In his befuddled state, he couldn't remember when she had seen him have a Vision. He supposed it didn't matter. He took a deep breath and let the air out. He was woozy. "How long did that take?"

"I don't know," she said. "It seemed like forever."

For him, too. And yet, it seemed like a blink of a moment, a single instant.

If only the Shaman were alive. He would be able to discuss the whole thing with her.

But she wasn't. She had died in Shadowlands with the others. He was alone. Leen didn't have the skills to interpret Visions. He wasn't certain if he had the skills either.

So many Visions. Something important must have happened. He brushed himself off and stood. Then the dizziness grabbed him, and he nearly fell. Leen caught his arm.

"Will you make it to Jahn?" she asked.

"I have no choice," he said, and wondered if it was true.

The Visions might have changed everything. Only he had no real way of knowing.

All he knew was that he had Seen Sebastian die. Again. And they were no longer Linked. He couldn't slide into Sebastian's body, to make Sebastian act quickly. Gift had to be by Sebastian's side when the Black King arrived. And something told Gift that the moment would be soon.

SIXTY-FIVE

SHE pulled herself off the snow-covered ground and shivered. Her mouth was dry, and her robe was covered with drool. Her body had left an indentation in the snow.

The air was frigid but clear. The sun wasn't warm here. It wasn't even friendly. But at least it provided very bright light that reflected off the snow. She couldn't travel far without getting what the locals called "snow blindness."

The Shaman wasn't even certain how she had gotten this far away from her cave. Her footprints were deep holes in the snow. She had walked. She had never walked through Visions before.

She brought a shaking hand to her face. Her lips and cheeks were already chapped. The Islanders in the village below had warned her that the mountains called the Eyes of Roca were cruel. She hadn't realized how cruel.

If the Visions had gone on much longer, she might have died.

The Eyes of Roca had no trees and rose higher, the locals said, than the Snow Mountains to the south. Like the Snow Mountains, the Eyes of Roca never lost their snowcap, but unlike the southern range, this one was considered unfriendly. Its name, after the Islander's most holy man (almost a god, as she understood it), was not a name of comfort, as it would have been in some countries, but a warning. *The Eyes of Roca are watching,* the locals said, and they seemed more concerned with their mythic mountain range than with the Fey in their midst.

For that, she was grateful. She doubted the Black King would make his way here quickly, and by the time he did, she hoped to be gone. She had Seen the cave that had hidden her since she left the Islander palace. But she hadn't Seen herself staggering out of it, in the middle of a Vision series.

Her feet were cold. She made herself stand, made herself walk back through the snow to her cave. Her fire was still burning near the cave's mouth. She hadn't been gone long. She pulled off her wet clothing and set it near the fire, then wrapped herself in blankets she had brought with her. She put snow in her pot, then hung it on the cooking wire over the fire. She would make herself some root tea, warm up, and contemplate what she had just Seen.

Even though she didn't want to.

At least fifty Visions had gone through her in that short span. She had never experienced a series like that before. Something major had happened, something so large that it disrupted the sure future and made fifty alternatives.

For the first time since she had escaped Shadowlands, she wished she weren't alone. She wished she had someone to compare Visions with.

Because the final Vision had terrified her.

She drew her knees up to her chest and rested her forehead on them. The shivering continued, even though she was warmer than she had been just a moment before. Perhaps it wasn't cold that made her shiver. Perhaps it was fear.

The images wouldn't leave her. All the Visions were clear, but the clearest was stained with blood. Blood upon blood upon blood. Fey blood. All over the world. The Fey were no longer reasonable creatures of war; they had become raving lunatics that ripped apart anything—anyone—who got in their path.

The Black Blood had turned on itself and had driven the Fey mad.

Her greatest fear.

And one of the fifty Visions. One path that this point, this change, might bring them to. She hoped Rugad had Seen it. She hoped Gift had Seen it.

Because if they hadn't, the Fey were doomed.

She wasn't certain what her own action should be. She had left Shadowlands, contrary to her own training, because she had seen her death at the hands of Rugad's Foot Soldiers. She refused to die there. She knew she had changed the Vision when, after she had left the Islander palace, she had collapsed into another Vision, one of this mountain cave, and evidence of a long life lived here.

Her life.

Rugad was skating very close to the edge of ruining his people. If she appeared before him, she would certainly die. Nicholas, sweet man that he was, wasn't Fey, and didn't have full comprehension of all that could occur. And young Gift, while he was a natural leader, had never experienced war. The only hope was Arianna, and she was as impetuous and headstrong as her grandfather, Rugar, who brought the Fey to this impasse.

She had already warned Nicholas's children what this fighting would do. She had warned Nicholas. And Rugad had been trained to avoid such things from birth.

Unless she got a clearer Vision, she would remain in her cave, on the side of this mountain, hidden from intrigue, and safe from the rest of the world.

From Rugad.

And maybe, even, from death.

SIXTY-SIX

NICHOLAS had his arm around Arianna. He wasn't watching her, though. He was looking at his son.

Sebastian huddled near the wall, arms wrapped around himself. He had said nothing since Arianna had explained her Visions. For the first time in his life, he looked lost in thought.

Nicholas let him be. Nicholas was shaky enough from Arianna's experience, not because of what she said as much as how she had looked. He had thought, for a moment, that she had been poisoned, that it had somehow taken longer than usual to work. He had held her, terrified that she was going to die like her mother had, hideously and quickly. But she hadn't. When Arianna had opened her eyes, he had felt redeemed.

She stood beside him now, watching the battle below. Her face held longing to be part of it, longing he understood. Part of him wanted to be below as well, but he knew better now. He knew that he didn't dare go, that she didn't dare go, that the fighting had to happen without them.

He had directed it from above. Now he could do nothing. Still, it looked as if he had done enough. Three-quarters of the birds had been startled into flight. The remaining flew in the faces of the attacking guards, but somehow Monte had prepared them. They stabbed at the birds, chopped at the birds, ripped out feathers and wings. Blood and feathers went everywhere. Birds screeched and so did Islanders. But he heard no real Fey victory cry. Nothing to make it sound as if the Fey were doing well.

From every window at the top of this tower, he saw Fey being slaughtered. At a high cost—for every two Fey, he lost one of his own—but he was still winning in hand-to-hand combat.

He didn't know how long it would last.

But while it did, it was glorious.

"Pa . . ."

Nicholas turned. Sebastian was pointing at the north window. Two dozen birds were hovering outside the glass, all of them very tiny. Their wings fluttered so fast that Nicholas couldn't even see them move. It almost seemed as if they were standing in midair.

The Fey on their backs were even smaller. He couldn't make out their features from this distance.

Arianna turned. She was frowning. Nicholas took a step forward and as he did, the birds tapped the glass with their beaks, not once, but dozens of times. The sound was terrifying and authoritative. The Fey on the birds' backs were waving their arms, obviously giving instructions. This was a planned attack.

The window cracked. Nicholas ran toward it. If he put some wood in front of it, he might be able to prevent their entry. He was halfway across the room when the glass shattered.

Something brown streaked past him. The cries from the battle below intensified, the screams, the shouts, the clang of sword against beak. The birds flew in, hovering together as one unit. Sebastian cried out hoarsely—

—and a small cat leapt into the air, batting the birds with its paws, and snapping its jaws. The birds scattered, but the Fey were shouting at them. Even though they were shouting in Fey, Nicholas recognized the word.

Attack.

"No!" he shouted in the same language. "That's my

daughter! That's the Black King's great-granddaughter. She has Black Blood!"

The words came out slower than he wanted, but the effect was the same. The birds backed off. Arianna jumped higher, catching one in her mouth, closing her jaws, shaking, and tossing the dead creature onto the ground. At the same time, she hit two more with her paws and stunned them.

The birds were backing up. Nicholas grabbed a poker from the fireplace and came to his daughter's aid, hitting the birds as if they were clods of dirt. They fell back, stunned.

Sebastian came over as well, slowly. He deliberately picked up the fallen birds and tossed them from the broken window.

Some of the birds went above Nicholas's head. Arianna kept jumping and snarling, but the birds were out of her reach. Nicholas kept swinging the poker, forcing the birds back. One went for Sebastian's eye, and Nicholas cried out again.

"He has Black Blood!"

And the bird backed off.

Then, as quickly as they had arrived, they left, their tiny force one-quarter its original size. Two more birds lay dead on the floor, and Arianna spat one out with what looked like, to Nicholas, reluctance. Then she ran back to her robe, crawled under it, and Shifted.

Nicholas clapped Sebastian on the back, and complimented him on his resourcefulness. When he turned, Arianna was adjusting her clothing. A tiny feather still hung from the corner of her mouth.

"We can't stay here any longer," he said.

"They can't kill us," Arianna said.

"I may not have time to explain next time," he said.

She nodded. "The other tower?"

"That's what I was thinking. Then we'll at least be able to watch and it might take them a while to realize where we are."

Sebastian was looking out the window. His large hands were shaking.

Nicholas slipped his arm around the boy's shoulders. "You didn't kill them," he said, knowing that was what bothered the boy. Sebastian was the gentlest of all of them.

He had been able to cup Arianna in his hands when she was a kitten without hurting her at all. He hated death, even of tiny things, like bugs.

So different from his sister.

"I . . . hope . . . not," Sebastian said. His voice shook.

Nicholas squeezed harder. Then he turned. "You ready, Ari?"

She nodded. She handed Nicholas his poker. It still had feathers on it. Unlike Sebastian, Nicholas wasn't upset about the deaths. They were attacking him and his children. They didn't deserve to live.

The sounds of the battle had grown progressively louder. The clanging, screaming, and screeching—the large birds were screeching as they attacked—seemed to move even closer to the palace. If the other birds returned, Nicholas wasn't certain how long his force could hold them off.

He needed a secondary plan. He would discuss that with Arianna when they reached the second tower. They would also discuss her Visions.

She was beside him. "We'll have to hurry," she said.

"I know." He glanced at Sebastian. The boy's face was set, as if he would use all of his concentration to get across the palace.

Then Nicholas pulled open the door—and immediately tried to close it. A dozen naked Fey, maybe more, flooded inside. They were carrying ancient swords, nicked by use and time. Nicholas recognized the swords. They had come from the Great Hall. These were Bird Riders in their Fey form.

They grabbed him before he could even raise the poker and held him fast. Their hands dug into his arms like talons. They grabbed Arianna and Sebastian as well.

"Don't!" Nicholas said in Fey. "They have Black Blood."

"We know," said the raven-haired female in front of him. Her hair appeared long, but it was feathered, and it hung down her back like plumage. "You'll come with us now."

"No!" Arianna said. She ripped her arm from their grasp. "You can't do anything to us."

"That's right," the woman said. She was holding Nicholas's great-grandfather's sword from the Peasant Uprising. She brought its tip to his throat, then smiled at Arianna and

Sebastian. "We can't do anything to you. But we can kill your father."

Arianna shoved the sword with her bare hand. It slid away from his throat. Nicholas backed up, only to be held by more Fey.

"Do that again," the woman said, "and your father dies."

"I'll get in your way," Arianna said.

"You can't be everywhere."

Nicholas felt sharp tips all along his back. He said nothing. The woman wasn't even looking at him. She was looking at his daughter.

"Ari . . ." Sebastian said, and pointed to Nicholas. Nicholas glanced down. Most of the swords were pointed at his body.

Arianna's eyes narrowed. She looked more like Jewel than she ever had. An angry Jewel. "Hurt him, and I'll kill you."

"I won't hurt him if you do what I say," the woman said.

"Give me your word," Arianna said.

"A Fey generally breaks her word," Nicholas said in Islander. "Your mother told me that, and I've seen it many times."

"He's right," the woman said in Fey. "But I'll give it to you if you want."

Arianna glanced at Nicholas. She wasn't prepared for this kind of situation. Somehow she had failed in his training. Not even Solanda had trained her for the difficulties of facing the Fey.

She swallowed. Nicholas's heart was pounding. His beautiful, impulsive daughter could save herself from this, and maybe Sebastian if she was lucky. But she couldn't save all three of them. And even if she did escape, she would have nowhere to go.

"All right," Arianna said. "What do you want?"

The woman smiled. She had that Fey beauty combined with a birdlike flatness in her eyes. The effect was that of a tamed wildness, a very dangerous wildness. "I want your cooperation," she said. "At least, until the Black King arrives."

SIXTY-SEVEN

"WAIT," Flurry said. He swooped down lower than he had been. They hadn't gone far from their resting place. The sun was still high, and he had good cover. Sparks were difficult to see in the daylight.

"I don't see anything," Cinder said.

"That's because we're not low enough." Flurry kept going lower, lower than he usually flew. Something had caught his eye. Something he had flown over a moment before.

There it was, on the side of the road. A Fey woman crouched beside the road, her hand resting on a man's back. Flurry hadn't seen the man at first. His clothing blended with the road, his skin and hair blending as well.

He was pulling himself up, slowly, and the woman looked terrified.

"I still don't see anything," Cinder said.

"Then you're not looking," Flurry said. He pointed. She hovered beside him, squinting downward. She inched lower, her wings moving rapidly to keep herself in one place.

"Oh," she said. Then she glanced up. "He's injured."

"He's had a Vision," Flurry said, not trying to keep the sarcasm from his voice. At least he knew they had the Black

King's great-grandson. But Cinder wasn't smart enough to realize that.

She wasn't reliable at all.

He sighed. He had to be two places at once. He had to stay here, with the boy, and he also had to get reinforcements. Cinder couldn't be relied on for either task.

"What're we going to do?" she asked.

He wished he knew. "Give me a moment."

He swooped down, hurtling like a spark from the sun. He brushed the boy's hair, flew past the woman's face, and then rose again. Images stuck with him. The boy was covered with dirt; his eyes had deep shadows, and he looked as if he had been crying. There was drool on the side of his face, his skin was wan and he appeared terrified.

But not as terrified as the woman—or, more accurately, girl. She was Infantry, wearing the old uniform that was in vogue when Rugar first left for the Isle. She too was filthy and her uniform was wrinkled. It smelled faintly of the Cardidas river.

She wasn't used to Visions, or the demands they made on Visionaries. She was panicked and frightened and angry.

She would be of no use to the boy, at least, not for a while. He would have to recover on his own.

Flurry nodded once, then flew up to Cinder. She was still hovering, one finger against her small mouth, as if she were deep in thought.

"You stay here," Flurry said, "and keep an eye on them. If they go anywhere, you follow. If they go off the road, you follow until you know where they're headed, then report back here."

"How will I know where 'here' is?"

Flurry glanced around. She had a point. It looked like most of the rest of the farmland here, the rolling fields and the road cut like a river between them.

He pointed to a small patch of brownish corn. This farmer hadn't realized his crop had bugs. "That corn is your landmark," he said. "I doubt you'll need it, but in case."

"Where're you going?"

"To get reinforcements. We can't capture him on our own."

"Other Wisps won't be able to help," she said.

He blinked at her, started to answer, then stopped. If she had misunderstood the instructions, how many others had as well? He was doubly relieved that he found the boy.

"I'm going to get Foot Soldiers," he said.

"There aren't any nearby."

He smiled. "That's where you're wrong," he said. "Rugad put pocket garrisons all over the southern part of the Isle. I just have to find the closest one."

"How do you know these things?" she asked.

He chucked her chin, unable to resist. "I just pay attention," he said.

She frowned as if she were trying to make sense of that. He didn't wait for her understanding.

"If you lose him, you'll be branded a Failure," Flurry said.

As her eyes widened in fear, he flew off. He didn't know if losing the great-grandson would make her a Failure or not, but he did know, after such dramatic examples of what happened to Failures, that she would stick to the boy like a burr.

He hoped that wouldn't make her do anything stupid.

He glanced back. She was still hovering, her tiny hands pressed together as if she were flattening a flower between them. She was worried.

Good.

That meant she would do her job.

Now he had to do his. He had to get reinforcements, and fast.

That boy was the reason Rugad came to Blue Isle.

Flurry couldn't afford to lose him.

None of them could.

SIXTY-EIGHT

THE troops had gone above. Servis was leaning against the stone wall, his knife out. He was using its tip to clean his fingernails.

Con was pacing. His breath was coming in shallow gasps. He had never faced a dilemma like this. The soldiers said the King knew, but what if they lied? What if they didn't know? He had to get above, he had to see. He had to know for himself.

"Servis, how far would you go to follow orders?" he asked.

"Dunna ask, Baby Aud," Servis said.

"I am asking."

"Tis me job ta follow orders."

Con turned. Servis was no longer picking at his nails with the knife. He had laid it across his leg, his hand on the hilt. He was watching Con.

Servis had misunderstood. He had thought that Con was asking what Servis would do if Con tried to leave. Con already knew that.

Servis would have to kill him.

And that was the key to orders, wasn't it? Doing what one had to, doing what was required.

Con didn't have orders.

He had a Charge.

He touched the vials of holy water in his pocket. Sometimes doing God's work meant using every available opportunity, no matter what the result.

He had a higher calling. He had to see the King.

"It's my job to follow orders, too," Con said.

"I canna let you leave, Baby Aud," Servis said.

"If you do, who'll know?" Con asked. "They're fighting above. They may not even come back this way."

"I'll know, Baby Aud." Servis's voice was soft. "I'll know."

Con nodded. And there lay his answer. Even if the King already knew, even if the King sent those troops, Con wouldn't be satisfied. He wouldn't know until he saw for himself, until he followed his Charge all the way through.

All he needed was a moment, a simple moment, and he would be able to fulfill his Charge. He knew the tunnels—or at least had a map of them. And if he were quiet, he would be able to see it all through.

With his thumb and forefinger, he worked the stopper out of a vial of holy water. "Don't you believe in a higher order?" he asked. "Don't you believe that God's work takes precedence over all others?"

"Dunna play such games with me, lad," Servis said. "I canna let ye go."

"But you're a believer, Servis." Con took a small step closer. He couldn't get too close, and yet he couldn't be too far either. He had to find the right point. "The Church teaches that God leads us all, even the King. And if God leads the King, then he certainly guides the King's guards. My Charge should have more weight than your order."

Servis sighed. His hand hadn't moved from the hilt of his dagger. "I dunna have the learnin ta think a these things, Baby Aud. Dunna make me. I'm a simple man and I will do simple things. Like follow orders."

"My orders are from God," Con said.

"N I only have yer word on that." Servis was growing agitated. He leaned forward. "I dunna know who gave ye the Charge or if tis false. I canna give up me orders fer yer Charge."

"But you would if you knew my Charge came from the Rocaan."

"Maybe. If'n I saw the Rocaan give yer Charge to ye."

"But you didn't. You only have my word. The word of a holy man." Con's fingers tightened around the vial.

"Yer a boy."

"I'm an Aud," he said, throwing Servis's words back at him.

Servis stared at him, then slid his hand off the knife hilt.

Con's heart made a small flip. Servis was listening. "There is another way I can convince you," Con said.

Servis put his hand flat on the ground. Con's fingers tightened on the vial. This would be the moment, if he were to take one. This might be his only chance.

But he kept his hand in his pocket.

"Keep talkin, Baby Aud."

"Come with me. Come into the palace and help me find the King. If at any time I put the King in danger, kill me."

"I was hopin we'd get through this without one a us killin the other," Servis said. "Na matter what ye have in yer pocket."

Con felt his face grow warm. "Just holy water," he said.

"I'm na Fey," Servis said.

"But I was hoping to surprise you."

Servis grinned. "Twould take more than water in the face ta surprise me."

Somehow Con believed it. He sighed. "Please," he said. "This Charge is my life, my future, and maybe the future of Blue Isle. We can't let it stop here, in this tunnel, with the Fey above us. We can't."

Servis grabbed the knife, and pushed himself to his feet. Con held his breath. Servis put the knife in its sheath. "Twould seem," he said, "that yer right. Tis a good compromise. I'll go with ye. Because yer right. No one'll know what happened here sides us. And we're little men in a big game. Tis better fer us ta do what we believe."

Con let out the breath he had been holding. "Thank you," he said.

"Dunna be thanking me," Servis said. "At least we're safe down here. If the Fey are winning above, goin ta the palace will get us both killed."

"That's a risk I have to take," Con said.

Servis clapped his hand on Con's shoulder. "Spoken like a fighter, Baby Aud."

"No," Con said quietly, feeling the need to correct Servis, a need as strong as his desire to go to the palace. "Spoken like a holy man."

"Ah, boy, have ye ever thought that maybe they're not so different?"

"They're different," Con said. But he spoke with a surety he no longer felt. The world was changing too quickly for him.

He only hoped he continued to make the right choices as it did.

SIXTY-NINE

ADRIAN hated the heat. He hated traveling in it, and wished that he could be on his farm, in the shade, waiting for the coolness of twilight to finish his chores. At least Luke was tending things. Luke would make certain the crops were taken care of and the house remained. If the Fey showed up, he was under instruction to give them what they wanted. Or, if he felt there were too many of them, he was to hide. Years ago, they had set up a number of hiding places on the farm, just in case.

Coulter walked ahead of Adrian and Scavenger. Coulter's chin was up, his eyes half-closed. He appeared to be following a trail that Adrian couldn't see. Scavenger was breathing heavily. He wore a dozen knives and two swords, the weight nearly crushing him. He had insisted on coming, but he didn't want to face his own people again unarmed.

He probably didn't want to face them at all.

Adrian had brought his old sword out of retirement, and he also carried a quiver full of arrows and the bow that Luke had made him the year before. He doubted they would do much good, but they were a start. He had some supplies as well. No sense traveling without food. They had no idea how long they would be gone.

Coulter was leading them down the road to Jahn. It made sense that Gift was going this way; his stated desire was to return to Sebastian.

The idea of fighting, any sort of fighting, terrified Adrian. In truth, he was no more a soldier than Scavenger. The last time he had gone to war to save his country. This time, he hoped he wouldn't have to fight at all.

The only one with any real power in this group was Coulter, and he still didn't know how to use most of it.

At least Luke was not involved this time. None of them felt good about leaving Luke behind, but it was his wish. He had no desire to fight the Fey again, no desire to be part of a force. He believed the Fey wouldn't even appear at the farm, and Scavenger agreed. Scavenger said the Fey were following an old fighting pattern, one that destroyed the center of power but left the wealth of the country alone.

It made sense to Adrian even if he didn't like it. He had a bad feeling about all of this, but he said nothing. His life was going to change again. The comfortable world he had been born into was long gone. The world of his imprisonment was destroyed, and the easy world he had built afterward was gone too. He didn't know what would replace them, and he wasn't sure he would live long enough to find out.

At least Luke was home and out of the fighting. Adrian couldn't bear it if his son got in trouble again because of Adrian's actions.

The corn was breathing in the soft wind. Adrian loved the creaks and groans of growing crops, the slight buzz of insects as they went about their business, the smell of greenery. That was his life, not this all pervading fear that started in his stomach and seemed to fill him.

Scavenger was ignoring the crops. He was scanning everything, the sides of the road, the road, the sky above it. Every few moments, he would lick his lips as if tasting the air. His squat body was in better condition than it had ever been. The work on the farm had given his arms a power that they hadn't had when he'd been in charge of the Fey dead. He was trimmer too, than he had been when Adrian met him, and his skin was even darker from his time in the sun.

But there were new lines on his face now, and his eyes seemed to be looking for something very far away. His nervousness was like a pervasive high-pitched whistle. Adrian was trying to ignore it, but somehow that seemed to make the whistle worse.

Suddenly Scavenger stopped. He bit his lower lip until it bled. As Adrian kept going, Scavenger grabbed his arm. The grip was tight.

"Get Coulter. *Now.*"

Adrian pulled his arm from Scavenger's grasp and ran the short distance to Coulter. "Hey," Adrian said. "Stop. Scavenger saw something."

"There's no time to stop," Coulter said.

Adrian took Coulter's arm, using a grip as firm as Scavenger's had been. "He's worried."

"He can't see anything important."

"He's been with them all his life. He might be able to see more than you."

Coulter stopped walking then. Two spots of color appeared on his pale cheeks. His eyes were dark blue, darker than they had ever been. "This better be important," he said, as if the decision to stop were Adrian's instead of Scavenger's.

Adrian said nothing as he led Coulter back to Scavenger. Scavenger stood in the middle of the road, his square head tilted toward the sky.

"What is it?" Coulter asked, the fullness of his displeasure coming through his voice.

Scavenger didn't reply. Instead, he pointed up.

Coulter followed the point. So did Adrian.

The sky was so blue, it looked as if it had been dyed by one of the Fey's Domestics. The wispy clouds from earlier were gone. The sun was directly overhead, and the slight heat shimmer that warm days sometimes had made parts of the air appear as if they were underwater.

Adrian didn't see anything. The sky looked the same all around him.

"What is it?" Coulter asked. "A Shadowlands?"

"I don't think so," Scavenger said.

"What? What do you see?" Adrian asked.

"Follow my finger," Scavenger said. "And you'll see a teeny tiny light blinking."

A light, in this sunlight? Adrian didn't think so. But he crouched, and followed the angle of Scavenger's finger. Then he saw it. A flash, like a sword in sunlight, only smaller. Much smaller. It disappeared, and then repeated, like a little warning sign.

He squinted, but couldn't see it any clearer. No wonder Coulter had thought it the entrance to a Shadowlands. It looked like one, only much smaller. Adrian still remembered the flashing lights against the darkness from the night he lost his own freedom, the night his life changed.

Shadowlands' lights flickered like this, but they formed a circle. This was a single light, so bright that it flashed in the daylight.

"What is it?" he asked.

Scavenger raised a hand and shielded his eyes. "A Wisp, I think."

"Why would a Wisp just float in the middle of nowhere? It makes no sense—"

"Shhh," Adrian said. Coulter sometimes treated Scavenger as the Fey would, with no respect at all. The idea that training, that magick was the only thing that made a being worthwhile went in early and stuck. Coulter never treated Adrian with disrespect, but at times, even Adrian felt the contempt. Full and rich and strong.

"He sees something, doesn't he?" Adrian said to Scavenger.

Scavenger nodded. "That's my guess."

Coulter finally understood. "Gift?" he said, his voice tinged with panic.

Adrian tightened his grip on Coulter's arm. "Either the Wisp is standing guard, waiting for more Fey to come, or the Wisp is standing guard, watching for Islanders."

"Either way, we're in trouble," Scavenger said softly.

"No," Coulter said. "*Gift's* in trouble." He swallowed, wrenched his arm free, and sat down. Adrian frowned at him. What an odd thing to do in the middle of a crisis.

"Give me a moment," Coulter said.

He tilted his head back and squinted, as he had been doing the night before Gift arrived. Suddenly Adrian understood.

He was looking for the lines, the ones he had shown them before. He was seeing where the magick was.

"There's only one right now," he said. "And Gift. But there was another Wisp not long ago."

"He went for reinforcements," Scavenger said.

"That's my guess," Coulter said. He glanced at Adrian. "They want Gift."

"I know," Adrian said.

"They can't have him. It will hurt us all."

"I know that too," Adrian said.

Coulter's thin lips pursed. "Then forgive me," he said and turned back toward the tiny light.

Before Adrian could ask what Coulter meant, a beam of light shot from Coulter's body. It was bright yellow, almost blinding in its intensity. Adrian had seen the boy shoot light before. He had been wrapped inside that light when they escaped Shadowlands. But he had never seen Coulter just aim light outward.

The beam looked rigid and tangible, like a pole leading from Coulter's body into the sky. The beam zoomed forward, ever increasing in length until it hit the blinking light. Adrian thought he heard a faint sound, like a scream, and then a puff of black smoke floated toward the sun.

Coulter's light disappeared.

Coulter buried his face in his hands.

"There's no time for remorse," Scavenger said. He put his hands under Coulter's arms and tried to lift him. The sight would have been comical—the short, square Fey trying to lift an Islander twice his size—if it weren't for Scavenger's panic.

The panic was infectious. This time the Fey wouldn't capture them but would kill them, no questions asked. Adrian wasn't certain if Coulter had the power to fight off an army of Fey.

"He's right," Adrian said. "Get up. We have to get to Gift first."

That reached Coulter. He pushed himself to his feet, staggered a moment, then stepped forward. Scavenger got out of his way, and Adrian stepped in where Scavenger had been. Adrian took one of Coulter's elbows. Coulter's face was raw. He had never used his powers like this. He had always used them to help, not to kill.

"It was a woman," he said. "She had been with Rugad for years. She was a Wisp, and she was worried she wasn't up to the task of guarding a Black Prince."

"She wasn't," Scavenger said. "She should have sensed you a long ways off. Now let's move."

He led the way, a short warrior wearing too many weapons. Adrian propelled Coulter forward. What he didn't tell Coulter was that there would probably be a lot of bodies before this was over. This death would only be Coulter's first.

The road turned slightly and dipped down into a field. At the bottom of the dip, Gift sat, his head in his hands. His posture was similar to what Coulter's had been only moments before. Leen knelt beside him, her hands fluttering around him, as if she didn't know what to do.

Coulter was in no shape to take charge of this, and Gift wouldn't listen to Scavenger. It was up to Adrian.

He let go of Coulter's arm and stopped in front of Leen. She had to look up at him.

"What happened?" he asked, afraid that the Fey had already been here, that they had cast some sort of spell that he had never heard about.

"He's had a Vision," Scavenger said. "Wipe off the drool, boy. It doesn't become you."

Gift raised his left hand and wiped the side of his mouth.

"Several Visions," Leen said. "They scared him."

"Several?" Scavenger sounded surprised, and even a little frightened.

"It doesn't matter," Adrian said, not caring about the details of Fey magick at the moment. "You had a Wisp above you, guarding you. The Fey know where you are. We have to get you out of here."

Leen and Gift both looked up. Adrian did too. The puff of smoke was dissipating. It looked like a small black cloud against the clear blue sky.

"You killed it?" Gift said to Coulter.

Coulter's eyes were red. His mouth trembled. "I had no choice."

"Seems like you have no choice a lot lately. Are you sure

that was one of the Black King's Wisps? Or was it my father?"

Adrian was about to speak, but Coulter drew himself together. "It was a woman named Cinder," he said and for a moment, his voice didn't shake. "Wind is dead. You know that. And Niche too. Don't blame me for what happened to them."

"How are you so certain? Were you Linked with them too?"

"One touch with your great-grandfather was more than enough, Gift," Coulter said. "You may not understand how much of a threat he is, but I do."

"If you really did understand," Scavenger said, "you'd be leaving now."

"That's right." Adrian finally took the opportunity to jump in. "We have to get you hidden, Gift. They know where you are."

"Please," Leen said. She clearly knew she was no match for the Black King's soldiers.

Gift looked at all of them, met their gazes, and didn't back down. "I'm going to the palace."

"That's suicide," Coulter said. "Sebastian is probably long gone."

"If he is, that's your fault," Gift said.

Adrian physically stepped between them. He crouched beside Gift, deciding to treat him as a boy who had lost everything instead of a man with more power than Adrian would ever have.

"Gift," he said. "We can argue this after we get you out of here. But they'll be back any moment. They left the Wisp to guard you and track you. They will know where you are—"

"He's not worth arguing over," Scavenger said. He shoved his way in, grabbed Gift by the hair, and pulled his head back. Then he put a knife to his throat.

Leen pulled her own knife.

Adrian reached forward.

"Stop," Scavenger said. "Another move from anyone, including you, Mr. Magick, and I'll slice this boy's throat."

"You wouldn't," Coulter said.

"I would," Scavenger said with such calmness that fear came into Coulter's face. "The Black King is here for his great-grandchildren. What'll he do when he gets them? He'll make them into him. Although Gift and his sister will be better than the Black King because they have more power. Only they don't know how to use it yet. I can solve this once and for all. I can kill this boy. And if I can get to the girl, I'll take away the Black King's reason for being here."

"But it won't stop anything, it won't change anything," Adrian said, trying to keep the panic he felt from creeping into his voice. It had been his mistake to bring Scavenger along. He knew the little Red Cap was impulsive and possibly crazy. He knew it, and yet he always thought that even though Scavenger had committed murder once, he would never do so again. Not with the provocation gone. "The Black King will still be here. He'll still have Blue Isle."

"But he'll have no reason to go on," Scavenger said. His grip on Gift was firm. Gift was moving. But he didn't look frightened. His entire body was slack, as if he were relaxing before sleep. Only his right hand was moving. Slowly. "If there's no one who can rule in the Black Family, there's no one who can conquer Leut. And if no one can rule, then your people have a chance to fight. If they kill the Black King—"

"You're crazy," Leen said. The tip of her knife was in Scavenger's back.

"Maybe," Scavenger said. "But maybe I have a good point. If the Black King fails to get his great-grandchildren, he loses. Even if he conquers Blue Isle."

"Let him go, Scavenger," Coulter said. "We'll get him out of here. We'll keep him away from the Black King."

"Will you?" Scavenger asked. "Because if you can't, we may as well kill him here. Now. Otherwise he'll be the death of us all."

"No," Gift said. His voice sounded strained against the knife. "Only you."

His right hand slid between his back and Scavenger's front with alarming speed. And, judging from the expression on Scavenger's face, Gift connected. Scavenger went white and gagged. Gift pushed the knife away with his left hand and turned, still keeping his grip on Scavenger's privates. He shoved the small Fey onto the ground and put a knee on his chest, finally letting go of Scavenger's groin.

Leen took Scavenger's knife.

"Never, ever touch me again, you little piece of filth," Gift said.

Scavenger growled and flailed at Gift. Adrian caught one of Scavenger's arms. Coulter caught the other.

"He's not filth," Adrian said. "He's Fey just like you. And he may have just saved your life, if you listen to him."

Gift spat on the ground beside Scavenger, and then stood. "He tried to kill me."

"He was showing you in the only way he thought you'd listen why it's so important that you stay away from your great-grandfather."

"My great-grandfather murdered my family."

"And he already touched your mind once," Coulter said. "We don't know what kind of tricks he has. Maybe he can manipulate your thoughts."

"If he can do that, I can do that," Gift said.

"You're eighteen," Adrian said. "He's got several generations on you, and that's several generations of practice. It's not something I'd want to risk, if I were you."

"You're the prize, boy," Scavenger said. He was still flat on his back in the dirt. "Don't you get it? If you walk into that city, you walk right into his hands."

"Listen to him," Coulter said. "Where you need to be is out here, fighting him."

Gift took a long look at Coulter. "But what about Sebastian?"

"He's got your sister. You warned her. Have some faith in her," Coulter said.

"She obviously loves him," Adrian said. "She almost killed you over him."

"What can I do?" Gift asked. "The Islanders won't follow me. And I can't attack my great-grandfather."

"You can't," Scavenger said. "But some of us can. It may be against the rules for Fey to attack Black Blood, but I've already broken rules. I don't care. I can kill him—without your official permission, of course."

Gift was finally relenting. "Why should I trust you? You just tried to kill me."

Scavenger shrugged as best he could with both his arms pinned. "I still might. It seems like the best option."

"You can't trust him," Leen said. "You can't trust any of them."

Coulter was standing very still. Adrian wanted to shout that Gift could trust Coulter, that Coulter had been there for Gift from the beginning, but Adrian said nothing. If Gift was too stubborn to figure that out on his own, well, then, Adrian couldn't convince him of it.

"We don't have much time," Adrian said. "They'll be back."

Leen looked at Gift. Gift was still staring at Scavenger.

"You know my great-grandfather, don't you?" he asked.

"Not personally," Scavenger said. "But I've been around him enough."

"Could he sway me?"

"Boy, he's swayed smarter and better people than you."

"Then why didn't he sway you?"

"Because I was a Red Cap. 'Filth,' as you so nicely put it."

"You tried to kill me." Gift's voice rose in self-defense.

"I won't hold it against you," Scavenger said. "But I still might kill you, if I think it's best for all of us."

Leen was still holding her knife. "You don't have the right to kill him," she said.

"I can do whatever I want," Scavenger said.

"No." Coulter's voice had power. It shook the area with its strength. "No, you can't. You won't touch Gift. I protect him. He's safe."

"No, he's not," Adrian said. "They'll be here any moment and this whole debate is moot."

"I want to know," Gift said, as if no one except Scavenger had spoken. "I want to know if you think I can win a battle against my great-grandfather."

"It would be tricky," Scavenger said. "You can't fight him directly. But if he never touches you, if he never corrupts you, you win. And then when he dies, you get the Fey anyway."

"Unless my sister does."

"You're older."

"But she'd have the Isle behind her."

Adrian's throat was dry. He didn't care about the arguments. He just didn't want to be stranded on this road when the reinforcements arrived. They might not touch Gift, but they would slaughter everyone else.

"This won't matter if the Fey show up," Adrian said.

"I don't think the Isle will support her," Scavenger said. "She's as Fey as you are."

"Then it doesn't matter."

"It matters." Scavenger shook with the force of his words. "It matters. He loses without an heir. He will have no one to give his empire to. Your uncles are nothings. If they were something, they would be here with the Black King. But he hates them. He wants you. And he'll get you, unless you're careful."

"How do I know I can trust you?" Gift said again.

Scavenger rolled his eyes. "I have to tell him," he said softly to Adrian. "Don't I?"

Adrian didn't know what Scavenger was referring to, but he decided to humor him. The quicker this discussion ended, the quicker they could leave.

"Yes," Adrian said. "You do."

Scavenger sighed, as if speaking this next were a great burden. "You have Black Blood, boy. You can't trust anyone."

Gift glanced at Coulter and then looked away. Coulter remained steady, staring at his friend.

He was wrong, Adrian thought. Scavenger was wrong. Gift could trust Coulter with his life.

"The Wisps who raised you are dead. The Islanders hate you because you're Fey, the Fey hate you for your soft Island upbringing. Your great-grandfather doesn't want you, he wants your potential."

"What about my father? My sister? Sebastian?"

"Your father? He never came for you, did he?"

"He didn't know."

"He says," Scavenger said. "And your sister cares more for your golem than you. And what of your golem? Hasn't he already taken your place? Your world is what you make it, boy, and the only way you make it yours is to trust no one."

"Not even you?"

"Especially not me. I still think we're better off with you dead."

Gift was shaking. Adrian glanced down the road. He saw nothing yet, but he wasn't really the one to look. Coulter seemed riveted by the discussion. And Leen was watching Scavenger carefully, holding her knife the entire time.

Gift crossed his arms. "What would my great-grandfather do with you?"

"He'd kill me," Scavenger said. "If I'd threatened his life."

Gift nodded.

"Let me live, boy, and you prove that you're soft."

Adrian swallowed. Scavenger had been a friend for a long time. Unpredictable, dangerous, but a friend. But he knew better than to interfere. Maybe when Gift pulled his knife or gave an order to Leen, then Adrian would interfere, but not until then.

"Or maybe I'll prove that I'm smart," Gift said. "You're the only one who has talked straight to me about this, no agenda at all."

"I have an agenda," Scavenger said. "I want the Black King out of my life. I don't want to live like a Red Cap ever again. And if it means I have to kill you to do so, I will."

"But you'll only live like a Red Cap under my great-grandfather."

"So it seems," Scavenger said.

"Which means you could give excellent advice to me," Gift said.

"As long as you watch your back."

"All right, then," Gift said. "Let's get off this road."

Adrian let out a sigh of relief. He let go of Scavenger's arm.

"No," Scavenger said. "I have to make one more thing clear to this boy. If it ever looks as if you'll fall into the hands of your great-grandfather, I will kill you."

"I'll remember that," Gift said. And it seemed, to Adrian, as if Gift had grown taller. He glanced at the others. "You seemed to think you have a plan to protect me. Let's get to it."

Scavenger got to his feet. Leen put her knife away, although she kept her hand on the hilt. Adrian stood, and Coulter took a deep, shuddery breath.

"They'll know where we're going," Leen said. "They know about the farms, you said so yourself, Gift. And now they know we're on the road. We have nowhere to go. You need to make a Shadowlands."

Gift put a hand on her shoulder. He appeared to be waiting for the others to speak.

Adrian didn't have any ideas. Leen was right. They couldn't go back to the farm, and they couldn't stay here. Coulter still didn't seem all himself.

Scavenger sighed. "Do I have to do all the thinking for you?" he snapped. "You can't make a Shadowlands. That's the first thing they'll look for. Think, people. They have *wisps* on you. Wisps. Wisps can't do anything. They can just observe, and they'll only do so from the air. The rest will come along the ground, according to the Wisps' directions."

Adrian smiled. He saw where Scavenger was going. "So we turn this to our advantage."

"Advantage," Leen said. "You are all more optimistic than I am."

"No we're not," Scavenger said. "Just more experienced. Come along."

He took her hand (making Adrian smile again—it seemed that Scavenger wanted to take her hand) and led her through the corn.

"They'll see the ears move," Gift said.

"Not if we hurry." Scavenger's voice was already muffled. Adrian shooed both Coulter and Gift ahead. They went, then Adrian followed with a final glance to the sky. Nothing. The smoke had dissipated. Nothing remained. A life, gone in an instant.

He shuddered. Coulter had such power, and he had never used it before. But he would use it again.

Adrian took a deep breath and disappeared into the stalks. He hoped Scavenger's plan was a good one. It would have to be for them all to survive.

SEVENTY

RUGAD strode through the palace gates. The sun was setting. It should have given the air the coolness of twilight, but the heat from all the fires lingered.

Heat and stench.

The air smelled of smoke and death. Already the bodies were decaying in the unnatural warmth.

Rugad kicked aside a sparrow stuck between its bird and Fey self. Bodies everywhere. The ground was littered with them and slick with blood. He put his hands on his hips and surveyed the mess.

It had taken most of the afternoon to get his stupid Beast Riders turned around. No one had outthought him like that before. No one had ever used his Beast Riders' nature against him like that. No one.

He had underestimated the Islander King even while cautioning himself against doing so.

Of course, it had cost the King many men. Guards lay all over the courtyard, their bodies pecked beyond recognition. Most had died with their arms over their faces in a vain attempt to protect their eyes. Once the Beast Riders had turned around, they had done the duty they should have done earlier.

Still, it served as a warning, and as a surprise. Unless Rugad was careful, the Islander King could get the better of him, even without the magick poison. Rugad had an adversary, and a good one.

For the first time.

Only Jewel's husband simply didn't have the troops. He had allowed himself to be surprised, he had allowed the Fey to get the upper hand in Jahn, and he had no way to get out of the city. He couldn't fight back any more than he already had.

Rugad knew this, but his own soldiers didn't, and they were jumpy. They had lost confidence—a brilliant strategy on the part of Jewel's husband, and one he could turn to his advantage if he knew how.

Rugad would never give him the chance.

Craw, head of one of the Bird Rider units, walked over to Rugad. Craw's bird form was a raven. He wasn't wearing it. Instead he was nude and covered with blood and offal. He carried a sword of a make Rugad had never seen before.

"The palace is secure," Craw said.

"You're certain?"

Craw nodded. "Checked it myself. We have a handful of prisoners in the kitchen, and the prize is in the Audience room."

"Take me there," Rugad said.

Craw smiled. He stepped over bodies, not seeming to care what he placed his bare feet in. His feet were less like human feet than talons anyway. They were black and scaly and probably had less feeling in them than Rugad's fingers.

Rugad stepped across the bodies, ignoring the blood. It didn't coat his boots; he wore magicked boots made for him specially by Domestics on Nye. He had been in worse carnage than this, but never in such unnecessary carnage. Birds and feathers were scattered everywhere.

His people had never panicked before.

Ever.

They would never panic again. He would see to that.

The main doorways stood open. A few bodies were scattered across the threshold, mostly Islander servants, from their clothing. The rest of the bodies in the stone corridor had been dragged to the walls and left for the Red Caps. Rugad had heard that Islander skin and blood had clean magick. He hoped so. They would have plenty of it to use.

If the Caps got to it soon.

The palace was impressive. Like the Tabernacle, the palace had a fortress's build with towers, turrets, gates, and impervious stone walls. Late in its history, someone had destroyed its defensive purpose by putting in decorative windows, not arrow slits. The later additions showed a people who had no knowledge of war.

But earlier—earlier someone had had need of protection.

He took all of this in at the great doors. They opened into several halls, one of them looking older than the others. "Where's my prize?" he asked.

Craw nodded toward the hall that had captured Rugad's attention. "We have them in the Audience room."

"Them?"

"Your great-grandson, his sister, and the King."

Rugad nodded. He wasn't ready to see them yet. "Did they put up a fight?"

"Not much of one." Craw hefted the weapon he held. "They had thoughtfully provided us with swords."

Old swords with dull blades. But, while Jewel's husband seemed to be a good strategist, he didn't know weapons.

"Excellent," Rugad said. "Is Wisdom here yet?"

"He just arrived," Craw said.

"Let him know I want a defensible place to set up headquarters."

"There is one several floors up," Craw said. "They call it the war room. It was built for defensive purpose. Only one door and no windows."

Sounded a bit like a nonmagick Shadowlands. Rugad nodded. "Take Wisdom there. Have him scout it and any other likely location. Then get the Caps here. With this heat, this mess will stink by nightfall."

"Yes, sir."

"The Audience room is through those doors?" Rugad asked, pointing.

"Yes, sir. The large oak doors on the other side of the Great Hall."

"You have sufficient guards?"

"Triple, sir. Their king seems wilier than we expected."

"My great-granddaughter is a Shifter. Warn your guards."

"Yes, sir," Craw said.

Rugad nodded at him, dismissing him without a word. Then Rugad went into what Craw had called the Great Hall.

He understood where Craw got the description. There were palaces all over the Galinas continent with rooms like this. Ancient palaces that dated back hundreds of years before the Fey invasion. The Great Hall was always used as a feasting and ceremonial room. He ran a finger along the stone. It was well cleaned but crumbly with age. The windows had been added later, and the bubbly glass even later. He glanced up. The roof had been rebuilt several times. He would have guessed that in the palace's first incarnation, the roof had been thatch.

Which meant there had probably been a fire once or an attack with fire. Whether they remembered it or not, the Islanders had war in their background. Serious war, the kind that demanded strong defenses and even stronger weapons.

Tables remained in this room, but they were cleaned. Apparently this had been where the banquet that Flurry interrupted had been held. He almost wished he had seen that moment; the Fey arriving in the middle of what apparently had been a large and important banquet. Even if the Islanders had no knowledge of their history, they did seem to know how to use the room.

He would use it well too. Perhaps it would even hold a ceremony to show off his great-grandchildren to the Fey.

He hadn't decided which of the children would lead. He would wait until he met them, until their talents made themselves clear. He suspected that the older would work, since he was raised by Fey, but this day had taught Rugad not to go strictly by expectation.

Across from the windows was a wall filled with weapons. He wound his way around the tables and stopped in front of it. So this was where his Bird Riders had picked up their ancient and dented swords. There were still a good hundred weapons on the wall, some rusted and unusable, but others that had years of use in them. His people were smart; they never let anything go unused.

Then he smiled. The Islanders, captured by their own weapons.

He adjusted his shirt and his pants. They were clean despite the wild ride over here. Bird shit and feathers had rained on him in the panic, but the Domestics' spell held. He had washed his face and hands before coming in, knowing that part of the impression of power came from his appearance.

He would meet his great-grandchildren with as much power as he could muster. This great-granddaughter, this Shifter, would need special attention; she had been raised by one of the most rebellious of the Fey.

He hoped that his people found his real great-grandson soon. It alarmed Rugad that he couldn't travel the Links anymore. That Islander Enchanter was a detail that he would have deal with, and soon.

He made his way through the Great Hall to the narrow corridor on the other side. It wasn't hard determining which room held the prisoners. The Fey guards outside were ridiculous in their numbers. They didn't mill, but they watched. He had never seen such nervous Fey faces before.

Jewel's husband had been smart. What he couldn't accomplish with his own troops, he accomplished with surprise. Rugad's people were spooked.

And his guards looked it. All of his troops, bloodied as they were, looked as if they'd lost instead of won. Rugad couldn't face a worthy adversary like this. If he were to take his own advice, he knew that he would have to stop underestimating the Islander King. If Rugad could see the fear, so would mighty Nicholas.

Unlike his son, Rugad learned from his mistakes.

Instead of going toward the Audience room, he turned his back on it. He would inspect the palace himself and find the best headquarters. Then he would insist that the Caps get to work around the palace, clearing out all evidence of the rout. The Islander bodies could remain, but the Fey bodies had to disappear or at least be hidden. He would bring in fresh guards after that, guards who didn't have a haunted look in their eyes. He would face the Islander King with strength, and absolutely no sign of weakness.

He could do that.

He stopped and mentally saluted the rival he had yet to meet. Rugad appreciated a worthy adversary. It kept him fresh. King Nicholas would lose, but he would lose after putting up a fight. A fight so good that it placed the future in doubt.

No man could hope to do better against the Fey.

Many had done worse.

SEVENTY-ONE

HE was just an old Aud gone bad.

His own words reverberated through his sleep. He shivered with cold and pain. His body ached from lying on the stone floor. He knew that Marly tended him while he slept, changed his bandages, kept him covered, and also kept him guarded. He could relax around her, and he wasn't certain why.

He just knew he could.

There was something that he was missing here, something that his sleep-and-pain-fogged mind hadn't grasped. Something important. Something life-or-death.

He was grasping toward it when voices startled him awake.

"... thought at first they'd made it ..."

"... a slaughter ..."

"... word is ..."

"... much worse ..."

He blinked awake and tried to sit up. Marly's hand was on his good shoulder, holding him down. He shook her off. He was hungry and thirsty and in incredible pain, but some of the exhaustion had worn off. The men stopped speaking when he sat up.

Yasep was watching him, darkened face suspicious.

"Go on," Matthias said. "You've obviously been on the surface. Let's hear the report."

Yasep jutted his chin out. If he reported to Matthias, then Matthias was the one in charge.

"Tis na right keepin secrets from him," Marly said. "Na now."

"She's right," Denl said. "We need him, if what they're sayin is true."

"What are they saying?" Matthias asked. He was careful to keep his voice strong, even though speaking hurt. His facial movement pulled on the scab that had formed over his wound.

Marly sat beside him and handed him a small cup filled with water. He took it, but didn't drink. He didn't want to appear too eager.

"They're sayin the Rocaan is dead," Jakib said. He was huddled near a box, and he looked terrified.

Matthias's heart thudded against his chest. He didn't want to know this. "How could that be true?" he asked.

"Holy water, tis na good," Ubur said.

"N the Tabernacle's been burned. I seen it myself," Denl said, "from across the bridge."

The Fey had figured out a way to fight holy water, and they had slaughtered the Rocaan. Matthias's head was spinning. If that were all true, then the Isle was doomed.

"Is there any way to confirm this?" he asked Yasep.

"Na without dyin," Yasep said.

"N tis worse," Denl said.

"Worse?" Matthias wasn't certain how much worse it could get. The Tabernacle, his home, his love despite the pain he'd caused it, was gone.

"Jahn's burned."

"The whole city?"

"Most a it."

"And the palace?"

"Surrounded, guards dead. If the King's alive, twon't be fer long," Yasep said.

So Nicholas's twenty-year gamble hadn't paid off. Matthias felt no satisfaction in that. He wondered briefly what had happened to the poor Aud who'd come through on his Charge, and then sighed. The boy was probably dead with the rest of them.

Or would be soon.

"What of his children?" Matthias asked.

Yasep shrugged. It obviously didn't concern him. Most of the Isle would feel that way. The children probably joined their great-grandfather. Despite himself, Matthias felt compassion for Nicholas. The man had made the wrong choice and realized it too late.

"Tis only a matter a time afore they find us," Jakib said. "The guards attacked outta the tunnels."

"And the boy came through from the Tabernacle side," Matthias said. "The Fey aren't stupid. They'll be down here in a matter of days."

"There's na anawhere else ta go," Yasep said. He ran his hands through his hair, tugged, and then bowed his head. Within an afternoon, he'd been defeated, the proud·man who hadn't wanted Matthias in the troop.

But Yasep had seen the destruction. To Matthias, it was simply something he'd imagined. Not yet real. He couldn't think of Titus as dead. In fact, he couldn't think of Titus as anything but that young, scared Aud who held the Secrets and the future of the Tabernacle.

Matthias had been horribly unfair to him.

He had been unfair to them all.

"I have to see," Matthias said.

"Ye can trust em," Marly said. "They wouldna lie."

Matthias shook his head. "I'm not accusing anyone of lying. But I have to know if the Rocaan lives."

"What's it ta ye?" Yasep asked. "Ye said yer na religious na more."

Matthias put a shaking hand to his head. "Denl, you understand, don't you, what it means if the Rocaan's dead?"

"Tis na ana one ta speak ta God."

"Crudely put," Matthias said. "And what else?"

"Tis na more religion."

Matthias nodded.

"What's it ta ye?" Yasep asked again. "Ye gave it up."

Matthias had to speak through his dizziness, through his pain. "The position of Rocaan. That's what I gave up. I'm still a Rocaanist."

"Tis just words," Yasep said, "and tis na important to us."

"If you believe that, you're a fool," Matthias said.

People around him gasped. Marly's grip on his arm tightened. "The Rocaan makes holy water."

"And it dinna work on these Fey," Jakib said. "I seen it meself."

"But holy water is only one of the Secrets," Matthias said. "The Rocaan knows a dozen others. I've been studying them. I know them. I was Rocaan. And if Titus is dead, I am the only one who knows them."

"All the more reason ta stay away from the Tabernacle," Marly said softly.

"You don't understand." Matthias eased forward, feeling the pull on his scabs. "There are legends in the Cliffs of Blood of magic swords that kill with a single touch. Of foods that shatter your enemy. These legends even tell of water that melts people."

"Like holy water," Denl said.

Matthias nodded. He had one of them. "And each of these legends corresponds to a Secret held by the Rocaan. There is a recipe for holy water. And instructions on how to make a sword. I was trying that one the day the Fey attacked me."

"It dunna matter," Yasep said. "If ye know, or he knows. It dunna matter."

"It matters," Matthias said. "If there are two of us, we can test the Secrets quicker. We can make weapons faster. We have to find him."

Marly put her hand on his arm. "We canna go. Ye canna go through the tunnels. N what if the Fey wait on the other side? We're all dead."

"Ye left em once afore," Yasep said. "Tis their problem now."

"But—"

"No," Yasep said. "Tis na sensible ta have ye both die. If the Rocaan is dead, so be it. If na, then he can fight, n ye can fight. From separate places."

Matthias rubbed a hand over his bandages. The argument was sound, but he didn't like it. He wanted to know if he were the only one left, if he was the hope of Rocaanism.

Of the Isle itself.

"Tis na smart ta die ta learn something ye can learn by bein patient," Marly said.

"Tis the word on the street that the Rocaan is dead," Jakib said. "The Tabernacle is burned. Twould seem right."

"Tis death ta go there now," Yasep said. "I willna let my people go there."

That was it. Matthias couldn't go alone. He wasn't sure he would make the hike without Marly beside him, without supplies, without someone to catch him if he passed out. He was still very weak.

And they were right. He would know eventually if Titus was dead.

If nothing of his past survived.

"Where do you suggest we go?" Matthias asked, knowing he was giving in by asking. "We can't stay here. The Fey will find us. They will locate these tunnels, and soon, if what the boy said was true."

"I dunna know a lot a places ta hide," Yasep said. "N if the Fey're as smart as they seem, they'll find em all. Tis only, as ye say, a matter a time."

Matthias stared at him. In his proud way, Yasep was asking for help. "How far east do these tunnels go?"

Yasep shrugged and looked away. Denl leaned forward, eager and terrified at the same time. "East?" he asked. "What's in the east?"

Matthias didn't answer. He wasn't going to justify himself, not yet. "How far?" he asked again.

"I been as far as Old Jahn goes," Jakib said. "The tunnels dunna end there. But I canna say they go much farther n that."

"The end of Old Jahn's good enough," Matthias said. "Is that part of the city on fire?"

"Tis mostly the west and south," Denl said.

"Let's hope it stays that way through the night."

"Ye'd better tell us where we're going in case we get split up," Yasep said. His voice shook, and he cleared his throat to cover it.

Matthias debated with himself for a moment. If they knew, they could tell the Fey if captured. But he supposed it didn't matter. With the loss of Jahn, of the Tabernacle, and of the palace, Blue Isle belonged to the Fey now. They would find and take over everything eventually.

"We're going to the Cliffs of Blood," he said. "It's remote, and the villagers didn't accept the palace's authority. They won't accept the Fey's either."

"Tis odd up there. They may na let us come," Yasep said.

"Jakib n I still ha family there," Marly said. "Do ye, Holy Sir?"

Matthias shuddered, remembering the way they had turned him out, left him for dead more than once.

Demon spawn.

Then he'd come to the Tabernacle and they'd accepted him, with his quick mind and his willingness to learn. They'd ignored his height, his unusual appearance, and had taken him for who he was. It wasn't his fault that he didn't believe in the Roca. He had tried. He had tried, the Old Rocaan said, too hard. Maybe if he had listened to the still small voice—

"No," he said. "I don't have family there."

But the Roca had come from the Cliffs of Blood. Rocaanism had been born there, and many of the Secrets had their origin there as well. Matthias had lived there for a while after he left the Tabernacle, and he learned that if he left the locals alone, they left him alone. The Cliffs were defensible, and they would be a good place to make a stand against the Fey.

If Matthias could find a weapon.

"I think if we're going to leave," he said, "we'd better go now."

"Yer in no condition to travel," Marly said.

"If I stay here, I die," Matthias said. He pushed himself to his feet. Like it or not, he led this small band of ragamuffins. His other band, the one he had come to Jahn with, was probably dead.

Like Titus.

And like Nicholas would be before the day was out.

Matthias's heart hurt. He hadn't thought he had any feeling left for these people. They hadn't listened to him. They had coddled the Fey and lost everything.

He would make a stand, and he would do it for them all.

He only hoped it wasn't too late.

SEVENTY-TWO

TRAPPED in his own Audience Chamber. The irony of it didn't appeal to him. Nicholas had never felt so angry in his life.

Nor so helpless.

It had looked for the good part of the afternoon as if his people would win. Then the birds had come back, clouds and clouds of them, like smoke before a fire, and they had landed with a vengeance. Their humiliation had obviously preyed on them, and they attacked like monsters.

His guards hadn't had a chance.

And he had watched it all, Arianna at his side. She hadn't said a word, not even when the birds started bringing the trophies to the windows in the Uprising Room.

But Sebastian had cried. Finally Arianna had gone to him and held him.

The Fey in the room had said nothing. They had watched the entire thing as if it were normal. Maybe Matthias had been right. Maybe they had no souls.

Then Nicholas had turned away from the carnage, looked at his half-Fey daughter, and remembered his all-Fey wife. The Fey made war; that was what they did. They were fierce creatures whose lives were defined not by how well they lived, but how well they fought.

And in this battle, Nicholas had fought well, but that had not been enough.

He stood near the dais in the Audience Chamber, looking at the family crest. Two swords crossed over a heart. How appropriate that had seemed to him once, when he loved Jewel here and created children with her.

"They're still outside the door," Arianna said. She came over to him, speaking softly, her hand on his arm. She was as aware as he was of the listening booths. He wasn't certain if the Fey had found them yet, but they would. They would. Just like they had found everything else.

"We don't have long," she said. "We have to come up with something."

Sometimes he forgot she was just fifteen. He put his hand over hers. There was nothing left.

"I could Shift and go under the door for help."

"To whom?" he asked softly, hoping she knew more than he did.

Then she shrugged. She didn't. She was just hoping that her father would save everything, that he would make it all better, like he did when she was a little girl.

"There's nothing we can do now," he said. "The Black King will be here soon. The best we can hope for is to negotiate."

"I won't work with him," she said.

"You might have no choice," Nicholas said. He had held out against the Fey for twenty years. His daughter—or his son by blood—would lead them. That was winning, of a sort.

Arianna went to Sebastian and ran a hand over his stiff hair. He looked at her, took her hand, and leaned it against his cheek. He still hadn't recovered from the loss of contact with Gift, and the death around him had terrified him so. Nicholas hadn't known how to comfort him.

Nicholas hadn't known how to comfort himself.

"There has to be something we can do," Arianna said.

"There's nothing we can do," Nicholas said, "short of murdering the Black King and putting you in his place. And we can't do that. The Shaman's warnings about the Black Blood are clear."

Arianna looked directly at one of the listening posts. "Tainting the Black Blood terrifies me," she said loudly.

Nicholas raised his head and so did Sebastian. She never spoke like that.

"I wouldn't make the madness fall on anyone."

Sebastian pulled her closer. "Ari, ... please ..." His grating voice had panic in it.

She kissed his head and eased out of his grip. "I'll always be sensible, Sebastian," she said.

She made her way to Nicholas, then wrapped her arms around him. He put his around her, and buried his face in her shoulder.

"I just got an idea," she whispered.

He started, but she held him fast.

"I can't kill the Black King, but you can."

"Arianna—"

"Shhh. If I grab a weapon, they can't attack me. If I throw it to you, you can kill him."

"Then what? They won't accept you as leader."

"They'll have to," she said.

"They'll kill you before you have a chance to think." Or me, he thought.

"Not if I Shift. Not if I can get you, me, and Sebastian out of here. Then the Islanders will still have their King, and any pretenders to the Black Throne will have to fight me. The Fey would be done. They wouldn't move anymore."

Nicholas shook his head. "It won't work," he said. "You can't even plan something like this. The Shaman was clear about it."

Arianna bowed her head. "But we could threaten him," she whispered. "Nothing could stop us from doing that."

"Except common sense," Nicholas said. "There has to be another way. We'll find it, Ari. We'll find it."

She raised her head. "But will we find it soon enough?"

"Ari ... !"

She backed away as the door opened. A Fey came in. He was young and dressed. The sword strapped to his side looked Fey-made. "The Black King shall be here shortly," the Fey said, his Islander accented on all the wrong syllables. "We are stationing guards in preparation for his arrival."

And to stop them from planning any more. Arianna's

bright gaze met Nicholas's. She thought the same. There were guards in the listening post. They couldn't have heard anything, but they didn't want their prisoners scheming together.

Guards streamed in. All were dressed, and several carried swords. It was the ones who didn't that worried Nicholas. They had long fingers and even longer nails. Foot Soldiers, who could kill with a single touch. He repressed a shudder. He had seen their work before.

Twenty-five soldiers came into the room and lined the walls. He supposed he should be honored. The Black King did consider Nicholas and his family a threat.

Nicholas went to Sebastian and put his arm around the boy. No matter what Arianna planned, there was no guarantee that Sebastian could move quickly enough to be saved. There wasn't even a guarantee that one of the Black King's soldiers wouldn't kill her.

Solanda had killed Rugar with no repercussions. It could happen again.

If Nicholas got a chance, he would try to talk Arianna out of trying anything. He would negotiate with the Black King, and if that failed, he would wait until the man died and hope that his children made the right choices. At least they would lead the Fey, at least Blue Isle would remain in the family.

And, he supposed, that was all that mattered now.

Everything else was lost.

SEVENTY-THREE

FLURRY hovered over the empty road. It was growing dark. His wings were tired. He hadn't flown this much in Nye. He doubted he had flown this much in his entire life.

And now Cinder was gone, leaving no clue as to where she went.

He shouldn't have left her. He knew better. He knew so much better. And yet he had. He had thought that she couldn't mistake these instructions, that she would understand the importance of them, that she would at least have left some sort of trail.

But he had been so cocky and confident when he spoke to her. He would be able to find them, he had said. He would know where they had gone.

Well, he had been up and down this road twice, he had checked the surrounding farms, and he hadn't seen anything.

The growing darkness was casting a blue shadow on the land, making everything very difficult to see. He couldn't make out details any more, where the road ended and where it began.

He couldn't *see*. And the Foot Soldiers would arrive at any moment, ready to take their prisoner.

They had none.

He would report to Rugad a Failure.

We had your great-grandson and then we lost him.

Flurry shuddered at the thought.

He flew lower. The rows of corn were broken slightly by what seemed like a trail. He had followed it before, and he was going to follow it again. He wouldn't be a Failure. He wouldn't let Rugad kill him as he had other Failures.

He just wouldn't.

He paused. Time to assume the worst. The boy was of Black Blood. What if he were worth Rugad's pursuit? What if he had seen Cinder and knew what she was? According to Wisdom, the boy had been raised by Wisps. He would know how to elude them.

And how did one evade a Wisp?

Look unobtrusive from the sky. Hide in something. Go inside. A Shadowlands wouldn't work because a Wisp would be the first to spot it.

The soldiers could always go an extra distance. Flurry could bring them back, blame them on being unable to find Gift.

Flurry could buy a little more time if he needed it.

The cornfield was his best and only bet.

He swooped lower, cursing the failing light. In the twilight, the broken corn looked like a river of blood in the middle of a moonlit sea. He already knew what was on the other side. A farm. The boy wouldn't be stupid enough to hide on a farm.

Would he?

Or was that wisdom? Wasn't that just the game that Rugad would play? Take the expected, use it to his own advantage.

Flurry flew lower and let himself glow, casting a tiny light on the trail below him. On the other side of the corn, a haystack. Then another, and another, all the way to the grain silo. Beyond that, the farmhouse itself.

He flew around the house first. The farmer, his wife, and five children were eating dinner, oblivious to the battle being fought across their land. They wouldn't be that calm if they were hiding fugitives. They wouldn't be eating that much if they knew about the invasion.

The house had no cellar, no basement, no underground hiding spot, at least not one he could see from the outside. And he needed to be able to see it from the outside, otherwise someone in that house had to be hiding the boy, and no one was.

He flew to the silo next.

It had three small windows, all of them at various levels in the silo. He peered in each, then flew in the lowest one.

The silo was empty. Wisps of grain littered the bottom of the bin, waiting for fall harvest. All of the grain normally stored here was either eaten or sold.

The boy couldn't be in here unless he were capable of changing size, like a Wisp, or Shifting to a tiny form. And, according to all Flurry knew, the boy couldn't do either.

That left the haystacks.

If he plunged in them, and the boy was hiding there, the boy would see Flurry and disappear before the Foot Soldiers arrived. Flurry had to look for something out of the ordinary.

If Flurry were hiding, he would take the center stack. Not too close to the farmhouse, but not too far either. Not too close to the corn, but not too far.

He swooped as low as he could get. The first stack wasn't really mounded. It was tied. Several bundles of hay stacked together and bound individually around the middle. Then they leaned against each other for support. A few strands of hay on the ground, but nothing much. Nothing more than the wind could knock free.

But the center stack. The center stack wasn't organized. It had several bundles in the middle, but they didn't seem to be leaning on anything. The twine around them appeared to be loosely tied. And there was hay all over the ground, hay of all sizes, much of it broken and trampled.

He hesitated a moment, ready to go in to look. But he could hear the soldiers now, marching on the other side. If the boy wasn't here, he'd let the soldiers play with the farm family. That would occupy them while Flurry searched again.

But he knew he wouldn't have to.

His search was over.

THE
CONFRONTATION

SEVENTY-FOUR

THE dizzy feeling he'd had after the series of Visions was back, behind his eyes. Rugad rubbed them. He had been on edge ever since then, but that strain seemed to be growing worse.

Rugad stood in the Great Hall surveying the weapons wall. Even though this was not his headquarters, it was, he decided, his favorite room in the palace. It was the only one that had a Fey feel to it. And he suspected that feel had come from the weapons still displayed on the walls.

He didn't like the morale he was encountering among his people. They seemed at best startled by the near-reversal, and at worst frightened of it. They seemed to think the Islanders had more powers than any other force the Fey had ever met.

If he left the rumors unchecked, they would only grow. And he knew that once they grew, once they became big, they would have a power all their own.

He had to nip it now.

He had chosen as his headquarters the very room that Nicholas had been captured in. The man had an instinct for fighting, a good natural instinct. The room, although it was open on all sides because of that bubbled glass, also provided a perfect view of the city and, Rugad suspected, an imperfect view of the areas beyond. It was large enough to use as a meeting hall and small enough that a man alone didn't feel overwhelmed.

The broken window was covered with a tapestry. He would get a Domestic on all the windows in the morning to get rid of the glass, and put in Fey glass that was defensively spelled.

The rest of the palace would need work of a kind he didn't have time for yet. He would let the Domestics remove much of the Islanders' personal items, but he would put them in storage. There was still much he didn't know about this culture, much that he needed to know, and he suspected some of this material would help him with that.

He had been startled, though, to find Jewel's portrait in a gallery filled with portraits of round, doughy, blue-eyed, blond-haired women. Queens and future queens, he suspected. He had stood before her for a long time, wishing he had done right by his granddaughter. He should have kept her on Nye and let Rugar destroy himself. But Rugad had had the vain hope that Jewel could pull it out, that she could take Blue Isle and save Rugad the trouble.

She had done the best she could under startling circumstances. At least she had left Rugad with two children from whom he could choose his own successor. The one thing he had learned in all his years of rule was that without a trusted successor, he was nothing.

He had the successor now. The problem would be trusting him.

Or her.

He hoped they were more Fey than Islander. He hoped they would understand the value in the Fey Empire and understand the kind of greatness it took to lead such an enterprise.

If Jewel's children proved not to be up to his expectations, he didn't know what he'd do. The grandsons he had left on Nye were nothing. They weren't even exemplary Fey. They had, surprisingly even to him, let him go, thinking that he would get stuck on Blue Isle and they would get the rule by default.

They hadn't even thought through what would happen if he took the Isle. Or if he found Jewel's children. And like Rugar's, their Vision was sloppy. The difference was that Rugar's had started good and gone down. Theirs was starting in a bad place and could only deteriorate.

So much rode on these great-grandchildren. And yet, now that he had one in his grasp, he was hesitant to approach her. He didn't want to find out that she was similar to her uncles on Nye. He didn't want to know that she wouldn't work as a successor.

Because that only left the great-grandson as yet unfound. And Rugad liked having two choices instead of one. At least with two, he might have a chance.

Still, he hadn't gotten where he was by agonizing over worries. He had gotten half a continent, and now this Isle, by taking action. And his next should be to finally meet his great-granddaughter and begin the process of wooing her over to his side.

In that, he was uncertain. He had never wooed before, and never with such purpose. His wife had felt honored being chosen by a member of the Black Family, as had every other woman he'd been with since she died. His people listened to him, as did other rulers he conquered. The idea of cajoling someone, of coaxing them to his side was as foreign as the customs on Blue Isle.

And then there was the problem of her father. The man was too smart. He had mounted a counterattack that, while not successful, had still hurt Rugad's people. And he had stopped the Fey once before. He had seduced Jewel, and he had more knowledge of the Fey than most.

And even more important, he was King. That carried a great deal of weight. Displaced rulers brought with them hope that they would rule again. In the past, it had always been Rugad's practice to kill a popular ruler, to stifle hope then and there.

But before he could make a decision about Nicholas, he had to see if Nicholas's daughter was attached to him. If she was, then Nicholas's death might count against Rugad. And he couldn't have that.

Too many questions, and none of them would be answered in the Hall. He was only using his time here to worry at problems he couldn't solve, at least not without more information.

He took a deep breath. The confrontation awaited. He had no idea what to expect.

He crossed the corridor and stopped outside the Audience room. Most of his guards were already inside. The others he had sent for stood outside. It was a measure of Nicholas's skill that Rugad would go in so heavily guarded that no man could get near him.

The guards were a mixture of Foot Soldiers, Infantry, and Beast Riders. The Riders were dressed and looked fresh. None of them appeared to have fought the battle earlier in the day.

Rugad turned to them. "Don't harm any of the prisoners," he said, "no matter what they do. But make certain they do not get near me."

The guards nodded. They had probably not needed the instruction, but he had given it for his peace of mind. Then with a sweep of both hands, he yanked the door open and went in.

His presence always caused consternation, and this time was no different. The guards inside backed away slightly. But the three forms in the middle of the room didn't seem too concerned. Rugad paused near the door, letting his own guards sweep around him until they reached their position.

And he watched.

The room was long and narrow. A dais stood above everything, with a crest, which surprised him. The image on the crest surprised him even more. Two swords crossed over a heart. He had seen the reverse of the same image in his only trip to the Eccrasian Mountains decades before. Two hearts pierced by a single sword. The oddness of it startled him.

The emotion only lasted an instant, but that was long enough for the Islander King to take advantage of the situation. He bowed, then swept up, easily the smallest man in the room. His yellow hair shone like a beacon among all the dark scalps.

"You must be my wife's grandfather," King Nicholas said in passable Fey.

Advantage to the Islander. The girl beside him drew closer. She was clearly half-breed. The Fey features always emerged strongest, but she had the look of her father about her face. Odd to think that when she had a narrow chin and upswept Fey features. But her skin was light, and her eyes pale. The birthmark flared off that pale skin like a brand.

In her eyes, though, Rugad saw Jewel. Determination, intelligence, and anger. He mentally saluted all three.

They pleased him.

He let the silence hang between them. It was the only way he could regain control of the situation. And he used it, not just to examine the girl, but also to look at the golem.

It appeared alive enough. He had never seen such an animated golem before. The person behind it was clearly powerful. But it had cracked once, shatter lines running along its face and into its clothing. Its eyes were bright too. He had only seen one golem like it, a golem fed with such power that it lived long after its animator was dead. His grandfather's golem. The old man had used it to rule in areas that he couldn't monitor. It was a second pair of eyes. He'd tried to do the same with a another golem, but it spread his power too thin. And, some said, the first golem was jealous.

This one watched him with an intensity that had a threat to it. The golem was guarding something, but what Rugad didn't know.

Yet.

"Girl," he said, deciding that ignoring the King was the best course. "What's your name?"

She glanced at her father. The look was small, but it told Rugad enough. They were Bound. Rugad would have to tread lightly.

"In my country," she said, her chin outstretched, eyes flashing blue, "it's discourteous to ignore the King."

Rugad suppressed a smile. She had even more spirit than he had hoped for. "I have conquered your country. You no longer have a King." He paused just enough for that sentence to sink in. Then he said, "I asked your name."

"A man does not conquer a country simply because he declares it so," the girl said. Her father touched her arm. She shrugged him off. So, the father was a bit overwhelmed by his impulsive daughter. Even better. Mighty King Nicholas had a weakness.

"No, he does not," Rugad said. "He conquers by bringing

in an invading army of overwhelming proportions, destroying the religion, burning the only city of note, and capturing the King. Now, girl, your name."

"Her name is Arianna," King Nicholas said. He did not look bowed or intimidated by Rugad's strength despite the interaction. He looked more like a man with an understanding of, and a dislike for, games.

This time, Rugad permitted the smile. "A name with history. Did Jewel choose it?"

"Jewel died as Arianna was being born."

"You can't tell me that you chose such a distinguished Fey name for your daughter by luck."

"No," Nicholas said. "No luck. I had good advice."

The guards were shifting. The movements were slight, but Rugad noted them. He was not facing a hostile enemy. He was facing one with a great deal of knowledge about the Fey. He had to acknowledge that.

"You married my granddaughter."

"She was a remarkable woman."

"And your people murdered her."

A shadow passed over the King's face. He still mourned her. He had loved her. Rugad had not expected that. He had expected a marriage of convenience, nothing more.

"One man murdered her," Nicholas said. "He was dealt with."

The phrase was vague. There was a story behind it, one that Rugad did not have time for.

"You expect special treatment because you married her," Rugad said, keeping his voice firm. "Because your blood flows in the body of my great-granddaughter?"

Nicholas was silent for a moment, his features smooth. The roundness of his face made him appear younger than he was, still a boy, yet another way to underestimate him. "When," he asked, "did I ask for special treatment?"

There was a faint note of contempt in his voice, just strong enough for Rugad to hear it and faint enough for him to claim he had never meant any disrespect.

"You asked for a meeting," Rugad said.

"It is customary in my land for rulers to meet and negotiate."

"When have you had the chance to meet or negotiate with anyone?"

"I negotiated with Jewel," Nicholas said.

Again, point to the Islander. Despite himself, Rugad liked this young King. Perhaps some of Arianna's spirit came from her father as well.

"So," Nicholas continued without much of a pause, "you're the one in error here."

The guards shifted again. A few looked at each other. Rugad noted the movements. No one spoke to the Black King that way.

No one.

"My people have already made an alliance with the Fey. You had no cause to come into our country, burn our city, attack our Tabernacle, or hold me hostage."

"An alliance?" Rugad said softly. "My people don't make alliances."

"Your granddaughter did." Nicholas took his daughter's arm and pulled her close. "My children are proof of that. This Isle is already part of the Fey Empire. By blood."

"Then why are yours the only half-breeds?"

"Because your people don't assimilate well."

Amazing, this man. Just amazing. He did not cower in the face of the Fey. He didn't hide in such complete loss. Still he fought. If Jewel were alive, Rugad would have commended her choice.

"My people don't assimilate," Rugad said. "We conquer. And that is where my granddaughter failed."

Color rose in Nicholas's cheeks. They flushed a soft red. Light skin had its disadvantages, then. It showed emotion so much easier than Fey skin.

"If you weren't so blind, you would see that your granddaughter did not fail." He pushed his daughter forward slightly. She looked at him with alarm. "Forever Blue Isle is allied with the Fey. The blood of our sacred ruler has mixed with your infamous Black Blood. We are a hereditary monarchy. My children, no matter whom I created them with, will rule. And you just destroyed their heritage."

"I didn't destroy anything," Rugad said before he could stop himself. "The wealth of Blue Isle remains intact."

"Are you so certain? Perhaps the cities on Galinas mean

little in comparison to their fields, but here, we had enormous wealth. The Tabernacle alone had not just wealth but history. Importance. And you destroyed it."

"I destroyed a threat to the Fey."

"If the Tabernacle threatened the Fey, then how did so many Fey survive all these years? You are ruthless for the sake of ruthlessness, and it has made you careless."

"Enough!" Rugad spoke so loudly that Arianna backed up. Her father caught her. Her father hadn't moved. Neither had the golem, who continued to watch Rugad with intelligent eyes. "The Fey do not ally. They conquer. And in that, Jewel failed. She did not conquer your people. The Islanders had no fear of the Fey, and you contributed nothing to the Empire, not one thing in twenty years. Goods and services in one part of the Empire belong to all parts of the Empire. Your trading stopped the moment my son stepped on your shores, and it has not resumed."

"Because we could not get off the Isle. We destroyed the maps and sent away our Guardian watchers long before Jewel and I even discussed marriage." His blue eyes were clear. His expression as guileless as Rugad's could be. "If you had sent ships, we would have filled them. Provided, of course, that they could have made it through the Stone Guardians and up the Cardidas."

He was brilliant, this King, and he was making Rugad look like a fool before his own guards. The Islanders had no knowledge of war. Rugar had been right. But their leader was unequaled in all of Rugad's experience. Never had Rugad met a man who could best him—even briefly—in conversation, and in war.

Anything Rugad would say at this point would sound defensive. So he decided not to address any of Nicholas's points. "Where is your son?"

"Beside me," Nicholas said.

Rugad looked at the golem. He looked back, the strength in his eyes matching Nicholas's. Yet Rugad could see no life around the creature. It was a golem. Later Rugad would check it for Links.

"Your real son."

"Sebastian is my son and has been his entire life."

"That creature is a golem," Rugad snapped. "It is a lump of stone."

"Stop it!" the girl said. "He's my brother. He's a person, just like you are."

"Oh, no, little girl," Rugad said. "I am very real. I do not shatter when cold."

"No," she said. "But you'd die if someone pierced you through the heart."

Several guards put their hands on their swords. Rugad glared at them, reminding them silently that they couldn't touch the girl. "As would you, child," Rugad said. He smiled at her and let the warmth he actually felt shine through his eyes. She was magnificent. All he had to do was make her his. "You understand, don't you, that I'm not here for Blue Isle. Blue Isle is, and has always been, the Fey's for the asking. I am here for you."

"For me?" She cocked her head slightly. "Well, you have me now."

Rugad shook his head. "I won't have you until you understand what you are."

She brought her eyelids down slightly. It had the effect of flattening her face, of making her seem distant and cold.

"Blue Isle is a tiny place in the center of the Infrin Sea. There are nine seas, and five continents. The Fey Empire stretches over three of those continents. If you work with me, girl, you will rule not only Blue Isle, but all of those continents, all of those countries, and you will have more power than you ever dreamed of."

"I don't dream of power," she said, but her voice wavered just enough to let him know that she considered it. "And I won't rule Blue Isle. My brother will."

"Your brother? Raised by my people with no love for your traditions?"

"He . . . knows . . . the . . . tra-di-tions," the golem said. His voice was raspy and hard. It made several of the guards jump. Rugad met each of their eyes, and they looked away. It would take days of work to get his troop back to its normal morale level.

"So," Rugad said, "you are my great-grandson's puppet."

"He's no one's puppet," the girl said.

"Oh, he's someone's," Rugad said, "or he would not have the life he does."

"Leave my son alone," Nicholas said.

"He is not your son," Rugad said. "He is a bit of stone."

"He is a man with a life of his own," Nicholas said.

"He is not living flesh," Rugad said, wondering how this man couldn't know that what he called a son was merely a magickal construct. He had thought the King brilliant. He had not expected this.

"He may not be living flesh," Nicholas said, "but he has a living soul—and it's probably purer than any of ours."

Rugad glanced at the golem again. He was constantly underestimating things in this place. A golem with a pure essence? A golem that had lived for eighteen years, a golem with a mind of its own? Perhaps it was more than a construct. But if it was, he didn't know exactly what it was.

"He had to have gotten his life from somewhere," Rugad said, hoping to draw the discussion away from the golem. "And he seems to know a lot about my great-grandson."

The golem didn't move. The girl did. She glanced from her father to the golem and then back to Rugad. "Leave him alone," she said.

"Why?" Rugad said, pleased at having discovered their mutual weakness, "when he's a direct link to my great-grandson?"

He took a step closer. His guards moved with him. He would see how far this loyalty went. "All I have to do," Rugad said, reaching toward the Golem, "is travel through him along his very powerful Link to find my great-grandson."

"Nooo . . ." the Golem said, wrenching his head back.

"It could, of course, shatter the Golem, but since he's not alive anyway—"

"You will not hurt him!" The girl moved with such swiftness that Rugad didn't even have time to shout a warning. She grabbed a sword off one of his guards, swung it over two other guards' heads, and shoved it at Rugad's neck. The sharp tip pricked his skin.

His guards lunged for her.

"Stop!" Rugad yelled. His adam's apple bobbed against the tip. It hurt. "You can't touch her."

They stopped.

His gaze met hers. Her eyes were almost clear. She didn't even look frightened.

"You don't know what you're playing with, girl," he said.

"I do know." She smiled. "I just don't care."

SEVENTY-FIVE

THEY hadn't gone far when the tunnel widened. A stench that Con couldn't quite identify filled the air. Ancient piss, a bit of decay, and something else.

"Ach," Servis said. "Smells like death."

Con shuddered. It did. But the smell was faint, as if it had been there a long, long time. Somehow Servis got ahead of him. He was pleased to have the guard's broad back and muscular arms facing whatever was ahead.

Servis held the torch high. "Walls're different," he said.

Con took a step closer. They weren't walls. They were open. Iron. Cells.

"We must be on the palace grounds," he said.

"Aye," Servis said, his voice warm with amusement. "We were on em when ye found me."

Con ignored that. He reached out, touched a bar. The metal was rusted. Flakes came off on his fingers. "No," he said. "I mean we must be close to the palace. This is a dungeon."

"I dinna think we had such places on the Isle," Servis said.

Then where, Con wanted to ask, had you heard of them? But he didn't. Even though Servis was bright, he lacked

Con's education, and it had been the only sore point between them when they had met the year before.

"We had some near the palace," Con said. "And I thought they were lost long ago."

"Na lost," Servis said, "but na used."

"Right now, anyway." Con shuddered. He didn't know what the Fey did. Did they take prisoners? Or did they slaughter everyone who got in their way?

Maybe it wouldn't matter. Maybe the guards were doing fine above. Maybe the Fey were being driven back.

He hoped so.

"Is this how you came?"

"Na," Servis said. "We dinna come through the palace. We passed that door long ago."

Con licked his lips. So it was on him and his memory of the map. He didn't really want to take it out here. He didn't want to stay in this place any longer than he had to.

"Well, let's keep going," he said. "And the first doorway we see, we take."

"N what do we do when we reach the palace?" Servis asked.

"Find the King," Con said, as if it were the easiest thing in the world.

He doubted it would be. He didn't know what would happen next.

The dungeon widened, and the cells continued down their own narrow passageways. The stench was stronger up close.

"Mouse," Servis said.

Con hoped so. He didn't think King Nicholas used this place, and he didn't want to find out otherwise. They kept going through the wide corridor. Some of the cells had straw in them, probably once used as pallets. A few had chains hanging from the walls.

Servis gaped at it all. "I dunna know," he said. "It seems a cruel place, and odd ta leave it empty."

"Who would the King have put in here now?"

"Fey."

"Twenty years ago, maybe," Con said, "but it didn't work out that way."

"Nay, it dinna."

They were silent for a moment. If King Nicholas had acted against the Fey instead of marrying into them, perhaps everything would be different now. Perhaps the Fey would have been too frightened to attack.

But Con had no real idea. He hadn't even been born when the Fey invaded Blue Isle. They were so much a fact of his life that he couldn't imagine Blue Isle without them.

The door was on his right, so encrusted in dirt and cobwebs that he almost didn't see it.

"Wait." He stopped, peered at it, and then realized that the door was solid, made of oak, and had no bars. He shoved on it, gingerly. Grime fell on his hand, and he shook it off. The door slid open with a creak.

Servis stuck the torch inside. The corridor was different from the others. It appeared older, like the corridors in the Tabernacle, with the stones placed to form a careful box. Bits of straw and fur lined the floor, and droppings covered the surface. Spiderwebs hung in great arcs from the walls and ceilings.

Clearly no one had been in here in a long, long time.

"This is it, I think," Con said.

"Check," Servis said. For the first time since they had started on this mission, he seemed nervous.

Con pulled out the map and they both studied it. From the drawing, it appeared that they were in the oldest part of the palace and that the corridor would take them up to the main floor.

They glanced at each other. This was the moment to back out if either of them were going to do so. The silence was palpable. Then Servis let go of his end of the map. The parchment flapped, and Con rolled it up, replacing it in his robe.

Little men, facing death for a Charge and a matter of honor. As Servis said, they would be the only ones who knew. But then, they were the only ones who needed to.

Servis led the way, one hand outstretched to wipe away cobwebs, the other holding the torch as close as possible so nothing ahead of them caught fire.

The corridor went straight for what seemed like forever,

then it veered upward. They turned a corner and found tiny steps, worn thin with time and use, that wound through a narrow part of the wall.

Con took the torch from Servis. This was Con's Charge, and his problem. Servis could follow if he wanted, but there was no sense in his leading.

Con braced one hand on the wall and held the torch with the other. The steps curved around, winding in a circle as they went up, a construction so ancient that only one part of the Tabernacle had it. Then the stairs dead-ended into a stone wall.

Behind it, voices spoke Fey.

Con glanced at Servis. His face looked yellow in the torchlight. The space that they were standing in was so small that they were almost on top of each other.

"Stairs dunna dead-end," Servis whispered.

"They do if no one uses them any more," Con said. "If someone built a wall to cover the entrance to the dungeon."

"Na," Servis said. "The wall's on the map. There must be a way ta open it."

Con felt the stone with his fingers. He didn't like the Fey voices. If they were loud enough to hear through stone, then there was a lot of them.

The mortar between the stones was crumbling. He felt nothing else.

Finally Servis had had enough. "Step back," he said.

Con did.

Servis pushed against the wall with his shoulder. Then he braced one foot against the far wall, and pushed with all his weight. The stone grated. Dirt and mortar rained on him, almost putting out the torch.

The grating sounded explosive in the small space. Con heard no more Fey voices. He imagined the Fey standing outside, watching the wall open, waiting with all their weapons for someone to emerge.

His throat was dry and tasted of dust.

They couldn't stop now. They had to go through. No matter what they found on the other side.

Sweat ran down Servis's face, cutting lines in the dirt. The stone wall moved slowly. If there were Fey outside, they had plenty of warning. Finally the wall had shifted enough that both men could fit through.

Con put a hand on Servis's arm. "Me first," he said.

Servis didn't argue. He stepped aside, and Con slipped through the narrow opening.

Into an empty room. The voices were down a hallway, as if they had moved on. Sweat prickled on his back. He motioned for Servis to follow.

The room was large, almost as large as the Sanctuary. Tables were scattered on the stone floor. One had been knocked awry by their entrance. Swords and other weapons covered the wall that they had entered. There were imprints of swords on many of the stones, as if there had been weapons there too, but they had been removed.

"Close it," Con said.

"But then we canna get back."

"There are others down there. The Fey don't need to find them."

Servis stared at him a moment, the realization dawning on his face. He had known that they were on a suicide mission, but apparently he had kept the option of escape open. It wasn't open any longer. He pushed the wall closed with his shoulder. The grating sound seemed smaller here. Con could understand why the Fey hadn't heard it.

Then Servis grabbed two knives off the wall. He stuck one in his belt, next to the sword and the other knife. Then he handed one to Con.

Con stared at it a moment. There were Fey here, and he had to find the King.

But Con had had no training with weapons. If he had to use a knife, it would mean that the Fey had gotten too close. He handed the knife back to Servis.

Servis opened his mouth, but Con shushed him.

Instead, Con took a sword off the wall. The sword didn't dislodge easily—it had clearly been there a long, long time. But it appealed to him. It looked like one of the decorative swords in the Tabernacle. The metal was thin and finely crafted, and unlike anything he'd ever seen before. It was also clean. No rust touched it, unlike most of the other weapons nearby.

Servis was looking down the passageway. "Tis a lot a Fey."

"I have holy water," Con said, not looking. He didn't want to know. He didn't have a lot of holy water.

"I hope tis enough," Servis said.

"Me, too," Con said.

They were armed, they were ready, and now they had to find the King. Con had no idea where to go now that they were inside.

"Ye'd think they'd put em in the dungeon. Mayhap they ain't found yet," Servis said, obviously understanding what Con was thinking.

"Then they'd be upstairs, wouldn't they?" Con said.

"Aye," Servis said.

Con turned. There had to be stairs all over the palace. He started toward the other doors when he heard a grunt.

He whirled. Servis was on his knees, the tip of a sword protruding from his stomach. Six Fey stood behind him. They were tall and thin, and looked nothing like the Fey that Con had grown up with. They all had proud expressions on their upswept features.

Con took out his holy water and pulled off the cork. His hand was shaking.

The Fey directly behind Servis laughed and pulled his sword from Servis's back. Servis grabbed his stomach and toppled forward.

"Oh, look," the Fey said in heavily accented Islander, "the little one has water."

"I'm scared," said another.

With a mumbled apology to the Holy One, Con tossed the holy water at them. They didn't back away like he expected. It hit the first Fey in the face and ran down his chin. He waited a moment, then wiped the holy water off.

"It doesn't work, little man," the Fey said. His gaze narrowed. "And now you have a choice. You can surrender to us, or we can kill you. Only I promise that it won't be as quick as your friend's death. I have some Foot Soldiers here who've been killing too quickly for their personal taste. They've been longing to take their time. I'll let them take it with you."

He had only a moment, and he didn't know what to do. He had his Charge, but it seemed like a lost cause now.

"Remember . . . the King . . ." Servis murmured, and then his mouth filled with blood. He gurgled, and died.

"You'll have to kill me," Con said, and held up his sword in a futile attempt to fight them off.

SEVENTY-SIX

THE hay scratched his face and made him want to sneeze. Gift crouched in the hay bale, Leen beside him. Sweat poured off him. He had never been so hot, filthy, and uncomfortable in all of his life.

The little Red Cap had found the hay and then instructed them to hide in the center bale. Gift was unaccustomed to taking orders from Red Caps, particularly fugitive ones. It both surprised and worried him that the Cap was intelligent. He had never thought of them as having much personality before. This one had personality, brains, and a willingness to kill anything that got in his way. Gift only associated that willingness to kill with Foot Soldiers. The fact that this Cap had it made him reassess all he had learned in Shadowlands.

They had been in the bale a long time now, and the Cap promised them that they'd have to be in it at least until dark. Darkness was a relative thing. Gift could feel the sunlight beating down on the bales, and the hay itself glowed in the sun. But it was dark enough inside for him to sleep. He wanted to catch up on the sleep he had missed, but the heat was making it impossible.

The heat, and the odd noises that had started a few moments ago.

The field had been full of noises. The cornstalks groaned in the warmth. They rustled in the slight wind, and so did the hay. But as time passed, Gift got used to those sounds. It was the new ones that bothered him.

Crunching sounds. The sounds of breaking leaves.

Leen reached over and grabbed his hand. Perhaps it was the farmer, inspecting his crop.

Perhaps.

But it sounded like there were too many feet for that.

He held Leen's hand tightly so that she didn't move. They hadn't expected Fey arrival on the ground. Perhaps his great-grandfather had decided to search every farm, every place that Gift could hide.

In that case, the old man was even more desperate than Gift thought.

The footsteps sounded closer. They were soft, more impressions than steps. It was almost as if he could hear the dirt packing under someone's weight.

Then the sounds stopped.

The hair on the back of Gift's neck stood on end. Leen started to move her hand away, and Gift gripped it even tighter. Someone was out there, near the haystack, watching.

Waiting.

Gift held his breath. His heart was pounding, his fingers trembling. He was sweating so much the people outside could probably smell him. His mouth was parched. What he wouldn't do for a drink.

Then he heard crunching on the far side of the hay bale. The strands around him shook. They were digging inside. He guessed it was probably too vain a hope to think that they wouldn't find him.

The crunching stopped and he heard a squeal. The Red Cap. Maybe they would quit with him.

"Who are you?" a male voice snapped in Fey.

"S-scavenger," the Red Cap said.

"What are you doing here?" the male Fey asked.

"I, ah, thought you were Rugar's people. They search for me sometimes."

"*Rugar's* men?" the male Fey asked. "Rugar has been dead for years."

"Yes, but his people keep looking for me. I'm one of the Fey who doesn't believe in the truce."

A lie. The little Cap had enough sense to lie. If he pulled it off, he would keep all of them hidden.

Leen slipped her fingers from Gift's. They still touched fingertips, but apparently his grip had grown too strong for her. He huddled in the bale, feeling the straw scratch his damp back.

"Why would you hide now, Cap?"

"I saw Fey. I thought maybe they were coming for me."

"We are Rugad's people," the male voice said. "We search for his great-grandson whom, we were told, ruled the Fey on Blue Isle."

"I didn't think anyone ruled the Fey on Blue Isle now that Rugar and his daughter were dead," the Cap said.

Gift bit his lower lip. Careful, Cap. They might see through this.

"The great-grandson would have to rule in that case," the male voice said.

"But he was a baby when they died. No one took their place. A bunch of Failures, the lot. No one even tried to fight."

Something wet fell down Gift's right cheek. He resisted the urge to wipe it away. The moisture had to be sweat. It couldn't be anything else.

Failures, the lot of them.

And they were all dead.

He should have died too. But he had been in Jahn, trying to save Sebastian, not realizing what else was at stake.

"If no one ruled, why were you hiding from them?"

"Because they hated me," the Cap said. "They said I was ruining all Jewel worked for."

"You're awfully clean for a Cap."

"I haven't been affiliated for a long time."

"And you made this entire mess by yourself?"

"I had trouble getting into the bale."

"It's a strange place to hide. Why didn't you go for the barn?"

"Because," the Cap said, "the Islanders hate me just as bad as the Fey do."

"You're just not very popular, are you?" the Fey asked.

"That's the bane of a Cap's existence," the Cap said.

"That's it, then," the Fey said. "Let him go."

Gift felt his shoulders relax. Leen's fingers twitched. They'd made it. The Cap had saved them.

Then hands parted the bale. Gift watched as long brown fingers pulled the strands of straw apart. Straw rained around him, as several pairs of hands gripped his shirt and pulled him free. Around him the same thing was happening to Leen, Coulter, and Adrian. Gift had trouble standing. He was weak and dizzy from the heat. Scavenger stood in the middle of a group of Foot Soldiers and Infantry, a look of dismay on his square face.

"You lie, Cap," said a Fey beside Gift. Gift turned just a little. The Fey had wings and a look of frailty. He was a Wisp. Gift's eyes filled, and he blinked, trying to force the water down.

"You are the real great-grandson," the Wisp said, "the one raised by Fey."

There was no use in denying it. Maybe if he talked long enough, he could set the others free.

"You've seen Sebastian?" Gift asked. "The Changeling?"

"The golem? Yes, I saw him, two nights ago, accepting the honor that should have been yours. But we stopped it. If you accept your great-grandfather's offer, you will rule not just Blue Isle, but the Fey Empire as well."

"What offer?" Gift asked. Coulter was watching him, straw poking out of his yellow hair like sticks.

"Your great-grandfather wants you to come peaceably with us. He will train you and you will succeed him as ruler of the Fey Empire."

Adrian's face was deep red. Sweat ran down it. The Cap looked angry. Leen had scratches from all the straw. She hunched, appearing wrung out.

"Where would you take me?" Gift asked. He was stalling for time, hoping the others would come up with something. Maybe even the little Cap. He seemed to be thinking the clearest.

"The palace," the Wisp said. "Your great-grandfather waits there."

Suddenly Gift forgot escape. The image of Sebastian standing before the Black King rose in his mind.

Sebastian, shattering.

"The Islander palace?" Gift asked. Bile had risen in his throat. It burned from his Adam's apple to his gullet. "The Black King is in the Islander palace?"

The Wisp smiled. "It's his now."

"But what about Sebastian? My father? My sister? What happened to them?"

"I thought they were nothing to you," the Wisp said.

"They're my family." Gift clenched his fists. He struggled against the hands that held him. "They're all I have left."

"And for that they matter?" the Wisp asked. There was a small note of contempt in his voice. Too small for the others to hear, but clear to Gift. Fey weren't supposed to care about others. Not when it got in the way of their own future.

"You can't touch my sister," Gift said. "She has Black Blood."

"I haven't touched anyone," the Wisp said.

Coulter made a small movement with his right hand, almost as if he were catching a ball that had bounced off the ground. A small light glowed through his fingers.

Gift licked his lips. "If Sebastian's dead, I won't do anything for your Black King."

"You should know," the Wisp said. "He's your golem. Isn't he?"

Coulter made the same small movement with his other hand. The light appeared there too.

"What's this?" A man cried out in Islander.

The farmer stood behind the Fey, his family around him. Adrian turned, so quickly he forced the Fey holding him to step back to retain their balance. "Run!" he shouted in the same language. "Run now!"

The farmer didn't need the instruction twice. He started to run, but some Fey started after him.

Gift tried to wrench away from his captors. The Cap was doing the same.

Suddenly Coulter erupted into flame. The Fey holding him screamed. The fire ran up their arms and along their clothing. Coulter moved away. He sent balls of fire into the grouping of Fey, and their boots ignited. The ground, though, didn't burn.

The Fey were screaming. The others were trying to put the fire out. The Cap grabbed one of his swords and hacked at the Fey holding Gift. Coulter came close, pointed a burning finger at them, and they backed away. Gift glanced at his friend in startlement, but said nothing.

Leen wrenched out of her captors' grasp. Adrian was still shouting at the farmer. Leen grabbed him, pulled him into the melee. The Wisp, in desperation, reached for Gift, and Gift shoved him as hard as he could, sending him backwards into the corn. Gift winced; he had probably broken the Wisp's wings and most of the bones in his legs.

Fey were screaming. The area smelled of burning flesh. Coulter grabbed Gift's arm, but the fire didn't run to him.

"Come on," Coulter said. "We only have a moment."

Gift let himself be pulled into the corn. As they reached it, Coulter's flames went out. Leen was following, Adrian and the Cap behind her. They were leaving a mess, a trail, and Gift didn't care. He was using the last of his energy to run.

"What was that?" the Cap asked.

"I've got a whole arsenal of spells," Coulter said. "They just aren't very powerful and they don't last long."

The Fey screams were growing.

"The farmer," Adrian said.

"We can't help him," the Cap said. He grabbed Adrian's shirt and pulled him forward.

"They'll be searching for us," Gift said.

"They won't find us," Coulter said. "You hurt their Wisp. They have to go by ground to get someone after us. If we can hide—"

They reached the end of the corn. Gift and Coulter broke through first. And stopped.

A row of Fey that extended as far as the eye could see blocked the cornfields. More Fey covered the road.

"They won't find us?" the Cap said as he burst out beside Gift. Adrian cursed and Leen moaned. "You don't have Vision, do you, Islander?"

"That's Gift's job," Coulter said. "Had any Visions about

this?" Gift shook his head. He'd had a lot of Visions this day, but none of them showed this. And most of them ended with Sebastian shattering.

"They're not going to take me," Gift said.

"Great," Leen said. "Where does that leave the rest of us?"

"Dead," the Cap said. "But they'll kill us whether they capture us or not. May as well go out fighting."

Without waiting for an answer, he brandished his bloodied sword aloft and plunged into the crowd.

SEVENTY-SEVEN

ARIANNA was breathing hard. The sword was heavier than she expected, and her arms were tired. She had used them as wings too much in the last few days.

Every eye in the room was on her. Every eye. The guards had their hands on their own swords. Her father was standing motionless beside her, and Sebastian was beside him. The Black King watched her, his eyes alive in his sun-wrinkled face.

"Do you know what will happen if you attack me with that?" he asked. He didn't even look frightened.

She knew, but she wasn't sure she believed. It was all Fey mumbo-jumbo, some of it true, some of it not. She wasn't sure she'd risk her family's lives for some Shaman's lie.

But then, if she killed the Black King, the guards would be free to kill her.

And her father.

"They say chaos will happen," she said. She sounded calm, and she didn't feel that way. Her arms were trembling. "But I don't believe it."

"Believe it, girl." It was as if they were the only two people in the room. She could feel his power. It radiated off him. He was used to command, used to being in charge. Even though her father had gotten the best of him in their verbal sparring, the Black King seemed undisturbed. Even now, looking down the mouth of his own death, he seemed undisturbed.

"If it's true," she said, "set us free."

"To what end?" he said. "I'll just capture you again."

"And I'll try to kill you again."

"You wouldn't," he said. "You wouldn't risk everything for nothing."

"You're not offering me everything. I get the prize after you die, whether you train me or not. I don't need you, old man," she said.

That did seem to reach him. He swallowed, a small movement, one the others might not even notice, but a movement all the same.

"If you kill me," he said, "you'll destroy everything the Fey have worked for. Everything."

She smiled. She had to shift her hand slightly to keep the sword up. "I've never seen what the Fey worked for. It's nothing to me."

"Chaos, girl. Brother against brother. Friend against friend. That's what you'd bring on this world."

"You mean," she said, "what you've already brought on it? My father is right. You didn't have to attack us. Maybe my brother and I would have worked with you. Maybe you should have found out first."

"You don't know what you're doing," he said. This time the desperation had crept into his voice. She had frightened him.

Badly.

He didn't know what she would do, what she was capable of.

She liked that. It gave her the edge she needed.

"And yet you want me to work for you," she said. "You want me beside you. You think I'm ignorant, but you'll let me rule an Empire."

"You're ignorant because you were raised among Islanders. That can be changed. You can learn."

"I was raised among my own people."

Her father took one step forward. It was a small step, but

it put him in her range of vision. She mentally thanked him for that. It made everything easier.

"The Fey are your people."

"The Fey are no more my people than they are my father's," she said. "Your people didn't want me. They wouldn't raise me. They left me here to die. If it weren't for my father and Solanda, I would be dead. So don't talk to me of my people."

"Those Fey are dead," the Black King said softly, carefully. "They were Failures. The Fey do not allow failure."

"Then what will happen to you, allowing a small slip of a girl to get the better of you?"

"You don't have the better of me," he said and reached for the sword.

She anticipated the move, and with her right hand, tossed the sword to her father. He caught it deftly, the sword moving as if it were designed for his hand. The Black King whirled, her father ran forward, and Sebastian screamed.

The guards were moving too, but she couldn't think about that. If her family was to escape, she had to act now.

She Shifted, and hoped she'd survive the process.

SEVENTY-EIGHT

THE Fey laughed as they charged him. Con swung his sword and sliced through three of them: the movement went through the neck of one, slicing off part of his shoulder; then penetrating the arm of another, cutting into his chest and out the other side; and into the third's stomach and out his thigh. The first's head fell backwards and landed with a splat. His body fell a moment later. The other two were cut in half, blood spurting from the lower half as the upper part of their bodies fell to the ground.

Blood fell on him like rain.

His arm wasn't even tired. He hadn't felt any resistance. If there weren't twitching bodies before him, he would have thought nothing had happened. It had felt as if he had sliced through air.

The other three Fey stopped as if he had commanded them.

"Back off," he said. "Back off or I'll kill the rest of you."

The sword was light in his hands. It was made of a material he had never felt before. Most swords were too heavy for him to hold.

Not this one.

His feet were wet. The floor was slick with blood. The three dead Fey lay between him and Servis, beside the damaged table. Then the remaining Fey started moving again. A Fey man came forward, his hands outstretched. He had such long fingernails that they looked like claws.

"Get back," Con said. "Get back now or I'll hurt you all."

A Fey was behind him, grabbing at his robe. Con whirled, nearly lost his balance, and stabbed at the Fey with his sword. The sword sliced through the Fey's arm at the elbow. The Fey clutched at the stump but did not scream.

A second Fey pulled him back, then snuck close to Con and grabbed the rest of the hand. Con watched, as appalled at it all as the Fey seemed to be.

He was vulnerable only if they took the sword. The sword seemed to have powers of its own.

He slammed his back against the stone wall. Now he could hold them all off.

But they weren't coming forward. They were staring at him as if he weren't human, as if he were something more than they were.

The second Fey drew his own sword and swung it toward Con. Con parried. The force of his blade against the other shattered the first. Metal clanged on the floor, and one piece splashed in the blood.

He wasn't even breathing hard. It had taken no effort to kill three Fey, seriously wound another, and destroy the fifth's weapon. Was this the power of a Charge? Was this why there were so few given?

Or was it the sword?

It seemed like the sword.

The two Fey who were left stared at him across the tangle of bodies. Fey faces, long, angular, narrow, male and female, were gap-mouthed with surprise. But six other Fey were running toward them from the corridor. They stopped when they saw the carnage. Half had swords. The others had those fingers with the long nails. Foot Soldiers, the ones who could slice off skin with a single touch.

He could hold them off, but he didn't know how long. The Fey had countless magicks. Sooner or later they'd figure out a way to get him. They would turn into something small and attack from above, or send a bolt of light at him or kill him with a thought. He didn't know how many of those things they were capable of, or even what they were capable of. He only knew that they would win. It was inevitable. One man couldn't win against hundreds.

Could he?

With God on his side?

They were watching him, staring at him, thinking as quickly as he was. A woman in the back moved and he brandished his sword.

"Don't move," he said, "Or I'll kill you all."

She stopped. Her eyes were big and brown. They caught the light, and seemed to reflect fear back at him.

"Tell me where my King is," he said.

No one answered. They were still watching him like he was a crazy man.

He had to use that fear.

He stepped forward, nearly slipping in the blood.

"Tell me!"

"In there," a man said in accented Islander, and pointed toward the corridor.

"Where all the others are?" Con asked.

"Yes," the man said. "In the Audience room."

Con should have known where that was, but he didn't. He didn't know any of this, except that there were eight Fey in this room, with the possibility of more all the time, and more than twenty Fey in the corridor beyond.

He could kill three with one stroke, but that might not be enough, especially with no one to watch his back.

But they didn't have to know that. They had no more idea than he did what he—or the sword—was capable of.

He muttered a silent prayer. If God helped him through this, he would devote the rest of his life to God's service.

"You get my King and you bring him here," Con said.

"We can't do that," the man said. "He's with the Black King."

"I don't care who he's with," Con said. "Bring him here, or I'll destroy each and every one of you. And your Black King."

"He can't do that," the woman who had tried to leave said. "He's an Islander."

"I'm a holy man," he said, "and I have more powers than

you ever dreamed of. How do you think I got here through your vast armies? Walked?"

"You're bluffing," she said.

"Are you willing to take that risk?" he said.

"We're dead either way," the man said. "It's either him or the Black King."

"I'll let your king go free if you bring mine," Con said. A bead of sweat ran down one cheek. His heart was pounding so hard he wondered if the Fey could hear it.

"You can't kill our Black King," the woman said. "If you could, you would have done so already."

He had no answer for that. They started forward and he swung his sword, wildly, narrowly missing the Fey in front.

"It's the sword," she said. "It's the sword that gives him his power. Get it!"

And they surged forward like one body, their eyes fixed on the sword in his hands.

SEVENTY-NINE

ADRIAN watched as Scavenger plunged into the crowd of Fey, swinging his swords, doing little damage. Foot Soldiers grabbed him and still he fought. Adrian swung his bow around and reached into his quiver. His hands were shaking.

For the second time in his life he would be a prisoner of the Fey.

If they let him live.

He wasn't about to let that happen.

Scavenger's fight was curiously silent. A few grunts, some groans, and a moan when the Foot Soldiers caught him. Leen took one step forward and stopped—she obviously knew what her people were capable of—and Gift looked as if this blow were one too many. Adrian lined up the arrow and shot at one of Scavenger's captors, hitting him the shoulder.

It didn't seem to make a difference.

But Coulter, Coulter seemed taller than he ever had.

He stepped into the middle of the group, in front of Gift. "Stop it," he said to the Fey. "Stop it, stop it, stop it."

The closest Fey laughed at him. But Coulter didn't even look at them. He sent a bolt of fire into the middle of the group. It landed—and exploded—behind Scavenger's captors. The Fey turned as one body—

—and the fighting stopped.

They couldn't deny the smoke that rose behind them, billowing into the sky, nor the fact that the day was hotter than it should have been. Fey were not stupid when it came to magick. They knew that Coulter had something, but what they weren't certain.

Adrian took out another arrow and lined it into his bow. Leen grabbed her sword. Gift took his knife. Suddenly they were a fighting force.

"I defend this member of the Black Family," Coulter said. "Defy me, and you'll all die."

"You're Islander," said a woman beside him.

"You're observant," he said, with a sarcasm that was foreign to him. "Let Scavenger go."

The Foot Soldiers didn't move. The wounded soldier, arrow sticking out of his shoulder, still held Scavenger. No one else moved either. The acrid scent of smoke rose behind them, and the heat seemed to be growing. Sweat ran down Adrian's face. He hadn't had anything to drink in a long time. He wondered how much longer his body could keep losing water and could remain upright.

"Let him go," Coulter said again.

They were waiting. It was obviously a test. They wanted to see what he was capable of.

Adrian felt a chill despite the heat. Coulter had said he had an arsenal of weapons, but not a lot of power. The Fey had a troop on this road and more weapons than Adrian cared to think of.

The bluff was the only thing that would save them. And Coulter didn't quite know how to do that.

Adrian kept the arrow in position, but lowered the bow slightly. "Do as he says." Adrian made his voice carry. "Or he'll kill all of you."

A sea of Fey faces, unimpressed.

"Can you Charm?" Gift hissed to Coulter, sotto voce, but Coulter didn't seem to hear him. Instead, he squinted, and Adrian thought he saw a small flash sparkle in the sun. As quickly as it appeared, it disappeared.

Then the Soldiers holding Scavenger staggered backwards. The first fell to her knees, blood seeping out of her eyes, nose, and ears. She stared at Coulter a moment before toppling forward. The other grabbed his head as if it hurt him. He staggered through the crowd of Fey. They parted like grass in a breeze. When he reached the edge of the road, he fell too, eyes open.

Dead.

The third, the one with Adrian's arrow, opened his eyes and mouth, let out a small squeak and fell over backwards.

Dead.

Coulter glared at them. The corners of his lips were blue, and his fists were clenched so tightly his arms shook. Adrian knew what this was costing him. Coulter had always been the peaceful one, the one who wanted to use his powers for good. They were forcing him into this for the one person he loved more than himself.

For Gift.

He obviously couldn't speak. Adrian had seen that expression before, just a few hours ago. The deaths were like little deaths inside Coulter.

"Do the rest of you want to die that way? Let us through," Adrian said.

"He can't kill us all," a Fey said from the back in Fey.

"Doesn't matter. The Black King will get us if we let the boy go."

"Can you Charm?" Gift whispered again.

"It won't work," Leen whispered back. "They're right."

Scavenger seemed to have recovered from his own fear. He scuttled back to the group, and as the Fey debated, he handed out weapons. He gave Gift another knife, and Leen an extra sword. Then he offered a knife to Coulter, but Coulter didn't even look at him.

Adrian waited, arrow poised.

Someone had to make a move, but it wasn't going to be him.

A tear ran down the side of Coulter's face. Followed by another. He closed his eyes, raised his hands above his head, and whispered, "Lightning," in Islander.

Instantly thunder boomed overhead. The smoke clouds reformed into storm clouds, and the sky grew dark.

"Duck," Coulter said in Islander. He was looking at Adrian now. "Please. Duck."

Adrian dropped his bow, grabbed Gift and flung him down. Scavenger did the same with Leen. Lightning rippled across the sky, then shot down in huge bolts, crackling as they came.

The air was charged. Adrian's hair rose on the back of his neck. Gift squirmed, trying to see, but Adrian held him firm. The lightning moved slower than real lightning, creeping down the sky. Adrian kept his head up, watching. Some of the Fey fell to the ground just after Adrian did. But others didn't. The eerie green light illuminated their faces, making them ash gray and too pale.

Then the lightning struck and the screaming started. Huge wails of agony. Adrian pressed his face against the dry ground. Sizzles rose over the screams, and a stench rose, a stench Adrian hadn't smelled since the first Fey invasion all those years ago. And this new smell wasn't quite it. It was thicker, less putrid, more acrid.

The smell of burning flesh.

His stomach turned, but he kept his hand on Gift. So far the lightning hadn't touched Coulter's friends, but Adrian didn't know how much control Coulter had.

So Adrian remained down as the stench grew and the screaming stopped—all except for one long, high-pitched wail. Gift scrabbled against the dry ground.

"Coulter," he said.

Adrian raised his head. Gift had understood it before Adrian had. The last scream belonged to Adrian's adopted son.

Coulter stood over a road filled with charred and burning bodies. A few Fey moved among the carnage, but those that did were whole. The sky was clearing, the clouds moving, the lightning gone.

And Coulter's mouth was open, his eyes staring straight ahead, unseeing, and he was screaming.

"Stop him. We've got to stop him." Gift moved out of Adrian's grasp and put his arms around Coulter. Coulter didn't move.

Scavenger stood too, followed by Leen. "We only have a moment," Scavenger said. "You can bet they already sent someone for help. And when those who are still alive recover, they'll be after us. We have to leave now."

Leen was looking over the bodies. A sea of blackened flesh. "He's an Enchanter," she said.

"It took you until now to figure that out?" Scavenger said.

Gift was still holding him, but Coulter hadn't moved. The scream had turned into a raspy wail.

"Get him moving," Scavenger said.

"Where?" Adrian asked. There was fire behind them and death before them.

"Not Jahn, that's for certain. And we can't go back to the farm. We only have two choices, east or west."

"Won't make much difference either way," Adrian said.

"There are Fey west," Leen said. "They slaughtered everyone in Shadowlands."

"Let's not decide here," Scavenger said, nodding toward a woman moving among the dead. "Let's just go."

"Let me get Coulter." Adrian moved Gift aside and gently put a hand over Coulter's mouth. Then he brought Coulter's head down onto his shoulder. Coulter bent rigidly, his entire body shuddering.

"Adrian," Coulter said. "Adrian." And then a sob poured out of him, followed by another and another. Coulter hadn't cried like this since he had discovered that his powers could harm, fifteen years ago.

That had taken an afternoon. They didn't have time now.

"It wasn't your fault," Adrian said. "Sometimes a man has to do this. Sometimes a man has to defend the people he loves."

"B-b-b-but—"

"No buts," Adrian said. "We have to go now, or this will be for nothing. They'll kill us all."

Coulter was still shuddering.

"Use my strength," Adrian said. "Use me. Lean on me. We'll make it together."

"And me," Gift said. He put a hand on Coulter's back. Coulter stood, saw the death before him, the death he had caused, and winced. Adrian pulled Coulter's face aside so that he couldn't see.

"We're going to go around this," Adrian said.

"Through is better," Scavenger said.

"Around. He won't make it through."

"We can't coddle him."

"We're not coddling him. I just want him to survive this."

"He's fine."

"Not inside, he's not," Adrian said. "He didn't have your training. He doesn't have your coolness or your stomach. He's Islander. We respect life."

Then he gasped. He hadn't meant to insult Scavenger. Scavenger had helped them for years.

But Scavenger merely shrugged. "I always thought that was a failing," he said, and started north.

Leen glanced at Adrian, looking a bit startled. But, surprisingly, color had returned to her cheeks. The Fey liked revenge. He had forgotten that. And this attack could be seen as revenge for her family.

She bent down, grabbed his bow, and handed it to him. He slung it over his other shoulder.

"Come on," Adrian said. Together he and Gift propelled Coulter forward. They moved as quickly as they could. Ahead, Adrian could see the end of the pile of bodies. Once they were around that, they could choose their route.

"Do you hate me?" Coulter asked.

"No," Adrian said. But it didn't seem to ease him. Coulter was waiting for Gift's response.

And Gift didn't answer.

EIGHTY

NICHOLAS caught the sword. It felt as if it had been waiting for him all his life. And he knew then that Arianna was right. With the Black King gone, she ruled the Fey and she would have Blue Isle.

But this had to be Nicholas's decision, not hers.

Nicholas didn't even stop to think. He ran forward. Out of the corner of his eye, he saw Arianna's clothes split as her legs extended, her torso grew and her face lengthened. She was Shifting.

Sebastian screamed.

The Black King was watching them both, looking startled. The guards moved too, but Nicholas couldn't think about that. He got within reach and swung the sword with both hands, using all the force he had. He was swinging upward, an awkward angle, but he couldn't go for the chest. The Black King's clothing had to be spelled. His neck and face were the only vulnerable places on his body.

As Nicholas moved, he felt all that rage, all the things the Fey had taken from him, all the losses he had suffered since he met them. His father, his kingdom, his real son.

Jewel.

Something slammed into Nicholas's back as he swung. Somehow he kept his balance, kept his focus. The Black King didn't move quickly enough, and the blade dug into the skin of his neck. It felt as if Nicholas were chopping into a tree with a dull knife.

The Black King choked and reached for the sword. Blood oozed out of the side of his neck. The weight on Nicholas's back grew. Arianna was nearly done Shifting, and the guards were coming toward him, their own swords drawn.

The Black King was staring at him in complete disbelief. Nicholas tried to pull the sword back, to attack again, but it was stuck. The guards' swords rained around him, but something pushed him toward the ground. He lost his grip on his own sword, and fell, landing at the Black King's feet.

Arianna's hooves pawed nervously. She had become a horse.

A horse.

She was brilliant, his daughter.

"Daddy!" she cried.

Swords clanged, just behind him, and he realized what had been pushing him.

Sebastian.

"No!" Nicholas cried and tried to roll over, but Sebastian was too heavy.

The Black King staggered back, hands on the sword, trying to pull it out, slicing his palms. Blood dripped on Nicholas. The guards brought their swords down. He kept trying to roll, but Sebastian—the stone boy—put his full weight on Nicholas. He couldn't breathe.

"Sebastian!" Arianna screamed. Her screams sounded like whinnying. "Sebastian." She reared, kicking at guards. She hit some of them, but not enough. Their swords clanged on Sebastian's back. Nicholas could feel the blows through Sebastian.

"Stop!" Arianna yelled. "He's of Black Blood."

But they must have known what he really was. They brought their swords down again, and this time, chunks of Sebastian flew past Nicholas's head.

Nicholas couldn't yell. He couldn't breathe. He wanted to tell Sebastian to get on Arianna, to ride away, but the air wheezed out of him.

"Sebastian, come up here!" Arianna yelled in Islander.

Then a sword whizzed down perilously close to Nicholas's face. He dodged with the last of his strength, and the sword hit Sebastian's cheek, lodging in one of the cracks. Sebastian let out a grunt, and then he rolled off Nicholas.

Sebastian's eyes glowed, and light streamed out of all the cracks in his body. For a moment he looked like a man who'd swallowed the sun.

Nicholas pushed himself up, ignoring his aches and his own dizziness. He grabbed Arianna's mane—it was the same fine black as her own hair—and reached for Sebastian. Sebastian extended his hand—it was glowing too—and then he mouthed something Nicholas didn't understand.

"No!" Arianna shouted.

The guards had backed away from him as if they knew what was coming. The Black King had slumped against the wall, eyes closed. He looked dead.

Nicholas took Sebastian's hand. Light traveled up Nicholas's body and filled him with a momentary warmth.

Then the light grew even more. It was blinding. Too much. Nicholas tried to pull Sebastian away from it—

And Sebastian exploded.

EIGHTY-ONE

THEY had made it beyond the carnage. They were now cutting across a grassy field a short distance from the road. The Cap insisted on a hurried pace. He hated being in the open.

Gift didn't blame him.

They had decided on the mountains to the east. They would either go to the Slides of Death or the Cliffs of Blood. Adrian had never traveled that far, and neither had anyone else. They would simply take the road with the most cover.

When they got there, they would decide whether or not to make a Shadowlands. Adrian had heard of caves and other hiding places in the mountains that might make a magickal construct unnecessary.

Gift kept his arm around Coulter. Coulter hadn't said anything since he sent the lightning on the Fey. He shivered every now and then, and he wouldn't have moved at all if Adrian and Gift hadn't propelled him forward.

Gift didn't know what it would be like to kill that many people with the flicker of a thought. He wasn't certain he wanted to know.

The stench of charred flesh clung to their clothing. Surprisingly, the Cap seemed the most bothered by it. He wanted to find the Cardidas or steal clothes. He was complaining almost constantly.

The others ignored him.

So did Gift.

It was getting dark. He suspected they would have to keep moving during the night. The farther they got from his great-grandfather's armies, the better off they'd be. But they needed food and water. He and Leen needed rest. Coulter probably did too.

Gift was about to mention it to Adrian when the world tilted. He felt oddly dizzy. The light was bright, and he was in that room, the room he'd seen earlier, the room in the palace. Guards were everywhere. His father's hand was on a sword that ran through his great-grandfather's neck. His sister was Shifting into a horse.

And Sebastian launched himself onto his father's back, knocking them both flat.

No! Gift shouted, but he wasn't really there. It was as if the barriers between him and the palace had lifted, like a curtain revealing a window, and he could see what was happening at that place and time.

The guards had their swords out. They were swinging at his father, but they hit Sebastian. Cracks spread through his entire body. Another sword hit him in the neck, making the cracks worse. He rolled off Gift's father. Light shone through the cracks. A brilliant light. The light that was Sebastian. Their father stood, cried out, reached for Sebastian. Sebastian reached back. Then his eyes moved, and he saw Gift.

"Gift . . ." he said. Light moved across his arm, up his father's arm, and headed toward Gift. Sebastian's body shuddered and then, suddenly, it shattered.

Bits of stone flew everywhere. The light, strong a moment before, became diffuse, scattering with the pieces.

No! Gift shouted again, but it did no good. He couldn't catch the bits of light.

Then the world tilted again. He was on the ground, dirt in his mouth, his hands in fists. Then he felt hands on his back. Coulter's hands. Adrian's hands. The Cap was sitting across from him, looking annoyed. And Leen stood, guarding them.

"Gift? Gift?" The voice was Coulter's. He had apparently aroused himself enough to respond to Gift's crisis.

Gift sat up, wiped the dirt from his cheek, and buried his face in his knees. Sebastian was dead. He'd seen it, the loss of his Changeling, his brother, his closest friend. And he couldn't stop it. He'd known about it for days and he hadn't been able to prevent it.

Sebastian was dead, but Gift had survived.

Somehow that made it worse.

"What did you See?" Adrian asked.

But it was Coulter who sat down beside him, Coulter who put his arm around him, and Coulter who pulled him close. Gift leaned against him and breathed.

Sebastian had died saving their father.

Sebastian had died so that their father could kill the Black King.

Sebastian.

Coulter's grip on Gift tightened.

Even if Gift had been Linked with Sebastian, he wouldn't have been able to stop Sebastian's death. Sebastian had been warned. He had known what would happen, and he had made a choice.

A choice to save their father.

A choice to save Arianna.

A choice that Gift couldn't have made even if he'd been there. His heritage prevented it.

At least now they had a chance. The Black King was wounded, maybe dead. In a few days, Gift might be able to get Coulter to reopen the Links. Then Gift could ally with his family to drive the army off their land.

Sebastian had done that for them. He might have saved them all.

But it didn't matter. Gift didn't know them.

He had loved Sebastian.

And Sebastian was dead.

EIGHTY-TWO

FOR a moment the world was as bright as the sun. Then as the light spread out, it faded and grew diffuse.

Bits of stone rained around them. The guards ducked. Several protected the body of the Black King. Arianna was screaming, but she had Shifted completely. Her clothes were in tatters on the floor, and she was a magnificent brown horse with a sleek black mane. She pawed at the empty space where Sebastian had been, and yelled for him.

Nicholas didn't even protect his head. Bits of his son bounced off him, leaving bruises that he deserved. The boy had died trying to save him.

And Sebastian had saved him, at least for the moment.

Nicholas couldn't mourn. He didn't have time. And he couldn't save Sebastian. There was nothing left.

"We have to get out of here," Nicholas said in Islander. If they didn't, Sebastian's death would be in vain. They had to move quickly. The Fey were in chaos from the Black King's death, but it wouldn't last. There were too many to fight. Nicholas's and Arianna's only chance was to flee.

But Arianna didn't seem to hear Nicholas. She was

crying for her brother, still pawing at the spot where he had been.

Rocks had fallen on her as well, but she didn't seem to notice.

"Arianna!"

Nicholas still had a hand in her mane. He tugged on it. But she made no movement. The guards that weren't around the Black King were crouched, protecting their heads. They wouldn't be down long, and when they got up, Nicholas didn't know what they'd do. Would they remember that Arianna was of Black Blood? Would they go after him?

He couldn't wait for her to recover. He braced a hand on her back and swung himself on.

She whinnied and rose on her hind legs—a horse response, which pleased him. And as she went down, he slapped her on the hind flank.

"We're going," he said. "Now!"

"Sebastian—" she said.

"Is dead. Make it worthwhile. Go!"

She did. She stopped at the door and kicked it down with her front hooves. Several dozen Fey swarmed outside, looking startled as a horse bolted past them. A few cried after them, but none gave chase.

Surprise. Surprise was working. But they had to hurry. If the Fey recovered, the two of them would die.

Arianna bolted through the Great Hall, past a bloody circle of Fey—did Nicholas see an Aud among them?—and out the main doors.

The stench in the courtyard was tremendous. The bodies looked even worse up close. Someone had lit the torches on the side of the building, but they didn't have to. The light from the burning city cast an orange glow over everything.

Twice. Twice in his life, he had lost all he owned in the space of a single day. At least this day, he still had his daughter. He had no idea what had become of his Fey son.

"Where do we go now?" Arianna asked. She picked her hooves gingerly over the body parts littering the cobblestone.

Nicholas glanced around. Fires to the south and west. Across the river, the Tabernacle burned. The air was full of soot and ash, and the heat was as intense as it had been in the middle of the day.

"We'll go north," he said.

"What about Sebastian?" she asked.

"He died so that we'd survive." Later he would comfort her. They could comfort each other. But this wasn't over yet. It wouldn't be over for a long, long time.

"North," she said, as if contemplating it. She made her way to the gate, then shook herself. He nearly lost his grip on her mane. She took a deep breath as if she were thinking, and then she said, "Grab on, Daddy."

He did, and she took off at full gallop. Nicholas leaned forward and wrapped his arms around her neck, and pressed his own head against hers. She was all he had left. His son, his home and his city were gone. His rule was probably over too. But that didn't matter any more. Arianna mattered. And he would protect her life with his own if he had to.

He glanced over his shoulder. No Fey were following them yet. But they'd search. They'd search and get revenge.

They would search, and unless Nicholas was very careful, they would find.

Nicholas was going to be very careful.

EIGHTY-THREE

CON swung his sword madly. And each time it connected, it sliced through something. Hands, fingers, arms, littered the ground around him. It got so that he didn't even want to look.

But he had to. The Fey were relentless. They kept coming at him, not stopping, showing no fear of his new-found power. Fifty, a hundred, he wasn't sure how many there were, only that he had to fight them, and he didn't dare move.

He didn't dare uncover his back.

And then a bang echoed through the Hall.

Everything stopped.

Fey in the corridor cried out, and then a horse appeared. It looked like no horse that Con had ever seen before. It was shorter than most, but still had the long slender legs. Its skin was brown, but its mane was deep black. It had blue eyes that whirled wildly in its angular head, and at the base of its muzzle was a shock of white hair.

The man on its back looked incredibly familiar. Only Con had never see him out of ceremonial dress. The King rode bareback, his hands gripping the long black mane. He was leaning forward and shouting at the horse as if it understood him.

Con saw all of that in a moment. Fey were shouting around him. He couldn't tell most of it—his own understanding of their language was limited—but he got some of it.

They were saying that Nicholas had killed the Black King.

Most of the Fey around Con were wounded. They were on their knees in the blood, tending their wounds.

The Fey that had been in the corridor were shouting, swirling toward the Audience room, searching for the dead Black King. None were following the horse.

Con thought that odd enough. He expected them to do something, to chase after the King, to call in reinforcements, *something*. But they didn't. And that didn't even answer how the horse had gotten into the palace in the first place.

Obviously someone had decided to rescue the King. And they had succeeded. The horse made it through the Great Hall, into the corridor and out the open front doors. For the moment, no one followed.

The Fey were in complete disarray. They were screaming at each other, wondering what to do about the Black King. It was as if they couldn't function without him.

Those that had been fighting Con moved away from him, headed toward the corridor, toward the Audience Chamber, fear on their faces.

Con moved along the wall, away from the carnage he'd caused. His feet were soaked with blood and his arm tingled. He wasn't tired, though. The exhaustion he had felt earlier was completely gone.

He reached the edges of the arching double doors and leaned sideways enough to monitor both the Hall and the corridor. The Fey in the corridor were looking in the Audience Chamber. Then they parted to let several Fey out. Those Fey carried a body on their shoulders.

The body was that of a large Fey man. His eyes were closed, and he had a sword protruding from his neck.

A Fey sword.

Maybe the cries had been right.

Maybe the Black King was dead.

The crowd of Fey followed their king, leaving the door

open and the Audience Chamber empty. The other Fey were tending the wounded behind Con.

It was his only chance to escape, and the wounded Fey were blocking his escape route. If he followed the horse out the door, he might lead them to the King.

He would hide.

And what better place to do that than in the room they had just taken the Black King from? They wouldn't go back in there, not for some time.

He rounded the corner, slipped off his sandals and wiped his bloody feet on his robe so that he wouldn't leave any prints. Then he crossed the hall, ducked into the room, and closed the door.

The room was bigger than he had expected. There were spears on the sides and chairs as well. A throne sat on the dais and behind it the crest of the royal family. Blood stained a portion of the floor in the center. The rest of the floor was littered with rocks.

The whole room tingled, like his arms did.

He set the sword down across a pile of stones and reached up to bar the door.

Instantly the room spun. It felt as if all the air had been sucked out of the area. Con slid backwards, and slammed against an invisible wall. Thunder boomed. He fell forwards and landed near the bloody patch.

The air came back. He could breathe.

But the tingling sensation was gone.

And so were the rocks.

Con pushed himself up on his hands and turned around.

A boy not much older than himself sat in the center of the room. He was nude. His body was grayish brown and webbed with lines. They looked like cracks. The sword was beneath him, its blade resting against his bare heels.

The boy lifted his head. His features were striking, Fey and not Fey. His eyes were filled with tears.

"My . . . family," he said, his voice halting and slow, not at all a match for those haunting eyes. "Where . . . are . . . they?"

Con squinted at the boy. Beneath the cracks, he looked familiar. Con stifled a gasp as the realization hit him.

The King's son.

Sebastian.

"Your father rode out of here on a horse," Con said. He didn't understand this. Where had the boy come from? The room had been empty a moment before.

Sebastian closed his eyes. A tear hung on one lid, then dropped on his cheek and slipped into a crack. He didn't appear to be breathing.

"What are you?" Con asked.

"Nothing . . ." Sebastian said slowly, "with-out . . . them."

THE RIVAL
[THREE DAYS LATER]

EIGHTY-FOUR

GIFT had never been so exhausted in his life. It had been five days since he'd had more than a few hours' sleep. The pace Scavenger insisted on was nearly impossible. They had covered more terrain and walked farther than Gift had ever done before. They were still walking, along a narrow brown path that wound along the top of a rise. The valley below them was covered with a haze of fog. The mountains ahead of them were covered with yellow light, as the setting sun shone its rays on their western face.

The others in his group looked ragged as well. Leen hadn't had any real sleep either. Her face was ash gray, the circles under her eyes so big that they made her look as if her skin had sunken inward. She had found them a cache of something Adrian called tak in an abandoned cabin, and that had helped a little. But not even the food was helping all the way. Nothing was.

Adrian, Coulter, and Scavenger had had more sleep. But they looked exhausted as well. Adrian had seemed so terrified when he faced Fey imprisonment; he had clearly vowed never to be taken again. He constantly worried about his son, Luke, who was still on the farm. But he kept saying that Luke would be fine, as if he were trying to convince himself.

Scavenger would have died before rejoining the Fey. He continually checked behind and above them to make certain they weren't being followed. He also insisted that Gift check within himself daily, to make certain no one had silently broken the seals on his Links.

Coulter was the one that Gift worried about. Since saving their lives, Coulter hadn't spoken more than a few words—and those had been in response to questions, or giving his opinion on the direction they should go.

Coulter not only looked tired, he looked haunted.

Gift wasn't certain how he would feel, with all of those deaths on his shoulders.

The group had finally reached the eastern edge of Blue Isle. The terrain was rocky here and covered with scraggly pine. The air was colder, even though it was summer, and Scavenger said they had been walking on a slow incline. Gift hadn't believed him until they reached the edge of a road, and an entire valley appeared before them, barely visible below the clouds.

They were following the Cardidas, watching it wind its way through the valleys, to the eastern edge of the Isle. And as they got closer, they could see the Snow Mountains to the south and the Eyes of Roca to the north. The Eyes of Roca were nearly twice as tall, jagged and bald on top. The Snow Mountains looked like hills in comparison, even though they were too tall to scale.

Or at least, they had been until his great-grandfather arrived.

Gift had only heard about this part of the Isle. He wasn't sure he wanted to see the part of the Eyes of Roca that drifted into the Cardidas, the part called the Cliffs of Blood. Nor was he sure he wanted to see the Cardidas end of the Snow Mountains either. Those rock formations were called the Slides of Death.

He hoped the group stopped before it went that far.

They really didn't have a plan, though. They knew they would have to find a place to hide. They had avoided villages and had ducked from any travelers on the road. So far, Scavenger believed that no one had seen them.

Gift hoped he was right. They needed food, rest, and time to recuperate.

Suddenly Scavenger stopped ahead. He held out his arms across the path so that the others had to stop too.

"Decision time," he said as Gift, who was bringing up the rear, finally reached the group. "This is our last valley. Either we descend and take risks with the villagers or we find a place in the mountains."

"How do you know this?" Adrian asked. He had never been this far east, and had said so a number of times. His lack of knowledge about the terrain seemed to bother him.

"Asked questions," Scavenger said.

"When?"

"For fifteen years. A man never stops worrying that the Fey will find him."

"Is there any place in the mountains?" Gift asked.

"Not in the Slides of Death," Scavenger said. "I've heard there's lots of places in the Cliffs of Blood, but we'll have to cross the Cardidas."

"I can't manufacture a ship," Coulter said. "Someone will have to see us."

"Either way, they'll have to see us, looks like," Adrian said.

"And how will they react to three Fey and two Islanders?" Gift asked.

"They won't," Scavenger said. "They'll take five Islanders across, no questions asked. Adrian will hire them."

"With what?" Adrian asked.

"We have more than enough barter," Scavenger said. "Any one of my weapons should do."

"And let's say that works," Leen said. "How're you going to turn us into Islanders?"

"I'm not," Scavenger said. "He is." He pointed at Coulter.

Coulter shook his head. "My powers aren't endless," he said.

"You're an Enchanter, aren't you?" Scavenger said.

"That's what you people call it," Coulter said.

Scavenger shrugged. "Then we don't have a problem."

Coulter shook his head as if Scavenger were daft. Gift frowned at them both.

"If your plan includes Coulter," Gift said, "the two of you should agree on it."

Scavenger sighed. "Your training is limited."

"My training doesn't exist. You know that." Coulter's fists were clenched. He was so on edge that Gift grabbed his hands, not certain what Coulter would do.

"An Enchanter," Scavenger said, "can do his own spells, like the one you used back there. He can also do, in a limited fashion, anything most Fey can do. Spies can alter their features to look like Islanders. You can do that too."

"But he can't do that to others," Gift said. He knew about Spies. Their powers were limited to themselves.

"Sure he can," Scavenger said. "A Spy spell is simply a mask spell. He needs to build one on all of us, and then stay close."

"You must think I'm God," Coulter said.

"I don't think you're God," Scavenger said. "I think you're someone who's lucky enough to have the kind of power I've always wanted."

Coulter threw him a look of such contempt that Gift felt it too, as though it were a physical blow. "If I could give it to you," Coulter said, "you'd have it." Then he sat down, brought his knees up to his chest and hid his face. Adrian looked at the others, then went to Coulter, sat beside him, and put his arm around him.

Gift pulled Scavenger a bit farther forward on the path. The mist below them cleared, showing the green tops of trees and a handful of cottages beneath them.

"You need to leave him alone," Gift said. "He's near the edge already."

"I would if I could," Scavenger said, "but he's all we got."

Gift frowned. "What about me?"

"Your fighting skills are poor, your leadership abilities small, and you have no magick," Scavenger said.

"I have Vision."

Scavenger nodded. "And look what good it's done us. You can't even tell us if your great-grandfather is alive."

"What does it matter if he is?" Gift asked, not certain he wanted to talk to this arrogant Red Cap any more.

"Then you have a problem. But if he isn't, you can rule the Fey, at least on Blue Isle."

"You just said my leadership skills were weak." Gift crossed his arms, and took a step forward. The mist was back over the valley, and a chill rose off it as darkness started to fall. "Besides, the Fey would never accept me as their leader."

"They will when I get through with you."

Gift shook his head. The Cap was full of odd notions. "What do you know about leadership?"

"More than you do," Scavenger said. "I got us here, didn't I?"

"Leading five people is different from running an empire."

"Maybe," Scavenger said. "Maybe not. But I think you should trust me. Because if you don't, I can't guarantee that you'll live much longer."

"My great-grandfather can't kill me."

"But he can find someone who would. It's simple enough. He doesn't even have to give a direct order."

A chill ran from the base of Gift's neck to his tailbone. He couldn't repress the shudder. "What are you saying?"

"I'm saying that it's you against him now. You have to face that."

"But you think he's dead."

Scavenger shook his head. "He might be dead. Your most recent vision showed that much. But the other Visions you described show him alive. And he's survived serious wounds before. He's not a man to underestimate."

"What if he is dead?" Gift said. He wrapped his arms around his chest.

"Then we return you to Jahn as soon as we get the news."

"And if he isn't?"

"We hide you until we make you his equal."

Gift turned and looked down. The Cap was staring into the valley as well, as if it gave him answers. "Do you think I can be?"

"There's a chance. You have his blood. You come from good stock. And they say he's here to find you. So he must have believed you could."

"A chance," Gift repeated. "That doesn't sound real positive."

"I've done the impossible before," Scavenger said. "No reason why I can't do it again."

He raised his gaze to Gift's face. Scavenger's eyes were dark and unreadable. Gift felt the scrutiny in them, and the concern. The problem was that Gift didn't want to be head of the Fey Empire. He didn't want to be his great-grandfather's equal. It meant making choices like the one Coulter had made in the field.

Choices Gift didn't have the stomach for.

Scavenger seemed to see the doubt. He frowned, and waved a hand in dismissal. "Get your Enchanter friend on his feet. We still have a lot to do and a long way to go." Then he walked away.

Gift sighed. His adoptive parents were gone. Sebastian was dead. He didn't know the fate of his real father and sister. And now he had to make choices about his own future.

His heritage had always left him no choice.

It left him none now.

He was born to rule the Fey.

It was time he learned how.

EIGHTY-FIVE

THEY had been walking since they reached the foothills of the Eyes of Roca. The countryside was rough here, full of rocks and broken terrain. The greenery was lush, though, something Nicholas wouldn't have expected. Pink flowers bloomed in the center of green leafy plants that Nicholas had never seen before. The air was cooler than it had been in the city, and he suspected it would get colder as they went higher.

There was snow on the mountain peaks.

He had read about villages at the edge of the Eyes of Roca. He would go there first, regroup, and think about his next plan. He knew they had only one hope, and he wasn't certain how to achieve it.

If the Black King was dead, Arianna had to take his place. But Nicholas had to wait until the Black King's troops had calmed down. He didn't want Arianna to die in some crazed revenge plot.

She was walking beside Nicholas. She wore a man's breeches and a coat too long for her. Her face was gaunt. All that Shifting, two days' hard gallop, and the last day's walk had exhausted her. She had Shifted one more time, from horse to dog, and had stolen the clothes.

She had also taken some for him—a blousy shirt that tied at the wrists, tight breeches, and a cloak that he carried over his arm. He didn't have the heart to tell her this was the same sort of outfit he had been wearing when he met her ' mother. Besides, he needed the clothes.

Nicholas had destroyed his blood-covered robe. He didn't want anyone to find it.

Their plan, once they reached the next village, was simple. Arianna would Shift again. She said she could look like one of the grooms (Nicholas hadn't asked why she had learned that), and they would go in as two men, looking for lodging and work. They would eat, rest, and wait for news. And while they did, Nicholas would make a plan to either regain his own throne or give Arianna her place among the Fey.

Both made him uneasy. There was a large part of him that wanted simply to disappear among these foothills, to become a nobody. The Eyes of Roca were the most inaccessible part of Blue Isle. Between the Cliffs of Blood and the Slides of Death, there was the Cardidas and little else. The eastern part of Blue Isle was the emptiest part, and the most mysterious.

But hiding wasn't fair to his daughter, and it certainly wasn't fair to his people.

They needed him now more than ever.

Arianna had said little as they traveled, and when she had spoken, it had been of Sebastian. Nicholas recognized those hollow stages of the first deep grief. He was grieving too, but it lacked the intensity he had felt when Jewel died. The boy had chosen his own end, and he had chosen well.

But oh, Nicholas would miss him. He would miss Sebastian's sweet smile and his halting voice. He would miss Sebastian's gentleness and his unusual wisdom. And he would miss the times they spent together as father and son.

But Nicholas had Arianna. He had to think of her now.

"Daddy," she said. She grabbed his sleeve. "There's someone ahead. Should I Shift?"

Nicholas squinted. There was someone walking toward them. The person was still too far away to make out.

"No," he said as he handed her the cloak. "Just hide yourself well."

He worried about her Shifting too much, particularly in her exhausted state. Solanda had once warned him that too much Shifting could lead to accidents like those Shifter children had. Nicholas remembered those days too well, the days when Arianna got stuck between shapes or Shifted to shapes that did not hold. He didn't have magick. He couldn't help her get out of it.

They had met a few other travelers on this road before. The cloak had hidden her enough to get by.

She put the cloak on, pulled its hood up, and bowed her head. Nicholas slipped his hand through her arm so that the passing traveler could draw his own conclusions.

But the closer they got, the more uncomfortable Nicholas grew. He recognized the stride as belonging to someone familiar. The approaching traveler also wore a robe and was taller than most Islanders.

Then Nicholas's mouth went dry. The hair, rising around the traveler's head like a nimbus, was white.

The Shaman.

Nicholas couldn't hide from her. And it was her duty to report to the Fey.

She stopped as though she had known that he recognized her. He kept walking, unwilling as yet to tell Arianna that the flight had been for nothing. When he reached the Shaman, he dipped his head once in acknowledgment. This woman had helped him whenever she could, but she had always placed her Feyness first.

As he would have done in her place.

She seemed thinner than she had before, and somehow younger. Color touched her cheeks, and her nut-brown eyes sparkled with warmth and intelligence.

"I've been waiting a long time for you," she said, and brushed her hand along his cheek.

"I thought you said we wouldn't see each other again."

She smiled. Her eyes were clear. No Doppelgänger had found her and killed her. It was the Shaman.

"You changed the future. It is unclear now."

He wondered at that, wasn't sure he wanted to know exactly what he had done.

He would ask later.

"Arianna," he said. "You don't have to hide."

She brought the hood of her cloak down. Her mouth worked when she saw the Shaman, but no sound came out. Then, unexpectedly, she burst into tears.

Nicholas folded her in his arms, and pressed her face against his shoulder. She was sobbing so hard that she shook. She had never cried like this before. In fact, she rarely cried. And she hadn't cried at all since Sebastian's death.

"What happens now?" Nicholas asked, his chin resting against his daughter's hair. She was shuddering in his arms.

"You come with me," the Shaman said. She was smiling.

Nicholas stroked his daughter's hair, and pulled her close. "We can't do that," he said. "I killed the Black King."

The Shaman's smile faded. "Would that you had, my son," she said. "Our lives would be so much easier. But he lives. And because he lives, you need protection."

"You're not going to take us to him?"

The Shaman shook her head. "Why should I?" she said. "To him, I am a Failure. He would kill me, then you, and make your daughter into a creature neither of us would recognize. No, Nicholas. I have come to help you."

He smoothed Arianna's hair away from her face, and then detached her from him. Her skin was blotchy, her eyes red.

"She lies," Arianna whispered.

Nicholas shook his head. "She never has before. She wouldn't take your life, Ari. She's the one who gave it to you."

"No," the Shaman said. "I merely followed my Vision and my heart. And now you both must do the same. We have a hundred futures ahead of us. We must choose the right one."

Arianna wiped her face with the back of her hand. "All those Visions? They mean we have choices?"

"A lot of choices," the Shaman said. "Your father did that for us by fighting back, by not going willingly into the Fey Empire."

"Why are you against the Black King?" Arianna asked.

"I am not against the Black King," the Shaman said. "I

am for you, and your brother, and a future that brings us peace."

"Do you think we can do that?" Nicholas asked. "We didn't manage it before."

"There is power in Blue Isle," the Shaman said. "We must learn to tap it."

"How?" Nicholas said. "We don't have much time."

"On the contrary, young Nicholas. We have to take the time. The Black King will make no moves until he has his great-grandchildren. We must make certain he will not find them. And then we will look for ways to defeat him."

"I don't know where Gift is," Nicholas said.

"I do," the Shaman said. "He is safe for now. Rugad will not take him. We have time."

"Time for what?" Arianna asked.

"Time to find the future that will change the Fey, child." The Shaman held out her hand. "Come with me. We will find that future together."

Nicholas looked at his daughter. He trusted the Shaman. He knew that she would do what she considered best. But Arianna was the unpredictable one, and she was the one they all needed.

Her gaze met her father's. Exhaustion and sadness poured out of her. She had no fight left. She needed the rest even more than he did.

Slowly she extended her hand until she took the Shaman's. The Shaman smiled. Then she extended her other hand to Nicholas. He took it. Her skin was tough as tanned leather, her fingers warm.

She had been beside him whenever he needed her, ever since he married Jewel. Someday he would find out why.

But for now he was willing to put his future and his daughter's in the Shaman's hands. She Saw everything clearly. She would guide them in the right direction.

For the first time in days, he felt hope.

EIGHTY-SIX

RUGAD leaned against a pile of pillows in the largest bedroom in the palace. He was told that it had been the King's—not Nicholas's, but his father's. The room overlooked a large garden and had bubbled glass built into the shutters. He was grateful for the ability to block the air from outside.

The entire city still smelled of smoke.

It had taken two days for the troops to put out the fires. According to Wisdom's most recent reports, half the city was gone. The Tabernacle was a shell, contents burned or destroyed. Wisdom said there were no reports of survivors.

Rugad needed to see for himself. He cursed the wound that left him imprisoned in this bed. If his guards hadn't thought quickly and left the sword in place, he would have died from blood loss.

One Vision had come true.

He remembered, vividly, wondering how long it would take Nicholas to chop off his head.

Rugad had never expected the attack. He cursed himself for that too, albeit silently. The wound had penetrated his voice box. The Healers promised that he would regain his powers of speech, but not soon. They were consulting with the Warders for a spell to repair the damage. Until then, he had to write his orders or use hand signals.

His loss of speech was demeaning and frustrating. The weakness was even more so. He couldn't get out of bed. His legs wouldn't support him.

The Healers said that a person of any age could have died from that wound. A person of his age should have. Only his stubbornness kept him alive.

His stubbornness and his concern.

He didn't have a successor yet.

His capture of the Isle meant nothing without that.

Blue Isle was a small oasis in the middle of a vast sea. He had known for decades that he could conquer this place. His son, Rugar, had never had his intelligence or his ability. His losses here meant nothing in Rugad's quest for success.

But Rugad hadn't come here just to conquer the Isle. He had conquered much bigger places, and would do so again.

He had come here for Jewel's children, and so far, he had neither of them. The girl was promising. Her fire and spirit were reminiscent of her mother. Her ruthlessness, though, reminded Rugad of himself. She must have gotten some of her courage from her father.

Rugad touched his neck. The man's attack had been swift and elegant. No other ruler, in all of Rugad's experience, had ever attempted an attack on him. No other ruler would have dared. Rugad suspected that young Nicholas had been more than a match for Jewel, a match reflected in their children.

He had no idea where his great-grandson was.

And even more worrisome, the golem, whom Rugad had thought destroyed, had reassembled himself with the help of one of the religious. The guard who had witnessed it all through the listening booth had gotten out too late to prevent their escape.

Rugad might physically own the Isle itself, but he did not own its heart. He wouldn't until the King was captured—and very publicly put to death.

A knock on the door made him sigh in frustration. He couldn't tell someone to come in or to stay out. He wished they would stop knocking. It didn't prevent them from entering, anyway.

And, true to Rugad's expectation, Wisdom entered without waiting for a response. He grabbed a chair, pulled it in front of the bed, and swung a leg over the seat. He had been Rugad's voice during these last few days, something that made Rugad uneasy. He would have to triple-check everything once he was on his feet again.

My great-grandson? Rugad mouthed. He had mouthed that question so many times that Wisdom apparently understood it.

Wisdom shook his head. He pursed his lips. Rugad didn't like the look. Something had gone very wrong.

"Your great-grandson is traveling with a powerful Enchanter," Wisdom said. "Two different troops of Foot Soldiers had him trapped. One found him in a field, and another on a road. Both groups were incinerated. The survivors are all badly burned."

My great-grandson? Rugad mouthed again.

Wisdom leaned back. He was clearly still frightened of his Black King's wrath, despite Rugad's condition. "Your great-grandson has disappeared. We've had Bird Riders searching for him, ground troops searching for him, and we've found nothing."

Rugad waited for the explanation.

"He had a night's head start on us. By the time we knew what happened, he had already traveled a great distance. We believe he's heading northeast, but we have people checking south and west as well."

Rugad grabbed his precious loose sheets of handmade paper. His hands shook, a weakness he didn't like Wisdom to see. Rugad wrote, *Check the city.*

Wisdom took the note. "He won't come here. We have a great presence here—"

Rugad grabbed the piece of paper, crumpled it and threw it at Wisdom. The paper hit him in the face. He blinked once, then said, "We'll search. My mistake."

Rugad nodded. Then he crossed his arms and closed his eyes, ending the discussion.

Both of his great-grandchildren were missing, and both were cunning. They wouldn't let him catch them. He would have to outthink them, and then he would need a strategy to bring them into the Fey fold.

If he could.

He was so old and so tired.

For all his victories it felt, at this moment, as if he had lost.

EIGHTY-SEVEN

So the Black King lived.

Nicholas sat in the back corner of the Shaman's cave. The dirt was soft beneath his blankets, the air warm. She had a fire built at the mouth of the cave, and she was tending it, her back to him.

She thought he was asleep.

He couldn't sleep.

He didn't dare. There was too much to plan, too much to do. And the first thing he had to do was acknowledge how his life had changed in the last few days.

When he was not much older than Arianna, the Fey invaded Blue Isle. With the help of holy water, and with Rugar's arrogance, the Islanders won. The Fey remained trapped within the Isle.

Four days ago, the Fey and the Islanders fought the Second Battle for Blue Isle.

The Islanders lost.

Nicholas leaned his head against the wall, the rock cool against his skull. Arianna slept beside him, shadows beneath her eyes, her hand resting on the blanket he had rolled up as her pillow. She was young, so very young, and impulsive.

But she was alive.

He had lost Sebastian.

But he had not lost Gift. The Shaman said she knew where to find the boy.

His two real children, born of Jewel. His assets. The Black King had come for them, and he did not have them.

That was Nicholas's first victory.

His second had come when he fought back, when he sent those Bird Riders flying. The Fey, thinking they were unbeatable, learned that they could be surprised. It had shaken their confidence. He had seen it in their eyes.

His third victory happened when he slid that sword into the Black King's throat. The Black King, leader of all Fey, was vulnerable. He could be defeated.

And Nicholas would be the one to defeat him.

He just had to plan. The Islanders had to know that their King lived. They would fight for him if they knew that. And if they believed they could defeat the Black King, they would fight even harder.

Nicholas had to act while the Black King was still vulnerable, before he put a complete stranglehold on the Isle. The Shaman would help him plan. Arianna had proven that she could think quickly on her feet. His son had survived.

He had tools.

He would use them all.

There would be a third battle for Blue Isle.

And he would win.

ABOUT THE
AUTHOR

Kristine Kathryn Rusch is an award-winning fiction writer. She has published fifteen novels under her own name: *The White Mists of Power*, *Afterimage* (written with Kevin J. Anderson), *Facade*, *Heart Readers*, *Traitors*, *Sins of the Blood*, *The Fey: The Sacrifice*, *The Devil's Churn*, *The Fey: The Changeling*, *Star Wars: The New Rebellion*, and, with her husband, Dean Wesley Smith, *The Escape*, *The Long Night*, *Klingon!*, *The Rings of Tautee*, and *Soldiers of Fear*. Her short fiction has been nominated for the Nebula, Hugo, World Fantasy, and Stoker awards. Her novella, *The Gallery of His Dreams*, won the Locus Award for best short fiction. Her body of fiction won her the John W. Campbell Award, given in 1991 in Europe. *The Fey: Sacrifice* was chosen by *Science Fiction Chronicle* as one of the Best Fantasy Novels of 1995.

Rusch is the former editor of the *Magazine of Fantasy and Science Fiction*, a prestigious fiction magazine founded in 1949. In 1994, she won the Hugo Award for her editing work. She started Pulphouse Publishing with Dean Wesley Smith, and they won a World Fantasy Award for their work on that press. Rusch and Smith edited *The SFWA Handbook: A Professional Writer's Guide to Writing Professionally*, which won the Locus Award for Best Non-Fiction. They have also written several novels under the pen name Sandy Schofield.

She lives and works in Oregon.

Come visit

BANTAM SPECTRA

on the INTERNET

Spectra invites you to join us
in our new on-line forum.

You'll find:

< Interviews with your favorite authors and
  excerpts from their latest books
< Bulletin boards that put you in touch with
  other science fiction fans, with Spectra
  authors, and with the Bantam editors who
  bring them to you
< A guide to the best science fiction re-
  sources on the Internet

Join us as we catch you up with all of Spectra's finest
authors, featuring monthly listings of upcoming titles
and special previews, as well as contests, interviews,
and more! We'll keep you in touch with the field, both
its past and its future—and everything in between.

Look for the Spectra Science Fiction
Forum on the World Wide Web at:

`http://www.bdd.com`

SF 30 7/96